QUEEN

OF CURSES

Book 2

Jessie D. Eaker

Jessie D. Eaker
jessieeaker.com

This is a work of fiction. Names, characters, places, and incidents are a product of the author's imagination. Locales and public names are sometimes used for atmospheric purposes. Any resemblance to actual people, living or dead, or to businesses, companies, events, institutions, or locales is completely coincidental.

Book Layout © 2017 BookDesignTemplates.com

Queen of Curses/ Jessie D. Eaker — First edition, Version 1.10
ISBN 978-1-7341293-2-8

To Becki

Contents

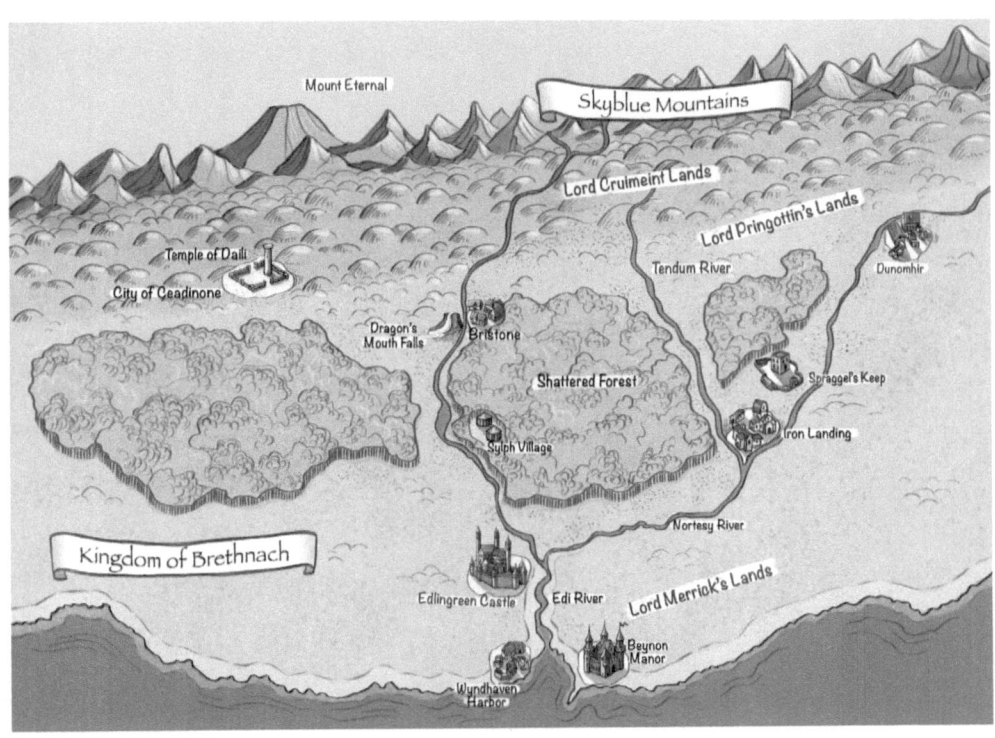

CHAPTER ONE

The Assassin

I brushed the soft end of the quill against my lips while I contemplated my journal. I had spent the better part of the morning gazing up at the rafters of the loft just over my head, trying to come up with a plan. Not a sweep the floor and empty the chamber pot type list—but a real plan. I was a knight now. And knights... well, they always had a plan.

Breathing in the accustomed scents of old paper and ink inside an even older and musty keep, I sighed. This was serious business. A world-famous knight should be able to quickly develop a plan. If you listened to the minstrels, the ancient heroes had one ready on a moment's notice. I didn't believe that for a moment, the minstrels embellished everything! I, on the other hand, tended to side with the historians who seemed to agree it took at least one sleepless night.

So I had a little bit of a deadline here. It was already mid-morning and the parchment in front of me was still blank. I would eventually copy my wonderful plan into my scroll journal. I wanted to be sure future generations could gaze upon it with suitable awe and wonder.

But where to start? The blank parchment stared up at me. There were so many things that went into forming a plan. You had to have men. You needed horses. And of course plenty of food. I nodded. Yes, a good meal was definitely hard to find on the road. I had learned this lesson quite well a few months ago as we raced Wort, a generally disagreeable man with an equally disagreeable magic weapon called *Havoc's Sword*. We had eventually managed to prevent Wort from stealing the powerful *Ruin's Shield*. I winced at the memory. Prevention might be too strong a word since I sort of broke both of them. But I didn't like to dwell on that. By my reckoning, any adventure you could walk, crawl, or even be carried away from, was definitely a good one.

I glanced to the left of my blank page and saw my likeness looking back at me. Zofie, actually Princess Zophia Olwenna Xernow of Bethnach, had taken pity on me when she saw my attempt at a self-portrait and drew a better one for me. I had to say she did a good job of capturing—in ink, no less—my masculine chin and rather square, twenty-year-old face. She had even shaded it to give the impression of my brown eyes and chestnut brown hair (for which my master threatened to kick me out if I didn't keep cut short). I was quite the solid representation of maleness. I sighed. She had tried to improve on the original slightly, but it didn't exactly work—the likeness still looked pleasantly plain (my mother's words, not mine).

From outside the nearby open window, I could hear the rhythmic rap of wood against wood in the courtyard. I swore to myself I wasn't going to look. I had my own things to do. Zofie and Risten were sparring in the courtyard. After our last battle with Wort, Risten was determined to pound everything she knew into our heads in as short a time as possible—and Zofie and I had the bruises to prove it.

Risten Brightmare was an attractive young woman, a half dozen years older than Zofie, and also a sword-master. Her blond hair had been pulled back in a long braid, and she was dressed in leather pants, white shirt, and red leather vest. When I first met her, I thought of her as having the deadly beauty of a she-wolf. Now, having known her for a while, it only reinforced that opinion.

But Zofie was the one that drew my eye. She was quite the beauty with long, dark red hair, blue eyes, pale skin, and a smattering of freckles across her nose. Today, she was wearing a loose white shirt, vest, and trousers to move easily while sparring with Risten. While a little winded from her exertion, she looked in excellent health for someone supposed to be cursed to death by her brother.

I propped my chin on my hand as I watched her and Risten trade blows. *Dammit! I'm not supposed to be gazing at her!* I quickly looked back down at my paper, realizing once again, I had become distracted.

I heard a particularly meaty whack and a howl of pain from Zofie.

"Focus!" yelled Risten. "Your mind is elsewhere today. I could have easily taken off your leg. Now start again." And the rhythmic rap of wood restarted.

I knew why Zofie was having trouble focusing. Spraggel was overdue. In fact, we all were a little on edge because of it.

She had penned a letter to Lord Dewi Merrick stating she had survived the attempt on her life and that she was innocent of her father's murder. She had closed by asking if he would support her against her murderous brother. Merrick and Zofie's deceased father had been good allies, making him Zofie's best hope for assistance.

Spraggel van Deviante, my elderly master, was carrying the message since he was the only one known to the lord who wasn't either supposed to be dead or wanted for royal thievery. They all voted against me carrying it because of my curse—which tended to give me bad luck and at the worst of times. Being the Thief of Curses was not all it was cracked up to be.

I looked down at the curse anchor on the inside of my left wrist. To the untrained eye, it resembled a darkly inked tattoo, but it was far from that. It was an oddly curved, almost flowing, triangle sitting angled on my wrist. Around the perimeter was what looked like tiny writing that could be runes, but were too small to make out. Inside the triangle was a single stylized eye, with its lid now closed. I had been told that it was an oddly shaped curse anchor. Even now, I got a chill looking at it.

Abhulengulus was the name of the curse in the old language—and he was a curse like none other. He had his own intelligence and personality. A quite disagreeable one, I might add. I generally called him Abe for short. When the eye on my wrist opened, he would talk to me—in my head, of course—and only I could hear him. He would even answer my questions if he felt like it.

But lately, he hadn't been feeling so generous. Ever since we stole the curses of Havoc's Sword and Ruin's Shield, not to mention arranged it so that Zofie's curse wasn't going to kill her, Abe had been strangely quiet. He had answered a few of my questions, but when I got to the more advanced ones, he would say I had to give the secret word before he could tell me more. I had gotten tired of having my questions rebuffed and stopped asking. Another strange thing since Abe had started speaking to me—my luck had stopped turning out bad... mostly.

Previously, everything around me went wrong: from soured milk to causing minor accidents as I walked down the road. But now, like Abe himself, things had been strangely quiet. I couldn't help but think something was up. And at any time, a really horrific event would happen. I shivered.

I pursed my lips as I considered Abe's curse anchor. While I had used Abe to save Zofie's life by modifying her curse, she was still cursed. Originally, it was a transformation curse, and every full moon, she would transform into a different animal. However, her curse also made her lose her original human form, and as each transformation occurred, it had been gradually killing her. But with the modification, she was returning to her true form, bit by bit. Within a few more months, she should be completely back to herself, and then I could remove the curse. But until then, she was unable to use her myst—a side effect of the original curse.

Ah, yes. *Myst.* The ethereal substance behind what some would call magic or sorcery. Myst could provide light in the deep of night or allow people to travel great distances within the blink of an eye. It could even be used to arm a weapon. While most people in the world (yours truly, excepted) could use myst to great effect, a select few known as myst seers could see and understand its inner workings. Zofie was among that number.

So for her, the lack of her myst skills was especially troublesome. In a sense, it was almost as if her left arm had been cut off.

Which is why the sword drills were necessary.

Outside the window, there was a particularly loud whack of wood against wood, and then Risten launched into a tirade about proper footwork. I guiltily looked down at my paper, realizing I didn't have much time. She would be coming for me next.

Taking a deep sigh, I knew I couldn't put it off any longer—it was time to write my plan. Now or never, as they say.

I dipped my quill into the ink bottle and boldly wrote the first two lines of my plan.

1. *Prove Zofie's innocence.*

2. *Restore Zofie to the throne.*

I stroked my lips with the quill again. There had to be a third step. There was *always* three steps. But what could it be? And then it hit me. I dipped my pen and wrote the final line.

3. *Protect Zofie.*

Which was likely going to be the hardest of all three.

I sat back congratulating myself. So there it was in three easy steps—a very simple plan. What more could one ask for?

I looked out the window at Zofie, her face a mask of concentration as she pressed an attack. I grew suddenly sad. There was actually a fourth step, but I could never write it down. I guess because it wasn't so much a plan, as a wish from the heart. One that could never happen. Zofie was a princess, and if I had my way (see step number 2), she would be queen. But me? I was nothing more than an apprentice scribe. Zofie had knighted me and even designated me as one of her suitors. But despite that, I was far below her station. Definitely not someone Zofie should seriously consider.

A foolish wish from the heart had no place in such a plan.

"Hold." I heard Risten say.

I glanced out the window. The sword-master stepped back, disengaging from their match. Risten didn't even look winded. Zofie, on the other hand, was breathing hard and seemed a little irritated. "Why did you stop? You keep stopping when things are just getting good."

Risten grinned. "Maybe so, but I've pushed you hard enough for today." She patted Zofie on the shoulder. "You're getting better. Your footwork is much improved. You might even stand a chance now." She looked thoughtful. "That's assuming your opponent is a greenhorn novice having an extremely bad day."

Zofie shook her head. "I think I'm a trifle better than that. You just can't judge properly because you're so damned good."

Risten rubbed her chin and considered her cousin. "I think you have a point. You really should spar with someone other than me." She turned toward my window and grinned evilly. "Coren! Get your ass out here! It's time for your beating... I mean practice."

I grimaced. Initially, I had been thrilled to receive instruction from one of the best sword-masters living. But lately, it had become a little— painful. I sighed. There was no way out of this one. I secured my papers from any wayward breezes and went outside to join them.

Risten held out her stick toward me as I approached, while I unbuckled my sword and gave it to her in exchange. She insisted I carry the weapon wherever I went.

Zofie had gifted it to me before I knew what it was, *Majestic*, the King's Sword. The blade had a rich history, and legend said it would pick the person qualified to carry it. I think Risten was a little miffed that it had chosen someone with such little sword experience. Something she was determined to fix as quickly as she could.

I moved to take my position, but Risten stepped close and whispered in my ear. "If you so much as put a bruise on her, I will cut your privates off."

"Don't listen to her, Coren." Zofie frowned and moved into her first stance, grinding the ball of her foot into the ground. "I can't hear her, but I know she's warned you not to hurt me. I *have* to master this. As your future queen, I order you to come at me with all you've got. Don't you dare hold back."

I looked from one to the other and couldn't help but think I was doomed. *Oh Creator,* I silently prayed. *Please save me.*

To my utter shock, the Creator did.

Risten straightened and turned toward the courtyard gate. She held up a silencing hand and we all strained to listen.

"Someone's approaching," Risten announced. She immediately took off at a dead run toward the keep. Zofie and I exchanged a glance and then took off after her.

The heavy oak door banged open as Risten led the way inside. My carefully stacked papers went flying in the sudden breeze. The two women rushed to the far window, which offered the best view of the road below us. I, on the other hand, went to collect my scattered papers.

Risten leaned dangerously far out the window. Zofie squeezed in beside her.

"He's back!" Risten announced. "Spraggel's coming up the road... but who's that with him?"

Zofie leaned out the window trying to get a better view. "Are you sure it's him?" she asked.

Risten nodded emphatically. "It's Spraggel, all right. He's easy to pick out. But I'm not sure about the other. A man for sure, wearing a large hat and dressed in Lord Merrick's livery."

Zofie slowly pulled back from the window and sighed sadly. "Only one man. That doesn't speak well for my request. It can't be anyone of importance—they would have an escort." She looked down. "That likely means that Merrick said no."

Risten put an arm around her cousin's shoulders and gave her a reassuring squeeze. "Ah, but think about it. Why send even one person if he was totally dismissing you?"

Zofie nodded. "You're right. It could be a messenger. Perhaps he wants to independently verify that I'm still alive." Zofie paused and glanced back toward the window. "But that doesn't sound right either." Zofie slowly drifted away from the window in thought.

Risten casually strolled over to where I was sorting my papers and handed me back my sword. She gave me a knowing smile and winked. I stared at her. *What was Risten up to?*

She looked over her shoulder in Zofie's direction, grinning mischievously. "Do you think you should run out to meet him? Like you did when you were eight."

Zofie gave Risten a puzzled look. "I'm not sure it would be proper. And the only time I did that was when...." She paused, her eyes flicking from me to Risten. Zofie looked horrified.

"What?" I asked.

Zofie shook her head in denial. "It couldn't be him."

Risten raised an eyebrow. "You could be right, but I'd bet my last coin it is." She patted me on the shoulder and leaned close. She whispered, "I'm looking forward to some fireworks."

Risten then strolled over to toward the door. Zofie shot me a worried look. But just then, I heard the soft clomp of horses arriving in the courtyard. I stood and looked to Zofie for some clue, but she avoided my gaze.

What is going on? I sighed. *I don't think I will ever understand her.*

I followed Risten out the door and stepped out into the morning sunlight, where two riders approached us across the open courtyard. One I could easily make out as Spraggel.

The other man was indeed dressed in the livery of Lord Merrick, with a coat of gold and a bold shade of green, plus a pair of dark trousers. Perched on top of his head was a broad hat that shaded his features. I could tell he was clean-shaven and broad of shoulder, but that was all. He was also lagging behind Spraggel and chose to stop a short distance away.

Spraggel pulled up in front of us. He carefully dismounted as expected for one of his advanced years and then stretched his back. "I'm not used to these long trips."

My master gave me a smile and a pat on the back but immediately turned his attention to Zofie. He gave her a slight bow, but then stepped closer and took her hands—his expression solemn. "I'm sorry Princess, but my trip was not successful. While the letter and the information I presented convinced Merrick you were still alive, he is refusing to back you at this time. He said to tell you that in his view of the current situation, going against the new king now would prove too risky."

Zofie's shoulder's sagged. "So, it was all for naught."

Spraggel brightened. "Not completely. Lord Merrick did say he would back you, provided you can provide undeniable proof of your innocence. While there is no love for the new king, he is afraid that without some kind of proof, the other lords won't side with him."

Zofie shook her head. "It's as I feared. None of the nobles will help."

Spraggel grinned. "Well, there is one." He rolled his eyes toward the rider behind him.

Taking his cue, the man nudged his horse forward. While still seated, he whipped off his hat in a sweeping gesture and bowed deeply from the waist. "Which is why I came," he said. "To help prove your innocence."

Zofie gasped. "Galvyn? Is that you?"

The man smiled. "Indeed, my princess. It is I, Galvyn Llewelyn Merrick. It has been a while, has it not?"

"I haven't seen you in five or six years."

He sat back up, threw a leg over his horse, and dismounted in a single smooth movement. "It's been five years, four months, and two days." He strode forward and took her hand, then brought it gently to his lips. "And every second has been torture."

He quickly turned to Risten and bowed to her, but not as deeply as he had to Zofie. "And my beloved Risten. You're as radiant as I remember. No doubt twice as deadly, too."

He went to take her hand, but Risten pulled back. "And you're still the sleaze I remember."

Galvyn was unfazed. He smiled and gave a slight nod. "As charming as always, my lady."

He then turned his smile on me. "And you must be Coren, the Thief of Curses." He extended his hand and we shook. I tried not to wince—his grip was so strong I could feel my bones cracking.

"I want to thank you," he said. "You have done a great service in rescuing her majesty. I am so glad you have brought my fiancée back to me."

My eyebrows went up in surprise. "Fiancée?"

But he didn't answer. Instead, he handed me the reins of his horse and leaned in closer. "Be sure he gets an extra handful of grain. I promised him if we made it today, I would treat him."

I looked at Galvyn in shock. "I'm not..." But I stopped when I realized he had refocused on Zofie and had completely dismissed me.

Zofie frowned. "Galvyn, while I admit, Father did declare you one of my suitors, it had not been considered an engagement."

Galvyn took Zofie's hand again before she had a chance to react. "It's true, your father never made it official, but as you can see, it's best to quickly bind your allies. And what better way than by marriage? After we prove your innocence, we can wed in grand style. And with my father's backing, I can easily bring the other lords around." He tenderly brought her hand to his lips. "Besides, what other choice do you have?"

Zofie's expression grew dark, and her face began to turn red.

Risten leaned toward me and whispered, "I told you there were going to be fireworks." She straightened and grinned evilly. "Ah, Galvyn. She already has another suitor. Someone who is just slightly better than worthless, which puts him above you."

Galvyn eyes went wide in shock. "Who is this cad? I will challenge him to a dual this instant. No one but I will have the hand of the princess."

I opened my mouth to reply, but then I thought otherwise. Maybe it was best if she didn't really consider me. After all, what army could I command? And if what we saw back on Mount Eternal was actually one of the Dark Avenyts, then we were going to need a *big* army.

Zofie, her face quite red, jerked her hand from Galvyn. She stepped forward and began to poke him in the chest. "I'm not some prize goat that can be haggled over. I will make my own decision about who I marry—if I ever do!"

Galvyn stood firm and grinned down at her. "Of course, my dear," he said in a patronizing voice. "You are the princess, and I am at your command."

Zofie trembled in fury and turned, taking two steps away before turning back.

Suddenly, the horse's reins jerked out of my fingers, and the steed trotted over to Zofie. She turned just as the horse nudged her. She pushed its head away. "Galvyn, I..." The horse took another step toward Zofie and nudged her so hard she staggered backward, landing awkwardly on her butt.

Galvyn reached for the horse's reins, "Now, now, Morning Glory. Don't be rude to my future bride."

Risten also reacted, putting a hand on her sword hilt and moving to put herself between it and Zofie.

Suddenly, the horse spun and gave a powerful kick toward Risten, which unfortunately caught her by surprise. It connected in her chest and sent her flying. She landed hard on her back and lay unmoving.

"Risten!" yelled Zofie and scrambled to her cousin's side.

Galvyn stood in shock as the horse wheeled and bucked again aimed right for him. Galvyn snapped out of it at the last moment and dodged with the horse's hooves barely missing him. Then the animal turned toward where Zofie knelt beside Risten and reared... aiming to come down right on her. I did the only thing I could think of, I tucked my shoulder and body-slammed the horse, bouncing off so hard I fell backward.

The horse staggered, catching itself mid-strike and barely missing the two women. Zofie was so focused on Risten, she did not notice.

While I got to my feet, Galvyn ducked under yet another kick and reached for the horse's reins. But the animal cleverly dodged and pulled away.

Galvyn shook his head. "What's gotten into you, Morning Glory?"

Much to our surprise, the horse answered.

"I'm not your damn horse," it said. "I carried your fat ass over hill and stream for the last three days! But that wasn't nearly as embarrassing as you calling me Morning Glory. Killing you is going to feel so good."

My eyes grew wide as realization struck. The animal had to be a human transformed into a horse. Which meant... an assassin!

The horse wheeled and gave another kick in my direction before it spun and galloped a short distance away. Then it abruptly stopped and turned toward us. I thought he might try to make another charge, so I hurriedly pulled my sword and planted myself in front of Zofie. As I did, Galvyn drew his own sword and prepared for the next attack.

Spraggel snapped out of his surprised daze and did what he usually did in these types of situations—he dug into his enchanted pocket. It was some kind of portal which connected with Creator knew where. While it seemed to have an infinite storage capacity, it was sometimes difficult to locate items.

"I know my sword's in here somewhere," I could hear him mumble.

The horse raised its head and I braced for it to charge, but instead it became enveloped in a purple glow—its outline gradually blurring. The equine shape quickly transformed into a tall, thin man, fully dressed in a stylish tunic and pants. He strode toward us even as the last of his glow was still fading.

He gave us a smirk. "Now that I'm free of that form, I can use my myst properly."

Oh, Creator. A myst user.

I tightened the grip on my sword and raised it toward him. I wasn't too sure how much good a sword was going to do against charms, but at least I could look fearsome. And Risten had taught me that having 'the look' would put you at an advantage. Only, I wasn't sure he was buying my whole fearsome thing.

The myst user held up his hand and continued to walk toward us, an evil grin on his face. Even I could feel his myst gathering. He was going to do something really bad.

"Abhulengulus!" I said under my breath. "Can I put a curse on him?"

The deep, dark voice of my curse answered. Even though I was used to him by now, I still shivered when he answered. And as usual, he was in a surly mood. *Ah, a question! After days of ignoring me, you suddenly need my help. Oh, I rue the day I got stuck with you!* He sighed dramatically. *No, you can't curse him until you steal his current curse. Remember, only one curse per customer. It's not all that uncommon for really strong myst users to take on a minor curse to protect against a really bad one.*

Unaware of the exchange going on in my head, Galvyn pointed his sword at the assassin. "You bastard!" he shouted dramatically. "Stop right this minute! I command it!" I was pretty sure he had practiced that line.

The assassin smirked. "Sorry, young lord. But I can't do that. I'm here to capture the princess and her cousin, or if that becomes impossible, kill them. And I honestly don't mind killing the rest of you as well." He looked toward Zofie. "But one must set their priorities."

He raised his hand and pointed to the princess behind me. Then with a wicked smile, he released his myst.

"Watch out!" Zofie yelled.

How does one protect against a myst attack? Technically it was called a charm, but that seemingly harmless name hid a wide variety of ways to kill someone. I certainly had no idea what to do. Risten had not included an attack like this in any of my training. So, I just did what came naturally. I stepped in front of it and brought up my sword.

I felt the power of his spell hit my sword, making it glow. The hilt grew hot in my hands, and I had time to be afraid of turning into something horrible or even disappearing into nothingness.

And then the strangest thing happened. His spell bounced off, striking a nearby tree and splitting it down the middle. The assassin gave me a 'how-dare-you' look.

"You deflected my charm," he stated matter-of-factly. He then quickly raised his arm and fired again.

The sword just seemed to move on its own, coming up to block the charm, and unfortunately, deflected it toward the keep, blowing off the heavy oak doors.

It had to be Majestic doing it. I grinned. This was going to be easier than I thought.

Off to the side, Spraggel had continued to dig in his magical pocket. He had amassed a sizable pile of items around his feet—an ink bottle, a shoe, and an hourglass. Plus, he was absentmindedly chewing on an apple he had come across. I was glad he hadn't found his sword yet.

The assassin paused, his confidence flagging.

"Give it up!" I shouted. "You can't get through me."

Furious, he raised his hand again and released another powerful burst of myst. My sword once more moved on its own and easily deflected it.

And to my horror, it headed right toward Spraggel.

"No!" I shouted.

Spraggel, completely unaware, was enveloped in purple light. He grimaced in pain, his apple falling from his grasp. He then began to shrink smaller and smaller until all I could see was a lump of gray fur lying on the ground.

Spraggel!

I gritted my teeth. This man was going to pay.

Out of the corner of my eye, I could see Risten slowly get to her feet. She was holding her chest. The horse's blow must have done some damage. Zofie rose with her and tried to hold her back, but Risten pushed her away.

Grimacing, she looked my way as she drew her sword. "Fool!" she yelled. "The King's Sword is not a toy. Get Zofie out of here before you kill us all!" She didn't wait for a reply. She turned her attention on the assassin and charged.

Galvyn joined Risten and they both attacked. Much to my surprise, the assassin pulled his own sword from Creator knew where. He hadn't had it the moment before. And he moved like a demon. His arms a blur, parrying every move Risten and Galvyn made.

I fumed in anger. This couldn't go on. I ached to rejoin the melee, but I would likely be a liability instead of providing help—my skill level was nowhere near Risten's or even Galvyn's for that matter.

"Abe," I said. "I need your help."

You idiot. What are you thinking now?

"Can I steal his curse and then put a curse right back on top of him?"

Are you kidding? You have to touch him to steal his curse, and the one he's using must make him stronger and faster than normal. You won't be able to even get close.

I shook with frustration. "Then what would you suggest I do?" I said through clenched teeth.

Run maybe.

"What!"

You heard me. Running is your best bet. He's too powerful for you. And isn't that what sword-bitch told you to do?

I shook my head. "I have to stop him!" I was frozen in place, conflicting emotions battling within me.

Risten got several swings in, but the assassin was ready and easily parried. Galvyn tried to help, coming from the other side, but surprisingly the assassin used his free hand to shove Galvyn away. As he stumbled, a portal appeared behind the young lord, and he fell backward through it. A heartbeat later, the portal reappeared facing downward about head high. Galvyn plunged out of it, landing hard on his back. He lay there, stunned.

With Galvyn out of the way, the assassin grinned evilly and turned to Risten.

Risten glanced in my direction and yelled, "Get her out of here!" I could hear the frustration in her voice. I was ignoring all of her training.

In our practices over the last couple of months, Risten had pounded into my head (and bruised body) that I had to protect Zofie at all costs. No matter if it meant leaving the sword-master behind. I wasn't doing my job. And I knew it.

I grabbed Zofie by the arm and tried to pull her away. "I need to get you to safety," I said. "We can barricade ourselves in the keep."

But she shook me off. "I'm not leaving." To emphasize the point, she scooped up her practice stick and brandished it like a sword. "He's got to be running low on myst. He's used a lot on the transformations and portals. Plus whatever acceleration curse he's using has got to be taking a toll. He's likely only got one good spell left. When that happens, we can rush him."

I glanced at Zofie. Her face was the perfect mask of fury and determination—a goddess with vengeance in her eyes. And if I hadn't already been infatuated with her, I definitely would have then. I raised my own blade to stand beside her.

Risten switched her sword to her left hand, her face a mask of pain. She had definitely broken something and was at a clear disadvantage. She needed to end this quickly. She rushed the assassin but pulled back at the last moment as a portal appeared in front of her. It quickly disappeared, but another appeared gradually herding her in our direction. He slowly advanced his eyes gleaming in delight.

"This has been fun, but I must bring it to a close." He raised his sword toward the sky and closed his eyes. For this one, sweat broke out on his brow and he shook with the effort. I could feel the myst massing... This was big.

A portal appeared beside Risten, dark and black, with cold radiating from it. I could feel a gentle flow of air moving into it. I didn't know much about myst casting, but I could tell this was different.

Zofie gasped. "That's a long-range portal. It could lead to anywhere in the world!"

I tried to pull Zofie away from it. But he blocked us and charged.

He attacked furiously. Risten and I defended but were forced back—closer and closer to the dark portal, until we were right in front of it. There was no way out. I could feel the cold from it, chilling my back. This was not looking good. Even though I would likely die, I readied myself to jump in and try to curse him.

Suddenly, a loud yell—actually a sort of "Yahhhh" war cry—came from behind the assassin.

Surprised, the assassin glanced over his shoulder. Risten used the distraction to shove Zofie and me to the side.

And then Galvyn attacked.

The assassin whipped around to defend, but at a full run, Galvyn plowed into him and knocked him backward. The assassin stumbled, caught his heel on the edge of the portal, and fell inside.

The surprise on his face as he fell was worth gold.

The assassin was enveloped by the darkness inside, and the portal snapped shut. The only evidence that it had even been there was the trampled grass.

Galvyn blinked at where the assassin had been. I think he was the most surprised of all of us. He grinned, sheathing his sword and squaring his shoulders.

"He should have known better than to tussle with me." He quickly turned to Zofie, brushing me aside, and took her hand. "Are you unharmed, my love? Let him show his face again, and he'll taste my steel. I'll do better protecting you next time."

An unexpected voice joined the conversation. "The key words there are indeed *next time*." We all turned toward the voice. It was high pitched, kind of gruff, and came from low on the ground. But the way it spoke—*Spraggel?*

A gray cat sat at our feet, gazing up at us with large, bright green eyes while its tail swished calmly back and forth.

"They will be back, your highness," the cat said. "Your brother definitely wants you dead."

CHAPTER TWO

The Cat Has an Idea

I gasped. "Spraggel! You can talk!"

The cat nodded. "I have been talking since I was a babe. And as my friends will attest, it'll take a little more than a transformation spell to get me to stop." He lifted his front paw and began to lick it.

Zofie knelt down in front of him. "You *do* realize you're a cat, don't you?"

Spraggel sighed and looked up from his paw. "Unfortunately, yes. I've been turned into one before, a long time ago, so I'm familiar with this form."

I shook my head. "You've been a cat before?" I just couldn't imagine my master being in a situation that would result in his transformation.

"Indeed," he said, standing and slinking over to rub against Zofie's leg. "In my youth, I made the mistake of pissing off the wrong myst user." He sighed. "But that's another story." He sat on his haunches and looked up at us. "This form is not a bad one, but I'm not overly fond of the instincts that come with it. And please don't tease me with a string. It's embarrassing."

Wincing, Risten put away her sword. She motioned Zofie over. "Can you look at this for me? He got me pretty good." She turned her back to us and opened her vest and shirt. Zofie bent down and must have probed the area because Risten's head jerked up with a hiss.

Zofie stood. "You're lucky. You only have a cracked rib and a nasty bruise. Likely going to hurt a lot though."

"Should you bind it?" I asked.

Risten began to carefully put her shirt and vest back. "No, the best treatment is to just let it heal on its own."

"You should at least rest for a day or so," Zofie said. She reached down and picked up Spraggel, cradling him in her arm.

Risten snorted. "Like that's going to happen with this latest attack."

Galvyn smacked his leg in frustration. "I can't believe we led an assassin here. We were so careful."

"And I was right there riding beside you!" said Spraggel, lifting his head in pleasure as Zofie scratched it. "A little higher dear. I'd forgotten how good that feels."

"Well, we can't stay here," I said. "They know where we are and could open one of those portals again at any time, likely send an army after us."

Risten nodded. "That's why we have to leave now. We could head north toward Dunomhir. Some of my old master's friends have gathered there."

I shook my head. "No, it's best to head to Iron Landing and hide out there. If we hurry, we can make it before dark."

Galvyn stepped over to Zofie. "Going to see my father would be better. I'm sure I can persuade him to provide shelter while we search for a way to prove your innocence. Beynon Manor would be the perfect place to hole up."

"Wait a minute," I said. "How do we know your father didn't send the assassin? Or you, for that matter. Maybe both of you are trying to get in good with the new king. You did lead him here."

Risten nodded. "I was thinking the same."

Galvyn gave us a look like we were clearly insane. "My father may not want to take on the new king, but that doesn't mean he supports him." He turned back to Zofie. "Besides, if he was going to sponsor an assassin, he wouldn't have allowed me to come." He grinned at me over his shoulder. "I'm his only heir." He pointed toward Spraggel's horse chomping grass a short distance away. "So why don't you start getting us ready to leave, while Lady Xernow and I discuss this."

I stood there shaking with anger.

Risten regarded Galvyn coolly. "We are *not* going to Beynon Manor. We're going north to Dunomhir. It's the perfect place to start building our army."

Galvyn gave her a strained smile. "Build an army? Surely you jest. Are these friends of your old master willing to incur the king's wrath?"

"Iron Landing would be better," I insisted.

But Risten ignored me and wheeled on Galvyn. She put her hand on her sword. "They're likely better friends than your father's men. That lot will sell her out the moment they lay eyes on her."

Galvyn leaned forward and stabbed at her with his finger. "I'll have you know my father and his men are very trustworthy."

"Uh, Risten, Galvyn," I said. "This is not the time."

Risten snorted. "Yeah, right. It's strange how they weren't at the party last year when old King Xernow was killed."

Galvyn's face turned red. "Are you calling my family traitors?"

Risten leaned forward. "I was thinking of something closer to *scum.*"

Galvyn inhaled sharply and reached for his sword.

"Will you *stop!*" Zofie shouted. "Don't I get a say in any of this?" Zofie looked from one to the other. "Both of you settle down. Your bickering is not helping."

Risten and Galvyn glared at each other a moment longer and then separated.

Spraggel looked up at Zofie from her arms. "Princess, as your designated senior advisor, I think all of these suggestions are too short-sighted." He paused and looked at each of us before turning his gaze to Zofie. "May I propose a slightly different plan?"

She considered Spraggel for a moment, as if she was ready to be done with all of us, but then closed her eyes and nodded. "I did appoint you to that position, so I must at least hear you out."

She placed Spraggel on the ground before us. He sat on his haunches, erect, and head held high. For a cat, he looked sort of regal. He put a paw across his chest and bowed to Zofie—which looked really odd. "Thank you, your highness." He turned to look at the rest of us. "I formally declare the Princess's court is in session. All of you, please be seated."

Why that foxy old... ah... cat. He called us to court so we had to listen to his argument and be bound by Zofie's decision. And Zofie knew it too. She smiled and nodded to Spraggel.

Normally, she would be sitting on her throne, but lacking one, she sat down cross-legged on the grass, her back straight and head held high. I had to say, she looked every bit the queen. With no other choice, Galvyn, Risten, and I sat down cross-legged in front of her with Spraggel in the middle.

Seeing that he had everyone's attention, Spraggel took a deep breath and rose on his four feet. "Thank you for hearing me out, your highness. I have listened to each of the suggestions and believe protecting you to be a priority, but it should not be our long term goal. What we should be thinking about is how to first prove your innocence, and second, get your throne back."

Galvyn leaned forward. "And pray tell how should we do that? From what you told me on our trip here, her brother set her up so that her myst signature was all over the old king. Any myst user worth their salt would see he died of myst depletion, and she was the one that drained him."

Risten slapped the ground. "But it wasn't her! That bastard Wynn set it up with a charm to draw from her father while forcing Zofie to defend herself. And even at the last, the bastard put a curse on her which forced her to draw out the last of the king's myst."

I noticed that Zofie sat very still, her face expressionless. I knew she felt extremely guilty for what had happened to the old King. This discussion had to be making her uncomfortable. I tried to move us along. "So master, how are you thinking of proving her innocence?"

Spraggel nodded. "Well, while I was waiting for Lord Merrick to see me, I was allowed the opportunity to look through his library. It was small...."

Galvyn interrupted. "A library? We don't have a library. Just a closet with a few ledgers off my father's study."

The cat flexed his shoulders in what I assumed was a shrug. "Anyway, while I was reading, I heard one of the king's captains talking to him about an ancient artifact called the *Mirror of Bygone Tears*. It is apparently something Wynn has approached your father about locating. Your father said it had been tried before with no success."

Galvyn looked at him suspiciously. "Why would my father be having a private conversation with one of the king's guard with you in his closet?" He leaned forward. "Wait. You're not telling me you were eavesdropping in his personal study."

"I guess it could have been his study. He did have a desk with some ink and paper lying around. And when he found me in there, he was quite perturbed." The cat raised his head. "But I did finally get to talk with him."

I just shook my head and looked down.

Galvyn shrugged. "And how, pray tell, does this mirror protect Zofie?"

Spraggel went back to washing his paw. "It doesn't protect her. Not in the least. However, I know a little about this device. It has the ability to show something from the past as it actually occurred. In other words, it's a way to show the Lords how Wynn pulled off the murder."

Spraggel paused and let us digest this bit of information. Having a neutral party reveal the past would definitely show how Wynn arranged and executed his plan, proving Zofie's innocence.

Zofie asked the question forming in my mind. "Why is Wynn looking for it?"

Spraggel gave another cat-like shrug. "Of that, I can't even offer a guess. It is strange that he would be interested in it."

"Perhaps he doesn't want Zofie to get it?" I offered.

Spraggel shook his head. "While it's possible, he only *just* learned that Zofie survived her curse. My sources say he's been making subtle inquiries since shortly after taking the throne. So there must be another reason."

We all paused as we thought this through.

Risten leaned forward. "Do you know where to find this mirror?"

Spraggel rolled his eyes upward. "Not exactly, but I know someone who might?"

"Might?" we all said in chorus.

Spraggel started licking his paw and using it to wash his whiskers. "Yes, he *might*. While I am more an expert on history and myst weapons, he's more of an expert on artifacts from the time of the Dark Avenyts. And this artifact is from that time."

Risten sighed, and with her elbow on her knee, propped her head on her hand. "But what about the second part of your plan—getting her throne back."

Spraggel turned to her. "That is something I think you will find extremely interesting. During the trip back, I happened to hear rumors of a rebellion building. Apparently, the new king is not liked very well, and many of the king's soldiers have either resigned or deserted."

Zofie shook her head. "That's very odd. Why would they do that?"

"Because there's a rumor circulating..." His tail swished back and forth excitedly. "That you're *alive*. And you're gathering an army in Dunomhir."

We all looked at Risten. That is where she had insisted we go.

Risten rolled her eyes. "I might have sent a letter to my master's friends there and mentioned a few things."

Spraggel turned back to Zofie. "So that is my plan. You and Coren travel with me to my friend to learn more about the Mirror of Bygone Tears, while Risten rides to Dunomhir to see about that army. This addresses both our strategic priorities."

Zofie considered Spraggel for a moment and then looked into each of our faces, returning to gaze at the cat. Then she smiled. "I like this plan. Will you each lend me your strength?"

Of course, we couldn't say no.

She was going to be our queen after all.

I wasn't looking forward to this visit.

I traipsed through the forest a short way from the keep, heading for where I thought the nymph's small pond lay. It had to be close by, but I wasn't exactly sure where. Usually, I tried to avoid her. She was a crafty creature though and had no trouble finding me when she wanted.

While I wasn't convinced, Spraggel thought she might be able to give us a disguise that would allow us to pass by the king's soldiers unnoticed. Being a creature of myst, her workings were more powerful than any myst user could generate. Spraggel had given me a couple things to offer her in trade, but they seemed a little *odd* to me.

I was no stranger to this particular nymph. Several years ago, when I had first come to apprentice with Master Spraggel, I had gone into the forest looking for firewood and mushrooms. I ended up knee-deep in an old pond with the nymph dancing around the edges laughing at me. Spraggel had warned me about her, saying the creature may look human, but her way of thinking was completely different from ours.

Zofie had offered to come with me, but Spraggel advised against it. Apparently, a male was needed, and I was the only male in our party with the proper *lack* of experience. Zofie had blushed a bright red at the comment, and Risten just cackled at having yet another piece of information with which to torment me.

I paused, took off my hat, and scratched my head. *Now, exactly where was that pond?* I remember being quite deep in the forest and was trying to figure out if I could find my way back out. Surely, I had to be close to it. I started forward again.

It was about then that I heard a woman singing. It was the most beautiful singing I had ever heard. There were no words to it that I could make out, yet it spoke to something in my heart, both thrilling and sad at the same time. I was drawn to it.

I laughed to myself. There was no way I was going to fall for that again. She would not trick me this time. I took a step forward and pushed water ahead of me.

What!

I looked down and realized I was standing knee-deep in an old pond.

How did I get here?

Dammit, I was sure I could beat her. I slogged my way to the edge, slipping twice before getting out on the moss-covered banks. I plopped down on the ground and took off my boots to pour out the water. Creator, I hated being wet.

As I emptied my other boot, I wondered where she could be.

"You're cute," said a high pitched, very female voice from right beside me.

I jumped, turning to find a lovely face only inches away and gazing at me intently. She had a pale complexion and bright green eyes—leaf green, actually. Her long brown hair was loose and flowed down her back with small violet flowers decorating her wavy locks. It took me a moment to realize the flowers weren't so much stuck in her hair as growing there. She was dressed in a long white gown of some gauzy material which seemed to ebb and flow like fog over a mountain, but at the same time did little to conceal her feminine charms.

She sat beside me with her knees drawn up to her chest and only her toes poking daintily out from under her skirts. She was smiling, seemingly delighted in my presence. "I wish I could keep you." She sighed sadly. "But my pond has grown too shallow to drown anyone." She took my arm and settled closer, leaning against me suggestively. "But won't you stay with me anyway? I'll take good care of you. Better than any human female you'll find."

I opened my mouth to speak but paused as I remembered Spraggel's warning: "*Be courteous. She will take offense very easily. Be honest with her since she will know you're lying and... well, remember what I said about being courteous. And whatever you do, don't promise her anything. A promise is a type of binding to them, and they get really pissed off if you don't keep your word. So pissed off, they will track you down to the ends of the earth."*

"Thank you for the offer," I said. "But I'm afraid I can't stay. I have someone I need to protect."

She pouted. "That's too bad. It's been so lonely out here. I haven't seen anyone since last you came..." She looked down in thought. "Was it yesterday?" She looked back up at me, confusion on her face. "No, you're older. It must have been before that." She sighed and frowned. "I can't remember."

From what I knew, her confusion was understandable. Time moved differently for her kind. They were extremely long-lived. Even though our last encounter was a few years ago, it likely seemed just yesterday to her.

And I wish she wasn't sitting so close.

I put on my best smile. "Dearest Lady, I was hoping you could help me. My friends and I are in need of assistance only you can provide."

Her left eyebrow rose. She leaned close again, her face closing the distance between us by half. She smelled of delicate flowers. "What is it you desire?"

"Three charms. Two for my friends and one for myself. They would need to disguise us and hide us from detection."

One corner of her mouth curled up and her eyes twinkled. "Would those needing them be cursed perhaps? Those require a special charm to cover both their body and hide their soul."

"Soul?"

She ran a finger down the front of my shirt. "Silly boy. Where do you think curses attach? Not your mortal body, but your bright and shining soul. All the better to sample your myst."

She traced a circle with her finger over my shirt across each of the curses I carried on my chest. She could evidently see them despite the material of my shirt. As it would be with any young male, I found her touch both pleasant... and disturbing.

"Yes, one of my friends is cursed, as am I."

She took my left hand, and pushing up the sleeve, gazed at my own curse. "Oh my. I haven't seen this one in a while." She looked up at me with a sly smile. "Is he still as obnoxious as a cloud of flies on a warm spring day?"

"Worse," I answered.

She laughed, her voice the sound of tinkling bells. She reached out a lone finger to touch the curse's eye but paused right above it. She shook her head. "No, I best not wake him. It would not be fair. He cannot speak to me without using his secret word, so I am sure he would find it frustrating."

My eyes grew big. "You know his secret word?"

She shook her head sadly. "No, I do not. And even if I did, I would not give it to you. That, my love, is something you will find yourself when you are ready."

I sighed. "I understand. So two of the charms will need to work with curses. Is this something you can do?"

She pulled away, frowning. "I can make such. But I require a high price for them." She looked at me hungrily. "What do you have to offer in return?"

This is where I had to trust Spraggel's advice—I couldn't see how this was going to work, but my master assured me the items were very valuable to creatures such as her.

I stood and swept off my hat, presented it to her with both hands. "I can give you my hat. It is a good hat—green to match your eyes and bearing the scent of a brave young man."

Her eyes betrayed her interest. "It is a good color, and that is a scent I love. I might let you have one charm for it, the simplest one, but that is all."

I handed the hat to her and she placed it on her head. She rose and stepped to the edge of the pond and gazed down at her reflection. She turned to look at me. "It is pretty. I think it suits me. What do you think?"

I nodded. "It does suit you. But then again, anything would suit one so beautiful."

She laughed. "You are such a flatterer." She grew serious. "And what about the other charms. For those, it must be something very valuable."

I hoped what Spraggel gave me worked. "Then how about a riddle?" I asked. "Something to occupy your mind while you stroll the banks of your pond."

She smiled, clearly intrigued. "That would be interesting. However, I would have to hear it to judge its worth. And once given, I cannot give it back, but if it is a good one, I could possibly give you one or two additional charms."

I stood up straight and looked at her levelly. "Here is my riddle. A young man is traveling through the forest when he encounters a large bear blocking his path. The bear says, 'Tell me something true and I will bite your neck in half. Tell me something false and I will squeeze you to death. After giving his answer, the bear let him pass unharmed. What did the young man say?"

The nymph put a finger to her pursed lips. "Ooh, that is a difficult one." She thought about it for a moment. "I do not know the answer, so please tell me."

"The young man told the bear, 'I will be squeezed to death.'"

The nymph clapped her hands and squealed in delight. "That was a good one. I will grant your charms." She pulled three flowers from her hair, took my hand, and placed them on my palm. She gently closed my fingers over them. "These will make those looking at you see something else, and any charms trying to see through will be confused. Just be sure to carry it about your person. Oh, and one word of caution. My flowers are delicate things. Never let them touch iron, for it will kill them instantly."

"Thank you," I gave her a slight bow. "You have my gratitude."

She stepped as close as a lover, her body against mine, and put her arms around my neck toying with the hair on the back of my head. She was just slightly shorter than I. The scent of flowers was intoxicating.

I stiffened in alarm. She was much too close.

"Tell me," she said, gazing up at me with a coy smile. "Do you have someone you love?"

I hesitated, not knowing what to do. I knew I couldn't lie to her, but I was afraid of what she would do if I answered. "I...."

She put a finger to my lips, stopping the answer. "Your beating heart tells me you have someone you desire, but your hesitation tells me you fear she might not find you suitable. You could stay here with me instead. I would love you."

"Thank you, my lady...." She put a finger to my lips, silencing me again.

"You may call me Autumn. Tis not my true name, but for you, I will answer to it."

I nodded. "Thank you Lady Autumn, but I cannot stay. My friends await me."

She leaned closer with her mouth to my ear. She whispered, "What does she think of your curse?"

I froze. I couldn't take a breath.

Autumn ran her caressing finger around my ear, across to my jaw and over to my lips. "True, your curse saved her. But do you think she could love someone who is tainted with not just a simple curse, but the curse of curses?" She played with a lock of my hair. "And what of your plan not to have any children—to keep from passing on the curse. The one you love is a ruler who must have an heir. Do you think she would wed you knowing that?" She gazed at me intently for a moment and then leaned close to breathe in my ear. "*I could break your curse.*"

My eyes went wide and my heart pounded in my chest.

Break my curse!

"How?" I whispered back to her.

She smiled. "I could give you a charm that would break any curse, no matter how old it is or how powerful. Make it so it never existed." She looked up in thought. "You would, of course, have to use it before winter start. Everything sleeps in winter, as do I."

I shook my head. "Abe wouldn't allow it."

She chuckled. "It being a charm, the old curse wouldn't be able to see it. A flaw in his making perhaps. Curses he can see a league away. But a charm... he is blind to it."

I stood transfixed as I took in the information. I could let Zofie's transformations return her completely human, remove her curse, and then break my own. I could rid us of both our curses. Permanently. That was an offer too good to pass up.

I shook my head. "How do you know so much about... everything?"

Her voice changed, losing its girlishness and taking on the tone of one of long years. "Your heart has not yet been claimed, allowing me to smell your youth and taste your goodness. You are as clear to me as water in a brook." She brightened, her voice returning to its girlish tone. "So what say you? Would you like this charm?"

Did I dare?

I swallowed nervously. "I... I don't have anything more to offer."

She gave me a one-sided grin. "Ahh, but you do have something to offer." She ran her hands through my hair, mussing it and then smoothing it down. "You could give me your promise."

My skin went cold and my heart pounded. I had just entered very dangerous territory. "A promise?" My voice cracked. "That is a very high price. What would you want me to promise?"

She smiled. "Not much. Just to return to visit me. Once every spring, when the ice melts from my pond and the leaves sprout from the trees."

"How many times would I need to return?"

She leaned back and tapped me gently on the end of my nose. "Just for the rest of your life."

"And if I fail to return?"

She smiled, widely, showing her teeth. Only they were not human teeth—they were the razor-sharp teeth of death. I stared in horror. But then she looked down, and her mouth was normal again. "If you fail to return," she said. "I would take your first child, to hold and to keep as my own. I will have my visits, one way or another."

I stayed still as I thought this over. I couldn't believe what she was offering. To be a normal person. To have a family. To be someone Zofie might actually consider. It was something I had only dreamed about.

I swallowed. "How would I do this promise?"

She leaned away slightly and made little twirls on my chest. "Say your promise and give your name. Then I will give you the charm and tell you how to use it."

I took a deep breath and let it out slowly. *Did I dare?* I could end my curse and make myself a real suitor for Zofie's affection.

Did I dare not?

I backed from her and bowed deeply. "Lady Autumn, please grant me the curse-breaking charm. For this, I promise to return to see you in the spring of each year until I die. I so promise... Coren Hart."

She smiled at me. But this was a different smile. It was one of victory. She stepped forward, took my head in her hands, and pulled me gently toward her. She kissed me lightly on my forehead. I felt a coolness on my skin where her lips had touched, but it quickly faded. "There, you have the charm. To complete it, you must say these words...." She then said a phrase in an ancient language I could not understand.

"I'm not sure I can remember those words."

She patted my cheek. "Have no fear, Coren Hart. The words will appear on your lips. Just say them willingly and with intent."

She then turned and began to walk away. "Remember, you must use the charm before winter start, or the solstice as you say. I will even send you reminders, lest you forget." She paused for a moment and looked over her shoulder. "The promise is mine now whether you use the charm or not. I will see you in the spring, my love. Please don't disappoint me."

I opened my mouth to reply and suddenly found myself at the edge of the forest, the sun high in the sky just past noon. I blinked, wondering where the time had gone. I looked down at my hand. I still held the three flowers. I couldn't believe I had succeeded. It all felt like a dream.

With a light heart, I started walking the path toward the keep. Zofie would be protected, and the end of my curse was near. As I walked, I absentmindedly rubbed a minor stinging sensation on my forehead where Lady Autumn had kissed me. Only my fingers felt something sticky. When I looked at them...

They were splotched with blood.

CHAPTER THREE

An Absent Master

My companions had the horses saddled and our essentials ready by the time I returned with the charms. We had agreed it best to get away as quickly as possible in case our enemies returned.

Risten had made quick work of her own preparations to leave, and with her horse beside her, was preparing to mount up when she saw me approach. Zofie stood close by, and although she didn't look happy about Risten leaving, she was putting on a brave face. Galvyn, on the other hand, looked like Risten's departure was making his day.

Risten gave me a lopsided smile when she saw me. "I thought I was going to have to leave without telling you goodbye." She stepped forward and wrapped her arms around me, pulling me close. I stiffened. She didn't normally do that. She whispered in my ear so the others wouldn't hear. "Keep an eye on Galvyn. I don't trust him. There's always been something odd about him. People do weird things when he's around."

My eyes went wide. *What?*

She pushed me back to arm's length and gently patted my face. "Remember, if you let anything happen to Zofie, I will cut your privates off."

She turned back to her cousin and gave her one last hug before mounting up.

Zofie looked up at her. "You still have the correspondor?"

Risten reached in her vest pocket and pulled out a rounded white stone. She held it up to Zofie. "I wouldn't dare leave it."

Zofie nodded in satisfaction. "Don't forget to use it."

Risten rolled her eyes, tucking the stone back in her vest pocket. "Yes, Mother."

Zofie grinned and stepped away from the horse. Risten turned her mount and urged him down the road. We watched her slowly move away. I, for one, was uncomfortable with her leaving. It meant Zofie's protection fell squarely on my shoulders. I prayed I was up to the task.

After Risten was out of sight, I turned to Zofie. "What is that correspondor thing?"

She continued to look down the road. "It's a charm I applied to two rocks, which will allow us to send messages back and forth. It requires a little more myst than most, but fortunately, Risten has enough to use it. I thought we might need one eventually." She sighed. "I just didn't think it would be so soon."

I cocked my head to one side. "You made it? But how? You can't use myst with your curse."

She looked over at me with a weak smile. "I made it one night between transformations while you were asleep. I... uh... borrowed just a bit of your myst to make it. I hope you don't mind."

It was one of the strange side effects of me controlling Zofie's curse. While I could modify her curse, she could pull myst from me. But only during those times her curse was resting—at the full and new moons.

"Of course, I don't mind. I'm certainly not using it."

She looked at me playfully, like she wanted to say more, but then decided not to.

As we gazed at one another, Spraggel spoke up suddenly. "So Coren, how many charms did you get from the nymph?"

I jumped. Zofie smiled, her eyes twinkling, and glanced away.

"I got three," I quickly answered.

"Really? That's excellent. I only thought you'd get one."

"But you told me three."

The cat swished his tail. "That was just to make you bargain harder."

I gave Spraggel a funny look and shook my head. My master's logic was sometimes lost on me. I wasted no further time in handing out the disguise charms.

Galvyn looked at his and frowned. "Do I need to say a word or something?"

I shook my head. "The nymph said it would disguise us. She didn't say anything about needing a word to start it. Only don't let the flowers come into contact with iron, which I assume also includes steel."

Zofie nodded. "Most charms start as soon as you put it on or stop when you take it off. So I guess you have to wear it."

Galvyn held it away from him like it would soil his clothes. "And just where am I supposed to put it? I can't carry it in my coin purse. Hang it out my ear perhaps?"

Zofie smiled, "You had no problem with that when we were children." She reached up and tucked her flower into her hair. She dropped her hands. "Well?"

My mouth fell open. Where Zofie had once stood was a well-rounded middle-aged woman with gray hair and plump round face. The travel cloak Zofie had been wearing had been transformed into a long shawl draped across her shoulders and a plain brown dress. The illusion persona was still Zofie—I could easily read her nervous expression. But she just looked very different. Galvyn had a similar reaction.

Zofie looked at us in apprehension. "Is something wrong?" She even sounded older.

I smiled. "You won't believe it. You could easily pass for a grandmother now. Even your clothes have changed."

"Really?" she asked in shock. She looked at her hands and then down her front. "I don't feel any different?"

Galvyn stuck his flower behind his ear. He immediately took on the appearance of an elderly man, hunched with age, and wearing an old tunic. His floppy hat had been replaced with a simple wool cap.

Zofie laughed. "You're an old man."

Galvyn couldn't help but crack a smile. "You're a fine one to talk, Grandmother."

I shrugged. "Well, I guess it's my turn." I stuck my flower behind my ear. I looked down at my hands and body but nothing seemed different.

Both Zofie and Galvyn stared at me in shock. "What?" I asked.

"Wow!" Zofie said in amazement.

Galvyn sighed in disgust. "Swap with me," he demanded. "You've obviously got mine."

Their gaze made me uncomfortable, so I pulled the flower from behind my ear and offered it to Galvyn. We swapped, but when Galvyn put my old flower behind his ear, he became the same old man.

Zofie chuckled. "It didn't change. Apparently, the charm decides what to show based on the person."

I put the flower back behind my ear and crossed my arms. "Can one of you tell me what's wrong with my disguise?"

Spraggel looked up at me, his tail rapidly swishing back and forth. "They're just surprised. The nymph decided you should be the most gorgeous hunk of male flesh anyone has seen in recent memory." He started licking his paw. "We might have a problem because the young girls are going to faint at the sight of you." He paused, his front foot frozen in mid-air. "In fact, some of the men might faint too!"

I frowned. I thought the nymph was going to hide us, not make us something conspicuous. I decided that disguise or not, I had best keep a low profile.

And so we started our journey heading toward Spraggel's friend, Hennion Tormaigh. He was supposed to be the best historical scholar in this part of the world.

Naturally, Galvyn rode my horse since his last one turned out to be an assassin. Which left me with riding an older packhorse. She was still in fit condition—I made sure all the horses were well cared for. She was a little more docile than I preferred, but fine none the less. It was more the principle of the thing. He could have asked first.

Of course, I said nothing about my promise to the nymph. I knew Spraggel would be upset, but I didn't regret my decision. I couldn't help but have a smile on my face. No more bad luck and no more putting up with Abe's obnoxious comments. The days of my dreaded curse were numbered.

It was late afternoon when we reached the edge of Lanting Woods where Spraggel's friend lived. The woods were just normal forest, and the road wandered through them like it couldn't make up its mind which way to go. And leaves were blowing everywhere. They had completed their final dazzling display of autumn color and were now floating down to carpet the way before us.

Something ahead caught my eye. "I think I see a house," I said, leaning forward in my saddle and shading my eyes with my hand. "Is that where Master Tormaigh lives?"

Spraggel, who had been riding just behind me, leaped to my shoulder and gazed toward it. "Why, yes it is. I see that bastard finally got around to fixing the roof. The leaks must have started getting on his books. Hennion never did take good care of the place."

According to Spraggel, Master Hennion Tormaigh was a bit of a hermit and had chosen a place in the woods well away from any town or village. I had asked Spraggel why he had not visited Hennion in the eight years since I had arrived. But he gave me a vague answer saying they were just having a little tiff right now and hadn't spoken to one another in ten years. Something to do with accusations of cheating at chess when Hennion was about to win. While I loved my master, it sounded exactly like something he would do.

As we approached, I could make out more details. The house was small—more of a cottage really—and in some disrepair, the garden both in the back and the smaller flower gardens in front had gone to weeds. The thatch roof indeed seemed to have been repaired recently, and the stone chimney looked in good shape. "I wonder if anyone is home," I said. "It looks deserted."

Spraggel sniffed the air and sat back on his haunches. "Someone was here not long ago. I can smell the smoke from what's left of their fire."

I pulled up in front of the house. Galvyn and Zofie pulled up even with me a moment later.

Galvyn flicked his hand toward the cottage. "Why don't you announce us," he said. "I'll stay here to guard her highness until we know it's safe."

I frowned at Galvyn in irritation, but couldn't really argue with him. It did make sense that someone protect her.

I dismounted and tied my horse to a hitching post in the front of the house and then went through a wooden gate, the hinges squeaking loudly as I swung it open.

"Hello!" I called, stepping to the door and knocking. "Anyone home?"

I waited but nothing came from inside. I turned to look at the others behind me wondering what I should do, but they just shrugged. I turned back and knocked again. Faintly, I heard shuffling inside, and then the door cracked open. A single eye examined me—the face it belonged to shaded behind the door.

I gave my most polite smile. "Greetings. We're here to see Master Tormaigh. My master Spraggel van Deviante has some business to discuss with him."

The person on the other side of the door remained silent. I saw the eye move to examine each of us, but then seemed to settle on Spraggel sitting atop my horse. A long moment later, the door slowly opened.

The owner of the eye was a young woman with dark hair just long enough to frame her delicate face. It was mussed as one just awoken from a deep sleep. Her feet were bare, and she wore a plain beige dress with a modest neckline and short sleeves. The garment hung loose on her but left no doubt she was of small stature. Even to my untrained eye, I could tell she had the potential to be a beauty if she wanted. But it was her ethnicity that intrigued me, evident from her eyes and shape of her face: she came from lands far, far to the east. I couldn't help but wonder what she was doing in this part of the world. I swallowed, suddenly nervous. Pretty young ladies had that effect on me.

She leaned against the door as if too tired to stand much longer and regarded me with disinterest, as if I was interrupting something important. "Master Tormaigh has spoken of a Spraggel van Deviante," she answered with a strong accent, unlike any I had heard before. "He said he was an old man, with a long gray beard, balding head, and always wore a gray robe." She nodded toward our group. "I don't see one such riding with you."

Spraggel bounded off my horse and stepped toward us, sashaying in the way cats do. "Hennion's description of me was accurate as of a few days ago, but as you can see, I've unfortunately wound up on the wrong side of a transformation spell."

She nodded calmly as if he'd simply told her the time of day. "Regardless, Master told me what to do should a Spraggel van Deviante come calling." She straightened and slowly closed the door. I heard the latch fall in place behind it.

Spraggel stood frozen—ears back and his tail straight out behind him. Even for a cat, I could tell he couldn't believe what he had just heard. Spraggel went up to the door. "You tell that bastard that I came all the way to see him, and this is how he treats me!" Spraggel began to pace back and forth. I had never seen him so agitated. "It's not my fault I sneezed," he yelled. "You weren't going to beat me anyway!"

Silence came from the other side.

"Hennion, you bastard! Come out, right this second!"

Still no answer.

Spraggel abruptly turned away from the door and stuck his tail up in the air in a most indignant pose. He sashayed back toward the horses mumbling under his breath. "Let's go," he said to us. "He's not going to help."

I looked back to Zofie. She looked crushed.

What's a knight supposed to do when his lady is disappointed?

I immediately stepped back to the door and began to knock. "Please open up. I need to speak with you for just a moment."

I knocked twice more before the door finally opened again. She didn't say anything, only looked at me.

"Hello again. My name is Coren Hart. You must be Master Tormaigh's apprentice. Could I speak to you for a moment? Apprentice to apprentice." I looked over my shoulder. "In private."

She considered me in her quiet way and then invited me in.

The inside of the small house was a disaster. Books, food, cooking utensils, and bedding were strewn about the interior. There was a small mat in the corner, which appeared to be hers—at least the bits of straw on her dress seemed to match what was in the mat. A rather large table sat in the middle of the room, and on the wall to my right rested a stone hearth, which I could see had a few barely smoldering coals inside. There appeared to be another room in the back that was closed off with a simple curtain.

She closed the door and looked up at me—her dark hair partially obscuring her eyes. She was clearly curious.

"Nice place," I said, looking around. It really wasn't, but I was trying to start a conversation. It almost looked like someone had fought a battle in the room.

She didn't say anything. Just stared at me.

A little uncomfortable with the awkward silence, but knowing I needed to get things going, I went with a tried and true conversation strategy: I said the first thing that came to mind. "We really need your master's help. We're looking for the Mirror of Bygone Tears. We have to find it."

She continued to look at me.

"Please," I begged. "I don't know what my master did, but perhaps there is something I can talk my master into doing to make it right."

She didn't seem moved by my little speech. In desperation, I went down on one knee before her. "Please."

And for the first time, her expression changed—a look of absolute horror. She immediately stepped forward and grabbed me by the arms, pulling me up. "No, don't ever kneel to me. I... I am not worthy."

And when I stood, she stepped back and sighed heavily. She ran a hand through her hair, pushing it away from her face and then letting it fall right back into her eyes. She seemed perplexed. "I can't help you," she said. "My master is not here. He's gone on a trip to my homeland, and I do not expect him back for at least two more months, maybe three."

I sighed in disappointment and sank onto a bench at the table. "Creator! We were so hoping he would help us." I pursed my lips thinking what our next move would be.

She studied me a moment. "Why are you even looking for the mirror? It went missing shortly after the war against the Dark Avenyts, and that was nearly a thousand years ago. No one has seen it since. Some scholars argue that it doesn't even exist."

"Because my master read that it could see into the past. One of my friends has been accused of a crime, and we were hoping it could prove their innocence."

She shook her head. "I have read my master's books and notes concerning the mirror. It is not something so trivial. Yes, it can show what has happened before, but it has some serious limitations. It was originally constructed to spy on the Dark Avenyts, allowing the king and his generals to see what his spies had seen. However, they could only see the actions of myst users, not regular people." She went over to the hearth and stirred the embers. "Also, it requires a special key to unlock it."

I sighed. "And I bet the mirror's been hidden somewhere, that naturally won't be easy to find. Those ancients sure were predictable."

She went to the cupboard, retrieved two cups, and measured some tea into each. She then returned to the fire, pulling off a battered kettle and pouring hot water into the cups.

"Exactly." She handed one of the cups to me, giving me a slight bow.

"Thank you." I returned the bow as I took the cup, and she seemed pleased. The tea had a pleasant rich aroma, and I inhaled it as I held it in my two hands. I continued, "Seems like it would be relatively easy to find using a myst locator charm. I'm assuming that's been tried before?"

She sat on the bench beside me and delicately sipped her tea. "It has. It is shielded somehow, so that doesn't work."

I nodded. "The myst caster that made that mirror must have been very talented."

She took a sip of her tea. "A woman made it. She was a genius even by our standards. Her name was Evelend."

I froze. "Did you say Evelend?"

Evelend was the person who made *my* curse—one of the few things we had learned about my curse from a book we had 'borrowed' from the priests of Dali.

She nodded. "But not much is known about her or her other creations. There are hints she made several more devices, but few records survived on what those creations were."

"Maybe you'll take a look at a book I have and see if you can read it? It came from the Temple of Daili and is in some kind of code."

Her eyes got big. "You got into the Temple of Daili? How in the world did you do that? No one but the high priest can see their books."

I grinned. "It's a rather interesting story involving some disguises, a large bird, and one female sacrifice."

She nodded excitedly. "I'll gladly look at it." Then her expression fell. "But I doubt it will do much good. From what I know of coded books, they require a word or phrase to make it readable. This was usually entrusted to a neutral third party. If it's an old book, then it will likely be forgotten by now."

I sighed. "That would just be my luck." I put the teacup down. "Well, I should be getting back to my friends. We're in a bit of a hurry." I nodded to her. "I thank you for the information and the excellent tea. Since we have no clues to the mirror's whereabouts, we will have to find another way."

She also put her cup down and stood. "This person you're trying to help must be someone very important to you... a lover perhaps?"

I chuckled and spoke before I thought. "No, Zofie is definitely not my lover. Her cousin would cut me in half if I got too close to her."

The young woman froze; I could almost see the gears in her head turning. "Your friend's name is Zofie?"

I cringed. My big mouth strikes again.

She continued. "As in Princess Zophia Olwenna Xernow?"

"Uh..." I backed toward the door.

She waved her hand and began pacing. "Which means the woman outside has to be her, although I thought she was younger—unless she is disguised. Which makes you..." she pointed to me. "The Thief of Curses."

I stood there speechless. *How did she figure out all that?*

She lunged forward and took my left arm, flipping it over to look at the curse mark on my wrist.

But she paused when she didn't see one. She grabbed the other arm, but it also didn't have one she could see. I felt sorry for her because my curse was actually there only hidden under my disguise charm.

She looked up extremely disappointed. "I guess... I was wrong. Master always said I jumped to conclusions." She suddenly turned and smiled wickedly. "Unless... you're disguised too. It would have to be a powerful charm, but doable." She pointed a finger at me. "If you really are the Thief of Curses, then I will help you find the Mirror of Bygone Tears."

"I thought you said you didn't know where it was."

She nodded. "I don't. But that doesn't mean I don't know how to find it. I ran across something in my research." She stepped toward me. "Now are you, or aren't you the Thief of Curses?"

I sighed and pulled out the flower from behind my ear. Her eyes went wide. She grabbed my left hand and stared at my curse anchor.

She whispered in reverence, "The Abhulengulus Curse."

I gently pulled my hand back. "Do you really know where the mirror is? I need it to prove the princess didn't murder her father. And if you don't, that's fine as long as you don't turn us in."

She looked up at me in shock. "Turn you in?" She grinned. "Surely you jest. Abhulengulus is one of the artifacts my master assigned me to research. This is Evelend's greatest work. I've got to find out everything about it."

I backed away slowly. "So, can you tell us how to find the mirror so we can be on our way? Time is short."

She grabbed my arm. "Oh no, you're not leaving me. This is a once in a lifetime encounter. I've got to hear your story... ask questions... I have to *know!*"

"But the mirror...."

She looked up at me in adoration. "I'll just have to come with you!"

She immediately released me and began flying about the room—opening a cupboard and pulling out a sack, going to another and throwing in an assortment of items from a metal spoon to wrapped provisions. She paused at a book she pulled out, then shrugged and threw that in too.

"I don't think it's a good idea for you to come. This will be dangerous. If Wynn catches you with us, it will be your death."

She ignored me and went to her straw mat. She grabbed up a blanket and draped it over her shoulders, and then lastly pulled a small pouch out from her mat and strapped it around her waist.

I continued. "We don't have a horse for you. No provisions either."

She stopped and stood in the middle of the room. She looked down in thought. "What am I forgetting?" She suddenly seemed to remember and went to a desk. She pulled out a loose bound journal and put it in her bag, along with a sealed bottle of ink and some small brushes. She bound up the sack and threw it across her shoulder. She smiled at me. "I'm ready."

I shook my head. "Didn't you hear me? You can't go with us. It's dangerous and you'll only slow us down."

She stepped close. "You'll never find the Mirror of Bygone Tears without me. But in exchange, you'll tell me all about your curse."

"Can't you just tell us now?" I started to say that I'd return later, but there might not be a later. My curse could be gone by then.

"Nope. I'm not going to let this chance pass. And don't think of going to someone else. I know more about it than anyone in the world except for my master. He had me do a bunch of searching in the old texts for him." She put a hand on my arm and looked up at me. "Please? Apprentice to apprentice, you of all people know how important this is."

I searched her expectant face. Doing the timeline in my head, I severely doubted Abe would still be on my wrist by the time we got back—assuming Lady Autumn's charm worked as advertised. So she would miss her once in a lifetime chance. Plus, we really could use a guide to the mirror.

I finally sighed in defeat. "Let's talk with the others and see what they think."

She grinned.

I pointed down at her feet. "If you're going on a journey, don't you think some shoes would be a good idea?"

She blushed. "I knew I was forgetting something."

After finding her very worn, but serviceable shoes, along with a worn gray cloak with a rip in the side, we went out to talk to the others. They had dismounted and were milling around.

Zofie's eyes went up when she saw I was without my disguise, but she said nothing.

Galvyn naturally had to make a comment. "Took you long enough. I thought perhaps you two had decided to have some fun in there."

Zofie gave him a deadly look.

"Everyone," I announced. "This is...." I drew up short and turned to her. She hadn't told me her name.

"Fumiko," she answered for me, bowing at the waist to them. "Just Fumiko. I am Master Tormaigh's apprentice. Unfortunately, my master is not here and won't be back for some time. I have suggested that you take me in his stead. I can help you find the mirror."

Zofie came forward. "You would do this for us? We would be truly grateful."

Fumiko gave another short bow. "I will do my best, princess."

Zofie's eyebrow went up. She glanced at me, knowing we had agreed not to reveal ourselves yet. "So you know who we are?"

I sighed. "She figured it out."

Zofie sighed heavily and took Fumiko's hands. "Then you know what danger you're putting yourself in. Should Wynn catch us, he would treat you as an accomplice."

Fumiko nodded. "I understand. However..." She looked over her shoulder at me. "I can't pass up the chance to study the Abhulengulus curse. The opportunity is too great."

Zofie looked perplexed. "So you're going with us because of Coren?"

Fumiko nodded. "Yes, princess." She looked down. "No offense."

Zofie glanced playfully in my direction. "None taken. It just means I'm going to have to keep a closer watch on my knight."

Galvyn cleared his throat.

Zofie grinned sheepishly and introduced Galvyn.

Fumiko gave him a bow also. "Greetings, young lord. You are Lord Merrick's eldest son. It is fortuitous you are accompanying the princess."

Spraggel jumped up on the hitching post, his tail switching back and forth. "So you know where the Mirror of Bygone Tears is?"

Fumiko pointedly ignored Spraggel and turned to me. "My master forbade me to speak to the one called Spraggel van Deviante. While I hold no grudge against him, my master said if I ever did speak to him without his permission, he would revoke my apprenticeship. Would you pass this along to him?" She glanced at him and then back to me. "Also, that I'm sorry he has turned into a cat, although my master usually talked about him like he was more of a dog."

Spraggel arched his back and hissed.

Galvyn sighed impatiently. "So where is this mirror?"

Fumiko shrugged. "I'm not sure. The exact location was never given."

Galvyn waved his arm in irritation. "Then please explain to me why having you along would help?"

"Because your family has the Wayward's Finder. It's ancient, but still effective at locating what was lost. And...."

I interrupted. "Wait a moment. You said that the mirror couldn't be found by myst locators."

Fumiko smiled. "It can't. But there are other ways of asking the question of where it is. Like the box holding it, or perhaps things about the land it's on. We can ask the finder some of these and pinpoint the location."

I looked up at Galvyn. "Would your family let us use this Wayward's Finder?"

Galvyn shrugged, but he looked a little unsure. "I suppose so. Father has it in a case in the library, although he hasn't let anyone use it in years." He scratched his ear. "Isn't there another way to find it? Going back to Beynon Manor is quite the trip from here."

Fumiko shook her head. "Sorry, that is the only myst object I know of that has the reach we'll need."

Galvyn sighed. "We can ask Father." Then he smiled. "I'm sure he'll let us since it's for my *betrothed*."

Zofie frowned but didn't correct him. She looked back to Fumiko. "I would welcome your help in finding the location of the mirror, but I think it's too dangerous for you beyond that. For your own safety, I would ask that we part company as soon as it is determined." She glanced at me. "Curse or no."

Fumiko looked disappointed but nodded. "Yes, princess. I understand."

Zofie turned to her horse, and Galvyn followed suit. But he wore a very unhappy expression.

Since we didn't have an extra horse, I volunteered to let Fumiko ride with me. As I reached down to help her up, I remembered something she had said earlier.

"Fumiko, you said a key is needed to unlock the mirror. Do you know where that is?"

She grinned broadly. "I've already found the key."

I looked at her in surprise. "Where is it then?"

She settled down behind me and patted my left arm. "It's your curse. The key to unlocking the mirror is you."

CHAPTER FOUR

A Maiden in Distress

Since we had a couple hours more of daylight, we pressed on a bit farther even though it meant we would be camping out for the night. To be considerate of our horses, Zofie and I switched off having Fumiko ride double with us. Galvyn declined to let her ride with him saying it wouldn't be proper for a young woman, especially a commoner, to be so intimate with him. I personally think he just never learned to share.

Fumiko quickly proved her worth by showing us a short cut. By taking what looked like a seldom-used trail, she led us through the woods and to a well-used path along the Tendum River. This would shorten our route by at least a day. If we followed the river south, it would lead us straight to Iron Landing. And from there, we could catch a barge to Beynon Manor where Galvyn lived. I had never been there, but from what I read, it was a castle in its own right. The only reason it was called a manor was to prevent insulting the king (and to get lower taxes).

Unfortunately, Beynon Manor, and Lord Merrick's lands for that matter, were on the coast far to the south-west. Which meant we had a lot of ground to cover until we reached it.

When darkness started making the rough path too risky for the horses, we made camp in a clump of woods just a short ways from the river. We only built a small fire and settled down with travel bread and dried meat. We also set aside our disguise charms afraid of overusing them or crushing the delicate flowers in our sleep.

Popping the last of her bread into her mouth, Zofie dug into her satchel and pulled out her correspondor. She held her hand out and placed the stone in the center of her palm. "I'm going to see if I can contact Risten."

Fumiko leaned forward. Her eyes got big as she realized what it was.

Zofie took a deep breath and closed her eyes. "Now, let's see if it works."

We all watched in anticipation as a blue glow enveloped the stone on Zofie's hand. "Risten?" she asked out loud. "Are you there?"

"SHIT!" came Risten's startled reply from the stone. "Don't do that!"

Zofie grinned. "Sorry, but we agreed I would contact you right after dark."

"Yeah, yeah. But I wasn't expecting you to scare me half to death doing it. I'm camping out here in the woods all by myself, and just as I'm about to fall asleep, your booming voice calls my name. I thought my heart was going to jump out of my chest!"

Zofie frowned. "Weren't you going to stay at an inn?"

Risten sighed. "I was. But when I stopped in a small village to water my horse, I overheard some merchants talking about soldiers patrolling the road. I thought it best to switch my route."

Zofie was clearly not pleased. "Risten, it might be too dangerous. Why don't you turn back?"

Risten laughed. "Not a chance. We decided we needed to connect up with my master's friends, and by the Creator, that's what I'm going to do."

"Risten..."

She cut Zofie off. "I'll be fine. Now turn this damn thing off before you attract something really nasty."

Zofie sighed. "All right. But be careful."

"Oh, and tell shit for brains that he better not slack off on his sword practice. He won't like what I do to him if he hasn't improved next time I see him."

I grimaced. Zofie looked up at me and smiled. "He heard you."

"And that goes for you too! You're only slightly better than he is, and that's not saying much."

It was her turn to grimace. "I'll do my best."

"Good! Now silence this thing and go to bed."

Zofie smiled wistfully as she covered the stone with her other hand. Its blue glow went out and she moved to put it away.

Fumiko was in awe. "That was amazing. I've got to write it down." She immediately pulled out her pen, ink, and unbound journal and began to write.

I yawned. I was dead tired from everything that had happened, so I was ready for my blankets. Spraggel had already curled up by the fire and was fast asleep. I glanced at Galvyn and noticed him watching Zofie as she readied her own place to sleep. He sat a little away from the rest of us, so I couldn't read his expression in the dim light. But he seemed to be watching Zofie's every move.

I was just finishing with my blankets when Fumiko called out to me. "Coren, will you sit with me," she asked. She was sitting cross-legged close to the fire with her journal spread across her lap. She patted the ground beside her. "I was hoping to talk about your curse."

I rubbed my eyes. I really didn't want to, but a deal was a deal.

Zofie raised an eyebrow as I plopped down beside Fumiko, but made no comment.

Fumiko sat up straight, as excited as if she was meeting the king. "Can I see your curse anchor," she asked.

I extended my left arm and she took it. She turned it this way and that, trying to see it better in the dim light, and seemingly unaware of how she kept brushing my hand against her chest. I was glad for the dim light so she couldn't see me blush. Once she found the proper angle, she asked me to hold my arm just so, and then quickly began to draw a sketch of it. It was a pretty good likeness, especially considering the conditions she was working under.

While she worked, Galvyn got up and went to where Zofie was watching us. He bent and whispered something in her ear. She glanced guiltily in my direction and then stood. "We'll be back in a moment. Galvyn wants to have a word in private with me."

I nodded, feeling an odd tightness in my chest as I watched Zofie and Galvyn walk away from the fire back toward the road. They were eventually lost in the darkness.

Spraggel, who was curled up beside the fire, opened one eye and watched them. He got up, stretched luxuriously as felines do, and then sauntered off after them. I snorted. I guess their request for privacy didn't apply to cats.

When Fumiko was done, she flipped to a new page and looked up at me. "I've heard the curse's eye opens when it's active. Can you make him do that so I can do another drawing with the eye open?"

I shrugged. "All right."

She grinned and hugged my hand to her chest again, watching the curse closely. I think my face was redder than the coals in the fire.

I cleared my voice. "Abe?" I said aloud. "Can you talk to me?"

He did not reply.

"Abe? Talk to me."

Still nothing.

"Abhulengulus, I command you to come forth right now!"

But Abe remained strangely quiet.

Puzzled, I shook my head. "I don't understand it. He always comes out when I call. I'm not sure...."

I broke off as Zofie stormed back into camp. Alone. She immediately went to her bedroll, jerked off her boots and threw herself down. We watched her in surprise.

She leaned up. "Do you mind if we go to bed?" she asked politely, with only a slight strain to her voice. "We need to get up early in the morning."

Fumiko and I exchanged a glance. She started putting her drawing materials away and I got in my blanket. Spraggel sauntered in and curled up beside my head. He leaned close and rubbed against my face. "A word of advice," he whispered softly. "Never, ever, touch the princess in a way she doesn't want to be touched. You will greatly regret it." He chuckled softly.

"What do you mean?" I whispered back.

Spraggel didn't say anything more, but I could swear he was smiling. A moment later, Galvyn limped into camp, a hand hovering near his crotch. He didn't seem to be doing so well.

Understanding suddenly hit me. "Zofie did that?"

Spraggel snorted. "Vanquished in one swift kick."

I closed my eyes, but I couldn't help but go to sleep with a smile on my face.

We arose at dawn the next morning and continued our travels. Galvyn, in his usual arrogant manner, decided he should take the lead for our meager party, leaving the rest of us to follow in his wake. Zofie, for her part, set her own pace and seemed content with letting him lead from as far in front as he wanted.

As we traveled, Fumiko was eager to ask questions about my curse, but Zofie's dark mood was infectious and dulled the conversation until even our newest member gave up. Zofie was indeed brooding, but I didn't think it was entirely Galvyn's doing. There seemed to be more weighing on her.

There was something on my thoughts too. Why hadn't Abe come forth when I called him? He'd never done that before. Unless it was the charm Lady Autumn had given me. She had said he would be blind to it, but perhaps she was wrong. Maybe he found out and was avoiding me, afraid I was finally going to be rid of him. I snorted. Not that it mattered. He was just a curse—an old and evil one, for sure—but still just a thing someone made. The sooner I got rid of him, the better.

We arrived on the outskirts of Iron Landing just before dark and dismounted to rest the horses and allow Spraggel time to scout ahead. We had been wearing our disguises all day, even though we only encountered a few people on the road. While we didn't have one for Fumiko, Spraggel thought she would be safe since she hadn't been associated with us previously.

Spraggel slinked out of the tall grass beside us.

"How's the road ahead?" I asked.

Spraggel's tail flicked back and forth in agitation. "Guarded. There is a checkpoint blocking the gate into town. They've set up some barrels and a wagon that you have to go around. I counted two guards, but there is likely a third somewhere close by."

Galvyn crossed his arms. "A checkpoint. Then they know where we're going."

Spraggel sat on his haunches, his tail continuing to flick back and forth. "I have to disagree, young lord. From the keep, there are only two ways to go, Iron Landing or Dunomhir. They've just staked out our likely paths."

Zofie nodded. "So, if we can avoid detection here, then they will have no idea what our goal actually is."

Spraggel stood. "That's why I strongly suggest we not get caught."

I nodded. "Sounds like a plan to me."

We moved to saddle up. Spraggel looked to Fumiko. "Child, remember to hang back and come in a little behind us. Our story is that we passed you on the road, but you're not with us."

She nodded in acknowledgment.

Spraggel stood and moved off toward the side of the road. "I'm going to scout ahead. They know a cat could be with you, so it's best I not be seen. I'll meet you at the Inland Sea." Spraggel then leaped off the horse and disappeared into the night.

The Inland Sea was Spraggel's favorite inn to visit on the rare occasions we came to town. Mikney de'Glougeman, the proprietor, and his daughter Maggie always did their best to make us feel welcome—although Mikney did not particularly like me. He seemed to have the odd idea I was chasing his daughter.

We all mounted up and pushed ahead with Fumiko on foot behind us. Only moments later, we rounded a bend in the road and encountered the checkpoint. As Spraggel had reported, it was manned by two bored guards wearing the king's livery of purple jackets and golden pants. They immediately stepped forward to block our path. "Declare yar'selves!" shouted the taller of the two.

I pulled up before them. "Good evening, sirs. We're from Dunomhir and we've business in town. My name is Rhen Corart and these are my parents. Gav and Fee."

He nodded toward Fumiko who was just walking up behind us. "What about the girl in back?"

She gave the guards a bow. "My name is Fumiko. My master has sent me for supplies. I am not with these travelers. They passed me a little ways back."

The taller guard nodded and looked at all of us. "The king 'as order'd a curfew," he announced, a little louder than he needed to. He had evidently been practicing but hadn't quite mastered that commanding voice yet. "No one's suppos'd to be out after dark, and we're check'n everyone com'n or go'n."

"Really?" I tried to look shocked. "This is the first we've heard about it. What brought this on?"

"Order came out this morn'n. Some dangerous traitors are supposed to be com'n this way. They're plott'n against the king. Four of'em, to be exact. One of'em even claimed to be the king's murder'n sister." He turned to the side and spat. "Thank the Creator, we all know that evil woman is dead." He wiped his mouth on the back of his hand.

Wynn hadn't wasted any time.

I swallowed nervously, making sure I did not look at Zofie. "So we can't go in? We've traveled so far and my poor parents are bone-tired."

He grinned. "We'll let ya in, after we check's ya." He motioned to the other guard. The shorter one marched forward and put a lens up to his eye. I tried not to look panicked. It was an *evincer*—a charmed piece of glass that could see through illusions. I just prayed Lady Autumn's charms were strong enough.

The guard stared at us, swinging the glass from me to Zofie to Galvyn to Fumiko and then back again. I could feel the nervous sweat trickling down my neck.

Finally he lowered the glass. "No illusions," he announced.

The taller looked disappointed and stepped to the side. "Get to yar lodging quickly." He grinned evilly. "I don't want ya getting mistook for traitors. If someone stops ya, tell them Odter let ya pass."

I gave a slight bow from my saddle. "Thank you, sirs. We won't cause any trouble."

I nudged my horse around the makeshift barricade and led the way into town and down the main street. Fumiko followed a short distance behind. Once we were out of earshot, I breathed a sigh of relief and pulled up to wait for her. I turned to say something to Zofie, but noticed she had tears in her eyes. Evidently, the guard's words had stung. She glanced at me and gave a quick shake of her head. So I left her alone.

The streets were empty and getting dark as the sun began to set. Most of the houses and stores were closed and dark—only a few had faint light from behind their shuttered windows. Our horse's hooves sounded loudly on the cobblestone adding to the unwelcome feel of the town.

A little further, we passed two of the king's soldiers questioning four civilians. One of the soldiers stared at us as we went past, but said nothing. I could feel their eyes on us. I thanked Lady Autumn once again for the wonderful charms.

After what seemed an eternity, we finally came to the Inland Sea. It was a welcome sight indeed to see an open door and a gentle light coming from the windows. It seemed the only ray of light in the town. As we drew up in front, I heard people talking and gentle laughter.

I sighed in relief. Maybe things were all right.

From inside, I heard a glass break and then shouting, followed closely by a female yelp and then a crash.

I sighed. Then again, maybe not.

"Stay here for a moment," I said as I dismounted and quickly tied my horse to a hitching post. "Let me see what's going on."

I stepped inside and immediately saw the problem. Two of the king's soldiers were inside. A big burly one had Mikney, the inn's owner, bent back over a table gripping him by the shirt, arm cocked and ready to punch. Mikney's nose was bloody. The other soldier wore the uniform of an officer—a captain, I thought. He was sitting on a stool and Maggie, Mikney's young daughter just barely starting to grow into her womanhood, was unwillingly sitting on his lap. The tray she usually carried was on the floor, as were several broken mugs and a spreading pool of ale.

Maggie tried to squirm out of the captain's grasp, but the soldier wouldn't let go. "Now just hold still girl," he said. "All I want is a little hug and a kiss. Surely, you've done that before."

Mikney struggled to stand, but another blow from the large man stopped him.

My anger rose. Maggie was one of the few people that had been nice to me in this town and in no way deserved this treatment. The last time I had seen someone abusing women, he got cursed into being a female himself. While I was sorely tempted to repeat that, it would definitely give us away. No, I would have to try something else.

"Are you the captain?" I yelled, putting a hand over my heart and breathing rapidly like I had run a great distance.

The man looked up, clearly irritated at having his fun interrupted. "What do you want?"

"Your men..." I gasped. "Down by... Ox Head tavern." I paused for a couple more gulps of air, then bent over with a hand on my knee. I pointed in the general direction. "They caught... four people... said I... should get you."

The captain jumped up, unceremoniously dumping Maggie to the floor. He motioned to the big burly guy, and they took off out the door.

I turned to watch them leave and smiled. I hadn't actually lied, but then again, I had best keep out of sight in case the captain returned.

Mikney slowly picked himself up off the table, dabbing at his nose and wincing when he realized it was broken. He muttered something in his native language that I didn't completely catch, but it had something to do with female dogs and the man's ancestry.

Maggie hadn't moved since being dumped on the floor. I knelt beside her, where she regarded me with an almost dazed expression.

"Maggie, are you all right?" I asked. "Did they hurt you?"

She slowly shook her head, tears welling in her eyes. She wiped them with the back of her hand, and I helped her stand.

She gave me a guarded look. "How did you know my name?" she asked. "Do I know you?"

I smiled. "I'm sorry young lady. I'm just a friend. Now let's get this cleaned up so you can go hide out in the back for a while." I leaned close and whispered in her ear. "It's Coren. I'm in disguise."

Her eyes went wide, and her eyes flicked over my disguise looking for some feature she could recognize. She nodded and bent to her task. I helped her to speed things along and then shooed her to the back, cautioning her not to come out.

Mikney, on the other hand, began to regard me with suspicion.

I stepped up to him. "There is something I need to speak with you about in private." I glanced around the room. It looked like all his customers had fled once the hitting started. But someone could still be lurking nearby "Perhaps we could go out back."

Holding his nose, Mikney nodded. He led me through the kitchen and outside to a small courtyard. I smiled. It was where Risten and I had fought a mock swordfight to settle a bet (she'd thoroughly kicked my butt). It looked empty.

While I was trying to decide how best to approach revealing my identity, Spraggel solved it for me. He slinked out from behind a woodpile and leaped up on a railing beside us. "Hello, Mikney," he announced. "Looks like you've been fighting again."

Mikney's eyes went wide, his eyes traveling from me to the cat.

I pointed to my feline master. "It's Spraggel," I offered and then pointed to myself. "And I'm actually Coren."

Mikney frowned. Looking back to Spraggel, he asked, "If you're truly the old man, then tell me why you keep frequenting my inn. Is it because you like my ale, or the way I serve my food?"

Spraggel sat down on the rail and cocked his head to one side. "The answer is neither. I won a bet a few years back."

Mikney shook his head in disbelief. "And I thought I got roughed up. What happened to you?"

"A myst user was afraid of my deadly blade."

Mikney looked at him skeptically. "Afraid of you maybe, but not your blade." He glanced around the courtyard nervously. "Please tell me you're not the reason the king's soldiers have everything locked tight?"

Spraggel's tail flicked back and forth. "Could be. Although it would be best for you not to ask."

Mikney gave a disappointed sigh. "I should have known."

Spraggel began to lick his paw. "When did all this start? The king's soldiers have always been a rough bunch, but this is way beyond that."

Mikney shook his head and looked off into the distance. "The curfew was announced just this morning. But we weren't really surprised. The tension's been building since you were here in the spring. Partly because the number of soldiers in town has been growing—and they're not very well-behaved. They certainly don't mind throwing a few fists to make an extra coin."

Spraggel sat up straight. "Sounds like recruiting standards have gone down."

Mikney shook his head. "Not gone down. Changed. And that's not all. About a month ago, the new king issued an edict that all myst users had to register with the local magistrate. Something about needing a ready list in case we were invaded. Any myst user found not registered by the Day of the New would be hanged." He wagged his finger at Spraggel. "Now, that one didn't sit too well with most people."

My master and I exchanged a look. Only about a quarter of the population were myst users. While they were definitely valuable, they weren't that rare. What exactly was Wynn up to?

Spraggel started licking his paw and washing his face. "Mikney, I hate to ask, but can you put us up for the night? There's five of us—two men, two women, and me, of course."

Mikney thought for a moment. "I only have a couple rooms to let and they're full. The king's soldiers make folks want to be indoors after dark." He thought for a moment. "The men can stay in the attic. Won't be comfortable, but it'll be dry. For the women... they'll have to sleep in Maggie's room."

Spraggel nodded. "I appreciate you doing this for us."

Mikney nodded and then turned to go back inside. "I best not be away too long. Just grab your stuff and head to the attic. I'll have Maggie bring you some food in a bit."

He started to step away, but paused. He looked at me. "Thanks for what you did in there."

I shrugged. "No thanks needed. You're my friends."

He looked at me a minute longer. He then turned to leave but called over his shoulder, "I'll still kill you if you bother her."

It was wonderful to be loved.

CHAPTER FIVE

The Announcement

I t had been a long day and I was exhausted. So after a quick dinner, I bedded down in the attic and immediately fell asleep. Of course, a dream was right behind.

It was one of those lucid ones, where you know you're actually dreaming, yet everything seems so real. I was back in the forest with Lady Autumn. The colors of the changing trees were vibrant reds and yellows. I could even hear a breeze gently stir the leaves. I was lying on my back on a soft bed of moss with my head in her lap. She leaned over me, gently caressing my face and smoothing back my hair. "When are you going to use your charm?" she asked softly. "I thought by now, you would have. Aren't you eager to be free of your curse and turn into an ordinary person?"

I wanted to answer; my mouth moved, but no sound came out.

She traced a finger over my lips. "I wonder if the princess would have use for an ordinary person. There are so many of them, after all."

I shook my head in denial. Zofie wasn't like that.

Lady Autumn smiled. "Are you sure? What could you possibly offer her? I venture that she's only using you. And once your curse is gone, you will be too." She leaned closer, a smug smile on her face. "Come to me after she breaks your heart..."

I awoke with a start. Spraggel was curled up and lying nearly on top of my head, his long tail flicking across my face. I tried to calm my pounding heart and turned over to get away from his irritating tail. I was still tired, but found myself wide awake. I was fairly sure I hadn't been asleep all that long. But every time I closed my eyes, all I saw was the smug smile on Lady Autumn's face. Had the dream actually been from her? Or was it my fears surfacing? I wasn't sure.

I couldn't help but notice the quiet in the room. While dark, enough light came from around the shutters to see that Galvyn's mat was empty. I couldn't help but wonder where he had gone. The outhouse most likely—the attic didn't have a chamber pot. I threw off my own covers and rose. Perhaps I should take a trip myself. Spraggel opened one eye to watch me get up, but it quickly faded shut. I shook my head. I think this form suited him better than being a human.

I quietly went downstairs, and after making sure no one was around, went out back toward the outhouse. I smiled as I remembered last spring. After my mock fight with Risten, Zofie had left a gift for me. Of course, I didn't know it at the time, but it was the King's Sword. She had told me later that she just knew I was the one to have it. I smiled. She must have at least seen something in me.

But the dream and Lady Autumn's words wouldn't leave me. Did Zofie really care for me, or was I just someone useful because of my curse? I shook my head. I had to have confidence. After my curse was gone, she would be able to see the real me.

I stepped out on the back porch, but froze when I saw two people standing in the courtyard illuminated by moonlight. I didn't have my disguise, so I stepped back into the shadows. I held my breath listening and was surprised that I recognized the voices.

It was Zofie and Galvyn. And they weren't disguised.

I looked closer and saw that Galvyn had one arm around Zofie's waist and was gesturing with the other. They were standing very close. "...Zof, I know you're fond of those two, but you have to think of the kingdom. Please, just come away with me. Using these disguise charms, we could easily get to Father and explain what happened in your own words. I'm sure we could convince him. Then we could be married, and with Father's backing, retake your throne. We wouldn't have to search for that accursed mirror." He leaned closer. "You and I would be unstoppable."

Zofie took a step back, slipping away from his arm. "Galvyn, I won't abandon Coren and Spraggel. I owe them my life. And besides, there is no guarantee your father would believe me."

"All the more reason for speed." The young lord took her hand and held it to his lips. "Then let's find a priest here. We could get married on the spot. Then Father couldn't argue with you since you'd be my wife. We could be marching on the palace within the month."

Zofie sighed, her shoulders sagging. "Gal...."

He cut her off by pulling her into a sudden kiss. Which lingered for a heartbeat longer than I cared to watch. But she shoved away from him. "Stop."

Galvyn went down on one knee before her. "Princess Zophia. Please marry me. With the Creator as my witness, I'll do my best to make you happy and serve the kingdom."

Zofie stared at him but didn't immediately answer.

I turned away and quietly went back inside. I knew what Zofie was going to tell him. Galvyn's arguments made perfect sense. What else could she do?

I awoke the next morning just after sunrise. I was lying on my side at the edge of the mat, and when I opened my eyes, the first thing I saw was a small flower growing through the floorboard. I thought it a violet—far out of season for this crisp fall morning. It had to be a reminder from Lady Autumn.

I rubbed my scratchy eyes. I was hardly rested. Thoughts of Zofie had kept me awake most of the night. So, I put my bedding away and left Galvyn still snoring in his bed. He had returned to the room shortly after me. I had pretended to be asleep, no mean feat since he had been loud enough to wake the whole inn.

Spraggel had gotten up early too—I guessed that was normal for a cat—prowling around Creator knew where. He had mentioned before bedding down that he intended to do some more scouting before we left. I hoped he didn't get into something.

I put my disguise back on and went downstairs to the tavern. Maggie smiled when she saw me and waved, as she expertly dodged through her early morning customers. She knew who I was now, and I received my usual bright smile from her.

Maggie pointed to a table in the corner and I was surprised to see that Zofie, hidden by her grandmother disguise, was sipping a cup of tea with the remains of her mostly uneaten breakfast pushed to one side. She was staring down at her cup—her expression of one deep in thought.

I sat down across from her. Zofie looked up in surprise and then smiled. "Good morning," she said. "Did you sleep well?"

I shook my head. "Not really, I had a lot on my mind."

Zofie nodded, looking thoughtful. "Me too."

Maggie returned and slapped down a plate with a hefty slice of ham and a small loaf of fresh bread, plus some of the same hot tea that Zofie had. She stood beside me with her hands on her hips. "Eat!" she commanded. "I put that aside for you this morning, so you better like it. If Father finds out...."

"Maggie!" came Mikney's voice. I looked over to find him glaring at me. His face was bruised and his nose swollen from his previous encounter, but I was still able to read his displeasure.

Maggie huffed and rolled her eyes as only young girls can. She went to see what he wanted.

Zofie's disguised face gave a wistful smile as she watched Maggie stomp away. "She seems quite smitten with you. You're all she could talk about as we got ready for bed last night." Zofie leaned forward and grinned. "We might have to change your name to Thief of Hearts."

I cut into the ham and took a bite. "I haven't done anything to encourage her." I shrugged. "I honestly don't know what she sees in me."

Zofie gave me a knowing smile. "Maybe I'll tell you one day."

"What?"

She shook her head. "Just kidding."

Maggie went into the back and came out a moment later wearing her jacket. She smiled and waved at us as she went out the door evidently on a mission for her father.

Zofie sighed and propped her head on her hand. "We had quite the conversation last night and stayed up much too late. It's the most fun I've had in a long time." She grinned. "We even pledged to be friends for life." Zofie looked toward the door that Maggie had left through. "I always wanted a little sister, and she is exactly what I had imagined one to be." The grin drained from her face and she sat up straighter. "If I do get the throne, I'd like to sponsor her—maybe give her a chance to be tutored at Edlingreen. But I don't know if her father would let her." She shook her head. "It would be such a waste if he didn't."

"I agree, she's definitely smart."

Zofie rolled her eyes in my direction. "She's more than smart Coren. She has the gift."

My eyes went large. "A myst user?"

She nodded. "I can see it in her. It's one of the few things I can still do with this curse on me. She's not that strong, but she has the ability to do some craftwork. With a little training, she could do quite well for herself."

I nodded. "There's always a demand for those that can build myst lanterns and other minor charms." I sat up straighter. "I guess I have another reason to see you made queen."

Zofie nodded distractedly but didn't answer. She had gone into her thoughts again.

I shifted topics trying to draw her out. "How was Fumiko?"

Zofie shrugged. "That girl could sleep through an apocalypse. She was out as soon as she hit the bed."

I nodded. "She's probably not used to traveling."

Zofie nodded. "She seems nice though." But she made no further comment.

I finished the last of my tea and pushed my plate away. "I'm heading out for a bit."

Zofie gave me a puzzled look. "But why? I thought we would arrange passage on a barge this morning?"

"We are, but last night Spraggel said he was going to scout the area and make sure we can do it safely. While he's doing that, I thought I would take the opportunity to pick up a few supplies. I shouldn't be long."

"Can I come too?" she asked.

I looked at her in surprise. But she didn't wait for an answer. She gulped down her now cold tea and started for the door while I sat rooted to the spot. She stopped and looked back at me. "Coming?"

What could one do?

I asked Mikney to let Galvyn or Spraggel know where we were going, and we walked down the street toward the market.

We walked side by side, not saying anything. I wanted to ask her about last night, but couldn't figure out how to approach it without making it look like I had been eavesdropping. Probably because eavesdropping was exactly what I had been doing.

I felt her hand touch my shoulder and she pointed. "That's the spot I first noticed you," she said, her mouth curling with the hint of a smile. "You were gawking at Risten and me."

I grinned. "Because I was amazed to see a woman, who I would later learn was your cousin, with this huge bird on her shoulder. The bird seemed to be following me with its eyes."

She nudged me. "It's because I was. I don't know what it was about you, but I couldn't take my eyes off you."

I chuckled. "You mean like now?"

Zofie playfully slapped me on the shoulder.

We laughed. And it felt good. We hadn't laughed together in quite a while. There had just been so much going on.

We turned a corner and came to the beginnings of the town market. Zofie was immediately drawn to the stall of a woman with lots of jewelry. One thing I had learned about Zofie while traveling with her was her attraction to anything shiny, especially if it could be worn.

She paused, lingering over a series of rings. The woman watching the stall claimed them to be pure silver. But as I assessed the condition and location of the stall, I knew they were more likely iron or pewter only dipped in the precious metal.

Thankfully, Zofie didn't spend but a couple moments looking before we were able to continue on to the market, where she stopped at another similar stall for another few minutes. When I finally got to the merchants I needed, we had stopped by no less than six different places looking at jewelry. I couldn't figure out what she was thinking. While she may be a princess, we didn't have the coins to spare for such.

I think she finally noticed my exasperation and paused in her looking. I breathed a sigh of relief and moved on to the purchases we'd need for our journey.

I went sparingly, only purchasing an extra myst lamp (used of course) and some travel food. I was hoping Galvyn's purse would help fund us since he'd already stated he preferred to stay in inns. But one never knew what one would encounter while out questing.

Our little excursion had already taken longer than I expected, and when I finished my last purchase, we found ourselves in the town square. There were a lot of people out crowding the streets, no doubt due to the curfew. But thanks to our disguises, no one paid us a second look. Unless we addressed someone directly, they tended to avoid us. In fact, I noticed that when we went through a clump of people, they mysteriously moved aside to let us pass. An interesting side effect of Lady Autumn's charm.

When I finished making my last purchase, Zofie put a hand on my arm. "Would you mind if we went in that shop?" she asked, nodding toward the building next to us. From the sign, it was a silversmith.

I turned back toward her and opened my mouth to protest. Over her shoulder, I saw a young couple holding hands, and the answer to why she was looking at jewelry hit me in the gut. She was looking for an engagement gift for Galvyn—and a ring was the traditional item. That had to be the reason. How could I have been so blind? I nodded numbly and let her pull me toward the silversmith.

The shop's door was open to allow the light and air into the room. Inside it was darker than I would have expected, and our boots made a loud clomping sound on the wooden floors as we entered. An older man looked up from a table at the back, a series of small tools scattered around him. On the one side of the room, was a case with a glass top. I was surprised to see such fine, clear glass since it was hard to make. Inside the case, I could see several rows of elegant necklaces, brooches, and rings. I had never seen the like except on the chests and fingers of nobles.

The shopkeep stood and walked over to us—his eyes wary. Even with our disguises on, we were not exactly the clientele that usually frequented his shop. "Good morning Madam and Sir," he said. "Can I help you with something?"

I was going to suggest that we leave before we attracted any unwanted attention when Zofie stepped toward him. Somehow even through her disguise, her noble birth shown through. "I lost a ring a long time ago—it looked silver, but it was actually white gold. I enter every shop I can find and pray that I find it. It belonged to my mother, you see."

The man seemed to soften a bit, but he still looked skeptical. "I'm sorry madam, but I only sell the rings I make here. You might try Malchalm's further down the street. He sometimes buys interesting items. White gold is rare and exactly something that would attract him."

Zofie nodded. "Thank you, good sir. May the Creator bless you." She gave a slight nod and started toward the door.

"Madam," the shopkeep called after us. "What exactly did this item look like? I can at least keep an eye out for it."

Zofie turned toward him and smiled. "It was a wide ring—something a woman would wear, with a vine pattern engraved around it. For a centerpiece, it had five small blue jewels arranged like a flower.

My mother never took it off, and it was supposed to become mine after she died, but it somehow got lost."

The man nodded. "I will watch for it."

Zofie nodded in return. "My thanks. I will check back upon my return trip."

The man nodded one last time and we left the shop. I was surprised. She didn't ask about a ring for Galvyn. I had been so sure. Could she have been covering up her true intent?

The words were out of my mouth before I could stop them. "Did you really have a ring like that from your mother?"

She nodded and gave me a wistful smile. "Yes, I did, or at least I was supposed to. Father gave it to me after Mother's death, and I had put it away until I was older. But somehow it went missing from my room. Father thought it might have been a servant, but none would confess to it."

Now, I felt stupid. Zofie wasn't looking for an engagement gift, she was looking for her mother's ring. "I... I hope you find it."

She shook her head. "I doubt I'll ever see it again." She looked up wistfully. "But one can hope. I remember it as clear as yesterday. Mother would often let me look at it as I sat on her lap. She never took it off. I'd run my fingers over its engravings and jewels. It was quite beautiful." She gave a heavy sigh. "It's sad really. I can remember the ring better than my mother herself. I asked Father about its history, and he said it was given to my mother by my grandmother."

I pulled her to the side as a cart passed. "Is your grandmother still alive?"

She shrugged. "I'm honestly not sure. I asked Father about my mother's lineage, but he wouldn't talk about it. Nor could I find anything about it in the family records. It was almost as if my mother just appeared on the face of the earth one day."

"Surely, the servants knew something."

She smiled mischievously. "They did, or at least a part of it. Apparently, when Father was a young man, he went overseas on a diplomatic trip. But the ship went missing in a bad storm, and he was thought to have died. Then nearly a year later, he returned very much alive." She paused while we stepped around a knot of people. "A month or so after his return, my mother appeared at the castle gates. When my father heard, he ran to meet her personally. It seems they met while he was missing." She sighed. "They eventually married, but it apparently caused quite a scandal on my mother's side. Although she had married a king, her family hadn't approved and cut ties with her. So I've never seen any relatives from her side." She sighed. "The ring was all I had of hers. I keep hoping that I'll run across it."

We were just entering the town square when a disturbance arose ahead of us. To our surprise, the king's herald rode into the square on a beautiful horse draped in royal colors. Accompanying him were two men on foot with long brass trumpets. They took position in the center of the square, with one of the trumpet players on each side of the mounted man. Then, they raised their instruments to their lips and blew loudly.

Traffic in the square and surrounding streets came to a halt—all eyes moved to the newly arrived men, and a hush fell over the crowd. Zofie and I hung back, afraid to get closer. Lady Autumn's charm was making us a small island in a large group of people. By hiding us, it was making us more visible.

After the trumpets were lowered, the Herald unfolded a piece of parchment and read from it.

"Hear me, oh hear me, townspeople!" he announced loudly, much louder than a man possibly could. There was no doubt some kind of myst charm helping his voice to carry. "I bring to you urgent news from King Branwynn Taggart Xernow. The king has learned there are those in the kingdom trying to spark rebellion among us. The king urges you not to believe their lies. He has offered a reward of a single gold royal to anyone who is brave enough to point out those spreading such talk."

Whispers arose among the crowd. A gold royal was a lot of coin. It was more than most of the merchants made in a year. Which would tempt many to turn in friends and relatives alike.

But the herald wasn't finished. He waited for silence to return. "Further, it has come to the king's attention that there is an impostor at large saying she is the king's dead sister, Zophia Olwenna Xernow. Be on the watch for this traitor. The king is offering a reward of *five hundred* gold royals for her—alive or dead."

A collective murmur went through the crowd. Just ten gold royals was enough for someone to live comfortably for life. But five hundred? That had to be close to everything in the royal treasury.

Zofie and I glanced at each other. I suddenly felt very exposed. Our only protection was our disguises. And if they should fail.... I shuddered.

Wynn wasn't playing games. Finding the Mirror of Bygone Tears had just gotten much harder.

CHAPTER SIX

Missing Daughter

We hurried as quickly as we could back to the Inland Sea. But when we arrived, we found a small knot of people gathered in front of it. I had visited the inn enough to recognize a couple of them as Mikney's neighboring shopkeeps. At first, I thought they were just gathered for a little conversation, but as we got closer, I could see that wasn't the case. They looked worried. When we walked up to them, we found the door to the inn standing open, with the interior dark and empty. I shook my head. It had been bustling just a few hours earlier.

"The inn's closed," said one of the men. "You'll need to get your things and find somewhere else to be this evening. I'm keeping an eye on things for him 'till he gets back. His daughter's gone missing."

"Maggie?" I asked, dread twisting my stomach. "What happened to her?"

He shrugged. "Not sure. Mikney said he sent her out on an errand this morning, and she didn't come back. He should have known better—other girls have gone missing recently." The man rubbed his forehead like he had an ache that wouldn't go away. "He thought it might be that Captain Rourke fellow that visited him last night and went over to the soldier's barracks to find him."

Zofie and I exchanged a glance—she looked as worried as I felt.

The man shook his head. "We told him not to go. That captain is meaner than a snake. I hope he doesn't get himself killed."

Zofie leaned forward. "Has anyone gone to inquire after him?"

The man looked down the street where a soldier stood propped against a wall. "We don't dare. Lately, if you ask too many questions, you get whipped or worse. Especially if it's about one of the missing."

I caught movement out of the corner of my eye and saw a feline shadow moving inside the inn. "We had best get our belongings and leave then. We don't want any trouble." Then before she could say anything, I grabbed Zofie's hand and pulled her inside.

Towing Zofie with me, I walked toward the back and caught up with Spraggel in the kitchen. He was sitting up perfectly straight on a work table with his tail curled around his feet. Galvyn leaned on the table beside him, the crumbs of bread and an empty cup indicating he had helped himself to some of Mikney's food. Fumiko was toward the back, watching out the door into the courtyard.

"About time you two showed up," Galvyn said, frowning. He too was wearing his disguise. "Maybe now we can get out of this Creator forsaken backwater."

I gave Galvyn a disgusted look and set the provisions we purchased on the table. "Show a little patience please," I said, irritation creeping into my voice. "I'm assuming you heard about our friends?"

Galvyn stood and positioned himself beside Zofie. "Friends or no, we have to get Zofie out of here. I was against this from the beginning. Now you've put her in danger."

My eyes went wide. I opened my mouth to speak, but Zofie interrupted.

"Coren didn't put me in danger," she said, picking up Spraggel and cradling him in her arms. He purred as she stroked his head. "If anything, I put those two innocents in jeopardy by coming here. They gave us aid." She looked up. "We have a responsibility to help them."

"No," Galvyn said, raising his voice. "I will not allow it. We have to get you out now."

While I didn't want to go along with Galvyn, I had to agree. "He's right," I said. "You shouldn't put yourself at risk. With what we heard in the town's square, a lot of people would be more than willing to turn you in if they can find you."

Fumiko called from the back. "I also agree. You shouldn't put yourself in danger."

Zofie pursed her lips clearly unhappy.

Spraggel raised his head. "Princess, I suggest Galvyn, Fumiko, and yourself go get the horses ready and meet us outside the town's north gate. While you're doing that, Coren and I will hunt for our friends."

Galvyn nodded in vigorous agreement. "See, even the cat thinks you should go. You and I need to leave now."

Zofie thought for a moment and then shook her head, determination written large on her face. I had seen that look before. It generally appeared when she had decided to do something, and not even the Creator himself could stop her.

"No." She paused and looked at each of us in turn. "I'm not leaving."

Galvyn stepped forward. "Zofie, that's...."

She held up her palm toward him. "I have to help them. You get everything ready and meet us outside of town. Coren, Spraggel, and I are going to find them."

Galvyn pursed his lips. "Then I'm coming too."

Zofie set Spraggel on the table. She turned to Galvyn, moving close and putting a hand on his chest. "Galvyn, we need an exit strategy and you're the best person for it. I promise not to put myself in danger. Won't you do this for me?"

Galvyn considered her for a moment and sighed heavily. "All right, but please be careful." He leaned forward, and before she could blink, kissed her—deeply. She staggered back in surprise, but Galvyn was already on his way. "Don't forget your promise," he called over his shoulder as he stepped outside in the direction of the stables. Fumiko followed right behind.

Zofie turned to me, her face bright red. I glanced away, a funny tightness in my chest.

Spraggel leaped down from the table. "Now that we have our roles assigned, I'm going to check out the soldiers' barracks. They're only a few streets over."

Zofie nodded. "Good idea. Coren and I will catch up to you in a moment."

Spraggel returned the nod and then leaped away.

Zofie put a hand on my shoulder. "Before we start searching, there is something I need from Maggie's room."

"There is?" I asked, confused.

She tugged on my arm. "Quickly."

Puzzled, I followed her upstairs. Maggie's room was very small with only a tiny bed and a few girl things—brush, combs, a small hand mirror—all laid out carefully on a tiny table. It looked—girlish.

"What do you need in here?" I asked, puzzled.

Zofie removed her flower from behind her ear and handed it to me—her disguise instantly dropping. She quickly slipped off her cloak and then sat down on the bed, where she began to remove her boots. "I need you to modify my curse. I need to be something that can track Maggie's scent. The best one Abe can do. When I was a wolf, I could smell things a mile away."

"But... but Spraggel has gone to the barracks." *And my curse might not be working*, I wanted to add.

Zofie shook her head. "I seriously doubt she's there. It would be too obvious. They've got to have a staging area somewhere."

I shook my head. "I'm not understanding where you're going with this?"

She stood barefoot before me. "Didn't you hear about the other girls going missing? Someone is running a slave operation. That's the only explanation. My father was trying to find out who was behind it right before he died. The pattern was to capture young girls and boys about

Maggie's age and then sell them. They move them fast too, usually on a boat or wagon within a day, never to be seen again."

My mouth fell open. "I knew there was a slave trade, but not on this scale."

She nodded. "Now quickly, change my curse. If I'm something with a keen sense of smell, I should be able to pick her out anywhere."

I gave her a pained expression. "Are you sure you want to do that? We tried accelerating your return to completely human back at the keep, but it ended up hurting you too much."

Zofie shook her head. "We don't have a lot of time to find her. Otherwise something..." She swallowed. "Something..." She looked away and took a deep breath. "I knew of a girl that was taken, and one of my father's men managed to find her before she left port." A tear came to Zofie's eye. "They had made an example of her, to put fear in the others and make them more manageable. They broke her leg and did other unspeakable horrors. Afterward, even though she was saved, she cried all the time and couldn't eat or sleep. She became a shell of the happy person she had been." She paused for a moment, tears bright in her eyes. "And then one day when her mother wasn't looking, she slipped away and drowned herself in the river." She took a deep breath and let it out slowly. "So I have to go after Maggie and any others that may have been captured. If I didn't..." she looked at me deadly seriously. "What kind of a queen would I be?"

I stared at her in shock—and admiration. I had never realized that Zofie had so much passion in her. And I couldn't argue with her logic.

"Abe! Wake up," I commanded.

Are you kidding? How could I possibly sleep through all this?

"Where have you been? You didn't come the last time I called."

I don't recall you saying the right words, he said sarcastically.

I didn't have time for this. "I need to modify Zofie's curse to be an animal with the best sense of smell. We'll also need some way to communicate. Can you do it?"

Of course, however, the bounds of the original curse restrict the modification to a relatively small set of animals. I will have to pick from those. Is that acceptable? Unless of course, you want me to mix animals. Her curse does let me do that. I guess I could put a donkey head on her body.

Zofie, only hearing one side of the conversation, motioned me to hurry.

"No mixing," I said. "I don't want her body any more messed up than she already is." Abe could be cruel sometimes in his quest for what he deemed was humorous. Another reason I wanted to be rid of him.

I stepped up to Zofie. "Are you ready?"

She nodded.

Using a single finger, I touched her high on her chest and opened my mouth to speak.

But Zofie grabbed my hand pausing me. "And don't tell Galvyn. He doesn't know about my curse."

I gave her a puzzled look. "What?"

She sighed heavily. "I'll explain later. It's complicated."

What was going on? I shook my head. "Any other last-minute instructions?"

She sighed and released my hand. She took a deep breath to steel herself. "Only that I hate doing this. It hurts so bad."

I smiled grimly. "You and me both." Then I said the invocation. "Abhulengulus. Modify Zofie's curse to forever change into an animal with an extreme sense of smell. And no mixing."

You're no fun.

Zofie was immediately enveloped by a blue glow, blazing bright enough to illuminate the darkened corners of the room. I winced at the pain on my own chest as the curse began to change her. Whenever Zofie transformed, her curse mark on my chest burned. But while my pain was bad, it was nothing compared to Zofie's. After all, curses were generally meant to torment the one bearing them. And Zofie's had definitely been designed to torment.

Gradually, her glowing blue form grew smaller as she shrank in size. Smaller and smaller she went until all that was left was a pile of clothes. Then the glow faded. I looked down in alarm. Where was she?

A red-haired rat poked its nose out from under Zofie's shirt. I could hear her voice in my head. *"Well, this is different."* She looked up at me, her whiskers twitching. *"And please, no jokes."*

She immediately scurried over to a pair of Maggie's spare shoes and ran her whiskers over them. I eyed her as I scooped up her clothes and boots and folded them into a bundle with her cloak. A rat? I guess I should have been a little more specific with Abe.

She paused and looked up at me. *"I've got it now."* She then bolted for the door and down the stairs. She was fast. I could barely keep up.

Outside we found the knot of people had dispersed. The lone soldier that had been down the street, now stood in front. I frowned. No doubt the reason the crowd had left. I really didn't have time to worry about it as Zofie scurried down the street.

As she made her way along the row of buildings, she would pause, sniff, and then go some more, all the while holding to the shadows. She seemed to know exactly what to do to help her blend in. Zofie had told me that she inherited the instincts of the animal she transformed into, but it always amazed me when she used them.

I paced her as she continued down the street. She abruptly stopped at the entrance to an alley.

"She became suddenly afraid right here." Zofie raised her head and sniffed the air. *"Then she went this way with two men. They were carrying steel."*

She took off down the alley. I had to run to keep up with her. We made several turns through the alley and came out on another street facing a small, nondescript house—tall grass on one side and an oak tree on the other. The house looked like it had seen better days.

Zofie and I held back. There was a wagon parked in front pulled by two horses. It had short sides and a rounded canvas top decorated with the faded picture of a large apple pie. The driver—a hunched man with a long beard and a balding head—paced impatiently at its rear. He seemed to be waiting for something.

"Her scent leads toward the house. I think she's still there. Her scent is very strong."

Suddenly a gray cat jumped in front of her, its ears back and ready to pounce.

"Don't Spraggel!" I yelled. "It's Zofie!"

Zofie froze and Spraggel continued to stare at her, his tail swishing back and forth. "So, I surmised," he said. "But the instincts in this form are quite strong." Spraggel bared his teeth. "I'm sorry, princess. But you're looking very nice today. Good enough to eat in fact. Ah... Coren, could you lend a hand here."

I inched forward and then quickly plucked Zofie up into my arms. Spraggel visibly relaxed and sat back on his haunches. "That was close." He raised his front paw and started licking it.

"So what did you find?" I asked.

"Nothing. There was no sign of them at the soldier's barracks."

I nodded. "We were afraid of that, so Zofie decided to track her scent. Which seems to lead toward that house."

Spraggel stood. "Then let's see if I can find her."

He took off across the street. He was quickly gone into some tall grass beside the house.

I checked to see if we were being watched and then slipped back down the alley. I set Zofie down, concealed between two rows of boxes and placed her clothes beside her.

"We better get you back to human form before you end up as someone's dinner." I quickly modified her curse, and while she was completing the transformation, I returned to the alley entrance. Zofie joined me a few moments later, her clothes and disguise charm back in place.

As we waited for Spraggel, two soldiers came out the front door dragging between them an unconscious and bound Mikney. The driver held aside the wagon's rear canvas and they unceremoniously dumped him inside. The wagon's driver spoke with them briefly while he reaffixed the canvas and then followed them back inside. I couldn't quite make out the conversation—they were just a little too far away.

A few minutes later, Spraggel darted back across the street and joined us.

"Maggie's not inside." He paced back and forth between us. "Mikney was, but I think you saw what they did with him."

"Let's at least get him out of there," I said.

But just as I was about to rush out, the door to the house opened. The driver of the wagon emerged, making his way to the front and hurriedly climbing up into the wagon seat. He briefly glanced at his cargo, before taking up the reins and starting the horses forward.

I couldn't let them get away. I ran after the wagon with Zofie right behind me—it wasn't moving fast, so I caught up to it quickly. I pulled the canvas back and peeked inside. Yes, Mikney lay unconscious where the soldiers had deposited him, but that wasn't the only surprise.

Zofie pulled up the other corner of the canvas—her eyes going wide and a hand going to cover her mouth. Maggie sat inside the wagon, her hands and feet bound plus a gag over her mouth. But the real shock was the other six captive girls about Maggie's age with her. And they all looked terrified.

I shoved the canvas aside and climbed in, before helping Zofie to join me. I peeked behind us to see if anyone had noticed our little trespassing. And true to form, they had—several soldiers came out of the house running after us. I shook my head. So much for doing this the easy way.

At the calls from the soldiers to stop, the wagon driver pulled the front canvas aside and spotted us. I dove for him and nearly got clubbed when I stuck my head out. I caught his arm and we struggled awkwardly for possession of the weapon. I managed to shake it from his grasp only to be dragged bodily outside. I lost my balance and landed on my back, forced painfully backward off the edge of the wagon seat. His hands grabbed my throat, and I futilely tried to break his hold. But I couldn't do it. He was just too strong.

Just as my vision began to go dim, I heard a thump and the man slumped over. Zofie stood behind him, holding the man's club and grinning wickedly. "Best thing I've done all day," she said.

I shoved the driver to one side and quickly grabbed the reins, urging the horses to a trot. The soldiers would eventually catch us, but maybe if we could make the town square, we could hide in the crowd. It was a longshot, but the best I could think of.

I glanced inside to see Zofie going to each of the girls. Many were now sobbing. As she freed them, she asked each one their name and gave them a couple words of encouragement or a brief hug. I turned back to the front and focused on guiding the horses. The streets were getting more crowded.

Spraggel leaped up onto the bench beside me. "Coren, my boy, you *do* realize you're headed toward the town square and are about to run out of street very soon."

"I know." I pointed my thumb behind me. "But if I slow down, the soldiers will catch up. I was thinking we might have a better chance of losing them if we went somewhere with a lot of people."

The square was right ahead of us. We needed a distraction—and it needed to be a big one.

And Zofie delivered.

Behind me, the princess began to rip off the wagon's canvas showing everyone around us the group of girls, now unbound, huddled inside and with Zofie standing in the middle of them. The image of the older woman instantly dropped as she jerked off her disguise charm. Zofie handed it to Maggie, pointing to Mikney and whispering something to her. Maggie nodded in understanding. Mikney was just starting to come around, his ropes having been cut off earlier. He looked up at us groggily.

We thundered into the square, but a large wagon blocked the path ahead, and people crowded the streets. I had no choice but to pull back on the reins and come to a halt. The people stopped to watch as we pulled in—a mixture of curiosity and dread. But then their eyes fell on Zofie standing tall in the bed of the wagon. A hush fell over the crowd with the only noise coming from the shouts of the pursuing soldiers.

I heard one of the girls in the wagon gasp, "I know you!" Her excited voice loud in the eerie quiet. "You're Princess Zophia." She turned to the other girls in excitement. "It's the princess. I saw her when we visited the castle. *The princess saved us!*"

I went to stand with Zofie, I pulled my own disguise flower and handed it to Maggie. I bent to her and whispered in her ear. "For you.

Wait until the crowd dies down and then use it to get you and your father to safety."

I started to turn away, but Maggie grabbed my arm. "Is it all right for us to have these? You and Zofie...?"

I nodded. "It's fine. You need them more right now."

Maggie looked at me in disbelief. She reached up and gave me a kiss on the cheek. "Thank you."

I smiled and gave her arm a squeeze. She knelt beside her father to help him sit up.

A murmur went through the crowd. They pressed close, their eyes wide in disbelief. I heard someone close by yell, "It's her! Princess Zophia's *alive!*"

Zofie raised her arms high. "People of Iron Landing," she shouted. "Hear me now. I have discovered who has been stealing your children. It was none other than the false king's soldiers stationed here. Be wary of them, but do not fear them. Hold them accountable!"

I shook my head. The king's soldiers were forcing their way through the crowd. We were trapped with nowhere to go.

"Coren," Zofie leaned toward me and whispered. "Modify my curse and don't hold back. *Now!*"

I hesitated. Doing two back to back transformations was going to be hard on her. I opened my mouth to protest, but saw just how close the soldiers were. I had no choice. "Abe," I said quickly. "Modify Zofie's curse to something that can get us away from here."

Zofie gave me a puzzled look. "That wasn't terribly specific."

I looked at her in horror as Abe laughed inside my head. It was a deep dark chuckle that reverberated within my skull and made my skin crawl. I had just given him a lot of leeway.

I opened my mouth to modify my command, but before I could, Abe answered.

As you wish.

Then I had no more time to think about it as the guards reached us.

Zofie was immediately enveloped in a deep blue glow—brighter and deeper in color than usual. She screamed as it took her and fell to her knees. I almost screamed myself. I could feel a massive myst draw through her curse anchor. The guards fell back at the sudden display of a myst working. They were trained well enough to know that swords were no match for a myst spell.

Suddenly the blue glow began to expand, growing larger, wings forming, and a head rising high. The wagon groaned as her weight increased. Zofie's clothes dropped to the ground, and I scrambled to gather them up.

When the blue glow dimmed and gradually went out, I found myself looking at an animal that only existed on banners and royal shields. It had the muscular body and hind legs of a majestic lion, yet the head, front legs, and wings of a magnificent eagle. The creature's back was the height of a tall man with a breast of pure white and its remaining fur and feathers the same shade of red as Zofie's own hair.

A griffin.

And Creator, she was beautiful. I gawked with the rest of the crowd.

Zofie raised her head and gave a loud squawk, then flapped her wings and began to rise. She reached out with her front claw, grabbing me about the waist, and began to gain height. Spraggel leaped onto my leg, his claws digging painfully into my pants. I reached down and pulled him up into my arms. Up and up we went, lurching skywards with every downstroke of her powerful wings. Once she had cleared the nearby buildings, Zofie gave another squawk and turned northward toward the edge of town.

When I looked down. Every eye below was watching us rise. Even the soldiers watched in awe. I couldn't help but smile. I would love to see the look on Wynn's face when he heard about this! The truth was out.

Princess Zophia was back!

CHAPTER SEVEN

Changing Fate

Zofie carried Spraggel and I outside of Iron Landing, and after making a wide circle, put us down in some woods on the north side of the town. I modified her curse to make her human again while Spraggel found Galvyn and Fumiko and led them to meet us. Galvyn made a big show of his reunion with Zofie, saying how worried he was and to never do something like that again. Fumiko was the one that asked the difficult question though.

"How did you get out of town?" she asked, clearly puzzled. "The soldiers almost didn't let us pass."

I opened my mouth to reply, not exactly sure what explanation was going to tumble out of it, but Zofie beat me to it. "I opened a portal for us." Zofie glanced at me nervously. "I moved it a little further out to make sure you weren't followed."

Galvyn raised his eyebrows in approval. "That's an impressive distance for a portal. I thought your specialty was shields." He shrugged. "But it doesn't matter. Regardless, you've gotten stronger since we were younger." He grinned. "My fiancée is not only beautiful and intelligent, she's powerful too!"

Fumiko didn't look convinced, but she asked no further questions.

Galvyn stepped toward the horses. "I want to hear more about your little adventure, but we had best be on our way. Be sure to put your disguise back on."

Zofie made a face. "Well, about that. I accidentally lost mine."

I raised my hand. "Me too." I tried not to look over at Zofie. Why was she trying to cover up our little adventure? We did some good today.

Galvyn wheeled on us. "What! You lost them! I...." He looked like he wanted to say more, but couldn't figure out how to chastise Zofie without pissing off the woman he was trying to persuade to marry him. He finally sighed and held out his flower to her. "Take mine. You've got to have one. I will just have to bluff my way through."

Zofie didn't argue. She took it and placed it behind her ear, her older woman disguise falling in place. "Thank you. I'll try to be more careful."

"Please do," he said, still angry. Then he turned his gaze on me. "And you had best leave us. They saw you with her, so you pose a threat."

"Galvyn," Zofie stepped forward and put a hand on his chest. "He's no more a threat than you are. Besides, I need my knight. He kept me from being captured and has proven himself time and again. He *has* to come with us."

Spraggel chose that time to reappear from scouting the area. "I must agree. I would be lost without my apprentice. Taking notes has gotten a little difficult for me."

Galvyn frowned. "Then how do you propose we hide him?"

Spraggel nodded. "I think we'll have to do this the old fashioned way."

He then sat and poked a paw toward his middle. It disappeared into his fur. My eyes went large. Don't tell me his magical pocket still worked! In the past, he had made a comment about how it was anchored to his body and not his clothes. I guess it didn't matter if he wore clothes or—fur.

He dug in the pocket for a moment, bent in half in the way that cats can do, and finally pulled out a small leather pouch hooked on a claw.

I immediately recognized it. It was his theater face paint kit. He would frequently make me dress up as some literary character to better learn the ancient plays. One time, he made me perform each part in a whole play. It had been fun. But I hadn't much cared for playing the ladies though. I don't look good in a dress.

Spraggel looked up at me. I swore he was smiling.

So that was how I came to be on the road heading to our next town wearing a fake mustache, black hair, and an eyepatch. The scar on my face looked pretty convincing too. Zofie had done a good job.

Our little rescue mission had caused us to change our plans. We had originally thought to catch a barge in Iron Landing and float down the Nortesy River to Wyndhaven Harbor. Beynon Manor was just east of there. However, since we had kicked the proverbial hornets' nest, every barge leaving Iron Landing was being searched and anyone suspicious taken prisoner. We thought it best to take a detour and use an overland route for a while longer. It would be slower, but we hoped much safer. Unfortunately, due to our hasty exit, we were still a horse short and would have to continue switching off until we either found another or took passage on a barge.

Midday found us settled into a comfortable pace not too taxing for the horses. Fumiko rode double with me, our horse a couple lengths ahead of Galvyn and Zofie. They were riding side by side, having a friendly chat with Spraggel cradled in Zofie's arm. I couldn't make out their words over the clomp of the horses' hooves, but they seemed to be having a lively conversation sprinkled with frequent laughs. They seemed to be growing increasingly comfortable with each other, and while I hated to admit it, it bothered me.

Would Zofie still have a use for me once my curse was gone? She had named me her knight. But would I go back to being a commoner

that she simply thought well of? I wasn't sure. And Galvyn wasn't helping. Zofie just seemed to be getting closer to him. And it made me very
uncomfortable.

I felt a small hand on my arm, giving it a gentle squeeze. "Are you
all right?" Fumiko asked. She leaned around with a look of concern on
her face. "You're being very quiet."

"I'm fine," I answered.

Fumiko sat a little closer than I was comfortable with. I shifted
away from her slightly, but she quickly shifted to close the distance.

"I was hoping we could talk some more about your curse," she said.
"We didn't get to finish our last discussion."

I sighed. I really just wanted to stew in my own misery, but I nodded anyway. I had made a promise.

Fumiko paused for a moment while she composed her thoughts.
"How long have you had the curse?" she finally asked.

I looked up and scratched my chin. "I got it when I was twelve, so I
guess that would make it about eight... no, nine years now. My father
passed it to me before he died." I looked down. "He drowned."

"I'm sorry," Fumiko said simply.

I looked forward and shrugged. Even after all that time, it still hurt.
"It was a long time ago. He was a kind and gentle man, always concerned for my welfare. And he did his best to teach me the family
business of raising horses."

She paused a moment. "You're apprenticed to a scribe now, so I
take it the horse business didn't do well after your father died."

I sighed. "No, it didn't. Mother just didn't have the knack, so she got
permission to sell it and then married my step-father. I always felt out
of place after that. And my curse didn't help. It caused bad luck at every
turn." I shook my head. "Although I don't remember it causing such
problems when Father had it."

Fumiko gently took my wrist and pulled it so she could see it. She
ran her thumb over it, the sensation making me shiver. Her touch was
so light. "That's because your curse must not have needed to change
his fate."

I looked over my shoulder at her. "Fumiko. While I will give you that Abe has caused me plenty of bad luck, he's never done anything close to changing my fate."

She looked at me in surprise. "You mean you didn't know?"

I shook my head. "Know what?"

She looked back to my wrist. "Abhulengulus is a very powerful curse. So powerful, he can manipulate his host's luck—those inconsequential decisions or events that could easily have gone one way or another. For instance, you're playing dice and you need to roll a two—your curse can influence their movement to make that happen. Of course, your overall luck has to stay equal to balance it all out, which is why you have bad luck from time to time." Fumiko licked her lips and leaned closer, her eyes alight. "But Abhulengulus can do more with this than just change a die roll. He can build on those small changes of luck to change your future. Influencing small happenings and even small decisions to make the impossible—possible. If timed correctly, he could influence a few dice rolls to win the game." She leaned back. "Or just as easily lose it."

I snorted. I wasn't convinced. "I've known for some time that Abe can change my luck. But my fate? That seems a little much."

She shook her head. "Coren, do not doubt me on this. Curses can only do what they were made to do. Abhulengulus has to ensure he is passed on to his next host. And to do that, he will manipulate your fate for his own means."

My mouth fell open as I considered the possibilities. "That means he could have engineered me falling into that flooded river so that my father would pass the curse to me..." I swallowed. "Even though it caused my father to die."

She nodded. "Exactly."

The full implication of what Abe could do hit me like a punch in the gut. Had Abe caused my father to die? Could it have been him all along? Was I carrying a cold-blooded murderer on my wrist? My head was spinning from the implications. And the reason my bad luck had died down, could it be because I was doing exactly what he wanted me to do? If I had not been completely sure before that I wanted this curse off me, I was doubly sure now.

Another thought occurred to me. I looked back at Zofie, who was gently stroking Spraggel in her arm. Could that be the reason I crossed paths with a princess? She had said there was something about me that attracted her. And I definitely had feelings for her. Did Abe make that happen? Were our feelings even our own?

Was what I felt for Zofie a *lie*?

I shook my head. It was too much to think about. "I'm... I'm not sure I believe it. There's no way he can be affecting me that way."

She leaned closer with a deadly serious expression. "If he's controlling your fate... subtly influencing those individual dice roles... how would you know?"

I stared at her in horror.

I wouldn't.

For the next couple of days, we continued our journey in the mundane way that such travels go. We wove our way along small roads and trails, trying not to attract attention. When darkness fell, we would camp, eat a light meal, and listen to Zofie as she contacted Risten. The sword-master kept us enthralled with her nightly reports—going into a humorous diatribe about one of her new party's peculiarities, only to make us gasp the next moment at her telling of close calls with the king's soldiers that now pursued her. Although she said nothing, I could tell that Zofie was terrified of something happening to her cousin.

When all was said and done, we would sleep under the stars and be back on the road at first light. Fumiko continued to interrogate me about my curse while Galvyn monopolized Zofie. Between the two of them, Zofie and I hardly had any time to speak. I wondered if they were *trying* to keep us apart.

On the fourth day out from Iron Landing, clouds began to roll in and we realized our luck with the weather wasn't going to hold. So as we came in sight of a small town, Galvyn announced that we were staying in an inn for the night. He for one didn't want to sleep wet.

It was late afternoon when we stopped, and while the others settled in, I used the opportunities to groom and care for the horses in the inn's stable. It felt good to be working with them. It reminded me of my father and the good times we had shared.

As I was rubbing them down, I heard someone step into the stable behind me.

"Would you like some help?" I looked up to see Zofie standing beside me, a timid grin on her face.

I couldn't help but smile, my mood instantly lifting at the sight of her. "I would love it."

She got a brush and took her own horse behind me and began to groom her. She had her disguise on, but I had grown used to it. While I could still see it, it also wasn't there—an odd trick of the charm. We worked in silence for a moment, and I tried to find something neutral to talk about.

"Where's Galvyn?" I asked.

Zofie snorted. "Need you ask? Drinking ale and explaining to the innkeeper how to make a fine brew. Fumiko, on the other hand, is asleep. Hit the bed and was out." Zofie stroked her horse and then paused. "You seem to like talking to her."

I shrugged. "She knows some about my curse. And I did promise to tell her what I could." It was my turn to pause before continuing. "I noticed you've been talking to Galvyn a lot too."

It was her turn to shrug. "We're old playmates. It's fun to reminisce about the things we did as children and catch up on the people we know. Other than Risten, he was the only other child I got to play with." She was quiet for a moment: all you could hear was the soft shuffling of the horses and the sound of brushing. "Our fathers decided when we were young that we would be married. I had no say in the matter. Didn't really even understand it at the time. Only that he was a fairly frequent visitor to the castle, and he kept stealing my dolls."

I stopped brushing and turned toward her. She must have felt my eyes on her back because she stopped and turned too. We stared at each other in silence for several heartbeats. I finally looked down. "I understand if you choose to marry Galvyn. He's got a lot more to offer than I do. And as queen, you have to consider those things."

"Are you withdrawing as one of my suitors?" she said, a hint of coldness in her voice.

I looked at her in confusion. "I thought... you and Galvyn..." I felt myself blush.

Zofie just looked at me innocently. "Thought what?"

I took the coward's way and shook my head. "Nothing." I switched topics. "Have you told Galvyn about your curse? The full moon is not that far away."

"No, I haven't. And I don't plan to. He won't take it well. His family has a thing about those with curses. And... well... I don't know." She diverted her eyes. "They consider anyone that has been cursed to be... tarnished." She turned her eyes to the ground, almost like she was ashamed.

I came around the horses and faced her. I lifted her chin until our eyes met.

"Am I tarnished?" I asked.

She gave a shake of her head. "Definitely not."

"Then you're not either. You are anything but tarnished. I won't let Galvyn, his family, or anyone ever imply it."

She smiled up at me and put a hand on my arm. "Thank you." We held each other's gaze a moment longer, until I suddenly realized how close we were.

I quickly turned and stepped toward a pouch hanging on the wall to put away my brush. A flash of color caught my eye, and I looked down to see a tiny spring flower looking up at me expectantly. This one was white with a purple center—beautiful, but it shouldn't be there. It had to be another reminder from Lady Autumn.

I turned back to Zofie. "How many more transformations do you think you'll need to be back to normal?"

She gave a half grin. "It should only take a few more. The transformation changes are more subtle now, so progress is slower." She sighed. "And more painful. The closer I get to being myself, the more the transformations hurt." She gave me a teasing smile. "Why are you asking? My knight is not going to desert me, is he?"

I shook my head. "I'd never leave you. No, I'm just eager to get my curse off."

She nodded and moved to put her own brush away. "That I can understand. Did Fumiko give you any hints on how?"

I glanced at the tiny flower. "Not really. I sort of... took a different approach." I turned fully toward Zofie. "I made a bargain with the nymph."

Her eyes went wide. "*You what!* Please tell me you weren't that reckless." She trailed off, her expression softening. "The nymph offered to remove your curse, didn't she?"

I nodded.

She looked at me for a moment and then gave a heavy sigh. "Definitely risky, but not something that comes along every day." She looked concerned. "Are you sure you're all right with this?"

"I've wanted this curse off me since the day I got it. I want it off right this very minute. I don't like it that you-know-who is inside my head watching everything I do. Plus I don't like that everything I touch sours." I shook my head. "But I also want to wait until you are completely back to normal. So putting it off for a little bit longer doesn't pose a problem for me. I do have a time limit though—Lady Autumn says I have to use the breaking charm before the start of winter." I ran a hand through my hair. "My only worry is that you won't need me anymore after my curse is gone."

She stepped forward and touched my chest. "I will always need someone with as much heart as you have."

She looked up at me, and I again realized how close she was. Her eyes searched mine, inviting me. I bent toward her. Our lips drawing closer...

"Coren!" Spraggel came strolling into the stable. "What the Creator's hell is this about making a deal with the nymph?"

Zofie and I jumped at the sudden intrusion. We quickly separated.

"Spraggel, you have impeccable timing," I muttered.

"Of course I do, young man. Timing is everything—a lesson I learned well. Reminds me of an event in my youth when I got the timing wrong and got turned into a cat for the first time." He paused for a moment as if collecting his thoughts, but seemed to catch himself and shook his head. "I mustn't get distracted. Now, what about the nymph's charm?"

Zofie gave me an amused grin and handed me her brush before moving toward the door. "I need to check on Galvyn to make sure he hasn't created a mess."

I watched her leave, unable to prevent myself from watching the way she moved, like music in motion. I hoped Galvyn appreciated just what an awesome lady Zofie was.

Spraggel cleared his throat. "Close your mouth Coren. You're gawking. Now tell me about the nymph!"

I broke my gaze away and squatted down in front of him. "It was just a simple bargain. Lady Autumn offered, and I accepted. Simple as that."

He gave me an intense stare and his voice became very stern. "When you're dealing with creatures of myst, there is no such thing as simple."

I shrugged. "What I want to know is how you found out? Were you eavesdropping on my conversation with Zofie?"

"I was *not* eavesdropping," he said indignantly. "This form has excellent hearing, and I just happened to be dozing right outside." Spraggel started licking his paw and using it to wash his face. "Now what did she make you promise? I pray it was nothing too hard."

I stood and began to put away the brushes. "It was just to visit her once a year. I figure that's something I can do without too much trouble."

"You didn't give her your name, did you?"

"Well..."

Spraggel dropped his head in frustration. "And the second condition? The one that takes effect if you can't visit her?"

I drew up. "Wait. How did you know there was a second condition?"

Spraggel resumed washing his paw. "There's always a second one. It's the one you have to watch out for." He returned to his washing. "So what was it?"

"She gets my firstborn."

Spraggel jumped to his feet, back arched and hissing. "Oh Creator's hell! Please tell me you didn't do that!" Spraggel had scolded me a lot over the years, but I had never heard him so frantically angry.

"Well, it's not like I'm going to have children anyway."

"Don't you realize that you're dealing with a creature of pure myst! Now that she has your name, she can do pretty much whatever she pleases. Which means you *will* have children."

My master was starting to irritate me. "Then I'll just have to make sure I visit her every year."

Spraggel sighed, pacing back and forth. "Coren, you still don't get it. She doesn't want the visits—she wants your child. Something will come up to keep you from getting there. It's inevitable!"

I was getting angry now. "Spraggel. This was the deal of a lifetime. For simply visiting her, I'll finally be able to get rid of this murderous thing on my wrist!"

Spraggel shook his head and his tail flicked with agitation. "I'm...." He turned away in frustration. "I just don't know what to say. I'm disappointed in you. You've let yourself be blinded. This is not going to turn out well."

"Turn out well, you say!" I yelled after him. "Curses generally don't."

Spraggel stalked out, which was hard to do for a cat, and I was left alone with the horses. My horse snickered and shook his head. I patted him gently. "Don't tell me you're going to scold me too?"

It eyed me in a horse sort of manner and stepped away signaling it was done with the brushing and wanted to get on with the more important business of eating.

I took my time finishing with the horses to allow myself a chance to calm down. I understood why Spraggel was upset, but this bargain was just too good to pass up.

When I couldn't drag out caring for the horses any further, I left the stable and headed for the inn's well. I thought I should wash up a bit.

As I was drawing up the bucket, I heard horses approaching the inn. Turning, my eyes nearly popped out when I saw three riders wearing the king's livery. They stopped in front of the inn and dismounted.

Oh, hell.

I stepped back behind the inn and wondered what I should do next. I had my sword with me, but I did not think I could take on all three of them.

The men secured their horses to a hitching post and went inside. I quickly moved to an open window and listened, praying I didn't have to jump in. I raised on my tiptoes and peeked inside. Galvyn was sitting at a table by himself, but the steaming cup of tea made it obvious that someone had been sitting with him. Zofie, no doubt, and I breathed a sigh of relief that she was able to hide.

One of the soldiers approached him, while one stayed by the door, and the other went into the back. "You there," said the soldier. "Where is your companion? We've received a report of a woman staying here that fit the description of one that interfered with the king's business in Iron Landing."

I nearly gasped. How had they spotted her? Zofie had been wearing her disguise every time she was outside.

Galvyn, on the other hand, didn't even blink. He picked up his mug of ale, leaned back in his chair, and let them bask in his arrogance. "Is that the way you address a lord." He continued to glare at them, his indignant righteousness growing. "Do you know who I am?"

The soldier suddenly looked uncertain and studied him more closely.

Galvyn held up his right hand and wiggled his fingers so the soldier could see the rather large ring.

The man's eyes grew wide. "No, Lord Merrick. I had no idea. But I thought you were older."

Galvyn dropped his hand and leaned back. "Appearances can be improved. Now, what do you want?"

"My lord..." he licked his lips. "I've been ordered by the king to check anyone who is the least bit suspicious."

Galvyn slammed his fist on the table. "Do I look like I came from Iron Landing?" His voice gradually getting louder. "*Do I?*"

The man licked his lips. "But the woman..."

"You mean me," came a feminine voice from the landing above them.

The men quickly turned to see Fumiko coming down a set of steep stairs.

"The lord and I were just chatting." She crossed the room to sit across from him. She picked up Zofie's cup of tea and took a sip. "He is a fascinating man."

The soldier looked from one to the other. Just then, the soldier came out from the back and shook his head.

Galvyn tried to take a drink from his mug, but he had drained it. He looked at it in puzzlement for a moment and then raised it up high. "Innkeeper!" he shouted.

The proprietor came out immediately and filled his cup. The man's hand was shaking—it was fairly obvious who had turned us in. While he poured, Galvyn asked him slyly.

"Innkeeper? Is there anything here these good soldiers might be interested in?"

The little man shook his head.

"Good." Galvyn looked up at the soldier with a self-satisfied smile. "Now, why don't you and your men go look elsewhere for this mysterious woman. She obviously isn't here."

The soldier didn't hesitate. He saluted, which indicated how rattled he was because the proper etiquette would have been to bow. He then went out the door with his two men in tow.

After the soldiers had ridden away, I went inside. Galvyn was still drinking, but Fumiko had drifted back upstairs, no doubt to check on Zofie.

I sat down across from him. "I was watching from the window. You handled that quite well."

He looked down into his mug and swirled it around. "Of course." He leaned forward, so close I could smell the ale on his breath. "It's because I'm something you're not. I'm a noble."

He leaned back and smiled. "You should remember that. Especially when it comes to Zofie. She and I are the same kind." He drained his mug, set it down, and rose. He looked down at me. "You are, and always will be, nothing but a cursed commoner." He then moved toward the stairs.

I wanted to be angry with him. Shout out at him. But for some reason, I couldn't muster up the fire.

Because sadly, what he said was true.

CHAPTER EIGHT

Fight

T he next day, we arose early and rode westward. We still had two more days of travel until we reached the Nortesy River. From there, we could catch a barge to Beynon Manor. The manor wasn't on the coast, but it was within a few hours ride.

We rode in silence. Spraggel was still angry over my bargain with the nymph and rode with Zofie. Zofie seemed lost in her own thoughts, yet preferring to ride beside Galvyn. Galvyn seemed to radiate confidence. The young lord almost seemed to have an invisible bubble around him that I wasn't allowed to penetrate. He barely acknowledged me. And naturally, Fumiko rode behind me, and for once, seemed to understand I didn't want to be talked to.

What Galvyn had said at the inn had really struck a nerve. He was right, of course. Zofie was different from me. I didn't live in the same world as her. While all this swirled in my head, my heart stubbornly refused to be convinced.

We were only about an hour from our last stop when I felt

something odd in the gait of my horse. I stopped and dismounted; Fumiko did likewise. I ran my hand carefully over each of his legs, noticing that his right front one felt just a tad warmer than the others. I stood and sighed in disappointment—the horse was showing signs of going lame. It was probably because of the additional weight he was being asked to carry.

Zofie and Galvyn had been riding in front of us, but Zofie pulled up a short distance ahead when she noticed us stopped. "What's wrong?" she called.

"My horse," I called back. "It's starting to limp. Probably from carrying both of us."

Galvyn was even further up the road than Zofie, but I could still tell he was frowning. "So what are you going to do about it out here? It's not completely lame yet, so just ride it to the next village, and we'll get a new one there."

I shook my head. There was no way I was going to injure this horse further. He had been with us our entire first quest to retrieve the sword. He likely just needed a little rest. "You go on ahead. I'm going to walk with him for a while to see if he gets any worse."

"Suit yourself," he called back and turned his mount up the road. He looked over his shoulder. "Zofie, stay with me."

Zofie looked uncertain. Her horse was eager to catch up with Galvyn's and started making a circle in the road.

"Fumiko," I said, fixing the reins so I could lead my mount. "You can go ride with Zofie."

She shook her head. "It's not safe to be alone on the road. I will walk with you."

I started leading the horse. "You don't have to."

She shrugged. "I don't mind. Master doesn't have a horse, so I'm used to walking wherever we need to go." She smiled. "Usually, it was only me going for supplies."

"Are you sure," I asked. "We still have a long way to go."

She shrugged again. "Then I guess we best get started."

I waved Zofie on, and she allowed her mount to turn in the same direction as Galvyn's, but at a slow walking pace. I think she was trying to split the difference between Galvyn and us.

Fumiko and I walked for a bit in silence. Up ahead, I noticed that Galvyn had stopped and was waiting for Zofie to catch up. He was saying something to her I couldn't hear.

I glanced at Fumiko. She was directly beside me, and I couldn't help but admire her exotic beauty. Curiosity got the best of me. "If I'm not mistaken, your homeland is far to the east, past the great Frozen Mountains. How did someone from so far away get to be Master Tormaigh's apprentice?"

Fumiko tended to avoid talking about herself, so I was surprised that she answered my question. "By accident, of course." She looked up and smiled as if tapping a very pleasant memory. "Master had traveled to my homeland to talk with a renowned scholar about some recently discovered ancient texts. My master is a great historian, but languages are difficult for him. When his interpreter took ill, he went to find medicine, but couldn't find anyone to help him. So he went through the city screaming at the top of his lungs that he was looking to hire someone that could understand his language." She shook her head and grinned. "Of course, no one understood what he was saying, and most thought he was insane. I happened to be passing through that same town. Since my family had insisted I learn the language at an early age, I heard him and answered. He hired me on the spot. While his interpreter healed, I helped him with his studies. I must have impressed him because he begged me to accompany him back to his home. Since my family had disowned me, I took him up on his offer." She gave a chuckle. "He didn't realize I was a girl until two months later."

I gave her a puzzled look. "Why would your parents disown you? That seems a bit harsh."

Fumiko glanced at me. I could tell from her expression that I had pressed too far. "I would prefer not to talk about it," she said seriously. "Let's just say, I deserved the punishment, but I have no regrets."

We walked on in silence for a bit. Up ahead, Zofie and Galvyn had pulled a little further away from us. They were riding side by side and in deep discussion—at least it appeared that way from Galvyn's excited motions.

Fumiko suddenly stopped and grabbed my arm with both hands. Her face a mask of concern. "Listen," she whispered.

I halted with the horse stopping behind me. I looked at her in shock as I heard it too. Riders. And they were riding hard.

She pulled me to the side. "We best get off the road."

But even as she spoke, it was too late. Three men on horses came over the rise galloping toward us. They didn't appear to be anyone's soldiers, but were instead dressed as merchants. They slowed as they drew near with us. I recognized the man in front from the inn we had stayed at.

He pulled up beside us and quickly swung down. "I'm glad I caught you," he said out of breath. He smiled and nodded toward Fumiko. "The young lady left something behind."

Fumiko looked at him coolly. "All my things are with me."

He stepped toward her and fumbled at his belt. "No, you definitely left something behind. It's right here." His hand whipped out a knife—a rather sharp one from the looks of it—and held it to her throat.

I reached for my sword as the other two moved into position beside me, one holding a club and the other one a knife.

"Don't move," their leader commanded while stepping completely behind Fumiko—the knife never leaving her throat. He pulled her against him. "Or the young lady here will get her throat slit."

Fumiko remained motionless, offering no resistance. Her eyes fixed straight ahead.

"Leave her alone!" I shouted taking a step forward, but knife-man held his own blade at my throat making me freeze in place.

Down the road, I saw Zofie start to turn in our direction, but Galvyn reached across and yanked her reins out of her hand. He turned and kicked his horse into a gallop forcing Zofie's to follow right behind. I could hear her yelling at him to stop.

The group's leader noticed them getting away, but didn't seem to care. He snorted and turned his attention back to us. "Looks like your friends have abandoned you. Their kind usually do."

He turned his attention back to Fumiko, running a finger down her cheek. His lips spread into a wicked smile. "She's a beauty. Such a delicate thing." He sniffed the air. "Needs a bath though." He grinned and ran his tongue along the side of her face.

Fumiko gave no reaction—only stared straight ahead.

I winced as my hands were jerked behind me and securely tied. "I'm nothing special," I said. "I certainly have no one to pay ransom. So, take my purse and bags and be done with it."

His eyebrows went up and he apologetically shook his head. "Sorry, but we don't want your belongings. It's *you* we want. I overheard that stupid noble talking back at the inn. He said you are one of those traitors the king is looking for. You're going to make us all rich."

"But we're not...." Club-man whacked me on the head with his weapon, and I fell hard to the ground. My world spun. For good measure, he kicked me in the ribs. I couldn't breathe.

"No talking, or we'll hit you again. I'm only keeping you alive because you're easier to carry that way. If you give us any trouble, we'll kill you."

I shook my head trying to clear it and then put my forehead on the ground. "Abe," I whispered. I prayed he was working, but he did not reply. "Abe," I said a little louder, earning another kick from one of the men. I gasped in pain, while Abe refused to come. I shook my head as the two men grabbed my arms and stood me back up on unsteady feet.

Club man pulled my sword and held it up. He whistled as he examined it. "Now that's a beauty."

Their leader laughed and ran his finger down Fumiko's face, continuing down her neck. He paused to play with the front opening of her dress.

My head swimming, I looked sadly at Fumiko. I had failed. I hadn't noticed them coming sooner. I hadn't gotten my sword out in time. I hadn't gotten Abe to work. So many things I should have been able to do, but didn't.

Fumiko stayed perfectly still. Her face showed no emotion as the man ran his finger along the edge of her dress eager to explore further. I saw her eyes glance to each of the men around her, taking in their weapons and the horses. Until her gaze finally rested on me.

She looked at me sadly. "Please don't hate me," she pleaded.

And then she moved.

Faster than I could follow, she grabbed the man's hand holding the knife and twisted it downward, using his thumb for leverage. She then tucked her head down and literally threw him to the ground on his back. She put her foot on his chest, and still holding his arm, twisted the limb hard. I heard something snap and he screamed in pain.

We all just stared at her in shock as she dropped the leader's arm, and on her toes, did a quick two steps toward the man holding me. Then her leg came up, sending the folds of her dress flying, and her foot sailing through the air. She connected with his temple three times in quick succession—the blows so fast their wind ruffled my hair. Knife-man released me and staggered back. Without his support, I collapsed to the ground.

Club-man finally acted. He dropped my sword and swung at Fumiko with his stick, but she quickly dodged, bending impossibly far back until she touched the ground with her hands. Then continuing the motion, her leg came up and delivered a solid kick to the man's chin. His head shot up at the impact, and he staggered backward and fell unmoving.

Knife-man recovered from his hits and brandished his weapon. He swung it at her in quick, deadly crosswise strokes, driving her back as she dodged. She quickly stepped inside his guard, grabbed his arm, and almost wrapping it around her as she backed up to him, she hit him twice in the face with her elbow and then another sharp blow to his body. He staggered and collapsed into a bush.

The leader of the group regained his feet and advanced on Fumiko. The broken arm hung limp at his side, but he held his wicked knife in his good one. "I'm going to kill you *bitch!*"

Fumiko tried to kick the blade out of his hand, but he dodged. They squared off, each looking for an opening. The man lunged forward, but Fumiko blocked him with her forearm and wheeled in a roundhouse kick that sent him sailing and her dress rising high as she spun. He fell flat on his back and didn't get up.

Breathing hard, she paused to make sure all her opponents were down and then retrieved my sword. She quickly stepped over and untied me—I could tell that her own hands were shaking. While I was trying to make sense of what had just happened, she gathered up their three horses and swatted two of them on the rear, sending them back down the road the way they had come. She then helped me stand on shaky legs and mount the one she had kept back. I leaned forward and interlaced my fingers in the horse's mane, trying not to fall off.

I must have passed out for a few moments, because the next thing I knew, I was leaning back with my head against something soft and my head gently swaying with our horse's motion.

My eyes opened, and it took me a moment to realize that Fumiko was riding behind me. She had been keeping me upright by reaching around me to hold the reins. Our original horse was tied to our saddle and trotting along behind us.

Fumiko must have realized I had awoken.

"How are you doing?" she asked.

"I'm all right, I think." I straightened and immediately regretted it. I groaned. I touched where the man had struck me in the head and then felt my ribs. I didn't feel anything broken, but I was going to have some really nasty bruises. I winced as I twisted to look back at her. "Thank you for saving me. I would never have guessed you could fight like that. You were amazing. Everything was so fluid—almost like a dance."

She wouldn't look at me, instead keeping her eyes fixed ahead. "Swear to me that you won't ever tell anyone about what you saw. Not even my master knows I can fight."

I sat up a little straighter and put a hand on my ribs. "I won't tell. But I don't understand why you would want to hide it. You were incredible!"

She shook her head. "I left that part of my life behind when I left my homeland. If you hadn't been in danger, I wouldn't have used it."

I paused for a moment. "Then I owe you an even greater debt."

Fumiko was quiet behind me for a little bit. Then she spoke, "I know how you can pay it back."

"My debt? How?"

She grinned. "Once you determine the location of the Mirror of Bygone Tears, take me with you to retrieve it."

"That's not mine to give. We'll have to talk with Zofie."

She looked up at me. "The princess will listen to you."

I shook my head. "I'm not so sure. She seems to be listening to Galvyn a lot lately."

Fumiko snorted. "He has an unfair advantage. But do not underestimate the princess. She'll figure things out."

"Figure out what?" I asked.

She just smiled and refused to answer.

A short while later, we encountered Zofie riding back toward us with Galvyn just behind. At seeing me, she almost broke into tears and gave me a fierce hug—which felt good, but really hurt my ribs. She apologized several times for leaving us behind, saying it took her a while to get Galvyn to let her horse go. She gave him an evil glare. I assured her that she had made the best move.

Galvyn coolly congratulated me on getting free, but was otherwise quiet. I think he was a little disappointed.

Then Zofie asked how we had gotten free. I wasn't exactly sure what to say.

Fumiko jumped in for me. "Coren managed to get his sword out. They fought with him briefly, but when he didn't back down, they gave up and retreated." She came over and laid a hand on my shoulder. "He saved me."

Zofie gave me a smile and a nod of satisfaction. "Well done, Coren. My knight did well."

My heart sank. But it wasn't like that. I hadn't done anything. *Couldn't* have done anything. I felt so fake at the praise. I looked down and mumbled something about not remembering what happened because of the blow to my head.

And so we resumed our journey. Fumiko again rode behind me on our newly acquired horse. She said nothing further about our little struggle, so I followed her example.

About mid-afternoon, we stopped at a small inn. It was larger than I would have expected for such a small village, probably due to its proximity to the Nortesy River which was only one day's ride away. Zofie and I had wanted to press on, even camping beside the road if we needed, but Spraggel for once suggested otherwise. He said we really didn't know what other surprises might await us, so being in an inn might make us a more difficult target. Galvyn readily agreed with Spraggel. He hated to camp.

Zofie, Fumiko, and I were all tired from what had happened that morning, so after I begged a pain potion from the innkeeper, we retired to our rooms. Galvyn chose to stay in the small tavern, preferring to drink his ale and try to engage the young barmaid in conversation.

I didn't sleep long, but felt much better afterward. My head no longer hurt and my ribs were manageable.

I put my arms behind my head and went through the fight earlier, trying to see what I should have done differently. I had failed miserably. Thank the Creator that Fumiko could take care of herself. But my mind kept circling round and round on one point: what if it had been Zofie? What would I have done then?

And why hadn't Abe come when I called? It had to be because of the charm Lady Autumn had given me. I didn't know if he had found out about it, or if it was perhaps interfering with him. Either way, it didn't matter. I would be done with him soon.

I frowned at a sudden thought. Maybe he was already gone.

"Abe?" I asked. "Are you there?"

I fully expected silence, but was surprised to hear him reply. *Yes, you stupid sack of meat, I'm here. Anxiously awaiting your next command. To think I have to serve you, someone just barely more intelligent than a monkey. And that's insulting the monkey.*

"Abe!" I exclaimed. "Where have you been?"

I've been attached to your arm. What did you think I was going to do, sprout legs and walk!

I rolled my eyes. "No, you haven't answered me."

Yes, I did. You called just now and I answered. In fact, I've answered every time you've called me.

I grew puzzled. He didn't sound like he was teasing me. "No Abe, I've been calling you for several days now and you wouldn't answer. In fact, I really needed you this morning, but you wouldn't come."

No, I... Wait. Where are we? There was an edge of confusion in his voice instead of his usual arrogance.

"We're several days down the road heading toward Beynon Manor. We're almost to the Nortesy River."

No, that can't be right. He seemed honestly puzzled, which was very uncharacteristic for the foulmouthed curse. *The last I remember, we were in Iron Landing and I modified the princess' curse. But after that, nothing until just now.*

"You're not tricking me, are you?"

Creator, no. If I were, you'd never know it.

"Then do you know why you didn't come?"

He paused for a moment. *No, I don't. It's like I just stopped working. I've never had anything like this before.*

I felt a little guilty about not revealing Lady Autumn's charm, but I couldn't afford to have him do something to stop me from using it. "You seem fine now. It's probably because you ran out of myst. I'm not a myst user, so I may not be producing enough to keep you working."

He hesitated. *That can't be it. You don't have any myst.*

I rolled my eyes. He could be so frustrating at times. It would be so good to get rid of him. I wish Fumiko was with me so she could finally talk with him. Which reminded me of something she had said earlier.

"Abe," I said. "There's something else I wanted to ask. Fumiko says that you can bend your host's fate to your will. Do you?"

Fumiko? Who's Fumiko?

"She's the girl that joined our party right after we left. She's Master Tormaigh's apprentice and is going to help us find the Mirror of Bygone Tears."

Right. He sounded a little uncertain. *I remember something about going to Master Tormaigh's. My memory gets a little fuzzy after that.*

"Now quit trying to distract me," I complained. "Can you control your host's fate?"

He gave an almost human sigh. *Without my secret word, all I can say is.... sort of.*

"What? That doesn't make sense. It's either something you do or you don't."

Well, in one sense I do change your fate, but it's only to protect you. And it's not something I consciously do. It just happens by reflex... like your heart beating or blinking your eyes. You don't think about it, because it takes care of itself. So don't blame me when something less than desirable happens because I have to balance out the good and bad luck. Which means you might end up with a broken leg, but it will keep you from dying from an arrow to the heart.

"Does that mean me meeting up with Zofie wasn't a coincidence? That you had it all planned out?" My anger was rising. "And what about my father? Did you kill him, just to keep me alive?"

Coren, that's not how it works.

"Oh really, then how does it?"

Abe didn't answer immediately. *Are you sure you want to have this conversation? You're not going to like it.*

"Yes, I do. I want to know all about it."

Abe sighed. *It's true that I have a part of me that can manipulate luck, but I can only swing the chances of something happening one way or another. Some might say that I can change fate. But there is one thing in this world that is stronger than what you call fate. It's a person's will. And that is something I can't control.*

"So what's that got to do with his death?"

Everything, you stupid sack of meat. Yuri, I mean your father, decided to save your worthless hide all on his own. Could I have prevented him from jumping in the river after you? Well, no offense, but I certainly tried. I caused him to slip in the mud, fall down, have his path blocked—but every single time, he pushed on until I had exhausted the possibilities. He was utterly determined to save you.

It was Yuri that decided your life was worth more to him than his own, enough so that he gave you the curse before you were ready. He knew perfectly well that once he gave up the curse, I had no way to help him. Oh, and by the way, did I mourn his death? I did indeed. He was one of the few hosts I've had that I respected, and why he gave up his life for you is beyond my understanding. So there! That's the answer to your last question today. I hope you choke on it!

And then Abe was gone. As if a door had been shut between us.

I rubbed my face. So it had truly been an accident. Or at least, my falling in the river was. But after that, my father had made a series of decisions to save my life. Perhaps I had been looking at this all wrong. Maybe instead of dwelling on the unfairness of it all, I needed to instead think about the gift he had given me.

And what about Abe. He had mourned my father—had liked him even. Which explained why he talked to me the way he did—he resented my living instead of my father. I hadn't considered that he could have the capacity for emotion, little alone mourn someone. He didn't want to be attached to me any more than I did to him. In fact, Abe had sounded almost... human.

I looked at my curse mark, suddenly uneasy. If Abe was intelligent and could feel emotion, wasn't that just like a human. Would breaking him be the same as murder? *I'm sorry, but I don't want you anymore, so I'm going to kill you.* The cold thought made me shudder.

Was I making a mistake?

The room was suddenly too small—I had to get some fresh air. I put my boots on and grabbed my sword. Until a few moments ago, everything seemed so simple. But now? I wasn't sure.

I threw open my door to find Zofie standing in front of it. She looked deep in thought and stepped back in surprise. She seemed embarrassed, but her expression quickly changed to concern when she saw my face.

"Are you all right?" she asked. "You look upset. I was just going to see what you were doing."

I sighed and ran a hand through my hair. "I'm fine. Only a little restless. The skirmish with those thieves this morning could have gone better. I thought I would fill two cups from one pail and do some sword practice."

Zofie perked up. "Can I join you? I have something I need to talk to you about anyway."

I shrugged. "If you don't mind practicing with a grump."

Zofie smiled. "While I've seen you a little testy before, I've never seen you as a grump." She moved to her room. "Let me get my sword."

She came back a moment later with it belted to her hip, and we moved downstairs.

"I just talked with Risten," Zofie said. "She contacted me for a change. Apparently, she is going with her friends to gather weapons. So she asked I not contact her for a few days. I think she's afraid I might yell out and accidentally betray her position. True to form, she reminded me that I needed to practice." Zofie screwed up her face and did the perfect imitation of her cousin. "If you're going to carry that sword, you damn well better be able to use it."

I laughed. That was exactly how Risten would have said it. She had told me something similar when I first got my sword.

Once outside, I pointed to a grassy meadow just beyond the stables. "Where's Galvyn? Wouldn't you rather spar with him?"

She rolled her eyes. "He's too busy talking to the barmaid to pay me any attention. He has a thing for blondes and big bosoms. Besides, you're *much* better company."

My heart almost skipped a beat.

When we reached the meadow, we warmed up a bit, going through our forms as Risten had taught us. It was a lot of work and it felt good. It took my mind off my other problems. Zofie may not have practiced recently, but her forms were perfect. No doubt it was all Risten would tolerate. I felt like a klutz next to her. She was all grace and beauty while I was jerks and jabs.

We paused for a moment to get our breath. Zofie wiped the sweat from her brow. "Would you care to spar now?"

I chuckled. "You'll have to be careful with me. I've been mortally wounded." I put a hand on my bruised ribs.

She smiled wickedly. "Good, then I might stand a chance of winning."

We each drew our swords and squared off. She moved into a perfect first stance, and I knew I could be in trouble. I had seen her spar with Risten, and from what I had seen, she was fairly good.

We traded a few blows to get used to each other. Not surprisingly, I was stronger than Zofie, but she was definitely faster.

I stepped back and lowered my sword. "Regardless of what Risten said, you're pretty good. When did you start learning?"

Zofie wiped sweat from her brow. "I learned some of the basics at a very early age. Remember, Risten started when she was twelve, and I was only five or six. Every time Risten learned something new, she would show me and I'd copy her. She even got a small wooden sword I could play with." She smiled. "I think she stole it from Galvyn."

She stretched her arms. "But I lost interest as Father introduced me to other things a ruler should know. Plus in my early teens, I came into controlling my myst powers and was assigned to Mistress Ginneley to train." She glanced at me with a wistful smile. "But one day I rediscovered swordplay. One spring day not too terribly long ago, I was dying to go outside. There was this one myst spell I was having trouble with, and it was stifling in Mistress Ginneley's study. Risten managed to get me free by pretending she needed a sparring partner. I fully intended to catch a nap under a tree, but Master Valervick, Risten's weapons tutor, caught us. So Risten and I had to actually practice, and I was surprised at how much fun it was—and how quickly I became winded. So I worked it out with my tutors to spar with Risten every day until she began to take on other responsibilities."

"Well, you've definitely gotten good at it."

Zofie turned her blinding smile on me. "Well, my knight, what do you say. Up for it? Ready to go all out."

I made a face. "I don't know...."

A corner of her mouth rose. "Risten would say something like, 'Is the big strong man afraid of a little girl?'"

I chuckled. "Yes, she would say exactly that. Only she'd add... Can't blame you, 'cause this little girl's going to kick your ass.'" I raised my sword and took my first stance. "So bring it on."

She smiled in return and went into her perfect stance, her sword held high. "Do not hold back, or I will be very angry."

And so we started, trading blows back and forth. She was indeed good, and we were pretty well matched. But it didn't take long for her lack of practicing to make itself known as she began to tire, and her movements became slower. I slowed down a little to match her. I didn't want to beat her too badly.

She gritted her teeth. "I told you not to hold back!"

"I'm not," I lied. I reasoned it wasn't her fault she was out of practice.

We traded a few more blows, me matching her, when she suddenly stepped back and threw her sword down. I froze in mid-swing. I was totally unprepared when she closed with me, grabbed my shirt, and threw me to the ground. I landed hard on my back. She leaned over me, her face red in anger. "I told you not to hold back!" She shouted, her face red. I never realized my sweet Zofie could get so angry. "You should have beaten me by now! I know you're stronger than me. I can't stand it when people coddle me. If everyone treats me like I'm a porcelain doll, how am I supposed to learn? How am I supposed to grow!"

"Zofie, I'm sorry."

She hit me on the chest, but the blow had no power. Tears came to her eyes, and she sank to her knees beside me. "I could have lost you this morning. And I couldn't do anything to help you. I hate my curse, and I hate being this stupid pretend princess. I don't know what's right for me or the kingdom. Creator, I hate it all! And Galvyn he... he...."

I felt the hot tears landing on my cheeks.

And it suddenly hit me. I never considered that Zofie maybe had fears and insecurities. No one to confide in. And she must be terrified—afraid she might make the wrong decision—and it might hurt someone she loved.

I sat up. She looked away, wiping tears and trying to compose herself. I reached out and gently turned her chin in my direction. Her tear-filled eyes were a mix of worry, dread, and anger.

"Zofie," I said softly. "I'm sorry. I promise I won't hold back again."

She gazed at me a moment before leaning close and looking into my eyes—her beautiful face dangerously close. I could see each and every freckle on her nose. "Liar," she said gently. "You're still doing it."

I heard steps off to my right. "Getting a little close to my fiancée there, aren't you!" Zofie and I both turned toward the sound. Galvyn was walking toward us. He stopped and clasped his hands behind his back. "And from the looks of it, making her cry too."

I rose and helped Zofie get to her feet. She wiped her eyes with the back of her hand. "We were just talking," she said.

Galvyn raised an eyebrow. "Talking is fine. Just remember your station. Judging from your tears, I'm assuming you told him?"

Her head came up in alarm. "Galvyn, now's not a good time."

Puzzled, I looked from one to the other. "Tell me what?"

Zofie took a step toward Galvyn and placed a hand on his chest. "Please don't!"

Galvyn grinned smugly and ignored her. "Tell you that she's chosen me. We're going to be married as soon as we can find this ancient mirror, or determine it can't be found." He rocked forward on his heels. "It was a good fight and all, but in the end, she made the best choice possible. For her and the kingdom."

I looked to Zofie, and she looked into my eyes. And in her expression, I saw hurt.

I wondered if she saw the same in mine.

CHAPTER NINE

Finding
A Finder

I have traveled with Spraggel many times over the years. Some of these trips had been hard or physically uncomfortable, yet I really hadn't minded so much. Those were only inconveniences. But, they did wear on one after a while, and at some point during the trip, I would wish it was over. I would want to get some good food, be safe and warm by the keep's hearth, or just sleep in my own bed. But in all my time with Spraggel, I had never been absolutely miserable.

Until this leg of the journey.

For the next several days we made our way toward Wyndhaven Harbor. First, arranging boat passage down the Nortesy and then floating down it until it reached the mighty Edi, and from there to Shallowmouth Bay, the gateway to the ocean. It wasn't an especially hard trip. The food was reasonable, but by no means fancy. We rode in the boat all day, so there was nothing more strenuous to do than watching the scenery go by. Fumiko kept me in constant conversation discussing my curse and the mirror that we sought. Spraggel would sometimes listen and add in a choice bit of history or trivia. It should have been an enjoyable trip.

However, I felt empty inside at the painful distance between Zofie and myself. I couldn't help but feel like it was she who was traveling down the river, while I was the one on the shore, and we were getting further and further apart.

The evening after Galvyn announced they were engaged, Zofie had talked with me privately. I could tell she was upset, but she kept a straight face. She tried to explain her reasons for agreeing to marry Galvyn.

She started counting them off on her fingers. "...his parents are wealthy, his family has a long noble lineage, and his father is well respected by the other lords." She shrugged. "It's the best possible alliance I could possibly make...."

"But do you love him?" I interrupted.

Her eyes widened in surprise. "I... I..." she stammered.

I leaned forward and took her hand in mine. "Do you love him?" I asked again softly. "Or if not that, can you even tell me that you just like him?"

Her mouth opened and closed a few times before she jerked her hand back and turned away. "It doesn't matter. I really don't have a choice."

I took a long shaky breath and let it out slowly. I thought I would be angry, I thought at least I would be hurt. But I wasn't. Instead, I only had an overwhelming sense of loss. "I understand," I said. "And I will do my best to serve you, as long as you need me."

She turned toward me, her eyes moist, but her lips in a genuine smile. "Thank you." And I knew she meant it.

"But," I said. "We will have to see how things stand after you are wed. I do not think Galvyn will be in favor of me staying."

She shook her head. "Galvyn *will not* tell me who I have around me."

I retook her hand and gave it a gentle kiss. "I think you and I both know that he can, and he will. I'm a threat to his security. One that must be removed."

She opened her mouth to deny it, but no words came out.

I bowed to her before turning to leave. "Good night, princess."

I felt her eyes on my back as I walked away, but she said nothing more. Calling her princess had been cruel—she hated for her friends to call her that. But I felt I needed to reestablish our relationship. I was now only her knight.

Since then, Zofie had been avoiding me. She kept a smile pasted on her face and laughed frequently. But I knew from our previous travels that the smile was paper-thin and her laugh a little bit exaggerated. I think Spraggel and Fumiko sensed it too, but they wisely decided not to say anything.

To pay for our river passage, we sold our horses—not that we could have afforded to transport them downriver anyway. It was the most logical thing to do, and I was able to get a reasonable price for them. But at the same time, I hated to see them go. They had been like old friends. It seemed like something else that I had to give up.

The final insult was that Abe wouldn't come. I called him several times during our trip, but he refused to show up. I had hoped Spraggel might have an idea, but he was also stumped. Fumiko asked about him every day—I think she began to wonder if I was lying.

It was a week after Zofie and Galvyn's announcement that we arrived in Wyndhaven Harbor, the largest town on the Shallowmouth Bay. Beynon Manor, Galvyn's home, was just to the north of the harbor proper, so this part of our journey was almost done.

Galvyn had wanted to simply walk up to his father's manor and announce our presence, but Spraggel argued against it, saying we needed to find out what was going on first. Things could have changed since he departed.

So after disembarking, we made our way to a tavern that Galvyn frequented called the Siren's Lyre. For the visit, Zofie loaned him her disguise charm while she, Fumiko, and I hid in a nearby alley. Spraggel of course, went around back to see what he could learn from there.

I was surprised when Galvyn rejoined us after only a half an hour. He handed Zofie back her charm. "I'm loath to admit it, but apparently,

Spraggel was right. Not all is well at Beynon Manor. There has been an unusual amount of traffic around it—most of them are the king's soldiers. Several have been stationed at the gates."

"Have they arrested Lord Merrick?" Zofie asked.

Galvyn shook his head. "From what I could gather, he has an escort from the king assigned to him, but otherwise has free rein."

"You don't think he's aligned with Wynn, do you?" I asked.

Galvyn looked a little unsure, but then shook his head. "There's no way he would align with the king. The taxes are killing our business." He thought for a moment. "But this doesn't change our plan. We slip into the manor, find my father, explain our engagement, and persuade him to let us use the finder."

Zofie leaned closer. "Going in through the front door doesn't sound like a good idea. Do you know a way we can sneak in?"

Galvyn rolled his eyes. "Of course I do. I've been slipping out ever since I was nothing more than a brat, but we'll have to do it at night. The servants have to be asleep for it to work." He glanced at Zofie, and I swear I saw him blush. "And you... ah... and Fumiko had best stay behind." He nodded. "In case it's a trap." He turned and patted me hard on the back, nearly knocking me over. "I'll take this one with me though. He can stand watch."

I rolled my shoulder blades, wondering if they would ever be the same. "I can do that."

Zofie gave him a suspicious look. "Why can't I come too? Seems it would be best if I made my case to Lord Merrick myself."

Galvyn shook his head. "I don't think that's a good idea. We have to go in through this tiny little tunnel, and I know how you don't like tight places."

Zofie paused, considering Galvyn closely for a couple heartbeats longer than I thought she should have. "All right," she finally agreed.

I looked up at the sky. "Since it's only mid-afternoon, I suggest we find a quiet inn and try to stay off the streets. It'll also give these two somewhere to stay while we're out."

Spraggel sauntered around the corner and began to rub against

Zofie's legs. "We're being watched," he warned us calmly "I suggest we move further into the alley."

We started down that way, Spraggel following us. After we had gone a short distance, he continued. "I noticed a couple men in regular clothes watching the back of the tavern. No swords and no uniforms, but there's no doubt they're looking for someone."

We emerged from the alley on a major street and turned toward the heart of the town. We hadn't gone very far when we heard a shout. "There they are!"

While every impulse I had said to run, I kept walking at the same pace I had been. My companions did the same.

I heard running behind us, and then a man brushed by me heading up the street. He and four others converged on a small party of three just a little ahead of us: two men and one woman. The woman was wearing a hooded robe that hid her face. They were joined a moment later by two uniformed soldiers.

We continued to walk toward them, not daring to turn aside, but flowing with the foot traffic around them. I swallowed and tried to ignore the sweat on my brow. Since the other pedestrians paid no heed to it, this was apparently a common event.

The soldiers encircled the party of three. I could hear them protest, but it was only a token complaint—they were clearly terrified. They ordered the woman to lower her hood, which she did, and long brown locks flowed out from it.

The taller of the two soldiers frowned. "I thought you said she had red hair."

One of the plainly dressed men answered, "It looked red to me, but it was hard to make out under the hood."

Just as we were pulling even with them, I saw one of the soldiers grab each of the men's left wrist and examine them. He looked up and shook his head. Their commander made a face and dismissed them with a wave. My back itched wondering when they were going to stop us, but they didn't approach.

After we had safely passed the soldiers, Zofie leaned over and picked up Spraggel so he could talk to us. "Seems like they're looking for three people," he quietly pointed out while licking his paw. "Earlier they were looking for four. They must not know Fumiko is now with us. Not only that, they're looking for a red-haired woman and a man with something on his left wrist. Interesting. It seems their intelligence is pretty good."

I whispered back. "But why did they not stop us? We sort of fit the description."

Spraggel chuckled. "It's probably because of the disguise charm. The nymph does good work, so while it is hiding Zofie's appearance, it's likely making all of us a little harder to notice."

Fumiko's eyebrows shot up. "You talked to a nymph?"

I nodded.

She grinned. "Then I need to talk to you about that too. They're fascinating creatures—and deadly too."

I rolled my eyes. Just what I needed to hear.

When we arrived at the Waterman's Inn, I couldn't help but notice it was a little—posh. Galvyn gave me a disgusted look when I mentioned it. "It's true a lot of nobility go there," he said. "But more importantly, they're used to people coming and going at all hours. Which means fewer questions. And if you're worried about paying for it, I will take care of everything." He started to go in, but I grabbed him by the shoulder. "Should you borrow Zofie's disguise again."

He gave me a deadly look for touching him. "I'm better off without it. There could be a reward out for me, but this place has a strict policy of non-interference. As long as we don't run naked down the halls, we'll be fine." He grinned. "Only the really wealthy ones get to do that."

So we went in and Galvyn obtained a single room for us all, and as I feared, it put a big dent in our purses. And true to Galvyn's word, the woman behind the counter didn't question us one bit.

But charged us extra for a cat.

Late that evening, Galvyn and I left Zofie and Fumiko in the room while we tried to slip into the manor. The streets were deserted and eerily quiet. Fortunately, it was a foggy evening which made it easier to avoid any patrols. Both of us had the hoods of our cloaks pulled up to disguise our faces—we left our one disguise charm with Zofie in case something should happen.

It didn't take us long to make it to the manor. It sat atop a hill with a tall stone wall around it. We observed the entrance from just down the street. It was well lit and I could see the guards wore the king's colors. We weren't getting in that way.

"All right," I whispered. "How do we get in? Over the wall?"

Galvyn looked at me nervously. "You have to swear you won't tell Zofie."

"What?" I asked, puzzled. "Not tell her about jumping a wall?"

He rolled his eyes. "No, you idiot. About the way we sneak in. You have to swear you won't tell Zofie."

I scratched my head. "Why?"

"It's a little embarrassing for her to find out. I'll tell her eventually, just not right now."

I shrugged. "All right, I swear I won't tell her, but I won't lie either. If she asks me directly, I'll tell her I swore not to say."

Galvyn gave me a disgusted look. "That will do." He sighed and shook his head. "You really don't know a thing about women, do you? You don't tell them everything. That's what they expect. They just want to be taken care of by their man. The stronger, the better. It's why you lost really. She was naturally attracted to my leadership instinct."

I snorted, not believing what was coming out of his mouth. "And I'm sure your father having an army had absolutely nothing to do with it." I pointed down the street. "Now, can we get this over with?"

He smirked but said nothing more.

He led us across the street and then down to the next corner. The building was plain, but whitewashed so that it seemed to shine in the dim light. There was no sign outside, only a short flight of stone steps and then a door. A well-dressed man, tall and broad-shouldered, stood beside it. The man eyed us as we walked up the stairs but didn't say anything as we passed inside.

I blinked in the strangely hued light inside. Myst lamps hung on the wall decorated with red shades giving the room an intimate warm glow. Inside were several scantily clad women reclining on thick cushions scattered about the room. They looked up as we came inside with a curious, hungry stare that made me uncomfortable.

Galvyn didn't hesitate and walked up to a counter with an older woman behind it. "I need to speak with Madam Ryleigh. Tell her Little Wolf needs to go home." He then pushed a silver piece over the counter toward her. She nodded. "Just a moment, sir."

She motioned to one of the young women sitting close by. The woman gave us a sultry smile as she slowly rose and sauntered through an open door. Her skirt was extremely short—swaying gently as she walked and displaying quite a length of attractive leg.

I swallowed.

Galvyn leaned close and whispered, "The girls here are best left alone. They may look pretty, but they're quite skilled at incapacitating someone, not to mention the weapons hidden around the room."

I glanced toward one of them, and she blew a kiss in my direction. I didn't doubt him. Females generally scared the life out of me. And those were just the normal, everyday variety. These were in a completely different category.

We waited, standing in the center of the room, while the women appraised us with their eyes. No one spoke. Galvyn seemed perfectly calm, but I was sweating.

The messenger returned shortly and motioned us to follow. We went down a long corridor with many doors similar to one of the fancier inns. At the end of the hall, we went down a circular staircase which led to a single door. She knocked once, and a muffled reply came from inside. Opening the door for us, she allowed us to enter and then closed it behind.

A middle-aged woman, Madam Ryleigh I assumed, sat behind a simple desk. Papers and a ledger were scattered across it. The office was small with one wall completely curtained. She looked up and gave Galvyn a broad smile. "So Little Wolf returns. If you will give me a few minutes, I'll make sure Candis is prepared for you."

Galvyn glanced at me and then waved her to silence. "Not now, madam. I just need to go home without all those soldiers getting in the way. I need to speak with my father."

"Yes, my lord," she smiled. "But wouldn't you like to take a few minutes with Candis. She *is* your favorite... and she's missed you so."

"She has?" Galvyn seemed surprised.

"Indeed. She said so only yesterday, wondering when her Little Wolf was going to return."

Something about the way she spoke didn't feel right. I knew without a doubt, she was stalling.

I stepped forward, raising my left wrist so she could see my curse mark. "How long ago did you trip the alarm?" I asked. "Tell me the truth because I am a myst caster and will know it if you lie. And if you do lie, I will curse you to forever be a toad." Without Abe working, that was not going to happen, but she didn't know that. She stared up at me with fear in her eyes.

Galvyn gave me a puzzled look, but then realization suddenly hit him. He wheeled on the woman. "Are you working with the king? How could you go against my father?"

The woman shook her head violently. "It was your father's orders. He told us that if you should appear, to keep you here until his men could fetch you."

"The alarm?" I said threateningly. "How long till they get here."

"I... I'm not sure," she stammered, her face white. "But it won't be long."

Galvyn immediately stepped around the desk and held out his hand. "The key, please. Don't make me search for it."

She got a devilish grin on her face. "You wouldn't dare. Although I might like it if you did."

He turned to me. "Toad."

I nodded. "A big fat one." I pointed at her. "I curse...."

"No! Please no!" She stood. "I'll give it to you."

She started to reach into her bosom, but suddenly bolted for the door. I grabbed her, and being overbalanced, we both toppled to the floor. We wrestled with her trying to get away, but I managed to pin her hands to the floor. She finally stopped struggling with her skirts in disarray and her blouse partially open. Both of us were breathing hard.

I blushed when I realized I had her in a very compromising position.

"Now give us the key," I demanded.

She glared up at me. "All right."

I released her right hand and she reached into her bosom, pulling out a single brass key. Galvyn grabbed it and went to the curtained side of the room. When he pushed it back, it revealed a narrow door. He unlocked it and motioned me to follow.

I released Madam Ryleigh and stood, offering my hand to help her up. She just glared at me. She stood on her own, fixed her blouse, and then stalked out the door we had entered.

I didn't waste any time. I quickly followed Galvyn, who locked the door behind me.

Darkness was so thick you could cut it. I listened to the sound of our breathing and the drip of water somewhere ahead. I felt along the wall and found it was rough rock—we were in some kind of tunnel. I reached inside my shirt and fished out my amulet which cast a dim glow around us.

Galvyn brushed past me, and I jogged after him down the tunnel.

"You have a tunnel going from your manor to a brothel?" I asked. "Isn't something wrong with that?"

Galvyn shrugged. "Our investments haven't been doing so well over the years and running our estate is expensive. Father has had to be creative to keep us comfortable in the lifestyle we deserve. The king taxes everything that moves through the port, so he had to find something that was below cover, so to speak."

"But a brothel?"

"Not only is it profitable, but it has some side benefits." He gave me an evil smile, and my dislike of him went up a bit more.

He continued, "Aside from the obvious ones, the workers are a rich source of information. We give the girls and boys a bonus for interesting tidbits of gossip. In fact, old King Xernow, Zofie's father, valued the information my father provided, although he had no idea of its source." He waved his hand around. "We own several such establishments. The one we came from only deals with nobility. The ones closer to the docks cater to a different sort of crowd and work out of our taverns. We bring women in from all over to have the best selection."

I stopped dead, and breathing hard, shook my head in disbelief. "Did I hear you right? You bring them in from all over? You mean you recruit them?"

Galvyn had to stop since I had the light. He turned to me defiantly. "Yes, we recruit them. Depending on their quality, we pay quite highly."

I could feel my face turning red. The memory of Maggie tied up in the back of that wagon came to me. "You mean you buy them? As in slaves?"

He harrumphed. "Not slaves. That's too crass a word. They're more like *servants*. They have to work for us, but we give them a portion of their earnings, and when they earn enough, they can buy out their contract." He motioned down the tunnel. "Now can we get moving, they'll be after us in a moment."

"And do they get a choice of how they pay back their debt, or do you force them to be prostitutes?"

He shrugged. "I don't really know. Father deals with that side of the business."

"In other words, you don't want to know."

Galvyn stepped toward me, clearly angry. "What has one of my family businesses got to do with running down this Creator damned tunnel! You want the Wayward's Finder, don't you?"

"Tell me! Are they forced into this?"

"I told you, I don't know. They're brokered to us through various channels. Some are convicted criminals, others are debtors." He turned to face back down the tunnel. "And some, I don't know how they ended up here." He pointed down the tunnel. "Now, can we get going before I jerk that necklace off you and go by myself!"

"Does Zofie know?" I was afraid of the answer.

He wheeled on me. "Of course not! That's why I couldn't bring her with us. And if you tell her, I will personally see you dead, curse or no curse." He looked down the tunnel. "She's exactly like her father with an inflated sense of justice."

I opened my mouth to speak, but paused at a sound behind us. We exchanged a glance. We were being followed and I didn't have the time to finish with him. "We're not done discussing this," I said.

We resumed running down the tunnel, trying to put as much distance between us and those coming behind.

The tunnel was a good bit longer than I anticipated, holding nearly level. We eventually came to a dead end with a set of circular stairs leading up. We quickly started climbing and came to a thick oak door. Galvyn put his ear against it and listened. He nodded in satisfaction.

Galvyn grabbed the handle of the door and then paused. There was a brief spark of blue light, and then the door swung open. As he pulled the door wide, he grinned up at me. "Myst lock. Only my father and I can open it."

We emerged into some kind of wine cellar with various containers stretching into the dark. Galvyn didn't hesitate, and I followed him down that long aisle of casks, barrels, and bottles. I gazed at the collection in wonder. "Does your father have enough wine?"

He looked around in disgust. "Actually, it's Mother's. She's expecting another war and wants to be prepared. She does like her wine."

The aisle came to an abrupt dead-end at a tall stone wall. Galvyn led me to a large square cut in the floor, and I couldn't help but wonder what it was.

We stepped into the middle of it and Galvyn simply pointed upward. Much to my surprise, the piece of floor began to slowly rise without making a sound. As we drew near the ceiling, I could see a similar square cut through it just big enough for us to pass through.

"What is this used for?"

"Mother had this myst lift installed because the servants complained so bitterly about carrying all that wine to the cellar. Of course, she had it extended one floor higher than father intended, so *she* didn't have to take the stairs either." He looked up. "Put out your light. One of the servants might see it."

I hid my jewel under my cloak as we emerged into what appeared to be darkened kitchens—the only light coming from the gently glowing embers in a large baking hearth. The lift continued its slow rise through the kitchens to the floor above, coming to a stop at the end of a dark corridor.

From down the hall, I could see light coming from under a door. And from behind it, came soft, but badly played music filtering toward us—extremely bad. I cringed at the torturous sounds the instrument made.

Galvyn leaned close. "That would be Mother. She hasn't been able to sleep well for the last few years and has taken to playing her gittern." He glanced down the hall and then back. "I personally think it's to keep Father out of her chambers. It's absolutely terrible."

While I hated to admit it, I actually agreed with Galvyn on something.

He put a finger to his lips and motioned me onward. He led me down the hall away from his mother's chambers to a single closed door. He quietly opened it and stepped inside. "Keep your light low, or the servants will see you."

I pulled out my light, but kept it shaded with my hand. Its feeble glow was enough to see that this was a bedroom.

"What is this?" I whispered.

"My room."

Galvyn strode to a shelf next to the shuttered window. On the shelf was a rather large wire cage. To my surprise, there was a rat-like creature inside—only it didn't have a tail. It seemed to know Galvyn though. It came to the edge and looked at him with eager eyes. "Honeycup, did you miss me," he cooed. "Have they been feeding you well." He pulled a small wooden box from the shelf and took out what must have been bits of food. Whatever it was, the little creature loved it and quickly scarfed it down. I shook my head.

While he fussed over his pet, I looked around. He had quite a few tapestries and pictures on his walls. It was too dark to make out the images. There was even a collection of small swords and knives on one wall, which looked more suitable for a child than a man.

"Coren," came Galvyn's frustrated tone. "Look in that dresser, third drawer down and bring me a box of treats. Honeycup needs some more before I go. They're his favorite."

What did he think I was, his servant? Then I realized that was *exactly* what he thought I was. I sighed and went to the dresser. It was an elaborately carved oak one. Opening the indicated drawer I didn't immediately see what he wanted. The contents were all jumbled. I pushed some stuff around until I identified the box he wanted. As I pulled it out, something small and metallic came with it. It sparkled as it fell to the floor.

I picked it up and carried over the box. "This fell out when I grabbed it." I held out a piece of some kind of jewelry. It had a wide band, but other than that I couldn't make out any details in the dim light. It seemed too small for a man's ring—a child's ring perhaps? I couldn't help but wonder where he got it. "What is it anyway?" I asked.

He shrugged, his attention focused on his pet. "I'm not sure where I got the ugly trinket. I've had it forever. Just put it back in the dresser."

I allowed my light to grow brighter so I could look at it better. That's when I caught a glimpse of something on the wall out of the corner of my eye. Looking closer, I realized it was a portrait—a rather large one. It must have cost a small fortune. I easily recognized the subject and marveled not only at its size, but the level of detail the artist had captured.

It was Zofie. A Zofie from a few years ago, but it was definitely her.

Galvyn finished with his pet and noticed my stare.

I pointed. "I can understand you like her and all, but isn't that a little excessive."

He glared at me. "I've known I was going to marry her for ages. Father wanted me to have a small reminder of what my bride looked like."

"Small?"

He harrumphed and turned away.

Just then I heard a noise in the hall outside, I quickly slipped the ring into my pocket and closed my hand tightly around the light to dim it. Galvyn stepped over to the chest and quietly opened the bottom drawer. He pulled out a couple of things I couldn't make out and slipped them into his pockets.

He next stepped to the window, quietly opened the shutters, and then looked up and then down. He surprised me by climbing up onto the window's sill. "Follow me." Then he stepped out.

What! We were two floors up. That would be enough to break a leg!

To my utter surprise, Galvyn seemed to stand on nothing. He beckoned me forward, and I reluctantly joined him on some type of invisible lift. He again pointed up, and we slowly rose to another window one floor up. It was unlocked, and we stepped through into a sort of study.

Galvyn turned on a myst globe. "Mother's not the only one to slip things by father. When Mother was having her lift installed, I bribed the workmen to put in one for me too. It's proven quite useful over the years, especially when Mother was angry at me and locked me in my room."

The study had highly polished floors and bookshelves along one wall. A working desk covered in papers sat to one side. In the center of the room was a dark wood case capped with the finest piece of glass I had ever seen. And inside sat—I couldn't think of any other way to describe it—a stick.

Admittedly a forked one, but it was still just a piece of finger-thick wood about as long as my forearm.

I pointed to it. "Is that the Wayward's Finder?"

Galvyn gave me a funny look. "What else would it be?"

"But it's a stick," I protested.

He rolled his eyes. "What did you think it was supposed to be? Gold or silver maybe? Of course, it's a stick."

"And *that* can find anything?"

"Yes, it can. It only requires a myst user to power it, but I've been told it can be quite draining."

"So, you're not going to use it?"

He gave me a puzzled look. "No, I thought you would. You're the Thief of Curses. Aren't you a myst user?"

I snorted. "Hardly. Abe provides the myst. I just cast the curses."

He glared at me in irritation but then turned to look at the case. "This is turning into a real disaster. I was hoping we could just use it here. My father will kill me if he finds out I've been in his study, little alone if I touch the finder."

"But you've been insisting that your father will help Zofie."

Galvyn leaned toward me in irritation. "And he will, after she marries me. He'll have no choice."

It suddenly hit me that Galvyn had no intention of talking to his father. "That's not what Zofie thinks."

He put his hands on his hips. "Didn't we just have a conversation about telling a woman everything? They have to be led." He looked back at the finder in thought. "Perhaps we should take it, and then maybe Zofie could power it."

And then I had my second realization of the evening: he still didn't know about Zofie's curse. She hadn't told him. While she carried that curse, she couldn't use her myst. Why had she kept it from him? I shook my head. I wasn't going to deal with that now.

"So, how do we get it out?" I asked.

We circled the case, finding a steel door in the back with a thumb-size depression in it toward the top. It was another myst lock. Galvyn pressed his thumb to it, but nothing happened. "That's odd. It won't open."

"Can't we just break the glass?"

"No, that's special myst reinforced glass. You can't break it. Nothing can." He stood and shook his head. "I can open everything else in the manor. Why not this?"

Suddenly the door to the library was flung open, and Lord Dewi Merrick, Galvyn's father, stepped into the room. "I can tell you why you can't open it," he said. "I removed my traitorous son from it."

CHAPTER TEN

Pointing
The Way

G alvyn froze in place. "Father!"

Lord Merrick stood just inside the door, and he was furious. "I can't believe you would steal from your own family to help that murderess."

I leaned over to peer around Lord Merrick into the hall behind him. I could see several men just outside with their weapons out. Once Lord Merrick stood to the side, they would quickly flood the room.

"She's not a murderer," exclaimed Galvyn indignantly. "And I would bring the finder back."

"Like you return all the other things you've appropriated."

"I am *not* a thief!" There was a shrill note to his denial.

Merrick just glared at him. "Now take me to the girl. I don't want to make this any more difficult than it already is."

I glanced at the case holding the finder. Galvyn said nothing could break it. But I knew something that would. Or at least it would if Abe would answer me.

"Abe," I whispered under my breath, hoping against hope that he would answer. "Are you there? Please be there."

What in the Creator's name do you want now! Abe was so loud, I could almost hear him echoing inside my head.

"You're back!" I whispered excitedly.

We've had this conversation before. I haven't been anywhere.

"But you wouldn't answer me... Oh, never mind. I have a question. Who can I cast the Ruin's Shield curse on? I need it to open that case. I understand it has to be a myst user."

Why don't you put it on butthead? He's the closest myst user. Although not a very strong one. It would work for at least a short time.

"It won't hurt him, will it?"

If you mean kill him, of course not. Hurt him? Damn right it will! Transformations are outright painful.

It looked like the conversation between Galvyn and his father wasn't going too well. Time to step in. I put a hand on Galvyn's shoulder and leaned closer. "I apologize for what I'm about to do."

He gave me a strange look. "And that is?"

"Well, I curse you to become Ruin's Shield."

A blue glow surrounded Galvyn, and he looked at me in shock. I immediately grabbed him by the neck, and he quickly collapsed into a large shield with me holding it by its middle support.

Lord Merrick stepped forward. "What did you do to my son? Change him back this instant!"

I didn't answer. Since the shield destroyed anything that touched its outer surface, I pushed it against the glass case. Despite whatever protections it may have had, that side vanished in a cloud of dust. I swiveled the shield toward Merrick, and through the newly created hole, grabbed the finder. It really was a stick. I then started backing away. "I think you know what this shield is. So please stay back. I don't want anyone to get hurt!"

Soldiers began to stream in the door. I backed to the window but quickly discovered the shield was too big to go through. I sighed, not really wanting to do this. I tilted the shield toward the wall, and pushing it forward, quickly made a shield size hole. I stepped out onto the myst lift.

I had a moment of panic as I wondered how to make it go down, but it started on its own, and I slowly began to drop. I held the shield over my head, facing upwards in case someone decided to throw something at me. And sure enough a few minutes later, I felt an impact and then saw a puff of dust.

"Don't shoot, you idiot!" screamed Lord Merrick. "That's my son!"

The lift stopped moving upon reaching Galvyn's room. I jumped up and down on it, hoping it would take me the rest of the way down, but no such luck. With no choice, I again opened a shield size hole in the wall and stepped into Galvyn's room.

Holding the shield away from me, I said the words to take the curse back, "Your curse is my curse."

Immediately the shield was enveloped in a blue glow and quickly transformed back into a confused Galvyn. He went down on one knee and threw up.

"I'm sorry for doing that," I said. "But it's the only way I could think of to take the finder and get away."

Galvyn slowly stood up. He wasn't quite steady on his feet yet.

"We have to hurry," I said. "Your father's just above us...."

But I never got to finish as Galvyn slammed his fist into my face. "*Don't you ever do that again!*" he spat. And he hit me again making me stagger.

I felt something warm leaking from my nose and lip. I dabbed at it with my fingers, and they came away bloody.

I glared at him. "I just saved your butt and you clip me for it?" I dabbed at it again staring at it in disbelief.

"If I had a weapon, you'd be dead," he said coldly. "Besides hurting like hell, being cursed is filthy. Only the weak are cursed. And in front of my father too!" He then went to a drawer and pulled out a piece of clothing and threw it at me. "Don't drop any blood, or they'll be able to follow us." He grabbed the finder from my hand. "And don't touch my family's belongings."

He glared at me a moment more before stepping to the door. He quietly opened it and looked both ways. He stepped out and I followed. But we only made it two steps down the hall before I heard heavy footfalls approaching from ahead of us.

Suddenly a door behind us opened: the one leading to Galvyn's mother's chambers. Silhouetted in the light streaming from the room stood a lone figure. With the light behind her, all I could tell was she was wearing a long dress.

"This way." She motioned us toward her. "Quickly!"

Galvyn and I ran into the woman's room, and she shut the door behind us. Looking around, I saw we were in a small sitting room, comfortably furnished with plush carpet, padded chairs, ornately decorated myst lamps, and a small serving table to one side. In one of the chairs lay the tortured gittern with a quill sitting beside it. I noticed two other doors in the room, one open, leading to what looked like a bedroom, and the other closed, possibly a closet.

The woman leaned against the closed door as she briefly considered us. She was a slender woman, a tad taller than me, and appeared to be in her early mid-years. Her shoulder-length hair was blond with streaks of white highlights. It was cut to frame her face, and she wore it loose. She was an attractive woman, and I imagined in her younger years she had stolen quite a few hearts.

The woman strode to the room's other closed door and opened it to reveal a tiny closet with shoes, dresses, and coats stuffed inside. There was no way we would fit in that. But just as quickly, she shut it again. Then she reached up to the top corner of the frame and tapped three times.

The second time she opened it, we saw what could only be a tiny study with a desk, chair, and several rough drawings on the wall.

"Inside," she ordered. "And stay quiet. If someone other than me should open the door, stand perfectly still and don't even breathe. I'll get you in a bit."

We did as she ordered, and she closed the door behind us.

I looked to Galvyn, and he answered the question on my lips. "That's my mother, Nadine, and these are her chambers."

"Did you know your mother had a secret room?"

Galvyn slowly shook his head and looked around. "I had no idea." He seemed just as perplexed as I was.

I shook my head. Galvyn's family kept a lot of secrets. Especially from each other.

I inspected the room around me a little more closely. I was dying to examine the charm that concealed the room, but didn't think that was wise at the moment. It had to be either a portal or an illusion. But I placed my money on an illusion since I didn't feel any disorientation when we passed into it.

The walls of the study were mostly bare wood, with only a few ink sketches decorating them, tacked up with pins. Most were of places, but there was a larger one hanging over the desk which caught my eye. It was a sketch of a young girl's face, no more than four or five. It was well-done. The paper was simply pinned to the wall and had yellowed, indicating it had been hanging there for a while. The subject's hair was pulled back with clips, and she had that open face smile all young girls did. There was no artist name on it, nor any indication of who the subject was, but for some reason she seemed familiar. I couldn't help but wonder who she was.

Sitting on a corner of the desk was a moth-eaten stuffed animal—a bear, I believe—with buttons for eyes and nose and a worn pink ribbon circling its neck. I wondered if it was connected to the little girl.

Suddenly, I heard banging coming from beyond our door. There was a pause and then the tromping of feet along with some agitated voices which I couldn't make out. Without warning, the door to our room flew open, and Lord Merrick himself stood in the entrance. Galvyn and I froze. The older man looked around, and to my surprise, didn't notice us. Instead, he seemed to be looking at something closer to the entrance. "I know you let them in," he called over his shoulder. "Where are you hiding them? The king will have both our heads for this. Besides, we need the reward." The lord reached out and seemed to shove things out of the way. He rapped on where the closet walls would have been, and to my surprise, I heard an answering knock. The illusion hiding us must be quite complex.

An irritated Nadine answered from just behind him. "I told you before that no one's here. Now have you embarrassed me enough, or do you want me to undress so your men can search under my skirts!"

Lord Merrick rolled his eyes and shook his head. "Why don't you just be quiet. Melodrama doesn't suit you. And I seriously doubt my men would be impressed by your old body." He stepped away from the closet door, but left it open. "Men, they're not here. Let's backtrack one more time."

Nadine stepped to the door and slowly closed it. Behind her, I could hear the noise of people leaving.

I whispered to Galvyn. "It sounds like your father has his sights on Zofie's reward. Are you sure he'll come around after you're married?"

Galvyn looked at me in irritation. "I never said Father would back her unconditionally. What I said was he'd be willing to consider it, if we could prove her innocence. Our being wed would surely help."

I pointed toward the door. "That didn't sound like someone willing to consider much of anything. And on top of that, he knew you were coming. Which means they've somehow learned how to track us, or.... you've been feeding them information."

Galvyn grabbed the front of my shirt. "I would *never* betray Zofie, regardless of what you think." He poked a finger in my chest. "And what about you. Zofie chose me, so you have nothing now. Perhaps you're passing information to collect the reward yourself."

It was my turn to get angry. "I've served her with nothing but full loyalty. She is more important to me than life itself!"

"Really?" He snorted. "Then why did you give up so easily."

I sputtered. The accusation floored me. How could he even think something like that? We glared at each other.

We were interrupted by the closet door opening again. Nadine stood in the entrance. "You can come out now. I think it's safe."

Galvyn shot me one last look of irritation and strode out the door. He brushed past Nadine with no acknowledgment that she had just saved him, little alone that she was his mother. It frankly surprised me. This was definitely one messed up family.

I paused in front of Nadine. "My name is Coren Hart and I thank you for hiding us. I know this must have cost you."

Nadine smiled, genuinely pleased. "Thank you, young man. My son could take a few lessons in manners from you."

Galvyn ignored the comment. "Is there a back way out of here?" he demanded.

Nadine closed the closet door and shook her head. "You know there's not. It would be best to wait a bit until the search spreads out."

Galvyn snorted at the comment and went to the serving table where he poured himself something from one of the decanters there. Nadine came forward and gently touched my face. "Looks like someone took a hit. And I bet it wasn't from my husband's men."

Galvyn snorted. "He deserved it."

She gave him a side-wise glance and then stepped to a small dresser. She took out what looked like a medicine kit. "Galvyn dearest. I could use a small drink myself. It has been rather stressful this evening. Would you pour me one from my special bottle? You know, the pink one?"

Galvyn shot her a nasty look. "I'm not your servant."

Nadine directed me to one of the chairs and opened up her kit. "True, but you are still my son, and I would hope you would do at least this much for your mother."

Galvyn snorted, and reached for a pink-tinted glass decanter. But as soon as he touched it, he froze in place.

Nadine looked over her shoulder at him and smiled. It was not a kind smile. "That should hold him for a few minutes."

I looked between them in confusion. "What...?"

She poured something medicinal smelling on a small cloth and began to wipe my nose and cheek. "This has a strong odor, but it will help with the bruising." She paused and looked into my eyes. "Rest easy. I'll not hurt you." She glanced over her shoulder at Galvyn. "And I'll release the spell momentarily. I just wanted a chance to talk with you privately."

I nodded and she continued cleaning me up. She seemed to be composing herself for something. "I've heard you're the Thief of Curses. Is that true?"

"I've been called that. But just because I have a curse, doesn't make me a thief."

She gave a half grin and nodded. "And I guess sneaking into a person's home and borrowing a family heirloom doesn't qualify you as a thief?" She smiled kindly at the taunt. "But I do understand why. And the why makes a big difference." She turned my head slightly. "And you're the princess's other suitor?"

I sat back a little nervous. "I was. But she's chosen Galvyn."

She nodded slowly and again looked over her shoulder at him. There was a complex mix of emotions on her face. "My son is a lot like his father. More than I had hoped. Don't get me wrong, I love my son. But he can be a bit... challenging at times." She turned back to face me. "I hope the princess knows what she's getting into. Sometimes, a short term solution isn't always the best one." She looked away for a moment with a wistful expression. "I have experience with that." She sighed, and we sat in silence for a moment as she fussed with me.

As she worked, I looked at her more closely. I noticed she continued to smile, but I sensed that her smile was her armor—a shield well used. And it spoke of someone accustomed to heartbreak.

Finishing her task, she sat back and began returning items to the kit. "And what of the girl that is always with the princess? A redhead, just like her. Isn't her name Risten? I met her once a while back. She seemed very nice."

I thought it a little odd she mentioned Risten. "Well, she has blonde hair now, just a shade darker than yours. Zofie's master changed it as part of a disguise. And as for *nice*, I don't know if I would describe her that way."

"Oh?"

I nodded. "I find her rude, demeaning, and sometimes just plain mean. But..." I looked in the distance. "Despite her foul words, she has a heart of gold and will do anything for her friends. She's someone I would trust with my life. I know Zofie does."

Nadine smiled and a tear came to her eye. "It makes me glad to hear that." She seemed to catch herself and cleared her throat. "Sounds like the princess has been fortunate to find someone like Risten. I'm sure she will be of assistance if the princess can regain her throne."

Nadine abruptly stood and returned her kit to the dresser. Then from another drawer, she pulled out a small leather pouch. She turned to me and placed it in my hand. When I opened it, there were several pieces of gold and silver jewelry inside.

"Thank you, but...."

She cut me off. "Take them. I no longer need them. And while it's not much, please use them to help the princess."

"But shouldn't you be giving this to Galvyn and not me?"

She smiled. "I've learned from my husband that you have to invest where you think the greatest return will be." She reached up and touched my face. "Please take care of the princess, and especially those closest to her." I could tell she wanted to say more. I could almost see the words on her lips.

For some reason, I thought of the sketch of the little girl and the stuffed bear; of Risten's comment that she had been sent to live with her father at an early age and she never knew the woman who birthed her; and that Risten's hair had been patterned after that same mysterious person. All those pieces pointed to only one conclusion.

My eyes went wide as it hit me. "You're Risten's mother."

She stared at me for a moment with that sad smile on her face. She then abruptly turned toward Galvyn. "I'd best free my son. Any longer and he'll grow suspect."

I stood and gave her a slight bow. "I thank you for all that you have done. I will not forget. Perhaps when all this has blown over, I will suggest the princess come visit you. And maybe I'll suggest Risten come with her."

A slow grin came to Nadine's face. The first truly genuine one I'd seen. "I would like that."

And then she turned and touched her son on the shoulder. He immediately unfroze.

"I'm sorry son, it's this one here." She pulled out a smaller pink decanter and poured herself a tiny bit into a crystal glass.

He looked at her sourly. "If you're going to order me around like a servant, then at least get your instructions right?"

She patted his face. "Yes, dear."

He rolled his eyes.

Nadine took a sip. "I think the noise has died down some. I will create a distraction so you can get a head start. I'm assuming you came in through the tunnel?"

Galvyn seemed surprised. "You know about the tunnel?"

Nadine frowned. "Of course I know. Your father started that accursed business while I was carrying you. It's why you don't have any younger siblings." She didn't wait for Galvyn's response. She strode to the door. "I'll go upstairs and draw them to me. Then you can sneak out." She then opened it and slipped out.

I wondered how we would know when the distraction was in place.

We only waited a short time before there was a blood-curdling scream from above us. Throughout the house, we heard boots running. Galvyn peeked out the door and then motioned for me to follow.

Galvyn led us back to the myst lift where we rode it down into the cellar. From there, we retraced our steps down the tunnel and into the brothel. Madam Ryleigh was nowhere to be seen. Galvyn showed me out a back way, and we began walking toward the inn.

When we reached an intersection, a gray cat approached us. "This way," Spraggel whispered.

Galvyn protested. "But the inn is in the other direction."

Spraggel rubbed up against my leg. "There's been a complication. The princess felt that waiting there was dangerous."

"Complication?" I asked.

But Spraggel didn't answer. He then took off at a trot, leaving us with no option but to follow. He led us through several alleys, and I know we doubled back at least three times. He finally seemed satisfied that no one followed us, and he started us toward the harbor.

By the time we arrived at a deserted warehouse near the docks, the eastern sky was just beginning to lighten. Spraggel entered easily through a small hole in the door, but we had to climb in a window toward the back. The inside was completely empty and looked like no one had been inside it for quite a while. Zofie and Fumiko emerged from a dark corner when they saw us. Spraggel was already in Zofie's arms having his chin scratched.

I immediately noticed something wrong. "Did something happen? You're not wearing your disguise," I said.

"It's broke," Zofie said flatly.

Fumiko pointed to herself. "It's my fault. I was brushing the princess's hair, and I was going to surprise her by letting her use one of my combs. When I went to put her flower back in her hair, it accidentally touched my ring. I always thought it was silver, but apparently it was just coated and I had worn it down to the iron underneath. The flower shriveled up instantly."

Zofie picked up the story from there. "And then we heard a commotion below us as a group of the king's soldiers argued with the inn managers. We snuck out and Spraggel led us here. This is the best he could do."

Spraggel spoke up. "We'll survive without the disguise. Now tell us, did you get it?"

Galvyn smiled. "Indeed we did. He pulled the finder out from under his coat."

Zofie frowned. "It looks like a stick."

I chuckled. "That's what I said."

Galvyn protested. "This is a family heirloom. It dates back to the time of the Dark Avenyts."

Zofie shook her head. "It still looks like a stick."

Galvyn held it up. "Look. I'll show you. You grab both of the ends and then invoke it by saying, 'Point me to' and then say the name of the object you're looking for. It will point you in the direction."

Zofie turned to Fumiko. "You said we couldn't seek the mirror itself, but we could seek out the case it's in. What's the case called?"

Fumiko pushed her hair back from her eyes. "It wasn't given a proper name. It was just mentioned that the mirror was kept in a case to protect it."

I frowned. "I thought you said we could find the mirror by finding what it was kept in?"

Fumiko put her hands on her hips. "I did say that, but it doesn't have a proper name. You just have to know how to phrase it so it will work."

Galvyn groaned. "So now you're telling me we can't use this to find it. I've only seen it work when the proper name was used."

"Don't blame me," shot back Fumiko. "I didn't know the thing required a proper name. Most advanced myst objects are smart enough to figure it out."

I shrugged. "Then we'll just have to try a couple different combinations. What was it commonly known by?"

Fumiko shrugged. "There were only a few mentions in the texts of something containing the mirror." She looked up and closed her eyes in recollection. "The first one I looked at called it 'a container.' The second called it 'a case'. And the last one…" She paused in thought and then looked up in surprise. "I… I can't recall."

Zofie nodded. "Then let's try what we know." She put a hand on Galvyn's shoulder. "You can try it however you want, but I'd recommend asking it to point us to The Container for the Mirror of Bygone Tears."

Galvyn nodded and gave a confident smile. "That's exactly what I was going to do. We think so much alike."

Zofie gave him a pained smile.

Galvyn dug in his pocket and pulled out a small round object. "We'll need to know what direction to go, so I brought my compass. It'll be easier to take a bearing that way."

"Good thinking," complimented Zofie.

Galvyn could only grin as he set the compass on the floor in front of himself.

We each took a step backward to give him room. He held out the finder and said, "Point us to the Container for the Mirror of Bygone Tears!"

I held my breath in anticipation as the stick glowed green—but it quickly went out.

Zofie frowned. "The spell activated. That means it's at least trying to work. Let's use the other description."

Galvyn did, with similar results.

The young lord sighed. "I saw this once before. Father was using it to locate some trinket for a friend, but they couldn't come up with the proper name."

I went to Fumiko and put a hand on her shoulder. "Was there anything else we could use for a clue?"

She looked very frustrated, almost angry. "The word is right there. Give me a moment to think." She stepped away toward a darker part of the warehouse.

Galvyn and Zofie were trying out different combinations. I glanced toward where Fumiko had gone and saw her squatting with her back against a far wall. She folded her arms over her knees and rested her head down on them. And then for the life of me, it looked like she went to sleep.

Concerned, I stepped toward her and squatted down beside her. She was indeed breathing regularly. She had always been one to fall asleep quickly, but this was almost instantaneous. I touched her shoulder, "Fumiko, are you all right?"

She almost violently seized my hand, gripping it tightly. When she looked up, her eyes were full of tears and she had a pleading look on her face. But the expression quickly changed into one of victory. She wiped her eyes with the back of her hand and smiled confidently. "Thank you, Coren. You helped me get the answer."

She got to her feet. She took me by the hand and led me back to the others. "The oldest text was in ancient Urticia, and the word it used for whatever held the mirror, had two literal meanings: One for a place to store protected items and the other a chamber with a high curved ceiling. The original translator chose the first meaning, which is where the terms case and container came from. But if you consider the timeframe, there was a lot of death after the Dark Avenyts war."

I looked at her puzzled. "What has death got to do with it?"

"Everything." Fumiko smiled. "Try using the word *crypt*."

Surprised expressions went all around our group.

"A container to hold those that have died," I mused.

Galvyn shrugged. "What have we got to lose?" He held the finder out and said, "Point us to the Crypt of the Mirror of Bygone Tears."

Once again, the object glowed green—but this time the glow strengthened. It grew brighter and the tip began to quiver.

Galvyn's eyes grew wide. "I... I think it's working!"

The finder suddenly jerked far to the left, nearly knocking Galvyn over, then wheeling back to the right. It quivered for a moment before moving again and turning Galvyn completely around to face the other way. And then the item froze in place.

I quickly grabbed the compass and held it just over the finder. We all looked at each other in shock.

The finder was pointing due south.

It was pointing out to sea.

CHAPTER ELEVEN

Out to Sea

T he crate came down heavily, making a loud noise on the wooden boards of the wharf. I jumped. I was nervous anyway as we waited for the cargo to be loaded on the ship. Loud noises didn't help.

"Hey!" Galvyn stepped toward the worker that had dropped it. "Be careful with that! It's fragile!"

"Shut yer hole," he shouted back, disengaging his dolly from the crate. "It'r in one piece, 'ren't it? If I wer'nt bein' careful, it'd b'n bits."

Galvyn's eyes drew down. "Do you know who I am? If anything is broken, I'll have your job."

The old worker rolled his eyes. "If da boss could'a found some'n else for t'job, he'd a'ready done it!" He then displayed a middle finger to Galvyn and strolled away pushing his dolly before him.

Galvyn stood erect and adjusted his jacket, daggers in his eyes as he watched the man heading down the wharf. "Peasants," he muttered under his breath.

He turned back to me and frowned. "Relax a little. You're so nervous you're going to give us away. And quit pulling at your collar. We're supposed to be rich merchants."

I immediately dropped my hand from my neck and restrained myself from touching it. The shirt was stiff and the collar was choking me. Not to mention the dress jacket was too tight and the boots too shiny. I personally couldn't see why we had to wear such fancy clothes. But Galvyn had insisted we look the part. Our disguise was completed using some of the materials from Spraggel's theater face paint kit. The young lord now brandished a long mustache while I wore my usual eyepatch and long scar on my cheek.

"I hope our cargo is doing all right." I leaned casually against the crate and knocked twice on the side.

It was immediately answered with two knocks from inside. Zofie had survived the rough handling.

I could safely say that this madness was all Spraggel's fault. He had explained his plan to us back at the warehouse. Since the trail to the mirror led out to sea, we were going to require a ship. While we could hire passage, getting Zofie onboard was a problem. Since we no longer had a disguise charm, we were going to have to sneak her aboard. Through his family connections, Galvyn happened to know someone that could do it without bringing in his father. We were able to quickly work out an arrangement. The fact the "special" cargo was human didn't even make Galvyn's counterpart blink. It made me wonder even more about his family's business.

A chill breeze, scented with the smell of the ocean, ruffled my hair, and rocked the ship tied to the wharf beside us. Her name was the *Wily Lass*. To my untrained eye, at least, she didn't look very wily. She looked kind of—*old*. She was covered in barnacles, her exterior paint was faded and flaking off, and her rigging looked just plain worn out.

And I was going to have to ride it in all that water?

I turned to Galvyn. "Are you sure the ship is safe?"

Galvyn grinned. "It was well recommended. I have to trust the captain knows what she's doing."

I eyed our vessel dubiously. "Have you done this before?"

Galvyn almost rocked with pride. "Take passage on a ship? Of course. That's something most nobles do at an early age. Although the accommodations were a little more... refined." He leaned closer. "Not having doubts about accompanying us, are you? I'm sure Zofie and I can find this stupid mirror without you."

I shook my head. "No, I'm coming. I just don't like water."

He patted me on the back. "You'll do fine." He grinned evilly. "Just pray we don't run into a storm. I've heard the waves are so big that they'll sweep a man over the side before he can call for help."

I couldn't help but imagine all that dark water coming over one's head. I shivered. I'd likely die of fright before I drowned.

He chuckled, enjoying my discomfort. "Seriously, storms can be bad, but the real problem is freebooters. I hear there's been an increase in their numbers. Apparently, the king decided his navy cost too much and cut back on supplies, as well as killing off a few captains. That didn't sit too well with the sailors, and many gave up protecting the shipping lanes and instead have decided to fund themselves via looting." He leaned closer. "After they steal the cargo, they slit the throats of all the passengers and crew of any ship they find."

I started to sweat.

Galvyn gave an evil grin. He dropped his voice to a whisper and leaned closer. "But the things you really have to watch out for are the sea wraiths. Some say they're not of this world. And those they catch are never seen again."

I'm sure my face lost all color.

Galvyn suddenly broke off his little scare session. He looked at something over my shoulder and drew himself up taller, straightening his jacket in a most regal manner. Behind me, I heard the sound of many feet on the wharf. I turned to see a short, thin, well-dressed man followed by two bored-looking guards. I groaned inwardly. It was the port inspector. It was his job to assess the tax on goods entering and leaving port. While we had made provisions for an encounter like this, we had hoped to avoid it. I prayed our plan worked.

Galvyn broke into a huge smile and gave a deep sweeping bow to the man as he drew up with us. "Best of the day to you, good sir. You must be the port inspector. I think you will find everything in order...."

"Open it." The short man commanded, nodding toward our crate. His accent marked him as being a local but from the richer, more sophisticated part of town.

Galvyn stammered. "But my good sir, it's only some fine porcelain I managed to chance upon. I...."

The man slapped the crate loudly with the flat of his hand. "Porcelain usually is packed in this type of container," came the flat reply. "But it usually *arrives* at the port, not shipped out. Now open it, or I'll have my guards here take an ax to it. Either way, it's going to be opened."

Galvyn leaned back, looking insulted. "Well, if you insist." He sounded defeated.

He turned to me and motioned for me to get on with it. I pulled out a crowbar that Galvyn had insisted I bring, and began working on carefully prying open the top.

"I haven't all day," announced the inspector.

Galvyn wrung his hands. "He's new, my lord. I apologize for the delay. Can't find good help these days."

The lid finally came free, and I lifted it aside to reveal a crate full of straw. The inspector came forward and dug through it until he uncovered several bottles of wine. As we all knew, wine usually shipped in barrels. That is unless it was an extremely valuable vintage.

"Hmmm. This doesn't look like porcelain to me. Looks like bottles of wine. I'd have to taste it to be sure, but likely a very expensive one, I must say." The inspector paused and glared at us. "You wouldn't by chance be trying to avoid the king's tax on fine wine, would you?"

Galvyn quickly replied, "Of course not. There must have been a mistake on the paperwork."

"Good," said the inspector. "Then perhaps you should properly adjust the paperwork and give me the tax."

"Of course, of course. And you can keep that bottle for yourself since you've been so understanding of my mistake." Galvyn reached in his coat pocket and pulled out a bag of coins he'd prepared in advance. He handed it to the inspector.

The inspector made the coins disappear into his own coat pocket. "Indeed," said the inspector as I repositioned the top and nailed it back down. "Some people think they can sneak anything by me. But I've seen it all. You'll not get one by me."

"True, very true," Galvyn quickly agreed.

The inspector and his men stepped away, headed toward the next ship.

I couldn't decide if this had been a real inspection or if it had just been for show. He had caught our "mistake" and penalized us for it. But the exchange of coins at the end made me wonder if perhaps the inspector knew the crate had a false bottom and the coin ensured he didn't look too far.

When the inspector was out of earshot, Galvyn leaned closer. "That went better than I expected. He could have made us unpack the whole crate."

I knocked on the side twice and received the two knock reply. Zofie was doing all right, at least. "How much longer until we board?"

Galvyn looked up at the sun which was almost directly overhead. "The captain said we would sail with the tides just after noon."

They must have been waiting for the inspector because when I turned, I saw the ship's captain approaching with one of her crew in tow. Ina was her name. She was a mature woman approaching her middle years, but not quite there yet. She wore loose dark blue pants, a white blouse and a dark blue vest, unbuttoned at the top. She was well-tanned and kept her dark hair cut short. She was frowning. We had met her earlier during our negotiations, and I fully believed that frown was permanently affixed into her face. "Is that all your cargo?" Captain Ina asked impatiently.

Galvyn perked up. "Indeed it is. Please handle it with the utmost care."

She pointed to the crate and motioned to her crewman. He was a man with huge muscles and a dark complexion wearing knee-length pants and an open vest. He also liked to frown.

To my surprise, the man squatted beside it and picked up the crate, lifting it to his shoulder. I was shocked. Just how strong was this man.

"Put it to the front of the hold," she instructed. "And Jomo, don't drop this one overboard like you did the last one."

Jomo grunted and then made his way toward the ship and up the gangplank.

The captain nodded her head in the direction of the ship. "You had best board too. I don't wait for stragglers." She turned without a reply and followed the crewman carrying the crate.

Galvyn straightened his jacket and strolled toward the gangplank. "We best do as she says. We don't want to be left behind." He paused and turned to me. "Have you seen that girl? She's cutting it a little close. What's her name?"

"Fumiko?" I asked. "I haven't seen her. She should have been back by now." By our original agreement, she wasn't supposed to be on this leg of the trip, and we should have parted company. But since I owed her, I asked Zofie if she could continue with us. I didn't mention that she had saved me, but instead said it would be good to have some kind of expert on the mirror.

To my surprise, Zofie readily agreed. She apparently really liked the young woman.

So Fumiko was still with us. Or at least she would be if she didn't miss the ship. She had gone to buy some personal supplies about an hour ago, mumbling something about her clothes.

"Well, you may want to go look for her," said Galvyn. "We'll be leaving soon."

I looked up and down the wharf and over to the shops and buildings along just back from it. No sign of her. I sighed. "I'll be right back."

I took off at a jog toward shore. She couldn't have gone far. I spotted a shop with a seamstress's sign and stepped inside. The proprietor said a woman fitting Fumiko's description had been there earlier, but she had left heading further into town. Following her path, I headed down the street and spotted a tailor's store. Strangely, despite the busy street, the door was shut and shutters closed. A sign on the door said they would be right back. I knocked on the door, but no one came.

I sighed, running my hand through my hair in frustration. I put my back against the closed door and leaned against it. Where could she have gone?

Suddenly the door opened behind me, and I staggered back. I would have fallen inside had a hand not steadied me. I turned to find Fumiko looking up at me. Only she was dressed very differently than she had been before. She had exchanged her simple beige dress for dark trousers, a white shirt, and neatly laced red bodice which greatly emphasized the curves of her slim figure. The transformation from plain girl to young woman left me momentarily speechless.

"You changed clothes." That sounded stupid even to my ears.

As was typical of her, she didn't even bat an eye. "Galvyn sent you to look for me, didn't he?"

"What?" I shook my head at the abrupt transition. "He did suggest it since the ship is about to leave. We better hurry."

She stepped the rest of the way out the door, grabbed my hand and pulled me down the street. She urged me to walk faster. "That bastard sent someone to delay me in that shop. I believe he intends to be rid of the both of us."

Just then, a gray cat appeared beside me. "I fear the young lady may be right. When I left, the ship was pulling up the gangplank."

We both broke into a run. We rounded a corner and had a clear view of the section of the wharf our ship had been tied to—only to see it wasn't tied there anymore. One of the crew was pushing the ship away with a long pole.

Spraggel looked over his shoulder. "I think I better go ahead." He put on a cat-like burst of speed, raced toward the edge, and at the last possible moment, leaped for the ship and flew through the air to catch the edge of the deck. He pulled himself up and looked over his shoulder at us before moving into the vessel. Even for a cat, that had to be quite a jump.

But what about us?

I looked up and saw Galvyn standing by the rail. He waved at us. "You'll have to catch up to us later," he called. "Don't worry, I'll take very good care of Zofie." He seemed delighted.

What had Fumiko said earlier? That the bastard had planned this? From the way he was smiling, I had no doubt that he had.

I looked around the wharf for a small boat. Perhaps a fast sailboat could catch them. Fumiko grabbed my arm and pointed. I followed where she indicated.

The ship had yet to raise sail, likely because the wind was blowing into shore and the tide had yet to fully start emptying the bay. Which meant the ship was drifting very slowly away from shore using the impetus of the last few pushes with their poles. The wharf itself was a rather long one and curved slightly outward, with other ships drawn up to it. I shook my head not understanding.

Then I saw it. The Lightman's Statue.

A lot of goods flowed into and out of the port, not to mention it was the pride of the region. A century or more ago, a series of bad nighttime storms had caused a number of large merchant ships to crash into the wharf. A wealthy lord at the time decided to install a larger than life statue at the end of the wharf closest to the ocean and keep a myst lantern on it at all times. That way the ships could see to avoid it. The statue was of a man leaning far over the water and a myst lantern held in its extended hand. It was supposed to be installed on a tall pedestal, but the lord ran out of funds and just had it mounted onto the wharf. It stood before us like an open invitation.

With the direction the wind was blowing, the ship would pass very close to it. In fact, I could see one of the sailors positioning himself with a long pole in case they came too close. I measured the statue's height with my eye. It might be possible to jump from the statue's extended arm on to the ship's deck.

We both took off at a run. Despite my longer legs, Fumiko easily outpaced me. She reached the statue first and climbed up it. She didn't even pause as she stepped out onto the arm holding the myst lantern.

To my great surprise, she walked across with perfect balance and without seeming to care that she could easily slip off. She looked back and motioned me forward.

"Quick!" she shouted.

I climbed the statue easily enough, but when I reached the arm, I balked. I didn't think it would be strong enough for both of us. I also thought this was a little higher than I bargained for.

Suddenly, the ship was below us—the sailor with the pole giving us a bemused look. Fumiko jumped. She sailed high in the air and easily crossed the distance to the ship. She landed gracefully on the deck, tucking to a roll and springing to her feet. I, on the other hand, didn't do so well. I got up my courage and ran out on the arm and jumped... to fall short and impact against the hull. I bounced and then fell. The shock of the frigid water almost made me suck the chill brine into my lungs. I came up floundering and spitting. A fear colder than the ocean depths seized me. *Water! I was in deep, dark water! I was going to drown!* I could almost feel its fingers reaching for me to drag me under. I thrashed in raw panic.

Suddenly a rope slapped me in the face, and in my hysterics, I grabbed it. The rope quickly drew taunt, and it began to drag me after it. I looked up to see Fumiko and another sailor pulling me in. Several others joined in hauling my wet and cold body onto the deck. Shaking and drawing in great gulps of air, I rolled to my back and looked up at the blue sky above me. I thanked the Creator that I had something solid underneath me. I was not afraid of dying, just so long as it wasn't by drowning.

The captain leaned over me breaking my view of the sky. She looked at me critically before announcing her opinion. "That was the stupidest thing I have ever seen, and I hate stupid. Pull something like that again, and I'll leave you to the sharks."

She turned on her heel and walked off. Fumiko knelt beside me and helped me strip off the soaked coat, shirt, and boots while one of the crew handed me a rough blanket. I eagerly wrapped myself in it and tried to warm up. Creator, I hated being wet.

I felt eyes upon me and my gaze drifted over to Galvyn who was silently staring at me. And he did not look pleased.

I leaned on the railing watching the sun touch the horizon as the *Wily Lass* plowed through the open water. Overhead the sails had been unfurled, catching not only the wind but the last rays of the sinking sun. We had long since left port and started our journey southward with only a few dedicated gulls still following us. I glanced over my shoulder. Galvyn and the captain were in deep discussion. She was expressing concern over our current course since there was nothing on the maps to indicate anything other than open seas on our chosen heading. Fumiko had consulted with them earlier, lending some additional information, but it did little to allay the captain's concerns.

I would have thought that Spraggel would have joined the conversation, but he had been mysteriously absent since he boarded. Only the Creator knew what he was up to.

Zofie was in the cabin she shared with Fumiko. After we had entered the open ocean, she had been let out of her hiding place. None of the crew seemed surprised to see her, which indicated to me they considered it normal for people to travel in crates. I couldn't help but again wonder about Galvyn's line of business.

I sighed, looking back to the horizon and berating myself for my latest failure. Sure, I had gotten on the ship, but I had nearly drowned. And not only that, everyone had seen me panic. A few of the crew still gave an amused chuckle when I passed them. Some knight I was. I got myself captured, and Fumiko had to save me. I had missed my ship and nearly drowned. Not the mention, the one person I truly cared about, had chosen another. I was used to bad luck, but several calamities in a row were a bit much. I seemed to be having one after another! Maybe when I got rid of my curse, I should retire and go back to being just an apprentice scribe. It was definitely a lot safer—and a lot dryer. I couldn't help but wonder what else could go wrong.

And I didn't have to wait long.

I felt a presence beside me. I looked up to see Zofie standing along the rail looking out into the ocean. She was wearing her cloak against the chill, but the hood was down, as was her hair—loose strands flicked across her face. She stood perfectly straight, and she looked... angry.

"Coren," she said, still looking off to the dimming sunset. "Galvyn told me about what happened when you borrowed the finder. I have some questions about your adventure." Her voice sounded strained. She was definitely angry. Maybe she had found out about the side business of Galvyn's family—and was upset that I hadn't come forward earlier.

Concerned, I stood up and faced her. "What's wrong?"

She wouldn't look at me and continued to stare off into the ocean. "Galvyn said that both of you had to go into a brothel to access the tunnel to his family's manor."

"That's right."

"Galvyn also told me that the brothel is just for appearances, and the women there are actually guards for the manor."

"That wasn't my understanding...."

She held up a hand, silencing me. "He also said you had threatened a woman there—and in fact were going to turn her into a toad unless she did exactly as you said. You had her so terrified she didn't dare disobey."

"That's mostly true," I said, scratching my nose and wondering where this was going. "She wasn't being very cooperative. Although, I did give her a scare, I wouldn't call it terrified."

She paused for a moment. Her hands locked on the railing. "So by your own admission, you forced that innocent woman to do a *special favor* for you against her will. You even touched her intimately. And the whole time, she was too terrified to stop you from taking advantage of her?"

I shook my head. "That's not what happened." I was starting to become a little irritated at what she was implying. "I had to get the key away from her, but I didn't touch her that way. And Galvyn told me it was a real brothel and not the only one his family has."

She still wouldn't look at me. "He said you would try to shift the blame. Just so you know, his family runs a series of fake brothels to gather information. His family had an arrangement with my father."

Something just didn't add up. That had been a *real* brothel. Even Galvyn's mother had mentioned them as such. I was being set up. "Galvyn's lying, Zofie."

She finally turned to look at me. And I realized I was wrong. Zofie wasn't angry—she was furious. "But why would he? I've known him far longer than I have you. He has no reason to concoct something like that." She shook her head. "I should have guessed something was up back in Iron Landing when that innkeeper Mikney, Maggie's father, hated you so much. He already knew your reputation." She jerked her head back out to the ocean. "I think your curse has given you too much power, Coren. And you can't handle it. You're using it against those weaker than you. Maybe it's a good thing you're getting rid of it."

I shook my head. "Zofie, I never did those things. Sure, Madam Ryleigh and I took a little tumble...."

She abruptly turned and fully faced me. "A little tumble, you say? Galvyn says you had her in a very compromising position, her skirts pulled up, and a hand on her breast. If he hadn't intervened, you would have..." She broke off and turned to look back at the sea. "I would appreciate it if you didn't speak to me henceforth. I have no use for a molester."

She started to turn away, but I grabbed her arm. "I'm not a molester. I didn't *do* anything."

She looked down at my hand and then back up to me. "Please remove your hand before I take it off for you."

"Zofie, I...."

But I didn't get to finish. Galvyn pulled me roughly around to face him and punched me. Dazed, I staggered back against the rail and slid to my butt. I could feel the blood start to flow down my face. I stared up at them in shock. Zofie looked at me with tears in her eyes and then walked away.

Galvyn rubbed his knuckles and shook out his hand. He grinned. "I told you to leave her alone. You should have stayed on shore." Then he turned away, catching up with Zofie and putting an arm around her shoulders.

I wanted to run after them and deny it. But what proof did I have? Zofie had already chosen to believe Galvyn over me. I bowed my head. He was right—they really were the same. They were nobles and only believed their own kind.

I leaned my head back against the rail and looked up at the sky. I could see an almost full moon and plenty of stars through the rigging. I shook my head. I was sick of this. I didn't belong, and I was tired of being abused. I quit. I'm done. I'm going home.

As I watched the moon and stars, they got blurry, and I felt a drop slide down my cheek.

CHAPTER TWELVE

Unexpected
Beacon

That night I didn't want to be in the tiny cabin I shared with Galvyn. So after attending to my bruised nose, which I was convinced would never be the same, I grabbed a blanket and went down into the hold to the crate that had been used to smuggle Zofie onboard. It took me a moment to find it. It had been latched shut, and to my surprise when I opened it, Spraggel leaped out of it.

"Thank the Creator you let me out," he called as he ran off. "I've been in there for hours, and even though I'm a cat, nature does call."

"How...?" I started to ask how he had gotten locked in there, but he was gone before I could say anything.

I shrugged and crawled inside, pulling out my broken amulet to shed a dim illumination into the interior. Although a little short, it was thickly padded. If I curled up, I had just enough room to lie down. Which I did with my back to the door. I left it cracked, and sure enough, Spraggel returned just a few minutes later.

"That feels so much better," he said. "I really didn't want to soil the inside, but I was approaching a breaking point." He curled up behind me. "I'm going to have to have a word with whoever locked me in."

His claim penetrated my depression. "One of the crew?"

"Doubtful." He sighed. "Probably just a mistake anyway."

I shoved my amulet inside my shirt and shut my eyes. But sleep was the furthest thing from my mind.

"What's wrong, Coren? I can tell something's bothering you."

"Nothing," I said.

"That bad, huh?"

"Yes, it is."

He didn't answer, and then we were quiet for a bit. Finally, the words just seemed to explode out of me. "Zofie's angry with me. Galvyn told her I molested a woman while we were trying to get in his manor."

"Did you?"

"Of course not. I did struggle with her, but it was just to get the key. All of Galvyn's facts are sort of correct, it... it's just not how things happened. I would never do those kind of things." I sighed. "What really hurts is that Zofie took his word over mine."

We were silent for a bit. The exhaustion of the day had begun to lull me to sleep, when Spraggel spoke. "Did you know there were rumors about the Merrick family? About their silver tongues?"

"What about it?" I remembered Risten warning me about Galvyn before she left us.

He sighed. "There are reports that they have influenced some people into doing things they normally wouldn't do. Most have laughed it off as being nothing more than good merchants. However, they are myst users. Weak ones at best, but still able to use it."

I rolled toward him. "Are you saying Galvyn is imposing his will on Zofie."

Spraggel shook his head. "That might be a little strong. It would take a curse to actually take over someone. But influencing their emotions... that might be possible. Bear in mind that while I had a friend that showed me quite a bit about myst users, I am not an expert. I could be wrong."

"How could I prove it?"

Spraggel chuckled. "You can't." He settled at my back. "Now get some sleep. I'll speak with the princess tomorrow. And have some faith in her. She's not stupid, so she will eventually see it for herself. And for the Creator's sake, don't make things worse."

I gave a short bark of a laugh. "I don't see how I possibly could."

"Coren, you have a talent for it."

Over the next three days, I did my best to stay out of everyone's way. This was a bit of a challenge since it was a tiny vessel, but I managed. Drifting to the bow of the ship when Galvyn was in the cabin, or into the hold when Zofie came out for air. Fumiko seemed to be the only one I couldn't avoid, and we talked for a bit about my curse. But I had nothing more to offer her.

On the third night into our voyage, the sky was clear and the air crisp with the full moon so bright it almost looked like day. Zofie would be transforming soon, turning briefly back to her neutral chimera state. Usually I was there with her, but tonight I thought it best if I stayed away.

So, I took my blanket back down to the crate for another less than comfortable sleep. It was dark in the hold, but I had learned my way around by touch. I opened the container and sensed something different. I leaned in and took out my amulet only to come nose to nose with Zofie. We both flinched back. She was sitting against the back of the crate with her knees pulled up to her chest.

"What are you doing here?" I asked in surprise. But I knew the answer even as I spoke the question.

"I'm going to transform soon," she said dejectedly. "Fumiko is asleep in our cabin, so I can't go there. And I can't do it out on deck, since the glow will illuminate the entire ship."

I nodded. "Makes sense. I'll find somewhere else to sleep."

I was surprised when I felt a gentle touch on my arm. "Don't go yet." She sighed sadly. "I need to tell you something."

I squatted down in the doorway so we were at eye level.

She looked down. "I wanted to apologize. I think I was too harsh on you the other night. And I'm very sorry that Galvyn hit you." She looked away embarrassed. "I don't know what came over me. I just wanted to hear your telling of the events, but I became so angry. I'm not usually that way. My emotions have been all over the place lately."

I nodded. Thinking of Spraggel's advice, I was afraid to open my mouth.

"Spraggel talked with me and told me that what Galvyn described was not you. That in his eagerness to win my favor, Galvyn may have misinterpreted the events. Fumiko defended you too, saying she thought you were a fine gentleman. She even asked me if it was all right for her to pursue you."

"Fumiko said *what?*" I shook my head. "What did you tell her?"

Zofie smiled. "That's between her and me."

She then patted the empty space beside her. "I know I shouldn't ask, and this is completely selfish on my part, especially the way I've treated you, but would you please sit with me while I transform. It always hurts a little less when you're near." She paused a moment looking at me. "I will understand if you don't want to."

I was torn. Was she just using me, because she had no one else, or was she genuinely sorry? I looked into her eyes and made my decision.

I gave her a reassuring grin. "You know I can't refuse. You're still my friend."

She smiled in relief and a tear came to her eye. "And you're a much better one than I deserve."

I eased into the crate and pulled the door shut behind me. I then shared my blanket with her. It took me a moment to settle because something in my pocket was poking me in the leg, and I just couldn't get it to move the right way. It was that stupid ring from Galvyn's room. I had tried to give it back to him several times, but he refused to even talk about it. So unsure what to do with it, I ended up carrying the trinket around with me.

"Did anyone see you come down?" Zofie asked.

I gave up on arranging my pocket and shook my head. "I don't think so. But Galvyn's going to notice both of us being gone." I poked her playfully. "He might think you're cheating on him."

"I doubt that," she replied coolly. Zofie looked down sadly. "I'm not even sure he would care. Just as long as I didn't embarrass him." She looked up into my eyes, and I could see she was deadly serious.

Was this the same woman that was laughing with me when we started our journey? It was as if every ounce of joy had been drained from her. I couldn't help but be reminded of Galvyn's mother and her sad smile. Was Zofie destined to follow that same path?

"Are you and he not getting along?" I asked.

She looked down and shook her head. "It's strange. Sometimes I feel so strongly for him, while other times, I can't stand him."

"Zofie, you...." I started.

But she cut me off. "And don't you *dare* tell me I don't have to. It will only make it harder. I *do* have to marry him."

"But Lord Merrick wanted to turn you over to the king!" I protested.

She shook her head. "Galvyn thinks his father was putting on a show for Wynn's spies. But after I prove I'm innocent and we're married, Lord Merrick will announce his support for me. Then the other lords will follow." She sighed. "It's the perfect plan." She gazed at me a moment. "Only it doesn't feel so perfect."

A quote came to mind. "*A thousand wise men can make a thousand plans to send a thousand troops into battle...*" I said. It was from one of the Poet's lesser works—one I particularly hated.

She barely lifted her head and glanced my way in irritation. "Coren, now is not the time for that." She returned her forehead to her knees. We sat in silence for a moment. Then she went ahead and completed the quote. "*...But have them undone by a single troubled heart.*" She gave a heavy sigh. "I didn't like that work anyway."

"Me either. Spraggel made me translate it." I shuddered. "Into Ancient Urticia."

She then rolled her head over again to look at me with a puzzled expression. "It was originally written in that language. Why would he have had you re-translate it?"

"He said he wanted to see if I could improve on the original."

"Did you?"

I grinned at her. "What do you think?"

She grinned back. "It was horrible, wasn't it?"

I rolled my eyes. "That's a secret between him and me."

She laughed.

"Did I make you feel better?"

"A little."

I made a bold move. I reached out, and taking her hand, gave it a gentle squeeze. "What's *really* bothering you? Are you worried Galvyn will find out about your curse?"

She looked at me a moment in surprise and then gave me a weak smile. "Seems I can't keep any secrets from you. I *am* worried. I'm afraid once he finds out about it, he will reject me. Which will be bad for the kingdom."

"You should tell him."

She looked away, her eyes sliding away from mine. "You're right. I should tell him, but I'm dreading it. I've been putting it off until after this transformation. I keep hoping it will be done, and maybe he won't have to know." She sat in silence for a moment. "It's not the only reason I'm hoping they're done. The transformations have become excruciating. That last one back to human form in Iron Landing was really bad."

I nodded. "I remember."

"It's like my curse is fighting my return to normal." She shook her head. "I am *not* looking forward to this one." She looked miserable. "Can you ask Abhulengulus to start my curse early? I really just want to get it over with."

My heart felt for her. I squeezed her hand. "Of course. But I have to warn you that Abe has been ignoring me lately. I think it's because of Lady Autumn's charm. Either Abe is protesting over it, or it somehow interferes with him."

She nodded. "Could you try anyway?"

She looked so pitiful. I wished I could do something to help. Then a thought occurred to me. "I wonder." I held up a finger. "Zofie, give me a moment. I want to ask Abe a question. If he'll answer me."

She looked puzzled. "All right."

"Abhulengulus," I said out loud.

Ho, ho! Came the reply in my head. *He used my full name which means he's feeling feisty. Aching for a fight. Bring it on, I like a good challenge!*

"Question one," I whispered.

Not three questions again, he whined. *I thought we were done with that. You've asked me almost everything I can tell you.*

I licked my lips. "I've seen you modify Zofie's curse to do different things, like making her bigger or adding different abilities. Can you modify Zofie's curse to not cause her as much pain."

I'm really impressed. You're starting to figure this thing out. Took you long enough. The reason she is in such pain is that during a transformation, her curse draws a tremendous amount of myst through her body. So yes, I can modify it so that it draws that myst from you instead. And no, it will not kill either of you, although it will hurt. You will both be sharing the pain equally. However... He paused for a moment for dramatic effect. *"I would advise against it. There might be... how should I say... unintended consequences, which naturally I can't tell you about unless you have the secret word. Fortunately for you, the effect will only be temporary for the time she is in her chimera form. At her next transformation later tonight, when she returns to the human form you gave her, the effect will no longer be noticeable.*

I grinned. So there *was* a way to ease Zofie's pain. "Thank you, Abe. You've been most helpful."

He laughed. *I meant what I said about those unintended consequences. Well, until next time.*

I looked up and found Zofie watching me. "It always amazes me how you talk to your curse."

I rolled my eyes. "It's not nearly that exciting on this end of the conversation. He's a real jerk."

Hey, I heard that!

I ignored him and leaned forward. "I think I know how to ease your pain."

Her eyes went wide. "How?"

I explained what Abe told me.

She looked at me skeptically. "You mean I have to draw enough myst from a non-myst user to power a rather myst hungry curse? That sounds like a recipe for trouble. That's how my father died."

"But there is something special about Abe. He says I'm not a myst user, and yet I've been in situations where I use a lot of myst. Maybe I'll find out more if I ever get this secret word. In the meantime, I trust what Abe says: it won't kill us. This might be a way for me to ease your suffering."

"Coren..." She looked into my eyes. "The transformation *is* quite painful. I would love your help, but it poses some risks to you. Are you sure you should do this for me?" She looked down. "Especially after what I said."

I waved it off. "I'm not concerned. Abe won't let anything happen to me. Although, he did say there could be what he called unintended consequences. He couldn't elaborate on what they were."

Zofie nodded. "That generally means there is a secondary effect. Like Spraggel's myst pocket. It is conveniently attached to his body, but there is no telling where things actually get stored." She mused for a moment. "I honestly wouldn't care if it turned me green, as long as I didn't hurt as much." She looked at me and touched my hand. "Why are you really doing this for me? You know that it's too much. You're not my suitor any longer."

I smiled. "I know. But if I didn't, what kind of a knight would I be?"

She blinked at me for using her own words. She returned my smile. "You are so damned annoying, you know that?"

"It's a talent."

She shook her head.

I held out my hand to her. "Shall we try modifying your curse now?"

Zofie sighed in resignation. "If you're determined, I will let you." She straightened. "How do we get started?"

Good question. I wasn't sure. I took a deep breath. "I think it would work like this."

I reached out a finger and put it on her chest where her heart was. "Abhulengulus," I spoke softly. "Modify Zofie's curse so that it draws myst from both of us."

In my head, came a reply. *Be warned that the change will initiate a transformation. Is this acceptable?*

"It is," I answered.

He laughed. *Watch out for those unintended consequences. This will be fun.*

Immediately, I felt a gentle warmth and then a flash over all my skin, as if something had briefly touched each and every spot of my body.

I couldn't help but wonder at the warning. There didn't seem to be anything amiss. I paused. Or was there?

I suddenly felt a sensation in my rib cage, like another heart beating inside my chest, and even though I was breathing, I could feel a different set of lungs expanding... and strangest of all, I could feel my finger touching my chest, only it wasn't my chest!

We jerked away from one another.

Zofie sat back and brushed her hair out of her eyes—I felt the strands of hair brush across my own forehead. Not only that, but I could feel a long braid swing against my back as she moved. I could even feel her emotion of startled concern.

What was going on?

"Zofie," I said. "Something feels odd."

"Tell me about it. I can feel you breathing." She quickly reached out and pinched me.

"Ouch! What did you do that for?"

In reply, she held out her own arm. "Now you."

I gave her a puzzled look, but did as she asked. My eyes went wide. *I felt the pinch too.*

"What's going on?" I asked.

Zofie shook her head. "Don't you see? He connected us up. We each feel what the other feels. We had a tiny myst connection between us before, but now.... He must have opened it up, we can now feel what the other feels."

My eyes went large. "The unintended consequences. I just didn't imagine it would be something like this."

She shook her head. "I...." She broke off as a sudden pain gripped her. I knew exactly what it was because I felt it along with her. And it hurt like hell. I reached out and grasped her hand. It felt like someone was shoving my insides around while they peeled off my skin and welded it back on with red hot irons. I was the one that wanted to scream. *How did she stand this?*

She was enveloped by a blue glow, and I held on for all I was worth. And then suddenly, it was over. My body felt cold with sweat and my shirt stuck to me. Only this shirt didn't feel quite that way.

She leaned forward. "Are you all right?"

I nodded weakly, wondering if my stomach was going to settle down.

She pulled my hand to her lips and kissed it. "Coren, that was much too high a price for you to pay, but you don't know how much I appreciate what you did. The pain wasn't nearly as bad as it has been. I can't thank you enough for it."

I ran a hand through my hair which was now damp with sweat. "How did you stand that before? It's horrible."

She smiled at me. "That wasn't nearly as bad as it had been. Not even by half." She looked down. "I guess it's really true that two can carry a burden much easier than one."

She began to pat over her body. It felt strange that I could feel each touch. "Coren could you shut your eyes. I want to see how much further I have to go before you can take this curse off me."

I looked down and shut my eyes. But it didn't help much. I could feel Zofie unfasten her shirt and pull it away from her body. "Hmmm, there's only a few feathers left on my chest. In fact, it looks almost like before." I felt her take off her boot. "And I do believe that my foot is back to normal." I felt her wiggle her toes. "Now maybe I won't hobble around as much when I'm between transformations."

I felt her pull her boot back on and refasten her shirt. Finally, she said I could open my eyes.

I raised an eyebrow. "So just a few more transformations until you're completely back to normal?"

"It would appear so. It will be so nice to not have to go through that every few weeks, not to mention being able to use my myst again."

We were silent for a moment. "Should we wait here until you transform again? If we wait, it will likely be another couple of hours. I could steal your curse and put it back. That would force the other transformation."

Zofie shook her head. "I don't want to risk it. You're already lending me your myst. If I overdraw it, then it could kill you."

I shrugged. "I doubt Abe would let that happen. I certainly don't mind trying."

Zofie frowned and rubbed the outside of her thigh. "Coren, I hate to ask, but do you perhaps have something in your pocket? I feel something digging into my leg, and I can't figure out what it is."

As a matter of fact, I knew precisely what it was since I had tried to shift it a couple of times. I moved around until I could reach inside my pocket and pulled out the offending item—the trinket I had gotten from Galvyn's room.

Curiosity got the best of me, and I pulled out up my glowing amulet to see it better. The piece was definitely finely crafted, but had to be the most unique piece of jewelry I had ever seen. It had an unusually wide band and was silver. Gold and silver inlays in the shape of vines and leaves went around it. And in the center was a flower made from five small blue jewels. It was oddly pretty, even elegant maybe, but not what I would call beautiful.

Zofie sighed and rubbed her leg. "That feels much better." She leaned closer. "What have you got there?"

I held it up. "Just a ring that I accidentally pulled out of Galvyn's dresser when we were in his...." I trailed off when I saw that Zofie's eyes had gone large in shock.

"It can't be," she whispered. She moved closer. "Can I see it please?"

Her hand was shaking as she held out her palm.

"Sure." I carefully placed the ring in her hand.

She turned it around and around in her fingers. It was almost as if she was seeing a ghost. She enfolded the ring in her hand and brought it to her chest.

"Coren, where exactly did you get this?" There was strong emotion in her voice, and tears were welling in her eyes. I could feel her pounding heart.

"What's wrong?" I asked in concern. "I got it from Galvyn's room. He called it an old trinket and said he couldn't remember where he got it. He said I could have it."

She nodded and smiled at me. "You surprise me yet again, Sir Coren. I have validated once more why you are my knight and why I was stupid to ever doubt you."

I shrugged. "So I'm good at finding things. But what is it?"

"It's my mother's ring." I could feel her joy. "The one that was stolen and I have been looking for."

"You mean Galvyn...?"

She nodded. "It explains a lot, really. His family used to visit us when I was younger to see how we got along. The brat must have snuck into my room and stolen it. That was why none of the servants turned up with it."

"When we were facing down Galvyn's father, he mentioned something about Galvyn having a history of stealing. I hope he hasn't retained that habit from his childhood." I chuckled. "Zofie, I think you should keep it."

Zofie held up the ring almost reverently. "I can remember sitting on my mother's lap and looking at it on her hand. She never took it off. She did explain that the flower in the middle was supposed to be lavender. They grew wild where she was from. And that the ring would be mine one day."

"I bet your mother was a fine lady."

Zofie sighed. "I was young when she died, so I don't remember her that well. And from what I've learned since, she was a bit of a mystery."

I frowned. "How so?"

"It was obvious Father loved her greatly. He would often talk about how she stole his heart the first time he saw her. But strangely, he wouldn't talk much more about how they met. He said he swore to my mother he would never talk about it—even to me." She cradled the ring in her hand and looked down at it. "The servants said she just showed up at the gates of Edlingreen, gave her name as Winstella Scurrlocke, and demanded to see the elder prince. When my father heard, he dropped what he was doing and literally ran to the gates to meet her. And upon seeing each other, they embraced as if they were very well acquainted." She looked up. "They were married not long after."

I felt sorry for Zofie. She hadn't known her mother well at all. I at least had known mine, and even though we didn't get along that well, I at least *knew* I didn't especially like her. Zofie hadn't had that chance.

There was only one thing to do then. I gently opened her hand and took the ring. She looked up at me in concern, as if I had just stolen her Mid-Winter's gift. I gave her hand a reassuring squeeze. I then opened the door to the crate and pulled her out behind me. She hesitated for a moment, but followed looking very puzzled. I led her to the patch of moonlight under the hold's open hatch, giving us a narrow view of the gently rocking sky and the full moon shining down in all its full glory. I turned to her and held her hand gently in mine. "Your mother said this ring should be yours one day. And so it shall." I thought for a moment, racking my brain for something appropriate to say, but finally settled for a quote from that sappy love story Zofie was always reading. I cleared my throat. "*Despite all manner of obstacles and against all odds, I have fought my way here...*"

Zofie didn't hesitate in taking it up. "*...to restore what was yours.*" A tear came to her eye.

I then took her right hand and slid her mother's ring onto Zofie's index finger.

Blinking back tears, she held it up in admiration. "I never thought I'd see it again. Thank you, Coren."

I gave a bow of my head. "My pleasure, your highness."

She sighed. "I wish you of all people wouldn't call me that." And then she did a double-take of the ring.

I dropped my own eyes to it and saw that the ring had started to glow in a deep red, almost violet in color.

"Ah... Zofie? Is it supposed to do that?"

She shook her head. "I didn't see it before, but there is a myst spell on it. It must have been hidden on the inside and activated when my finger slid through."

"What's it doing?"

Zofie opened her mouth to answer, but didn't have a chance before our whole world turned blindingly white.

The intense flash lasted for just a moment, sending a narrow beacon of radiance high up through the open hatch. It dissipated just as quickly as it arose.

I blinked trying to clear my vision. "Are you all right?" I asked. I blindly felt for her hand and then took it.

"I'm fine. It blinded me for a moment, but my sight is coming back."

I shut my eyes, seeing only the glowing afterimages. "What the Creator's hell was that?" I opened them and blinked, finally being able to focus on her.

She touched the ring on her finger. "That was an old spell. It's called a myst beacon. It's fallen out of use, but in times past it was used for announcements."

"Announcements?"

Zofie looked at me. "Someone thought it very important to let the world know I had put the ring on."

CHAPTER THIRTEEN

Sea Wraith

I stared at her for a moment not understanding. "You mean there was a myst spell on it to tell the world, 'Hey Zofie's wearing this ring?'"

She nodded, her eyes wide in shock. "It would appear so. Mother never mentioned anything about this."

Above us, I heard the stomping of many feet and shouting. It was immediately followed by all the crew storming down the steps in the hold. They were carrying an assortment of knives and clubs, and none of them looked happy. Galvyn was among them accompanying Captain Ina.

"So these are the ones that set off that myst signal," said the captain. "No doubt trying to send a message to the freebooters so they can find us on the open seas. Since the new king took over, they've been becoming extremely bold."

I couldn't help but wonder if what Galvyn had told me back in port was true. Did they really kill everyone on the ships they looted?

"I've told you they are innocent," said Galvyn. "They would no more want freebooters than you do."

"He's right, captain," I said. "We set it off by accident. I was returning a ring to her, and when she put it on, that bright light went off."

Ina seemed to notice me for the first time. After a few flicks of her eyes, I could see her mentally dismiss me as unimportant. She turned to Zofie and gave her a more appraising stare. She reached toward her, and I moved on reflex to block. But an unexpected force jerked me up by the collar into the air—I dangled from the long arm of Jomo, the big sailor that had single-handedly carried Zofie's crate onboard the ship. From my new found height, I saw Zofie's stare bring the captain up short.

"Dear captain," she said calmly. "Would you be so bold as to touch your kingdom's princess without her permission?"

Ina snorted and pulled her hand back. "The princess is dead by the king's own hand. You are nothing more than a slave we're transporting."

Zofie narrowed her eyes. "Am I? Are you sure?" The two stared at each other intently. It was nerve-racking.

The captain paused for a moment, suddenly unsure. But she quickly caught herself. "Very convincing, even the red hair."

And just at that moment, Spraggel made his appearance. He always seemed to have impeccable timing. I wondered where he had been hiding. The cat leaped up on a nearby crate and sat down regally with his tail wrapped around his feet. "I assure you, captain," said Spraggel. "She really is Princess Zophia Olwenna Xernow. And I am her senior advisor."

Everyone stared at Spraggel in disbelief. Spraggel stood up on all four legs and took half a step forward. "I really am."

A sailor at the back spoke in amazement. "The cat's speak'n."

"And it's gray," said another.

"It's an omen," the first whispered.

And a low murmur filled the hold.

The captain's face turned red. She rounded to confront her sailors. "Don't be spouting that superstitious nonsense! It's probably just someone with a myst spell on them. Nothing more."

"But captain," one man softly protested in back. "It's *gray*."

"I don't care if it's pink!" she shouted. "It doesn't change a thing!"

She turned back to face Zofie, her face flushed. She said more softly, "That's right, it doesn't change a thing." She straightened her jacket. "Whether you're the princess or some impostor, the king is looking for you."

"Captain," Galvyn leaned forward. "Let me explain."

Ina wheeled on Galvyn and pointed a finger at him. "You be quiet! Do you take me for a fool! You said I would be transporting a special person, but you didn't mention it was high-risk cargo. And on top of that, they've set off a myst beacon which had to have been seen for over twenty miles. Whether you intended to attract the freebooters or not doesn't matter. They're going to come." The captain paused. "And I pray to the Creator that it doesn't attract a sea wraith." A murmur went up among the crew. Several of them made warding signs.

The captain turned back to us. "Overboard with them!" she shouted.

The men didn't move.

The captain rolled her eyes. "The cat can stay."

The men roared and pushed forward to grab us. Zofie, Galvyn, and I were promptly hauled up on deck. Outside, the full moon shone brightly casting a dim shadow across the water. The only real light came from a few lanterns hanging from the fore and aft on the ship. The other crew members shouted and jeered as we were bodily carried and held against the railing. Upon seeing the black water below us, I struggled to get away, but they were too strong. I stared down at the dark depths in horror.

"*Captain!* Avast! Ship ahoy!" cried a sailor from the crow's nest.

The crew paused, and the captain strode up the steps to the poop deck. She pulled a far-lens from her pocket and pointed it where the sailor on watch was pointing.

"Is it a freebooter, captain?" one of the men asked anxiously.

As the captain stared out to sea, I strained to see what I could see from where I was pinned to the railing.

The captain slowly lowered her lens, her expression grim.

"Freebooter, captain?" the crewman asked again.

She leaned on the rail, steadying herself. "Not any freebooter I've ever seen. A vessel, aye, with no mast or sails, yet it's lit up with so many lights it almost glows. And it's approaching fast." She bowed her head. "And worse, it's moving against the wind."

Curses and warding signs went through the men. They obviously knew what it was.

The captain was crestfallen, covering her eyes and shaking her head. But a moment later, she caught her bearings and began shouting orders. "Quickly men, douse the lights and raise the sails! We'll try to outrun them. *Quickly!*"

The pressure holding me to the railing released as the crew went about the captain's orders—our crimes suddenly seeming unimportant.

Zofie couldn't help but ask. "If it's not freebooters, what could it be? Another merchant ship?"

The captain glowered at her. "Oh no. You've attracted something much worse. I've only seen something like this once, many years ago." She turned and looked toward it. "It's a sea wraith."

Spraggel appeared walking calmly along the railing toward us. The four of us huddled in a tiny group trying to stay out of the way of the running men.

"What the hell is a sea wraith?" I asked.

Spraggel sat and began licking his paw. "No one knows really—very few return from an encounter to tell the tale. And those that do have their memories scrambled either by a myst spell or some very traumatic experience." The cat put his paw down and looked up at us. "However, what the reports do say is that it appears suddenly on the horizon—a black ship during the day and a glowing one at night. It's picked up quite the reputation over the years as being something to be avoided at all costs. Most of the sailors believe it's the angry spirits of those lost at sea."

Zofie sighed. "Then the chances of outrunning it are slim."

Spraggel stood on his four legs, his tail waving behind him. "Those that avoided the wraith, say they didn't outrun it. But rather the wraith mysteriously turned aside."

"A myst spell could do all those things," I offered.

Spraggel nodded. "True, but they would have to be an extremely strong myst user to sustain it for any length of time."

I thought for a moment. "I don't know. I'm not that strong, but I can use a lever to move a boulder many times my weight. Maybe it's something like a myst lever helping them move more efficiently."

Spraggel cocked his head to one side. "I take it you don't believe they're supernatural entities."

I looked at the approaching ship. "Oh, I definitely believe in the supernatural. But that ship approaching looks man-made to me."

Spraggel looked over his shoulder in the direction of the wraith. "As it does to me." He sighed. "Whatever it is, we'll soon find out." He looked up in thought. "I wonder how I could record this so it would survive. A paper in a bottle maybe. Fumiko might write it up for me."

I had forgotten about her. "Where is Fumiko?"

"She was sleeping in her cabin earlier." Spraggel jumped down. "I'll check on her while you two figure out how you're going to save us."

Galvyn snorted. "Save us? I think you're overestimating them just a tad." He then stepped toward his own cabin. "I think I had best prepare myself for battle. Looks like a nasty one is brewing."

Going to find somewhere to hide more likely, I thought. I watched him leave.

I turned to Zofie, and she gave me an inquisitive look. She was no doubt having the same thoughts as me. How could we possibly save the ship? I knew nothing about sailing, and Zofie was still cursed and had no myst to use.

Zofie sighed. "I wish I had some myst left. There are several things I could do."

"Could you do a myst spell to move us faster?" I asked.

She shook her head. "I doubt it. It takes a lot of myst to physically move a large object like this ship. Same for the wind to blow against the sails, you've got to move a large volume of it to get any appreciable effect." She shook her head. "No, I wouldn't approach it that way. If we tried to outrun them, they could just keep chasing us until we exhausted ourselves." One side of her mouth curled up. "No, I would approach it in a completely different way. I'm good with shield spells, and you can do a lot with them." She looked down. "But that's just a fantasy right now."

I felt an itch on my nose, and Zofie absentmindedly reached up to rub her own face. The linkage from the curse modification was still with us. My eyes went wide. A sudden idea formed.

I stood straighter. "I could channel the myst to you through your curse."

Zofie stared at me in shock. After a moment, she shook her head. "That would be extremely dangerous. Just because you were able to provide enough myst to ease my transformation, doesn't mean you suddenly have an unlimited supply. You have no idea how much you really have."

I pointed toward the approaching ship. "And having them bearing down on us isn't extremely dangerous? Besides, I'm sure Abe will cut it off if it becomes too dangerous."

She considered it for a moment. "All right. But I'll only draw the minimum."

We ran to the poop deck and explained our plan to the captain. She was not pleased that we were still on board, little alone trying to convince her to let us try to help. "Why should I let you further endanger my ship? For that matter, you could be making it so they can easily capture us."

I was getting a little irritated with her. We were trying to help. "Listen, if we had wanted to stop you from running, we would have already done it! Do you think you could have stopped us?"

She considered us for a moment. "Do you really think you can pull it off?"

Zofie nodded. "I'm sure of it."

She gave a flick of her hand. "Then be about it."

"And one more thing, captain."

She gave Zofie an exasperated look. "And what might that be?"

"Change our course toward the other ship. With the wind at our back and full sail, we will approach them fairly fast. But when you see the blue sphere, change direction. Doesn't matter which way."

The captain stared at her a moment and then smiled wickedly. "Might as well. If we survive this, no one will believe I charged a sea wraith."

She turned to the helmsman. "Bring her about! We're going to charge that bitch! And light all the lanterns! We want her to fear the *Wily Lass!*"

The deck leaned as the course correction took hold, and the wraith moved to be directly ahead of us.

I hoped Zofie knew what she was doing. She led the way to the middle of the ship. She quickly stripped off her boots and stood barefoot on the deck. When I gave her a puzzled look, she quickly explained, "I need to feel the ship. A physical contact is always better for what I'm planning." She put a finger to her lips in thought. "I'll need my hands for the spell, but we'll also need to maximize the myst flow." She fixed her gaze on me. "Stand behind me and put both hands on my waist. That should do it."

I did as she asked. But she huffed and looked over her shoulder.

"Coren, on my waist *under my shirt.*"

I blushed. "Zofie, that's a little... intimate."

She frowned. "Coren, I went around naked for almost a year. I lost my modesty a week or so into that. For that matter, you've seen me naked."

"But now you're... a girl."

"I always have been. Just think of it as if we're dancing."

"I can't dance."

"About time you learned. Now, we haven't got time for this. Put your Creator damned hands on my waist."

I reluctantly did as she requested. I tried not to notice how soft and warm her skin was.

Zofie raised her hands and positioned her feet like she was digging in for a battle. She took a deep breath... but paused. "Are you sure about this Coren?" she said softly, none of the previous irritation in her voice. "I really don't want to kill anyone else. Especially not you."

I glanced over her shoulder at the now rapidly approaching ship. With the change in course, it was getting much closer. I could make out the bright lights coming from its deck. And now I could hear a deep and regular thumping coming from it.

I nodded. "I'm sure. I trust you." And then on impulse, I leaned closer and whispered in her ear, her hair tickling my lips. "As you once told me... don't hold back."

She looked over her shoulder at me and smiled. "You know just the thing to say to a lady. Now let's dance."

Zofie looked forward and raised her face to the sky. She took a deep breath, letting it out slowly—and then the spell started. I felt a tingle in my hands where they touched her and a deeper pull from inside me. I couldn't tell which sensation came from me or which from Zofie.

Suddenly around us appeared a black veil, dark and semi-transparent like smoke without a fire. It quickly rose around us encompassing the entire ship. I looked up and saw it hovering over us like a giant dome. But through it, I could still see the dim outline of the full moon.

I looked over Zofie's shoulder and could still see the wraith ship closing down on us, it appeared blurred, but I could still make out the lights on its deck.

"How are you feeling?" Zofie asked. "Any tiredness or weakness?"

I shrugged. "I feel fine. I can tell you're drawing on me, but no pain or discomfort."

"You are so strange," she mumbled. She took a deep breath. "Now for the hard part. I just created a weak shield which changes the light. They won't be able to tell what we're doing."

"And what are we doing?"

"Making us disappear."

A bright blue sphere rose up around us inside the smoky barrier. It expanded, surrounding the entire ship all the way up to the top of the tallest mast.

This was the signal the captain had been waiting for. "Hard to port!" she yelled.

The deck tilted and began to move out of the smoky barrier, taking the blue bubble with us. But then the sails went slack, and the ship started to lose its forward momentum.

"Zofie, we've lost the wind. We're going to be dead in the water."

"I know," she whispered. "It won't matter. We're invisible to them now. All they can see is the illusion."

As I looked, the smoky barrier seemed to take on a ship form: hull, masts, and sails. My eyes slid off it as I tried to make out the details. It was there, but not. And it was on our original collision course with the sea wraith.

I tensed, waiting to see what would happen. Every member of the crew held their breath. The thumping from the wraith grew so loud I could feel it vibrating in my chest.

Suddenly, the wraith ship slowed and changed course, its thumping growing momentarily slower as it barely missed the smoke illusion. As it sailed on past, the sea wraith changed course banking hard to port to follow it. In the process, the sea wraith came close enough to us that I could indeed tell it was a ship: a strange one with a sharp bow and no sails or masts—only a single structure rising from the middle of the vessel. Once it had completely turned, the thumping became louder again, and it was soon fading into the distance chasing the illusion.

I breathed a sigh of relief. "It looks like we did it...." I started. But I stopped when I noticed a brief flash of color in front of me. Peeking out from the strands of Zofie's braid was a tiny flower—it swayed gently in the breeze. Lady Autumn was reminding me again.

Why now of all times?

Suddenly, I felt a searing pain in my chest and I staggered back. The connection between us broke, and the blue sphere around us collapsed. I tried to catch myself, but my body would not respond. As I fell to the deck, I could see the distant illusion change to smoke and then dissipate.

I began to tremble and landed hard on my back. I looked up to see Zofie kneeling over me yelling something. And beyond her, I saw Fumiko emerge from her cabin running a hand through her sleep mussed hair. As consciousness faded, I heard Fumiko muttering to herself. "What did I miss?"

And then I was out.

CHAPTER FOURTEEN

The Portrait

W hen I opened my eyes, the weak light smacked me and made it reverberate through my beaten and bruised skull. I groaned and promptly shut them again, wishing I could fall back unconscious. I ached all over my body and generally felt like horse manure. I groaned again. That was when my stomach decided it needed attention and simultaneously made me feel nauseous and starving. I couldn't figure out how it did that.

I felt someone touch my cheek, and I risked cracking an eye to find Zofie leaning over me. Concern was written large on her face. I was definitely in my cabin bunk. Memories of the wraith, Zofie's spell working, and my sudden collapse came rushing back.

What the hell had happened?

"You're finally awake," Zofie said softly. I could see a wetness in her eyes. "I was afraid I had killed you too."

I opened my mouth to speak, but nothing came out. My mouth was totally dry. I swallowed and tried again. "Water," I croaked.

Zofie reached beside the bunk for a cup, while I tried to sit up, but my body just wasn't interested in cooperating. She had to help me lean up enough to take a few sips.

"What... happened?"

Zofie set the cup down and sat beside me. "Myst depletion. I sucked almost everything out of you. One more second of draw, and you would have died. You've been unconscious for two days."

I stared at her in shock. Through the porthole I could see it was dark, so it must be late. "Two days?" I shook my head and regretted it. I ran a hand through my hair to make sure my brains weren't leaking out. "What about the sea wraith?"

"It was pretty distant and heading away from us when you passed out. Thank the Creator it kept on going even after the spell ended."

"Did I really run out? Everything was fine until I suddenly lost consciousness."

"That's the only explanation. Usually, there's signs, like weakness or feeling faint. But I must have been drawing on you so heavily that you didn't have time to notice."

She patted my arm. "I bet you're starving. I'll see if there is anything to eat."

"What about your transformation?"

She shrugged. "It started just before sunrise after you collapsed. Quick and painful. I was afraid it might draw from you and finally kill you, but it seems I bore the whole cost." She looked down at her hands in her lap. "I deserved it for hurting you."

She quickly turned away and stood up to leave. "I'll be back in a bit with something to eat. It's about midnight now, so I don't know what I can find."

Something about Zofie's manner bothered me. It was more than just me getting hurt. "But that's not all, is it?"

She paused at the door and turned to me in surprise. I saw her start to deny it, but then she sighed—a deep aching one. "Galvyn was furious that I cried over you. He just couldn't understand why I should care about a commoner." She shook her head. "He's not the person I thought he was." She paused before continuing. "And on top of that, I suspect he's been manipulating me... or my emotions at least."

"Spraggel talked to you, didn't he?"

Zofie nodded sadly. "I didn't believe him at first, but then I began to see a pattern. It's very subtle. But now that I'm alert for it, I think I can avoid it affecting me." She shook her head sadly. "But the fact he would do that to me. Someone I trusted...." She raised her head and stiffened her back. "But if I intend to be queen, I will have to see my way through this." She moved to the door.

"Zofie," I called after her.

She paused in the doorway and looked back at me.

"Thank you for watching over me."

A slow smile came to her lips. "And you are most welcome, Sir Coren. I have truly picked a worthy knight."

She closed the door softly behind her. I felt for her, but knew I could not interfere. Zofie was going to have to figure this out for herself.

I reached for the wooden cup beside my bunk. My hand shook as I took another sip.

Coren! We need to talk!

I nearly dropped the cup at the booming voice inside my head. It was Abe. He had never instigated a conversation with me before.

I carefully set the cup down and rubbed my temple. "All right, so talk. But take it easy on me. You didn't stop Zofie from overdrawing my myst and nearly killing me."

That's what I wanted to talk to you about. While I hate to ask—and I mean I really, really hate it—I need your help. Something's wrong with me. I... I think I'm broken!

"Broken as in not being able to steal curses?"

Something like that.

That wasn't much of an answer. "Is Zofie overdrawing my myst and you being broken related?"

Abe snorted. *You haven't got any to overdraw.*

"Then where did all that myst come from?"

I... I'm not allowed to answer.

I sighed. "Let me guess. The secret word thing is preventing you."

Which is why I need you to hurry up and find it. I need to talk to you intelligently, and I can't with this muzzle on! You have no idea how frustrating this is! If I can talk about it, maybe you and the princess can figure it out.

"All right. What exactly is happening?"

I'm having periods where I stop functioning. I just freeze up. And I'm not sure how long they last.

I shrugged. "I don't see what the big problem is. So you take breaks."

You don't understand Coren. I can't...." He paused. I could feel him struggling for words. *"Do certain things if I'm not working. Which means I can't... dammit, this so frustrating!* He paused again. *My influence will... dammit all!*

Realization suddenly dawned on me. "You are trying to say that you won't be able to protect me."

I cannot answer that question, but it is a possibility. So it's in your best interest to find the stupid secret word!

I was getting irritated. "How am I supposed to do that? I have no idea where to find it."

Come on, Coren. I've... dammit...how can I say this? I've said things which might help one should they choose to use it.

"You've given me hints?" I asked in surprise.

What do you think I've been doing? All you need.... My curse went suddenly silent.

"Abe?" I asked.

No reply.

"Abhulengulus, answer me."

But the inside of my head was quiet. I began to wonder if perhaps Abe really was broken.

I went to take another sip of water and noticed a flash of color on the side of my cup.

A tiny flower was nodding at me.

For the next several days, it rained. It was a misty sort of rain that left one feeling damp even when inside. It put everyone on the ship into a sour mood. The seas reflected the feeling and rocked the small vessel to and fro. I, along with some of the crew, had to resort to a myst charm to keep our stomach settled. Galvyn of course made a show of not needing one. Just another way for him to point out his superiority. I was *really* starting to dislike the man.

I made a quick recovery from myst depletion, and Zofie kept a check on my condition until I felt strong enough to get out of bed. But once that happened, she started avoiding me—staying in her tiny cabin with only Fumiko attending her. I think her guilt over injuring me reminded her of what had happened to her father. Plus, I think she was avoiding Galvyn.

While Galvyn and I were supposed to share the cabin, he didn't bother me while I recovered. I think Zofie demanded that I be left alone and for him to find other arrangements. I wondered if he was sleeping in the crate.

During this time, I was mostly left to myself. Abe continued to be silent. I tried to read some, and write in my journal, but the rocking of the ship made it difficult. So I mostly just slept.

After roughly a week of poor conditions, the sun finally came out and the seas calmed, allowing us to come out of our cabins for some fresh air. To celebrate, the captain suggested the sailors have a sword sparring competition. It served to keep the crew sharp in case of freebooters, but it also offered a chance for a little recreation.

So at mid-day, we gathered on deck and cleared a spot barely big enough for two people to square off. All of us gathered around to watch, passengers included, as the sailors sparred with wooden sticks. The men were jovial about it, but took the proceedings quite seriously. The object seemed to be to strike anywhere on the body, except for the head, neck, and groin. Hits there were forbidden—one player was still on probation from a previous competition.

The sailors had a few matches with much cheering and bets being placed on the favorites. Then Galvyn decided to join in. Being trained to the sword since birth, the sailors were no match for him, and he easily dispatched even the best. The sad thing was, he didn't try to win so much as strive to humiliate them. Of course, Galvyn gloated over every win which made even the sunny day start to go dim.

After his last victory, Galvyn wiped the sweat from his brow and drank a bit of diluted wine.

"Is there no one else that would take me on?"

The sailors glanced among themselves but no one spoke.

Galvyn looked to me. "What about you, Coren. Care to go against me?"

Across from me and behind Galvyn, I saw Zofie give a slight shake of her head. While I wouldn't mind getting my ass kicked for Zofie, I would not do it without her permission.

"Sorry, I'm not a match for your skill. I will decline."

He snorted.

"I will." The voice came from up on the poop deck. Leaning on the rail and smiling down at us was Captain Ina. "But you'll have to sweeten the pot a bit."

Galvyn frowned. "I don't fight women. There's no sport in it."

Her eyebrows went up. "How about a gold piece says that I tap you not once, not twice..." She held up three fingers. "But three times."

The sailors cheered. Remembering my own go with Risten, I had learned that women were no gentle sex. They could be quite deadly—or in my case, quite painful.

Galvyn gave an amused shrug. "A foolish wager, but I'll take you up on it. I'm always eager to take a woman's charms."

The captain gave him a smile. While her lips curled up, her eyes were daggers. "I bet you are."

The captain joined us on the deck with the crew cheering her on. She pulled her shirt out of her trousers and tied it up securely up under her breasts. The big sailor handed her a stick and whispered something in her ear I couldn't hear. She grinned and nodded.

Captain Ina and Galvyn squared off against each other. Galvyn went into his starting form and the captain just stood there loosely, one corner of her mouth curled up into a grin. "On the count of three?" she asked.

Galvyn nodded, and the crew went silent. The captain started counting, but just stood there when she called the last number. Galvyn didn't hesitate. He charged and swung—only the captain wasn't there anymore and had neatly danced behind him. She hit him on the butt with her stick and stepped out of his reach. The crew cheered.

Galvyn's eyes went up in shock. "You're fast." It was a statement.

The captain grinned. "You have to be careful when dealing with fast women. We sometimes have our secrets."

This time Galvyn approached her a little more cautiously. She danced to the side and he tracked her. "Oh, and what secret is that?" he asked, never taking his eyes off her.

Galvyn lunged; she parried; he countered... and she ended up behind him, giving his butt another painful whack.

Galvyn's clenched his teeth in fury. "You're very fast, but I have your measure now."

She grinned. "No man can truly know a woman."

And she launched at him. Galvyn was instantly put on the defensive, and her well-timed blows drove him back. He had no time but to defend. The sailors scrambled to get out of the way. Then she dropped suddenly and swept Galvyn's legs out from under him. He landed hard on his butt. I saw it, but wasn't sure I believed it. I had seen that type of move before. From Risten.

The captain regained her feet and put the tip of her stick on Galvyn's chest. The stunned man stared up at her.

She grinned down at him. "I think I will have my gold now."

Galvyn protested. "That was no fair. You're a Creator blasted swordmaster!"

"As I said, no man can truly know a woman's secrets."

His face red, he jumped up and stomped off the deck for his cabin.

Captain Ina straightened and tossed her stick to Zofie, who snatched it out of the air.

"Why don't you and the other girl take a turn," her eyes glinted in mischief. "Every woman needs to know which end of the sword is which."

Zofie looked to Fumiko, who shrugged. They stepped out to the center of the sparring area.

"Do you know how to use a sword?" asked Zofie.

One of the sailors handed her the other stick. Fumiko sighted down it. "In my lands, we do it differently, but I have received a little training with a mock sword. Ours is more rigid in the forms, while your style is looser. I think I can do this."

Zofie smiled. "I won't be too hard on you."

Fumiko stood up straight, directly facing Zofie, the stick held before her. Her hair shaded her eyes, but it seemed her whole demeanor changed, more focused. "You never know, I might surprise you."

I stood straighter as something in my gut tightened. I thought back to the encounter with the kidnappers on the road. Fumiko had definitely surprised.

Zofie's eyebrows went up. "All right. On three then." She fell into her form.

Fumiko gave a slight nod. And when the count was done, the two leaped at each other.

Zofie used the same quick strokes I remembered from our earlier sparring. She was fast with good footwork. Fumiko clumsily blocked her, barely getting her stick in place, but she seemed to catch the rhythm as they traded blows. Zofie tried to score a hit, but Fumiko managed to block. Zofie pressed her harder—

And Fumiko suddenly changed styles. Her stance became looser, her grip on the stick went to one-handed, and—she grinned, only it wasn't a friendly grin.

Fumiko's pace quickened; her blows coming fast and furious. Zofie was taken by surprise, but defended the blows. And still, Fumiko increased the rhythm. She spun, nearly catching Zofie off guard, then spun the other way. Then the power behind the blows increased, driving Zofie back until she was at the railing. Both women were breathing hard. That's when I noticed a change in the strikes. They were no longer intended to score a point—they were intended to hurt or even kill. I rushed forward to stop them.

Suddenly, Fumiko did a twisting motion with her mock sword, and Zofie's weapon went sailing into the ocean. Fumiko reared back to strike—and just in time, I grabbed the stick. She wheeled on me, jerked the weapon from my grasp, and swung at me. I blocked with my arms—which hurt quite a bit—and when she reared for another strike, I grabbed her and pulled her tightly against me.

"*Fumiko!*" I shouted. "What are you doing?"

She struggled for a moment and then blinked up at me through the strands of her hair. Puzzlement and then sadness came over her face.

She dropped the practice sword as if it were something hot. She looked down, refusing to meet my eyes. "I'm... I'm sorry. I shouldn't have picked up the stick. I thought..." She looked up at me with tears in her eyes and pulled back. I released her. She glanced toward Zofie and mumbled an apology before fleeing to her cabin.

I went to stand beside Zofie. "Are you all right?"

Still breathing hard from the exertion, she nodded. "What was that all about?"

I shook my head. "I wish I knew. But I think there is something about our traveling partner she hasn't told us."

I stood in my usual spot on the ship's railing, watching the sun slip behind the horizon. A few puffy clouds floated above us, catching the last rays of the day and displaying brilliant shades of orange and purple. The undulating ocean had a calming effect, and I desperately needed some tranquility to ponder a simple question: *How much further was it?*

It was the same question on everyone's mind. And our time was running out.

While the Wayward's Finder pointed us in the direction of what we sought, it gave no indication of distance. So we really had no way of knowing how far we had yet to travel to reach this mysterious Crypt of the Mirror of By-gone Tears. Or worse, if it even still held the mirror.

Galvyn worked with the helmsman to take a bearing using it every morning and evening. And according to it, we were right on course. However, we were steadily drawing down our provisions and approaching the half-way mark. The captain had decreed that if we didn't encounter something in the next two days, we would have to turn back. I did not relish returning empty-handed.

I sighed and glanced up at the poop deck where Galvyn was talking with the helmsman. While the ocean had been unusually calm during the afternoon, the weather on the ship had been a little stormy. And Galvyn had been the eye of the storm.

Following the match with the captain, he continued to feel his wounded pride. However, he dare not say much to her, so he followed me around and found fault with everything from what I was eating to the nature of my birth. And when I just ignored him, he turned his unspent ammunition on Zofie criticizing her also. Zofie didn't hesitate to return his volley, and the two had a rip-roaring argument—easily heard by everyone on the ship. She stormed off to the cabin she shared with Fumiko and hadn't come out since.

Fumiko hadn't been much better. Since the little sparring adventure, she had isolated herself too. I had tried to coax her out to speak with me, but she declined. From what little Zofie would say, Fumiko huddled with her notebook and brushes in the farthest corner of her bunk, not saying anything, unless she was spoken to.

Ah, Fumiko.

I smiled. Sometimes I enjoyed talking with her, and other times I dreaded it: she would pump me for everything I knew from The Poet to my learning of ancient weapons. She had been most amused over my story about Spraggel making me go up on the roof of Revenhill Keep during a thunderstorm. Plus, she seemed particularly interested in my father's death and the passing of Abe to me. In exchange, she would freely share her knowledge of historical artifacts and legends.

But strangely, if the conversation drifted toward her past or her homeland, her answers became evasive and vague, saying she had previously lived an uninspired life filled with nothing but humdrum. Based on how she defeated those kidnappers on the road and the way she handled the practice sword, she had definitely had more than a humdrum life. From my brief encounters with her abilities, I would say her training was on par with Risten's. I shuddered to think what would happen if the two should ever come to blows.

Spraggel was the only one enjoying himself. He sat on the ship's upside-down dinghy and was telling stories to some of the crew. Yesterday he had been playing dice with them which had been interesting since all he could do was bat the die around.

When the sun had slipped completely behind the horizon, I pushed up from the rail and headed toward my cabin. From up on the poop deck, Galvyn gave me the evil eye to make sure I wasn't heading toward them—or Zofie.

I went to my cabin. Thankfully Galvyn would not be back for a while. He tended to drink wine in the evening and try to talk the men into some game of chance. It wasn't late enough to sleep, so instead, I took out my oil and cloth and then pulled out my sword. Sitting with it across my lap on my bunk, I began to wipe it down. The salt air was especially hard on steel, so I wanted to be sure I kept it completely rust free and ready for use at a moment's notice. Risten had drilled into me the importance of a well maintained and ready weapon.

I wondered how Risten was faring. She should have contacted us by now, but Zofie's correspondor had remained silent. Zofie had worried about it so much she had tried to contact Risten herself, but with no luck. We both hoped Risten had not gotten into trouble.

I ran the oiled rag over the sword while inspecting it for any signs of rust. Every time I held it, I was amazed that I possessed something of such beauty. It was perfectly balanced and highly polished, with a simple dragon worked into the guard. The sword was very old and had been sharpened many times over the years. Despite being well cared for, it showed some age with a few nicks and scratches that could not be polished or filed out.

I ran the cloth over the sword's fuller or the central grove of the sword, and not for the first time, puzzled over the inscription faintly visible there. A series of letters had been inlaid into it using a different metal and in no language that we could identify. They were faint, but visible in the right light.

Zofie was just as puzzled by them as I was. Spraggel and Risten thought they were perhaps the name of the sword's maker. But to me, it seemed too long for someone's name. I thought it a phrase of dedication, like *draw me only for justice,* or some such. I sighed. Maybe if things calmed down, I could research it a bit more.

There was a knock on the door. My heart jumped thinking perhaps it was Zofie, but when I looked up, I saw it was Fumiko.

"May I come in?" she asked sheepishly. She was clutching her leather binder to her chest.

I motioned her forward. "If you trust being alone with me in my bedroom."

She entered, closing the door behind her. She perched on the edge of my bunk still clutching the binder. "I trust you. I'm not the one you want after all."

I winced. "Is it that obvious?"

Fumiko nodded. "However, sometimes people change their minds." She blushed. "But that is not why I'm here. I wanted to see if you can get your curse to open. We haven't tried in a while." But then her eyes fell on the sword. "That's a beautiful weapon. Is that Majestic, the King's Sword?"

She leaned closer, and I detected the faint scent of flowers. Was she wearing perfume?

I cleared my throat. "It is indeed. Zofie gave it to me."

"When you became her knight?"

I shook my head. "Actually, it was before that."

Fumiko gave me a puzzled look.

I sighed. "She gave it to me at the beginning of our journey to find Ruin's Shield. She had only seen me once and didn't even know I was cursed."

Fumiko shook her head. "So she gave you the sword before you had proven your worth to her. I just can't imagine someone giving away something so precious to someone she didn't even know." She looked up at me, and then embarrassed, glanced back down. "No offense."

I smiled. "None taken. I asked her about it much later, and she said she just *knew* I was supposed to have it."

She looked up at me with large eyes. "So the sword chose you. There is a legend that says the King's Sword chooses who will wield it."

I shrugged. "Either that or Abe manipulated my luck so that Zofie would give it to me."

She shook her head. "I don't think so. While there are no detailed writings on it, there are legends about the sword. That out of every generation, it will choose who will wield it and best protect the kingdom."

"Please tell me it's not another Abe."

She chuckled. "Definitely not. While its forging dates to around the Dark Avenyts, it seemed to have been made a little later than your curse."

"And speaking of my curse, it has not awakened for several days. I'm beginning to wonder if something is wrong with it."

I stood and put my sword and oil away. Fumiko watched me silently. The binder that she had clutched to her chest drifted to her lap. When I turned back, I almost did a double-take. She wasn't wearing her bodice which wasn't that uncommon for her in the evening. But her shirt, well, it wasn't laced like she normally did it, leaving a little more of her chest visible. I swallowed and looked away. It likely came undone from carrying her binder.

I sat back down beside her on the bunk, a safe distance between us.

Fumiko looked down. "I really came here for something else." She reached into her binder and pulled out a single piece of paper. She stood in front of me and bowed slightly from the waist. "I apologize for striking you. I'm not sure what came over me." She held out the piece of paper to me with both hands. "I drew this for you."

I took the paper and turned it over. On the other side was a profile of me leaning on the ship's railing. My eyes went up in amazement. It was so detailed—done in a fine charcoal and shaded to present the shadows. She had done something to the paper to lock in the picture. I was impressed, to say the least.

"While I can't say much for the subject, it's wonderfully done," I said in amazement. "You're quite the artist."

She blushed. "I'm not that good. It's just something that I do from time to time."

She sat back down beside me, closing by half the safe distance we'd had before. "I have others if you'd like to see." She didn't wait. She pulled her binder into her lap and scooted closer until our shoulders touched. She excitedly opened it and leafed through the pictures she had drawn. There were some of Zofie in various poses—I think the princess may have been posing for her. There was Galvyn, the ship, various sailors, and from earlier in our trip, pictures of multiple inns, our horses, and miscellaneous other people. There were also quite a few pictures of me. Most not as detailed as the one she had gifted me, but still recognizable.

When we were done, she closed the book and set it on her other side. She looked up at me—our faces were dangerously close. I didn't have a lot of experience with women, but my first impulse was to run.

Fumiko reached over and took my left hand. She turned it over so that my curse anchor was visible. She gently traced its outline with her finger. "I wonder why he won't awaken." She pulled my hand to her chest and looked up at me again. She tucked her wild hair behind an ear. Her deep brown eyes looked up at me. She seemed to be waiting for something.

She gently reached up and touched my cheek. "You have such a kind face."

She moistened her lips and moved closer.

"Fumiko..." I croaked.

Just then, the door flew open and Zofie stood in the doorway. "Coren, I've just been talking to the captain...." she drew up as she took in the scene in the room.

Fumiko leaned away and jumped to her feet.

Zofie's eyes went wide. "Excuse me. I... should have knocked." She looked down and then stepped out.

Fumiko gathered up her binder and again clutched it to her chest. "I had better go."

And she fled the room.

I shook my head, not sure what I was going to do about her. I was afraid she wanted more than I could give her right now.

I looked down at Fumiko's picture lying on my bunk and smiled. I did appreciate the gift though. I would have to figure out a way to incorporate it into my own journal. My eye traveled to the lower corner where she had signed it. But there was something in tiny letters beneath it. I stepped closer to the light to make it out.

There, in tightly written letters was written:

Do not trust her.

CHAPTER FIFTEEN

The Island

At mid-morning of the next day, a single shout brought everyone up on deck. Spraggel and I were deep in conversation. He sat on the upside-down dinghy while I paced in front of him. We had been debating over what we would do if we didn't find the mirror. And at that point, it wasn't looking good—we were due to turn back the very next day. We had tried to beg some additional time, but the captain wouldn't hear of it.

"We are four weeks out with nothing to show for it," she had said. "If we were going to find something, we would have already found it."

That's why the sudden announcement so surprised us.

Land ho!

The cry was from a sailor atop the highest rigging of the mainmast. Spraggel and I stared at each other in shock.

Passengers and crew alike rushed to the bow to get a glimpse of the dark patch on the horizon. Zofie and Fumiko were right there with us—the two women chatting excitedly. Smiling widely, Zofie stepped over to me and gave me a quick hug before she picked up Spraggel and scratched under his chin. Galvyn, I noticed, hung back. Come to think of it, he had been quiet all morning.

After the initial shouts of joy, the crew set about preparing to make landfall while Fumiko, Galvyn, and Spraggel went to make their own preparations. That left Zofie and myself standing alone at the bow, watching the land gradually approach. Her hair was loose, and the stiff breeze whipped it back and forth. From her posture, I could tell something was on her mind.

Staring straight ahead without looking at me, she finally spoke. "I'm sorry I entered your cabin last night unannounced. I didn't mean to interrupt."

I chuckled. "You didn't interrupt anything. I like Fumiko—just not that way."

But Zofie said nothing and continued to stare straight ahead. I suddenly realized that Fumiko trying to kiss me was not what concerned her. No, it was something much more.

Zofie finally took a deep breath as if steeling herself. "What I was going to tell you last night is that I talked with the captain, and she confirmed something I was afraid to admit. I had overheard a couple of the crew talking about visiting a brothel back at the port, and I recognized its name. It was one belonging to Galvyn's family. So I cornered the captain and managed to find out Galvyn has been twisting the truth. His family's brothels are real, and they have been known to employ... slaves. The captain has even transported some of them." Zofie paused for a moment to push a strand of hair behind her ear. "Last night, I confronted Galvyn and told him I didn't appreciate being lied to."

She paused, and I turned to look at her. She seemed to have more to say, so I kept quiet to let her finish.

She shook her head sadly. "He then used his myst ability in an attempt to influence my emotions. He... he tried to make me trust him and his explanations. I have suspected he was doing something like that, but to actually catch him doing it, to feel him try to make me feel things I didn't want to." She shivered. "It made me feel violated. And it made me quite angry. I told him to stop trying to use me."

She paused again, gripping the railing tightly. "I expected him to get mad and stomp off. But he didn't. Instead, he just gave me a smile and admitted that it was true. And then he asked me a question I found hard to answer."

She pushed her wayward hair behind her ear. "He asked if I wasn't also using him. Wasn't I just as guilty? Using him just to get his father's backing and pushing aside my own feelings just to have it." She paused. "He said he was just helping me deal with it."

She turned toward me. She wore a sad expression—not heartbroken, more disappointed. "I had to admit to myself that what he said was true."

She looked down and sighed. "I finally told him he's not the man I thought he was, and I could no longer consider him a worthy suitor. I broke off our engagement."

I was shocked. "What did Galvyn say?"

She sighed sadly. "That I would take him back. It was only a matter of time."

She looked so miserable, I wanted to take her in my arms and comfort her. But at the same time, I knew it was the wrong thing to do. She was in her queen role right now. She had been forced to make a hard choice, and she had made it. I thought it spoke volumes to the kind of queen she would be.

She looked back toward the approaching land. "You knew, didn't you? You knew he was using his ability on me. Why didn't you say something?"

I paused, considering my answer. "Because you wouldn't have believed me. Any accusation would only make me look jealous."

We stood silently for a moment, then Zofie nodded. "Unfortunately, that's exactly what would have happened. I'm disappointed in myself. I nearly chose the wrong path because of my shortsightedness. I've got to be a better queen than that if my people are ever going to prosper."

"Zofie, you may be a princess, but you're only human. I'm just glad you figured it out before you did something irreversible."

She looked at me and I at her. Our eyes met. "Like drive away the only person I can really trust."

I took a deep breath. "I'll admit, seeing you with Galvyn broke my heart, but you didn't drive me away. I will always serve you, and I will always be your friend for as long as you want me."

It was my turn to look out into the ocean. "But if you're hinting I could return to being one of your suitors, I must decline. My heart couldn't take it if someone came forward and you had to choose them. I can't blame you really. I want what's best for the kingdom, too."

I turned to look at her. "I think we've both learned that there is a chasm between us. You're a noble and I'm not. Right now, we're linked by our curses, but once those are gone, I don't think you'll need me anymore." I had to tell her what I really felt. "Just as there is a real live person beneath the princess disguise, there is also a real live person attached to this ancient curse. Until we each can accept that person underneath, there is no hope for us."

Zofie and I gazed at each other for a moment longer, and then she turned to look toward the island. "You're right, Coren. And I'm so very, very sorry about what happened."

I reached over and put my hand on top of hers. "And I'm sorry too."

Her hand turned over and tightly grasped mine. "I'm not giving up on us, you know," she said, not looking at me.

I smiled. "Neither am I."

By late in the day, we could see that it definitely was an island with a couple small mountains rising above the ocean. There was also a reef surrounding it, forcing the captain to sail around the perimeter looking for a decent place to go ashore. Unfortunately, we found none, and as the sun began to sink, we were forced to drop anchor a safe distance away. The captain ordered that our landing party make ready for disembarking the next morning.

Being too excited to sleep much, I met Zofie and Fumiko up on deck just as the sun lightened the horizon. The morning itself was naturally chilly with a nippy breeze blowing across the water and reminding us that winter was only a month away. We all wore our cloaks to hold our warmth and keep out the fine ocean spray.

Much to my surprise, Galvyn joined us just a few moments later. I thought that since Zofie had broken off the engagement, he wouldn't want to. But upon seeing my surprise, he smiled and leaned close, whispering in my ear. "Did you actually think I would miss this? There is no way I'll trust my future wife to a commoner. She'll come back to me, it's just a matter of time. She's got no other choice."

I wanted to punch him, but decided to take a different approach. I whispered back. "I think you underestimate her. I'm confident she'll come up with something none of us will see coming. I just hope I'm there to see your face when it happens."

He just glared back at me.

As we were preparing to leave, Captain Ina came by and made it perfectly clear that while she had agreed to our passage, she was having nothing to do with exploring some myst protected island. The crewman accompanying us was going to look for water and supplies, but that was it. Should anything troublesome arise, then she was pulling out whether we were on board or not.

The dinghy only held five so the well-muscled Jomo accompanied us. Zofie and Fumiko sat aft with Spraggel curled up in Zofie's lap, and Fumiko, clutching her leather binder, which she had wrapped in her travel sack. Galvyn positioned himself in the front of the boat and abstained from helping. Not that I was surprised.

I, being the gallant one, said I would help row us to shore. It couldn't be that hard. By the time we reached the beach, Jomo hadn't even broken a sweat, while I thought my arms were going to come out of their sockets.

Our landing was uneventful. The reef shielded the shore from the ocean waves, so we easily grounded the dinghy and stepped out to dry ground. The beach itself was a mix of small black rocks and gray sand which stretched into the distance on either side of us. Other than the sound of the wind and surf, it was deadly quiet—not a seagull or even a crab could be seen. It was a little unnerving.

After the others climbed out, I helped Jomo pull the boat high enough up on shore to be safe from being washed away. Then without a word, he went off up the beach looking for drinkable water.

Galvyn took a reading using the finder. It pointed toward the interior and the highest mountain on the island. I sighted up it. It didn't look *that* high, but neither had Mount Eternal, and it was the highest mountain on the continent.

I went first trying to blaze the best path through thick seagrass and stubby cedar trees. The land quickly became much steeper, and the ground began to sprout tough bushes which I had to hack through using my sword. The nippy breeze continued to push at our backs and sway the vegetation, but with the heat of our exertion, it began to seem rather pleasant.

Our progress was slow, and I wondered if we would even be able to reach the crypt before having to turn back.

And then I stumbled across a road.

Well, actually, I fell over it. I had looked back to answer one of Galvyn's questions when my foot caught on a low rock, and I fell flat on my face. From my new vantage point, I could tell it wasn't just a single rock, but actually a series of stones, laid in a perfect line, stretching upwards toward the mountain top. Only a few feet away from it, running parallel to the first, was another matching row of stones. And in between the two rows, there was just clear sand and gravel—no vegetation,

"It's a road," Fumiko observed, stepping over me to stand between the rows of stone. "It must lead to the crypt." Without waiting, she clutched her binder to her chest and turned up the road. Galvyn followed right on her heels.

Zofie squatted beside me and touched my shoulder. "Are you all right?"

"Yes—just being my normal, klutzy self."

She patted my shoulder reassuringly. I moved my arms to push up but paused at the sight right in front of my face. A small orange flower was growing out of the sand. I blinked. I'm sure it hadn't been there a moment ago. I sighed and stood. No doubt another reminder from Lady Autumn. Strange, I mused. Up until this leg of the journey, I had been desperate to get rid of my curse. But I hadn't even thought of it recently. Strangely, I was more concerned about Abe *not* working than removing him. I counted the days in my head and realized that the beginning of winter wasn't that far away. If I was going to break my curse, I would have to do it soon. I made a mental note to talk to Zofie about it when we returned to the ship.

The road did indeed align with our intended direction, so we followed it, finding the way a little easier. At least I didn't have to spend time hacking through the brush.

The further along the road we traveled, the more distinct it became with well-placed stones lining the surface. As we climbed upward, the vegetation on either side of the road became sparser, giving way to mostly short grass. Until finally, as we pushed up an especially steep grade, we came to the top of the summit. And sitting in the center of a small grassy area at the end of the road was a small stone building.

The structure looked old, with its stone weathered and worn, and covered in places with thick green moss. The building itself was tiny— about three times longer than wide and just large enough to hold someone's remains. The roof was also made of stone and rose to a central peak. A door with an engraved arch over it was on the side facing the road. The emblem for the Creator was carved into the stone above the door marking it for a place of reverence. To all appearances, it really looked like a crypt.

We paused in front and surveyed the area. From our high vantage point, I could make out our ship anchored beyond the reef and the beautiful water surrounding the island. I could even make out Jomo leaning against the boat. It was definitely a peaceful place, perfect for someone to take their final rest.

Galvyn walked up to the giant door and looked it up and down. He laid his hand flat on it and gently pushed. "Seems pretty solid. Warm too. Warmer than the air. That generally means there is myst running through it." He pointed out the lines where the door met the sides. "Zof, if you were to apply a myst shield along these lines, it should open right up".

I glanced in her direction. She was frowning. Apparently, Galvyn still did not know Zofie was cursed.

Zofie shook her head. "Not now, Galvyn. Let's try not to destroy this ancient relic if we can help it. It's only been here for about a thousand years." She turned to Fumiko. "Any idea on how to get in?"

Fumiko shook her head. "This must be the container that was mentioned in the old texts, but there was no mention of this island or even the mountain we're standing on. This is completely new territory for me." She looked frustrated.

Galvyn just waved toward the door. "Zof, it would be a lot faster if you just used your myst. I know you're strong enough."

Zofie sighed, clearly irritated. Galvyn seemed to have a talent for getting on her nerves. "I'd prefer not to," she said. "It could accidentally bring down the whole thing. Let's at least *try* to open it first."

Galvyn frowned, but held his peace.

I stepped closer to the door and looked it over closely. It took up most of the width of this end of the structure and went all the way from the floor to the arch a foot over my head. I rested my hand on it and could tell Galvyn was right; the door was warmer than one would expect. I ran my hands across it, carefully feeling for some hidden latch. In my exploration, I dislodged a chunk of the moss about as big as my fist. It plopped to the floor at my foot, leaving the rock underneath exposed. I started to move on in my exploration, when something on the freshly uncovered rock caught my eye. It looked like some kind of carving.

Encouraged, I began to pull away more of the moss, gradually enlarging my initial spot, and revealing some type of pattern carved into the door's surface. The ever prepared Fumiko, handed me a cloth which I used to wipe away the remaining dirt.

When I was done, I stepped back to see a large circle with eight symbols engraved into its circumference. The symbol at the top was easily identifiable as the griffin, which usually represented the king. And the one just to the right of it was a crown like a queen might wear—but the rest were unfamiliar to me. Oddly, there was a blank spot for a ninth symbol at its bottom, but it was empty. I couldn't help but feel it represented a broken circle.

"It represents the Sage Council," stated Fumiko behind me. I turned to look at her. She blushed and clutched her binder tighter to her chest. She looked down and added. "This must be their memorial."

Spraggel leaped down from Zofie's arms, and in cat fashion, strode over to examine the symbols. "It could be. Jonathan Xernow the First put together the original council to fight the Dark Avenyts." He turned to Fumiko. "What makes you think it represents that council?"

Fumiko sidled up to the door and pointed to one of the symbols. "The original council had nine members, which included both the king and queen themselves. Plus, each of the council members had a particular skill." She pointed to a figure on the bottom right. "See the symbol with the triangle in a circle? That's for alchemy. And the one just above it, that's for metallurgy." She paused and scratched her head. "But one is missing. I see symbols for all the others..." She touched each as she recited them. "...Chief Advisor, Healer, Treasurer, and Army Commander." She stepped back and scratched her head. "But there should be one more for Myst Adept...."

Galvyn cut her off. "Enough with the history lesson. We don't have all day to debate this." He turned to Zofie and pointed his thumb toward the door over his shoulder. "Just use your myst to open it. I've seen your shield charm and it's pretty powerful. It should be more than enough."

I shook my head. "I don't think that's a good idea. It could damage the mirror."

Fumiko nodded in agreement.

Galvyn stepped to Zofie, pleading with her. "Come on, Zof! Just do it."

I groaned. He was really pushing her. I was suddenly glad she couldn't use her myst. Galvyn might not live through it.

Fumiko reading the situation, took half a step back and clutched her binder more tightly to her chest. And Spraggel just watched intensely.

Zofie crossed her arms. "Coren's right, we might do more damage than good."

Galvyn huffed. "Not likely. Just quit making excuses and do it. With your level of myst..."

"Galvyn," Zofie said quietly. She searched his face and seemed to come to a decision. Dropping her arms to her side, she took a deep breath and let it out slowly. "There is something I haven't told you."

"Really Zofie, you've got the power...." He broke off. "What did you say?"

"I said there is something I haven't told you about myself."

"If it's that your myst powers have grown, I already knew that."

She shook her head sadly. "No Galvyn. It's not that." She glanced at me and seemed to draw strength from it. "It's that I'm cursed."

For the next few heartbeats, all we heard was the rustling of the brush in the wind.

Zofie reached to the neck of her cloak and pulled both it and her shirt aside, revealing the top of her chest. There, sitting just under her collarbone, was a black symbol. It was about as large as a gold royal and perfectly round with complex symbols around the edge. Inside the circle were the shapes of four animals and the phases of the moon.

It was her curse mark.

"You see this Galvyn. Wynn put it on me the night he murdered Father. Because of it, I transform into an animal every full moon, or at least I did until Coren fixed it. This curse sucks up all my myst, so I have none to use."

"But what about that time on the ship? When you cloaked us in an illusion?"

"I used Coren's. If I'm between transformations, our connection allows me to draw from him. But I nearly killed him doing it." She released her collar, covering her mark. "Now, let's find another way in."

But Galvyn wasn't satisfied. "You're cursed?" There was no mistaking the loathing on his face. "My future wife bears a filthy *curse*?"

She looked at him levelly. "Your future wife likely will not. Whoever that might be. But one thing is sure, it won't be me."

Galvyn sighed. "Zofie, don't say that."

She snorted and gave a sad smile. "Oh really." She held out her hand toward him and stepped forward. He flinched back.

"You think I'm tainted now, don't you? Unclean. Dirty."

He held up his hands and took a step back. "Now Zofie, it isn't like that. I'm sure we can find a way to get it off you."

She shook her head. "You still don't get it. I broke off our engagement not just because you lied and kept secrets from me. No, it was because I was becoming just like you. And that's not who I want to be. I'm done with lies. This is what I am. Too bad if you don't like it. I *will* become queen, and I will do it *my* way!"

She drew herself up and strode over to the stone door. She placed her open palm against it, just over the symbols. "I am Princess Zophia Olwenna Xernow," she announced. "I am the rightful ruler of Brethnach, and I command you to open!"

Much to everyone's surprise, each of the symbols on the door lit up with a bright blue glow. It only lasted a moment before they faded.

All except the griffin. The symbol for the kingdom.

"Interesting," observed Spraggel, rubbing against Zofie's leg. "You instinctively knew what to do. And it recognized you too. I'm going to have to do more research on the Xernows when we get back."

But the door didn't open.

"What now?" I asked.

Spraggel nodded. "Usually in ceremonies, there are three representatives. Maybe it needs three members of the council to be present to open it."

I frowned. "But they're all dead."

Spraggel looked up at me. "Coren, pick me up and hold me close to the circle."

I did as he requested. He reached out a paw and touched the symbol for chief advisor. It immediately lit up.

Spraggel laughed. "Looks like the current holder of that office will work. Remember, when Zofie held court on top of Mount Eternal, she appointed me to be her chief advisor."

Zofie shook her head in alarm. "The only people I appointed were you, Risten, and Coren. But Risten's not here, and there is no symbol for Coren."

I looked at the blank spot. "Maybe there is."

I stepped to the carving and reached out to touch the empty space. Two heartbeats later, a symbol glowing an angry red appeared.

And it was the exact likeness of my curse mark.

We were startled by the sound of scraping stone, only it wasn't the door. Instead, a small section of the doorframe levered out, revealing a slot in the stone.

I rolled my eyes. "So that was just to get to the keyhole. Now we need the key."

Zofie looked to my sword. "I think you have it, Coren."

I knew immediately what she was referring to. I pulled out the blade and held the King's Sword up to the slot. It was just the right size.

I inserted the blade and pushed it home.

Immediately there was a loud grating sound, and the door slowly swung inward. Cool air wafted from inside. If ancient had a scent, the air from inside carried it.

As we watched, myst lights came on inside the small room, one at a time from each of the four walls. All the walls were bare, except the one across from us which had a beautiful mural on it—two dragons, one dark, one light locked in battle. In the center of the room, there was a large dark hole. We stepped closer and saw a narrow set of circular stairs leading downward.

Spraggel was the first to step to the edge and peer down the stairs. The light did not penetrate far, but it looked pretty deep. I stepped outside and returned with a couple pebbles. I tossed one into the center of the hole. We heard it ping against the stairs a couple times, but we didn't hear it hit bottom.

But we did hear a loud screeching sound reverberate up the passage.

We all looked at one another with wide eyes. "What was that?" asked Galvyn.

Spraggel sighed in exasperation. "It's the guardian, of course. All royal tombs are supposed to have them."

Zofie moved to the first step and carefully stepped down on it. At her touch, a myst light in a wall sconce came on a short way down the staircase. I was thankful that we wouldn't have to do this in the dark. However, it also meant that whatever was down there would know we're coming.

Zofie cautiously went down a few steps and then turned to look back at us. "You don't have to come if you don't want. This is my battle, not yours."

I chuckled. "What? And miss all the fun?" I stepped behind her, and Fumiko followed on my heels.

Spraggel leaped into Zofie's arms. "Indeed. I wouldn't miss this for the world."

Galvyn hung back. I could see him calculating the risk involved. Especially for a woman who outright rejected him.

I turned to him and smiled wickedly. "Not afraid are you?"

That snapped him out of it. He huffed and followed us.

Zofie seemed disappointed he was coming.

We started down the stairs. They were in good shape for having been built a thousand years before. There was some dust, but not what I would have expected. And the myst lights set into the walls at regular intervals would brighten as we approached and then extinguish after we had passed. I couldn't decide if they were showing us the way, or using the light to hold us captive.

After seeming to go down forever, we reached the bottom of the staircase. The myst lanterns that had regularly appeared along the wall, abruptly stopped, as if they too were afraid of what lay ahead. The last few steps were only dimly illuminated with long shadows across the floor and wall. Beyond the last stair, we could make out a large entranceway but could see nothing beyond it, only total darkness.

Zofie was in the lead and paused on the last step. She had been carrying Spraggel, but she put him down on the step beside her. She glanced at us, but no one said anything—all of us afraid to break the silence. She took a deep breath and then stepped forward.

When her foot touched the threshold of the entranceway—the lights went out. We were plunged into total darkness.

Fumiko gave a startled gasp, and Galvyn whispered a curse. I froze in place and immediately reached in my shirt to pull out my amulet. But then I paused. *There had to be a reason for this.* So I waited, and as my eyes adjusted, I saw tiny glints of light shining through the entranceway above us. *Stars?*

One by one they appeared. And as I watched, some of the lights began to take the shape of the constellations I was familiar with. An empyreal tapestry of pin-pricks that was somehow more beautiful than any clear night I had ever seen. Then I started. There were also stars below us. It was extremely disorienting, almost like one was floating in a sea of stars.

Then directly in front of us, far in the distance, easily a couple hundred feet away, a dim glow appeared—a single beam of light shining down from the ceiling. It gradually began to lighten, revealing what looked like a platform with three sarcophagi arranged around its edges. And in the center of them, directly under the light, was a single pedestal.

"The mirror!" I heard Fumiko gasp behind me

Her voice sounded strange to my ears. Muffled even. We were underground and in an enclosed chamber. A big one, but a chamber none the less. There should have been an echo. Yet the sound of Fumiko's voice barely seemed to carry to me. It was almost as if the chamber didn't want to break its long silence.

"It's beautiful," said Zofie beside me. "I felt her hand on my arm."

"Indeed it is." I took a hesitant step into the mass of tiny lights on the ground before me and found it solid.

Spraggel sniffed the air. "It can't be this easy. There has to be another trap."

I took another step forward. "You never know. Maybe we got off easy this time."

"Coren, don't...." warned Zofie.

I took a second step, and then a third... But on the fourth, I made a discovery—there was no ground there.

I fell. And landed in my favorite element.

I plunged into cold seawater and came up spitting and gasping for air. Good thing I wasn't wearing my sword, or I would have been dragged to the bottom.

I floundered in near panic at the deep dark water around me. Galvyn just laughed, content to let me panic. Zofie managed to grab my hand and pull me to the edge. Then with Fumiko's help, I dragged myself out. I lay there panting, dripping wet, and very cold.

I looked back to the edge of the water. The ripples from my plunge caused the field of stars to rock back and forth, showing it was actually the lights from above reflected in the water's surface.

Water. Why did it have to be water? I hoped the Creator was getting a good chuckle out of this.

"Are you all right?" asked Zofie.

Galvyn continued to snicker behind her.

I pulled off my soaked cloak and let it drop beside me. "Other than being totally embarrassed and completely wet," I said. "I'm fine."

Spraggel stepped to the edge. "At least we now know about the water barrier. Now the question is, how do we get across?"

I began to work my way to my feet, and Zofie stood with me.

Fumiko was walking along the water's edge. She had brought her own glow charm: a stick of some sort. After walking a short distance away, she called back to us. "It ends in a wall over here. This ledge goes right up to it."

I walked, dripping all the way, along the edge in the other direction and found the same.

Meeting back in the middle, we considered our situation.

"We could bring the boat from the shore," Zofie offered. "We might be able to talk that sailor into helping us."

Galvyn shook his head. "There is no way he will consent to that. If it were to get stuck down here, we wouldn't be able to get back to the ship." He had sulked all the way down the stairs, but now that I'd embarrassed myself, he seemed to be in a much better mood.

Spraggel slowly strolled around and between us in the frustrating way cats do. He paused and sat on his haunches. "Cats are excellent at navigating in dark spaces, and my senses tell me something about the water doesn't sound right."

"You mean the way the sounds are muffled?"

Spraggel nodded. "Well, there is that, but I sense something else affecting the ripples in the water." He stepped to the edge. He peered down into the depths. "Coren, would you lower your charm into the water? Don't let go of it, of course, just let it dangle below the surface."

I did as he asked, taking off my charm, kneeling, and slowly lowering it into the water. The illumination carried quite well below the surface, allowing us to make out a long shadow, just barely covered and extending toward the platform in the distance.

Spraggel laughed. "Just as I thought. There is a bridge, but it is just under the water. No doubt the level of this mote has risen over the years."

I was already wet, so I thought I would try this out. Holding my charm in front of me, I probed the water with my foot. Barely a toe deep, I felt something firm. I put weight on it and it held. I shuffled further out, carefully probing as I went. There was indeed some type of narrow stone path just under the water, and barely wide enough for someone to walk on. I continued to make my way across it, until I stood four or five paces from the edge. I held my arms out and turned to face my companions. "Come on in the water's fine," I shouted.

Zofie didn't hesitate. She scooped up Spraggel and stepped into the water, making her way toward me. Fumiko went back to the entrance and laid down her book, safely away from the water. Then she followed too.

Galvyn hesitated. He seemed about to balk, but after watching Zofie for a moment, he gingerly stepped out himself.

Fumiko and I held the lights and tried to illuminate the way for the others. The bridge was very narrow with no guards on the side, just a flat pathway. So a misstep could easily send one off the side. I tried to focus on my task and not be distracted by the dark water on either side of us. I didn't want to be embarrassed by another panic attack. I just prayed that we didn't get halfway across and find it broken.

I came to a dark patch in the path and probed it with my foot. I wanted to make sure it wasn't a break. But it proved to be just some kind of seaweed. That's when I noticed ripples on the water. And they seemed to be coming from my right side. I held the light in that direction but didn't see anything.

Odd. I wonder what stirred the water.

I turned to face my companions.

My mouth fell open and my eyes went up. Behind us was the biggest crab I had ever seen. It easily towered twice over us. I opened my mouth to give a shout.

But it beat me to it. The creature gave a high screeching yell and moved to attack.

CHAPTER SIXTEEN

The Mirror

T he fact it moved so quietly to get behind us had to be due to the weird acoustics of the chamber. The thing was huge—and unlike any smaller crab I had seen. Its body was too short to be a lobster, yet longer than a typical crab. It had a distinctive head with antenna and spikes surrounding it while its mouth stayed in constant motion, opening and closing. But it's most prominent feature was its giant claws, covered in sharp spikes and huge in proportion to its body. They could easily snap a person in half. It clung to the pathway using three of its legs.

Galvyn wheeled and drew his sword. Zofie put Spraggel down and did the same. I reached for mine but realized that I had left it at the entrance to hold the door open. I pulled out my knife instead. Wouldn't be the first time I'd fought without a sword.

As we took defensive positions, Spraggel made a strategic retreat, and Fumiko wisely followed, moving carefully around us. The path was barely large enough for her to pass. Which also meant we could only be able to attack the creature one at a time.

"Let's try backing away from it," called Zofie.

We began a slow retreat, but the creature screeched and moved forward, reaching for Galvyn.

The young man stepped toward it and swung his sword, landing a solid blow. However, it bounced off the creature's hard shell, not even making a scratch. Galvyn switched strategies and aimed for the head. The creature moved faster than I would have thought and batted the sword away with its huge claw. Galvyn attacked it again, but the creature simply grabbed his sword and yanked it out of his hands. I heard the blade snap in its huge claws.

Disarmed, Galvyn tried to step back as the crab swung a huge claw to bat him aside. Unfortunately, Galvyn lost his footing and one of the spikes covering the monster's claws caught him in the stomach. Zofie caught the young man as he fell and dragged him back.

Blood welled up from the wound and spilled into the water around us. The wound looked deep, and he was losing a lot of blood.

"Curse him!" Zofie shouted.

I didn't understand at first. I thought she was angry at him getting hit. But when I looked up at her, she was focusing on his wound.

"Do it quickly!" she tried to stuff some of his shirt into the wound. "Curse him to be some inanimate object. It will freeze his current state. We can remove the curse later when we have physicians to fix him." She then stood and began to swing at the beast herself.

A light went off in my head. Of course. All the people I had stolen curses from had resumed living where they left off. Time had quickly caught up with them, but with the right doctors and myst users, it might be possible to save someone. But with Abe being broken, I could only pray that it worked.

Galvyn shook his head weakly. "No," he whispered. "I'll kill you if you do. I'd rather die."

"Then kill me later," I said. I put a hand on his arm. "I curse you to become Havoc's Sword."

Immediately a blue glow sprung up around him. He rapidly transformed into the deadly sword I was familiar with—one that could cut through anything. I noticed it glowed a faint blue in the dim light, a testament to its power. I picked it up and stepped behind Zofie, where she was furiously fending off the creature's claws.

The giant crab gave a frustrated hiss and snapped forward. Zofie shifted to avoid and slipped. I pulled her against me and swung the sword at the same time. For once, luck was with me and I caught the giant just right. The attacking limb was cleanly sliced off.

The crab screeched and leaped into the water, submerging out of sight. Zofie leaned against me breathing hard, seeming reluctant to move. "Do you think... it will be back?" she asked.

"I don't think Crabbie will return soon, but we should stay alert."

"Crabbie?" She gave me a puzzled look. "Where did that come from?"

I shrugged. "The name just seemed to fit."

Zofie shook her head.

Then her eye caught the sword. She straightened and reached for my hand. She guided me to hold the sword up in front of her. "Galvyn, I'm sorry to do this to you, but it was the only way to save your life. I hope you'll forgive me."

I gave her a puzzled look. "Why are you taking responsibility? I'm the one that put the curse on him."

She touched my cheek. "Father always told me that I was ultimately responsible for my orders, not my subjects. And I was the one that commanded you to do it."

"I could have refused."

Her hand stayed on my face as she considered me. "True. I'm glad you didn't." A slow grin came to her face. "Disobeying this princess will have severe consequences."

I smiled. "I'm not afraid to die."

She leaned closer a twinkle in her eye. "There are some fates worse than death."

"Come look what I found," Fumiko yelled. We looked in her

direction, where she waved excitedly on the platform. She had already traveled the rest of the bridge.

Spraggel was beside her, shaking the water from his legs. "Indeed, it is quite remarkable."

We quickly covered the rest of the bridge and joined them up on the raised platform. The platform itself—just a hand's-breadth above the surrounding water—was roughly oval in shape and appeared to be carved out of the same stone as the floor and walls. Arranged around the edge were three stone sarcophagi—each an oblong square—made of light gray granite and engraved with simple square shapes. A thick stone slab covered each, and I judged one far heavier than all of us put together could lift. I prayed that whoever made their final rest inside them, stayed asleep.

In the very center of the platform, a slender, cylindrical pedestal rose from the floor—almost a high table—made of highly polished white marble and elegantly carved in an intricate weaving pattern. A single bright myst light shone down on it from above. On the stand, resting in a shallow impression, was a shiny black orb just slightly smaller than my fist. Its darkness was in sharp contrast to the white marble, seeming to almost eat the light touching it.

"Is that the Mirror of Bygone Tears?" I asked in disbelief. "It looks more like a piece of obsidian than a mirror."

Fumiko snorted. "Mirrors come in all kinds of shapes and can be made from many materials. Obsidian used to be popular because it was so shiny."

Zofie couldn't take her eyes off it. "Obsidian in jewelry means truth," she said reverently.

Spraggel, having reclaimed his perch in Zofie's arms, also chimed in. "And it used to be made into weapons. It could be made very sharp."

I looked at them. "So can we just take it and go?" I reached a hand for it.

Fumiko slapped it aside. "There is likely some kind of trap. Legends say it's protected."

Zofie stooped over to bring it to eye level. "Yes, I see it—a faint myst glow around it, which means an active spell. You can't see the glow because the overhead light washes it out. No telling what it will do."

"We have this." I raised Havoc's Sword. "It could cut through any protections."

Spraggel shook his head. "Not very wise. I'd use that sparingly. Remember what happened when that blade and Ruin's Shield were used against each other. The irresistible force against the impenetrable object. It nearly killed us all."

Fumiko began examining the stand, circling it. She paused on the far side. "I think there is a better way to unlock it."

We moved to join her and saw the pedestal had another part on the back, not readily visible from the front. A small square of marble extended out from it. Imbedded in the square was the imprint of a life-sized hand, as if someone had pushed it into the marble. But the real surprise was on the wrist of the impression. It was a symbol I knew quite well.

"That's my curse!"

Fumiko nodded. "Indeed it is."

"So you think my curse can open the protections on it."

Fumiko nodded. "Remember when I first joined you, I said you were the key to getting the mirror." She took my hand and turned it over so we could see my curse mark. "According to the texts, the original Thief of Curses was responsible for hiding the mirror. Something about it being too powerful to leave loose in the world."

"But," I protested. "It just shows people's pasts. How can it be too powerful?"

Fumiko grew serious. "Because it can show the past of any living myst user. It could be some deep, dark secret that no one is supposed to know. And it will show it to everyone present when the device is started. No secret is safe. Also, it doesn't have to be the person who requests the information. You can look into *anyone's* past."

I shrugged. "So it shows my deepest secret. I might be embarrassed, but it won't kill me. That still doesn't seem like something powerful enough to go to all this trouble."

Fumiko looked to Zofie. "Ask the princess. She knows the power of secrets."

Zofie looked uncomfortable. "Let's get this over with. We should get back before the captain leaves us."

"So what should I do?" I asked.

Fumiko shrugged. "I guess you put your hand in the impression. It should open the protections." She held out her hand. "I'll hold Galvyn... er... Havoc's Sword for you."

I handed it to her and then stood nervously before the handprint. I licked my lips. I glanced at Zofie, Spraggel, and then Fumiko holding Havoc's Sword. For some reason, I felt uneasy. It couldn't be this simple, could it?

I looked back down at the impression. This place must just be getting to me. "All right. Here we go."

I aligned my hand and wrist with the impression and pressed down. The stone was cool to my skin and smoother than I expected. And nothing immediately happened. I looked up at my companions and opened my mouth to speak, but I never got that far.

Suddenly, my world changed. I was standing in a place of all gray: everything around me, as far as the eye could see, was a dull color— like a thick fog on a brightly lit morning. And it was deadly quiet—as if sound didn't exist there. My eyes went wide. This was a place I had been in before when I had attempted to separate the shield and sword during their fight.

It was the place curses lived.

Standing before me was a stick-figure, the kind a child might draw to represent a person, with nothing more than lines for arms, legs, and body. But the head was different. It was larger than a normal man's, perfectly round, and contained the image of the pedestal. The figure was close enough that I could make out all the intricate details of the picture. And if I looked really closely, I could almost make out tiny gears moving inside it.

The being seemed to be waiting for me. "So you are the new Thief of Curses," it said, which was surprising since it had no mouth. "I am

honored to meet you. I have slumbered long awaiting your arrival."
He paused and considered me for a moment before continuing. "But
unfortunately, something is not quite right. Abhulengulus is not able
to greet me." The thing gestured off to one side, and I saw lying on
the ground another stick figure curled up as one sleeping on their
side. The symbol inside its large head was of the stylized eye on my
wrist. Only the eye was closed. I could also see the tiny gears inside,
but they were either not moving or moving so slowly my eyes couldn't
detect them.

"Abe said he thought he was broke."

The figure shook its head. I couldn't say where I got the impression,
but I felt he was sad.

"He is not broken," the being said. "Something is interfering with
his running."

"Interfering?"

"Indeed. And you do not have the secret word to help him. Which
means I can't truly justify you having the mirror. I hope you'll forgive
me. I do not do what I wish, but what I was made to do."

"No!" I shouted, suddenly finding myself back in my body beside
the pedestal.

Immediately, the heavy stone lids to the sarcophagi slid back and
fell heavily to the floor. A life-size statue of gold sat up in each of them.
They were human-shaped, with elongated head and limbs, but without
any facial features—just a smooth expressionless head. They bore no
weapons because the hands of each ended in a single sharp spike. To
my horror, they quickly climbed out to face us.

Spraggel leaped from Zofie's arms and moved to stand beside
Fumiko. He shook his head. "Animated stone statues protecting the
mirror. Such a cliché. They could have been a little more original."

Zofie drew her sword and squared off with the one closest her. The
golden man paused only a moment before attacking, using both arms
as one would swords.

Fumiko didn't hesitate to use Havoc's Sword, quickly cutting the
approaching golden figure into pieces which fell at her feet. She looked

back at the rest of us with a strange satisfaction in her eye.

I pulled out my knife and prepared to fend off the monster's blows as best I could. "Fumiko!" I yelled. "The sword!"

And then she did the strangest thing.

She reached across the pedestal, plucked up the mirror and stuck it in her purse. Then she grabbed Spraggel, tucked the surprised cat under her arm, and ran back across the bridge.

"Fumiko!" I called. Thinking perhaps she was trying to get Spraggel to safety. But then she paused about halfway across the lake, raised the sword and struck down behind her into the water several times, before continuing her run to the other side. Where she had struck, the dark water began to churn, and I felt a rumble through my feet. My eyes went large. Fumiko had just destroyed the bridge.

But I couldn't watch her. The golden man was stabbing and slicing at me. I blocked with my knife and dodged under his follow-through. Its movements were slow but deliberate. I couldn't help but feel it was herding me as I carefully backed around toward Zofie.

Zofie's golden man was quicker than mine and was raining blows down on Zofie faster than I could follow. I heard her suck breath and step away from her opponent. She held a gash on her side. I could see blood leaking around it.

This was not looking good. In the distance, I could see Fumiko reach the entrance. She retrieved her sack, stuffed Spraggel into it, and fled through the open door, slicing the supports as she ran back up the stairs. The chamber shook as that portion of the cavern collapsed. The golden men staggered and paused for a moment allowing Zofie and I to turn back to back. But the respite only lasted a moment before the golden men resumed their slow advance.

"Coren," said Zofie. Her back pressed up to mine. "I'm sorry I got you into this."

"Don't apologize. I don't regret my decision one bit."

She sighed. "In case this is the end, I wanted to tell you that... I love you. I have from the moment I first saw you."

"You say that *now*?" I yelled in surprise.

She didn't wait for a reply. She shoved off from me and squared off with her opponent.

Mine closed on me, and I didn't think my knife was going to be able to counter the attack that was coming. I prayed to the Creator for something, *anything* to happen.

And it did.

COREN! Shouted Abe in my head. *What the hell are you doing? Why are we in the cavern of the mirror? And why the hell are they trying to kill you!*

I grinned. Abe was back. I could steal a curse now. I leaned forward and touched the gold man. "Your curse is my curse!"

But nothing happened. And the golden man raised his arm to strike.

Stupid. It's charmed, not cursed. That won't help at all!

"Then I'm about to die."

He chuckled. *You wish.*

Suddenly, I heard a deafening screech, and a giant claw closed around the golden man. The crab beast had climbed up on to the platform and appeared none too happy that something was messing with its lunch. It dragged the golden man off into the depths with it.

Apparently, Abe's ability to influence my luck was operating again. "Abe, I could almost kiss you," I said.

Now that is disgusting!

I immediately wheeled and blocked a blow heading toward Zofie. Just then, the crab monster reappeared and grabbed the other golden man, dragging him off the platform.

Holding her side, Zofie collapsed against me. I quickly pulled her to one of the now open sarcophagi and peered inside. It was thankfully just an empty stone box. I swept her into my arms and placed her inside. I then climbed in beside her. It was large for a coffin, but still a tight fit for two people.

Zofie was breathing hard and holding her side. She was bleeding a lot—her shirt was soaked.

"Stay still," I whispered. I took the sword from her bloody fingers.

As I suspected, the crab beast reappeared, apparently finding the golden men not to its taste. I could hear its legs clicking against the stone of the platform as it searched for us. I gripped Zofie's sword in my hand, still wet from her blood. At one point, I could see it over the sarcophagus lip as it searched for us.

But for some reason, it didn't think to look inside the box. After searching for several minutes, I heard it slip back into the water. I raised up to check if it was gone and could only see ripples where it had entered the water.

Zofie was looking pale, and she was starting to shiver. She was going into shock.

I pushed a strand of sweaty hair out of her face. "You know what I've got to do, don't you?"

She nodded and shut her eyes.

"Abhulengulus," I said. "Trigger Zofie's transformation."

As you wish.

The blue glow of her transformation curse enveloped her, and she tensed at the sudden pain. Her curse was set to force a transformation whenever she was wounded—to make sure she lived to suffer. I had only accelerated it. The part where I shared her pain was also still active, and it hit me with a vengeance. I ached along with her, but neither of us dared to make a sound.

In moments, it had completed and the blue glow left us. It may have been rude of me, but I held Zofie in my arms as she recovered. Based on what she told me a few moments ago, I didn't think she would mind.

Zofie reached up and touched my face. "Thank you," she whispered.

I shook my head. "Thank me when we get out of this," I said softly.

Through our shared connection, I could feel her rapidly beating heart, the stickiness of the drying blood on her side, and the hard stone pressing into her hip. There was something else too. A kind of contented feeling. It strangely mirrored my own.

We lay there side by side for a moment. I finally broke the silence. "I can't believe Fumiko betrayed us. I thought she was our friend."

Zofie nodded. "As did I. We talked a lot on the ship. I thought of us as having grown close. To think she stole the mirror. I know I should be angry, but I can't help feeling just... sad."

I nodded. "I know what you mean. Do you think she was working for your brother?"

Zofie sighed. "I'm not sure. It could be she just has plans to sell it. It could fetch a high price to the right buyer."

I shook my head. "That just doesn't sound right. She was an apprentice like me, and you don't go that route if you want riches. Plus, why did she also take Spraggel? I can't help but feel we're missing something."

I sighed. "I don't know how we're going to get out of this one. And we need to do it quickly, or the ship will leave without us."

Zofie turned my face to hers. "We'll figure out something. And as for your performance, I think you did quite well. You saved my life yet again."

I smiled. "And you didn't do too bad yourself. Risten would have been proud of the way you fought Crabbie."

And I realized just how close we were inside that stone box. I felt her heart rate accelerate as we looked into each other eyes. Her lips were so close to mine. I leaned toward her...

Suddenly, the light illuminating the platform went out, plunging us into total darkness.

"Creator! What else is going to happen?"

And right on cue, I got my answer. *Coren!* yelled Abe in my head so loud I thought my brain was going to shake apart. *We need to talk!*

I groaned. "Abe, I don't have time for this. I've got a little thief to catch, and a boat I don't want to miss, so stay quiet unless you have a suggestion on how to get out."

Well, as a matter of fact, I do know a way to escape. But if you're going to be that way about it, I'll just keep it to myself.

"Escape? You know another way out?"

Not... talk... ing. You blew me off.

"Abe, tell me what it is?"

Is that the way you talk to someone who has something you want? You insulted me!

I drew in a frustrated breath. "I'm sorry I got upset with you. Will you please tell me how to get out of here?"

That's better. But I'm not sure you mean it.

"Abe!" I said in frustration.

Oh, all right. Now this bit of information falls under the heading of keeping your ass intact. Notice how all this water has been in this cave for a long time. Doesn't it seem a little fresh for that? Fresh enough at least to keep that giant crab alive and give it something to eat.

"So you're saying there's an underwater link to the ocean."

Yes, monkey brains. That is exactly what I mean.

I heard water moving and then the click of claws on stone. It was pitch black, so I couldn't see where the giant crab was. I held my breath as it moved around the platform. I heard clicks right beside our stone box and felt that at any moment, it might strike out at us. But the clicks moved on and then I heard the faint sound of water.

I turned to Zofie. "We need a way to explore under the water. Abe says there is a connection to the ocean. We could swim down, but we don't know how deep the water is or when Crabbie might decide to show up."

"I know how," said Zofie. "But it's risky."

"With Crabbie out there, I'll consider risky."

She took a deep breath. "I shouldn't even suggest this, but I'm between transformations. I could encircle us with a myst shield with enough air to stay underwater for a short while. But I'd have to draw myst from you. And the last time we did something like this, I almost killed you."

"Well, staying here isn't doing us any good either. If you think you can do it, then I say let's try it."

"I will do my best not to take too much." She thought for a moment. "Unfortunately, the bubble I form will want to float because of the air inside. So I'll need something really heavy to pull us under the water."

"You mean something as heavy as a stone box."

She patted my arm. "I like the way you think, but we'll still need something to push us into the water."

I sat up and took her hand, pulling her to sit beside me. "Get your bubble ready. I know just how to get things going." I pulled out my amulet which seemed extraordinarily bright after being in the total darkness for so long. "Hey, Crabbie!" I shouted. "We need a little help here!" I banged on the side of the box.

I didn't have to do this long before I heard the sound of water moving outside the range of my light. A few moments later, the giant crab came into view. It skittered right toward us, waving its one remaining claw.

I settled back down into the box.

Zofie squeezed my hand tightly, and I felt a tug in my chest. Around us sprang up a sphere glowing a gentle blue and large enough to hold the sarcophagus. Simultaneously came a loud popping sound as the sphere engulfed the stone box and a circular shaped piece of the ground underneath.

The crab seemed unaware that anything had happened. It charged forward and ran right smack into it. We rocked forward, up the side of the depression left in the ground, but it wasn't enough to push us over the edge. We settled back into the hole.

I stood and waved my arms. "Come on, big boy. I know you got more in you than that!"

The crab screeched and charged again, hitting the sphere with more force. The bubble moved, teetered at the depression's lip for a moment, and then began to roll. The frustrated crab shoved on it again, and we began to move toward the edge of the platform. I looked over the side of our box and saw that the myst shield had cleanly cut through the supports holding the sarcophagus in such a way to keep our box upright as the sphere rolled. The crab hit us one more time, which was enough to push us off the edge of the platform.

We fell a few inches, hit the water, and started to sink. But to my surprise, we stopped with the top part of the bubble still above water—

we still floated despite the fact we were sitting on a piece of solid stone. I heard water gurgling below us, and I looked over the edge. Panic hit full force.

"We're taking on water!"

"I know," Zofie said calmly. She gave my hand a reassuring squeeze. "We're still too light, so I need to take on a little water to make us sink. Don't worry. I got this. Now be quiet a moment and let me concentrate. I want to take on just enough to go below the surface, but not enough to send us to the bottom."

Gradually we sank deeper, with the last of the surface disappearing overhead. And it hit me that I was sinking into all this deep, dark water. The same black water that had killed my father.

I was going to die.

I suddenly couldn't breathe. I'd been exposed to so much deep water lately, I thought I was over my fear. But it was still there, waiting to grab me. I looked up wide-eyed as we moved deeper, my hands shaking. It took all of my willpower not to leap up and claw at the sphere. I turned panicked eyes in Zofie's direction, and I suddenly realized she could feel my fear through our link. She would know how cowardly I really was.

Instead, she squeezed my arm. "I know you're afraid, Coren, and it's all right. You've shared my pain, let me share your fear."

I swallowed and slowly nodded.

She took my hand and placed it over her heart. "Focus on my breathing. Feel my lungs slowly expand and then slowly release. Feel my heartbeat and let yours match mine." Zofie pulled back to smile at me.

I looked at her wild-eyed, not sure I could do what she asked. *Air! I needed air!* And I then I felt something come back through our shared link. A calmness. A tenderness. Acceptance. And gradually, I felt my fear ease. It didn't go away, but I took comfort in the steady beat of Zofie's heart and the feelings she was sharing. I couldn't help but wonder how she could be so strong.

When I had some semblance of control, Zofie put her arms around me. "Don't be afraid, my brave knight. I'm here with you."

"I don't feel very brave." My voice shook as I spoke.

She gave me a squeeze and quoted from one of those accursed epics she reads. *"One that stares into Death's eyes and doesn't feel fear is a fool."* She paused for me to finish it.

I knew the quote. *"However, the one that stares and trembles in fear, yet continues to stare, is truly brave."*

She looked up and pointed off into the water. "Look how beautiful it is."

The blue light the sphere emitted increased in brightness. Beyond, I could see fish swimming, attracted by the light of Zofie's sphere. They nibbled at the outside thinking it was some kind of new food. She increased the brightness some more, and I could even see the bottom—an eel swam just over the surface. I knew it was just to distract me, but it was working.

Zofie's comfort with being in the water made me suspicious. "You've been underwater before, haven't you?" I asked.

She nodded. "Mistress Ginneley, my myst teacher, insisted I learn this in case I should ever be in deep water. I learned how to enclose myself early on." She smiled. "Plus it gave Risten and I an excuse to go swimming when my bubble would accidentally fail."

Suddenly something slammed into the sphere again. Our crab swam just outside, still determined to eat us.

"So how do we find this hole in the cavern?"

"Well, I was hoping the current would pull us toward it. I've been adjusting the size of our bubble to make us float levelly in the water, but other than our pet crab pushing us, we don't seem to be making much progress."

I thought for a moment. "What if you extinguish all the lights. It should be late-afternoon outside now. Maybe we can see the light from it?"

Zofie looked at me like I was crazy. "I can't do that. Whenever myst is working, it always has a glow." She thought for a moment. "But I might be able to change its color." She shut her eyes.

A moment later, the light shifted to yellow, back to blue, and then a purple. It finally moved to a deep purple. "How's that?"

"Not so good," I answered, the color was rough on the eyes, but still too bright.

I considered the bubble for a moment. I had read about a strange theory in one of Spraggel's books that talked about colors we couldn't see. I had always wondered about that.

"Zofie, what if you keep changing the color beyond purple."

"Beyond purple? How can I change it to something that doesn't exist?"

"Trust me."

"All right." She refocused on her task, and the light changed—going to a deep purple, then a very deep, almost black-purple, until it finally disappeared from sight.

"You did it!"

I put my amulet away, and we waited for our eyes to adjust. Out pet crab slammed into the sphere and let us know it was still out there.

Then I saw it. A very faint glow coming from our right. I pointed it out to Zofie, and we began to move toward it. I asked her how she was doing that, and she mentioned it was something to do with the shape of the bubble and rising and falling.

Our pet crab would help us along occasionally, shoving us in the right direction. We found the hole and it turned out to be man-sized—and thankfully too small for our crab friend.

It was also too small for the sarcophagus.

Zofie studied it for a moment. She rubbed the temples of her head. She must be feeling it too. For the last little bit, I had noticed a headache creeping up the back of my head. The air inside with us was going bad.

Zofie sighed. "I'm not exactly sure what to do? I was hoping the hole was bigger. I can drop out the sarcophagus, but then we'll float straight up. I could also just drop the bubble, and we could swim through, but

I have no idea how far the surface is above us. We might not make it."

"Could you extend your bubble through the hole and allow us to crawl through it?"

She looked at me indignantly. "Do you realize how difficult that is? The bubble naturally wants to be a sphere. When I warp it into other shapes, it takes all the concentration I have to hold it." She rubbed her eyes. "Plus, every time I do something like that, I draw from your myst. I don't want to nearly kill you like I did last time. Forcing a tube shape is going to be difficult."

"What choice do you have?"

She sighed. "Your logic is so frustrating sometimes."

I grinned. "Glad I'm good for something."

She took a deep breath. "The air in here isn't helping. I'm having trouble focusing."

She held up a hand, and the end of the bubble began to extend through the hole. Zofie crawled toward it. "I need to go first to see how to direct it. But stay close to me. I don't know how long I can hold this shape."

Zofie moved first and squeezed into the bubble tube, and I followed directly behind her. Crawling through it was difficult because the bubble itself had very little friction, almost like glass, and was also a little springy. Suddenly, I bumped my head on Zofie's behind.

"Coren, I'm at my limit. Are you close enough that I can drop the sarcophagus?"

"I believe so."

"Good." I immediately felt the edge of the bubble touch the ends of my toes.

We continued through and reached the other side, then Zofie reformed the bubble for us to float up. But without our ballast, we went up rather explosively from the deeper water just outside the island's reef, blasting upward a good twenty feet above the ocean's surface.

For those few dizzying seconds we were airborne, we had a very good view of the island's reef and the shore beyond it. Zofie did something to help us soften our landing, but it still hurt.

She opened the top of the bubble to let in fresh air which never tasted so good. The headache and fuzziness immediately began to fade.

Zofie collapsed in exhaustion and rubbed her temples. Directing the myst like that must have taken a lot out of her.

"Are you all right?" I asked.

She looked up at me with one eye closed. "Just tired and a splitting headache. I'm a little out of practice in the more advanced myst workings. Nothing that a good night's sleep won't cure." She sat up. "How about you? Feeling tired or weak?"

I shrugged. "A headache, same as you, but I feel mostly fine."

Her eyes narrowed. "Curious. You seem to have an inexhaustible supply of myst. However, that one time on the ship something happened to it."

"Abe has been saying he's broken. Although the pedestal curse told me that something was actually interfering with the way he works."

Zofie seemed intrigued. "Was there a pattern to him not working? Was it at a certain time, or were you doing something?"

I shrugged. "I think it might have something to do with Lady Autumn's charm."

Zofie shook her head. "Charms and curses are two different things. One shouldn't affect the other." She leaned against the side of our bubble and rubbed her temple again. "Maybe we should talk about this later when the hammers in my head stop."

I looked around us. We were a good ways out from shore. With the sun setting low on the horizon next to the island, that placed us on the eastern side. The ship should be close by. Of course, the current was pulling us further out to sea. "We had better figure out how we can get back to shore and then back to the ship. You're going to need to transform again tonight, so we can't stay in the bubble too much longer."

But she didn't answer. She was looking at something behind me. She squinted and shaded her eyes, looking into the distance. Then her face broke into utter disbelief. "No, no, *NO!* It can't be." She leaped to her feet, the bubble beneath us rocking.

"What?" I turned.

At first, I didn't see anything, just the ocean stretching to the horizon. But then I spotted it. A long way out in the ocean was a ship, with sails billowing out in the wind and heading away from us.

It was the *Wily Lass*. They had left without us.

I breathed a sigh of disappointment and turned back to Zofie.

Tears were running down her cheeks. My ever-smiling, maddingly intelligent, and unbelievably resourceful princess was crying.

"They left," she said simply. "We'll never get home now. Galvyn will be a sword forever. And I'll never get my kingdom back." Her legs failed her, and she crumpled to her knees—her face screwed up and she openly wept.

I didn't know what to do, so I took her in my arms and she cried into my shoulder, her hot tears soaking into my shirt.

"I've failed!" she moaned. "I've let them all down! All my people. All my friends. Everyone I've cared about!" She sobbed a bit more. "And Father will never have justice."

I stroked her hair as she cried it out. My princess had finally reached the end of her rope. After all, she was only human. I wondered how long she had been holding in her fears. Afraid to even admit them, lest they come true.

And so she sobbed for a good quarter-hour, and I just quietly held her, the calm sea gently rocking us. And even though she was racked with sobs, she managed to keep her half-bubble together so we did not drown. I was filled with admiration. She was so strong, and I tried to share the feeling with her through our common link.

It must have worked because she finally sat up and rubbed her eyes. She was quite a sight. Her hair mussed, her eyes red, her nose running, and her shirt ripped and covered in blood. But I couldn't help but smile at her. I tilted her chin up and gazed into her eyes.

"We'll figure something out. We always do."

I raised my head at a faraway sound. A soft thumping. Where had I heard that before? Zofie heard it too and glanced at me in concern.

We looked toward the sound which came from the direction of the setting sun. But being so low on the horizon, it was difficult to make out anything in the glare. Then a shadow caught my eye. I held my breath in fear as the shadow resolved into something entirely unexpected coming around the edge of the island.

A large ship was speeding toward us, the thumping sound getting louder as it approached. Only this wasn't the ship we had arrived on. In fact, it was one we had tried to avoid.

It was the sea wraith.

CHAPTER SEVENTEEN

The Sea Wraith
Returns

Zofie stared in disbelief. "How did it find us?"

"Probably my curse trying to make sure we don't drown. But I really have to question its methods this time." I looked at her. "I don't suppose there is a way to quickly get to shore?"

She sniffled and wiped the last of her tears on her shirt sleeve. "I'm exhausted, and I don't dare try to reshape this bubble into something that could maneuver—it's all I can do to just hold it together."

I sighed and looked back to the approaching ship. It was nearly upon us. "Any suggestions on what we should do?"

"Smile."

I looked at her. "You're kidding, right?"

She shrugged. "You have a better idea? Maybe the stories about them are all wrong. Father always taught me that when entering a tough negotiation, be sure to smile. Sometimes, it's the only weapon you have."

So with no other choice, Zofie and I plastered smiles on our faces and waved to the approaching ship.

The sun was almost below the horizon by the time it reached us. And the vessel was much larger than I thought. You could have lined up three ships the size of the *Wily Lass* and *still* had some left over.

As we had seen earlier, it had no sails, yet it moved at a decent clip. It slowed as it drew up with us—our bubble bobbing in its huge wake. Then with a tremendous churning of water behind it, the ship came to an almost complete stop.

"Ahoy, two-person craft," called an emotionless female voice. "You will board our ship, or we will sink you. Decide quickly." She then repeated it in two other languages. It boomed from the ship above which meant some kind of myst amplification.

A rope was thrown to us, and I used it to draw up with the ship's hull. We then climbed up a rope ladder to the deck.

While the sun gave up its last rays and sank behind the horizon, the deck stayed brightly lit from powerful myst lights just overhead. Surrounding us were four women all wearing basically the same thing: black pants, coming only down to the knees, and white short-sleeved shirts that molded tightly to their bodies and left their well-muscled arms bare. I surmised it was some kind of uniform, but one that did little to hide their feminine forms. I couldn't help but blush.

Two of them held swords at ready, and from their manner, I had no doubt they knew how to use them. Beside them stood a younger female with arms folded across her chest. I thought it odd that she had a large gray feather just stuck behind her right ear. She looked at us with a haughty expression as if daring us to do something.

The remaining female was older, with a few streaks of gray in her hair and large silver loops hanging from her ears. She seemed to be the one in charge.

"What language do you speak?" the leader asked in lightly accented Ellish.

I opened my mouth, but Zofie answered first. And she was in full bore princess mode. I had seen her do this before—her demeanor demanded respect. "Ellish is fine. Andronise or Urticia will also do."

The woman grinned. "Declare your weapons now. If we find any on you later, we'll kill you. Don't think to test us because we ran out of humor several days ago."

Zofie stood her ground. "Will we get them back?"

The leader sighed. "Does it matter?"

Zofie cocked her head to one side. "Indeed it does. I claim noble rite of passage. You will properly store and return our weapons to us. Then treat us with the respect of our station."

The woman frowned, clearly not liking being ordered around. She stepped forward and grabbed Zofie by the throat. "We do not honor your barbaric customs."

Zofie smiled. "Then perhaps you will honor my blade."

The woman returned the smile. "Do you challenge me?"

"Only if I have to."

The two women glared at each other a moment more before the leader shoved Zofie back and released her. "Turn over your weapons now, and I will make sure they're set aside for you."

Zofie unbuckled her sword and handed it to her, as well as her knife. My sword was either still on the island or Fumiko had taken it, so all I had was my knife. The leader passed the weapons to the nearer of the two guards.

The leader stepped back, and the young woman with the feather came forward. She plucked the item from her hair and held it up in my direction. She closed one eye and used it to sight toward us. "He carries a curse and is not a myst user. He's got a broken light charm, plus another much more powerful charm...."

There was a spark and she yelped, releasing the feather. She frowned and shook out her hand. "The charm is protected. I hate those." She bent down to pick up her feather. "Whoever gave it to him is very powerful, but the charm appears to be dormant."

She then turned toward Zofie and held up the feather again. "Despite the blood on her shirt, she is not wounded. She is a master class myst user and also carries some kind of transformation curse.

She's harmless though, since it has drained her powers. She is also wearing a charmed ring..." Her eyes flew open. "It's the Blue Lavender ring!" She turned to the leader in confusion. "And it's active."

The leader wheeled on Zofie. "Show me your hands! *Now!*"

Taken aback, Zofie did as she was told.

The leader bent to examine them. Zofie only wore her mother's ring which is what the leader seized on. "Where did you get this ring?"

"It was my mother's, recently returned to me by my knight. It had been stolen and missing for several years."

The leader looked up and seemed to study her. Her voice softened. "What was your mother's name?"

"Her name before marrying my father was Winstella Scurrlocke."

All the bravo from the leader suddenly left her. She looked at Zofie and seemed to see her for the first time. She gently reached out and touched a loose strand of Zofie's hair. "And your mother. Where is she?"

"She died bearing my brother when I was but a small child."

The woman nodded as if confirming something she already knew. "And what is your name?"

"Princess Zophia Olwenna Xernow."

"Olwenna?" The woman blinked in surprise. She thought for a moment and then motioned us forward. "Come with me."

The leader stepped toward the ship's central tower. Zofie and I exchanged a glance and followed, with the other women coming behind us.

We entered through a door and then went up a series of steps until we reached the top. Inside was some kind of wheelhouse with thick glass on the fore and open to the outside on the sides. It was well lit from several myst lanterns affixed to the ceiling. Several young women were inside with one standing before a ship's wheel and two others poring over a table with a map—a large dial was next to it which I assumed was a compass. There were gauges and valves across one wall painted in a variety of reds, yellows, and greens.

Sitting to one side of the wheelhouse in a well-stuffed chair was an older woman wearing a long tunic and black pants. Her silver hair was cut short like the others, and she too had long earrings. Only hers were gold. While she appeared frail, her eyes were sharp and focused as she looked out the open window at the multicolored horizon—the sun had just settled beyond it. She spoke without looking. "What fish did you catch today, Captain? At least one keeper, I hope?"

So the woman escorting us was the captain of this vessel. That explained the air of authority.

The captain moved in front of the elder, standing erect, head up, and placing both her hands behind her back. "We have indeed found something unusual today." She nodded toward us.

The elder's eyes roved slowly in our direction and examined us critically. I felt like a fish looking at the fisherman that had just caught me, wondering if I was going to be released or eaten.

The captain motioned toward Zofie. "This woman wears the beacon. She is claiming noble rite of passage and says her mother's name was... Winstella."

It was like all motion in the room ceased—none daring to move. Even the woman standing in front of the ship's wheel stayed perfectly still—eyes forward, head straight, holding her breath. The elder looked like she had just bitten into a very sour fruit. She considered Zofie for several moments while I wondered what the hell was going on.

"Winstella," the elder said, feeling out the sound of the name in her mouth. "That's a name I haven't heard in some while." She considered Zofie a moment more, flicked her eyes to the captain before returning the gaze out the windows to the front. She settled into her seat. "I'm surprised at you, bringing such to me."

The captain's face grew red. "I thought you might be interested to know of her legacy, Mother."

"You forget your place, Captain!" spat the elder. "On this bridge, I am the *Guardian*, as you well know." The elder flicked her hand in dismissal. "I know of no Winstella."

The captain gave a stiff nod and then motioned for us to leave.

The elder spoke after her. "Also, treat her as you would any of the dross. She is nothing special."

The captain cocked her jaw and then, without another word, directed us out. Zofie tried to ask her about the elder, but the captain refused to talk. We were taken down the stairs and into the ship's interior to what appeared to be a brig—having several empty stalls barely large enough for someone to lay down in. The front and sides of the stalls were open, but secured by iron bars. These too were lit with overhead myst lanterns. Zofie and I were put in separate cells and locked in.

The captain turned to leave with her escort close on her heels. "Someone will be down to see to you shortly."

"Please captain," called Zofie. "What was that exchange with the elder about? And what does it have to do with my mother?"

The captain stood stiffly for a moment. "You have brought unrest to my ship. I suggest you remain quiet and not cause problems for the crew. I mean you no harm, but it will not go well for you if you do."

"But..."

"Silence!" she shouted, then lowered her voice. "No more. I have duties to attend to." She sighed. "And you must address me properly. My name is Captain Olwenna Scurrlocke."

Zofie's eyes went large.

The captain nodded. "Indeed, the family name is the same, as is your middle one. That's because your mother was my older sister. And the little devil named you after me."

After the captain had departed, we were left alone for a while. The thumping that had paused while picking us up resumed, so I assumed we were moving again.

Zofie clung to her cell's bars and rebuffed my attempts at conversation, saying she wanted to think for a bit. She seemed a little shocked she had relatives among the sea wraiths. Of course, I might be too.

I, on the other hand, looked around my cell searching for some way out. Not that I expected to find one. These people seemed to be experts at taking captives. I wondered what their purpose was. Slavery came to mind, and indeed there had been people taken. But not nearly the numbers one would have expected. Spraggel and I had spent one whole evening on the *Wily Lass* talking about it. He said most had no recollection of what happened after their ship had been boarded. Many told stories of monsters and eating people alive, while others told of beautiful mermaids that seduced men and women alike. Spraggel seemed to think these stories were nothing more than someone's wild imagination or false memories given to those returned. I couldn't help but wonder what would happen if there wasn't a ship to put you back on. I guess we were going to find out.

After a careful search, which didn't take more than a few minutes, I could find not a single weakness in the cell. Also, the only indication of outside conditions came from a single small portal in the entry door. With the bright lights both inside and out, it was hard to tell if darkness had really fallen. Surely the sun had set by now. Which meant Zofie would transform soon.

"Coren," Zofie said softly.

I looked up.

"I want you to take my curse," she whispered. "I need to be able to start using my myst. I'm close enough to being completely back to normal. I can make do for now."

I shook my head. "Zofie, you need a few more transformations to get back completely. You don't know if your insides are back to normal yet."

She frowned. "It can't be helped. I need to do something to get us out of here. And I've drawn way too much from you already."

"I'm not sure it would help us to escape. Even if I took your curse right now, you would not be able to do myst workings for several days. And I get the impression they're going to seal our fate a little sooner than that. I know it's inconvenient, but it does give you a bit of protection."

She lifted her chin and looked me in the eye. "Coren, I don't want to do this, but as your queen, I order you to take my curse."

My eyes went up. So she wanted to play like that, did she? "And as your knight, I refuse. At least for now. Having this curse on you may limit your ability, but it also prevents you from getting a worse curse." I ran a hand through my hair. "After we get out of this, you can remove me from your service for insubordination if you want."

She was not pleased with me. So I tried to change the subject. "What have they done to these bars?" I ran my hand over them. "They're made from iron, and we're at sea, yet they have not rusted."

She walked over to the bars between our cells and ran a hand over one. "They've been charmed not to. As well as the hull of the ship. Notice how it looks like wood, but it's more like a metal. It's had its internal structure changed to resemble something much stronger. Also, everything on here is myst resistant. I can see it since I'm a seer, but it's very subtle."

"If it's myst resistant, then that means they're concerned about someone with myst damaging the ship." I thought for a moment. "Is there such a thing as myst weapons?"

Zofie sighed. "Actually, there are, but they've fallen out of use. I believe you saw some of them in Dali."

Indeed I had, the priests had gathered quite the cache of old weapons—that is until Risten and I got hold of them.

We were silent for a moment. I leaned through the bars. "I wish they would feed us. I'm starved."

Zofie grinned. "Me too. I think we missed lunch."

I moved to stand in front of her. "Well, we were a little busy. Hard to believe we were nearly killed four times today."

Her eyebrows went up. "Four? I only remember three." She started counting on her fingers. "There was the first crab attack, then the gold men, and then the crab thing again. What am I missing?"

I smiled playfully. "I fell in the water."

She looked at me a moment in surprise and then returned my smile. "For you, I'll let you have that one. Although I think you were treading water pretty well."

"And you've definitely gotten better in your sword work. If that thing had been human, you'd have gotten him for sure."

We looked at each other for a moment, and then I reached through the bars to enfold her one hand in my two. She looked up at me, and I could see from her eyes that she was nearly exhausted. I pulled her hand to my lips. "Did you mean what you said in the crypt?"

"You heard that, did you?"

"Loud and clear."

We considered each other a moment longer. I opened my mouth to speak. "I...."

Just then, the door to the brig opened. Zofie pulled her hand back, and we both turned to face our visitors. Captain Scurrlocke and the young woman with the feather entered. To my relief, they both carried plates of food.

The young woman took the feather from behind her ear and waved it toward us. "Now you two be good for a moment."

I blinked and found a plate of food sitting on the floor of my cell. There was also one for Zofie in hers. The captain and feather woman were in different places on the other side of my cell. What had just happened? They couldn't have been that fast.

Zofie bent down for her plate, unconcerned with the sudden transportation of the food. "Showing off a little bit, aren't you? You really didn't need to use an abeyance charm on us. We would not have tested you."

The young woman smiled. "I wanted to remind you that escape is impossible."

Zofie snorted. "Like we could take over this ship by ourselves."

"Why is Zofie locked up anyway?" I asked. "Isn't she supposed to be getting noble rite of passage?"

But the captain ignored me and spoke to Zofie. "We have so much to talk about, I'm not sure where to start."

"I have quite a few questions myself." Zofie sat on the floor cross-legged and began to eat. I did the same.

The captain chuckled. "I bet you do. They all do. Geneene," the captain nodded toward feather woman. "Will be back in the morning to start the induction conversation. But I will tell you a few things now.

First, this is my ship, the *Angel's Dawn*. It's the pride of my people, and we call ourselves…" and then she said a word I didn't recognize. She smiled. "In Ellish, that means The Keepers of Long Past Secrets."

"And what do you keep?" asked Zofie.

"Things of import left in our care by the Marked One. The island you were just on was one, which, I understand, has been damaged."

I jumped in. "Zofie and I were trying to respect it. It was one of our party who caved in the entrance to trap us."

Geneene's eyes flicked in my direction, but they again chose to ignore me. I was a bit perturbed that they wouldn't acknowledge me. Was it because I was a commoner? Or maybe I had done something to offend them?

Zofie noticed too. "I apologize for the damage," she said. "As my knight mentioned, the one that trapped us destroyed the entrance. We were merely seeking the mirror to clear my name and help regain my throne from my brother. He murdered our father and set me up to take the blame."

The captain nodded. "I had heard as much. Our nature is to keep to ourselves, but our recruits frequently bring news of the rest of the world."

"Recruits?" Zofie put her plate down. "You mean those you take as slaves?"

The captain's face turned red. "We do not take slaves. We offer all a chance to stay with us if they wish to follow our customs, but we never force anyone. You too will be given a chance after you learn more about us."

Zofie stood and walked toward the bars in front of the captain. "I'm afraid I won't be able to stay. As I mentioned, my knight and I must return to stop my brother."

The captain's face grew pained. "You present certain… complications. I must insist you go through the indoctrination, so you know more about us."

Zofie pressed further. "Perhaps if I spoke with my grandmother.

Maybe she would see it differently. The elder we spoke to earlier was her, wasn't it?"

The captain gave a heavy sigh. "I would not advise it. She is indeed your grandmother, but you should never speak to her as such for two reasons." She held up a finger. "One, your grandmother and Winstella had a... falling out. I had hoped that enough time had passed that the anger had faded. But she is a proud woman, and her anger still burns." The captain put her hands behind her back and began to pace. "The other reason is that she is our Guardian... our leader in your terms. More than a queen, less than a priestess. She oversees keeping us ready for the Marked One's return and the final battle."

I put down my own plate, wishing I'd had a little more. It could have used a little more salt, but it was certainly the better food I'd had recently. I looked up to see Geneene's eyes cutting in my direction. What was it with these people? I stuck my tongue out at her. The young woman just rolled her eyes.

"Then how does it relate to this ring?" Zofie held up her hand. "It obviously means something—something important. Yet you haven't taken it from me."

The woman smiled. "It wouldn't matter if I took it from you. It's already spoken."

"Spoken?" Zofie pressed closer to the bars.

The captain nodded. "When the beacon went off. It showed the world who the next Guardian was. It has been lost since your mother left and took it with her."

Geneene was becoming increasingly bold in her glances at me. I wiped my mouth. Did I have something on my face?

"But why would she..." Zofie paused. I could almost see the gears in her head turning. "Mother..." Zofie's eyes grew large. "Mother ran away, didn't she? She was supposed to be the new Guardian."

Captain Scurrlocke smiled. "You've already figured it out. You have your mother's quick wit." She shook her head. "Yes, and guardianship passes from the mother to their oldest daughter."

Geneene forgot herself and openly stared at me. She pulled the feather from her hair and held it upright, sighting along it in my direction.

"That's right," continued the captain. "You're the next Guardian. And it's just in time too. Mother is not doing well. Which is why we must get you indoctrinated as soon as we can. That curse you carry will pose a problem, but we can figure something out, I'm sure."

"Why would my curse..." Zofie trailed off as she considered the ramifications. Her eyebrows drew down. "You mean you curse your Keepers? What on earth for?"

"It's a sign of their dedication. To prove their seriousness to our mission. It comes with several advantages." The captain made a dismissive gesture. "You'll find out more about it during your indoctrination."

Geneene studied me with her feather. I felt a little uncomfortable, like a bug under an enlarging glass.

"But I have other responsibilities," protested Zofie. "I have to stop my brother."

"I'm sorry about your brother, but you have a much greater role. Maybe we can find something else to do about him."

"Then what about Coren over there. I notice you don't seem to want to recognize him."

The captain shrugged. "The man is already cursed, so we have no use for him. When we harvest a male, we apply our own curse to make them a little easier to work with. Our thralls are all happy with their new role." She turned to look at me for the first time. "Instead, he will be turned back out to sea."

"Thralls?" Zofie's eyebrows rose. "You mean like slaves?"

She smiled. "We are not so barbaric to force people against their wills. Our thralls serve us quite willingly."

Zofie frowned. "When you take away someone's will, how can they not serve willingly?"

Coren! I flinched as my curse's voice boomed inside my head. *Both those people have curses I can steal. Oh, and the princess is about to transform.*

Geneene's eyes suddenly went wide. She swiveled to sight the feather at Zofie and then back to me.

"Dammit," I whispered. "Why did you just wake up?"

He laughed. *So the young Keeper would see me. I've got a reputation as a troublemaker to maintain. Besides, it will keep you alive a little bit longer if they find out about me. See you later!* And then he was gone.

Curse him!

Geneene immediately stepped to the door of my cell. It opened with a loud click at her touch. She reached down and grabbed my left arm and turned it over to see my curse mark.

"Captain," said Geneene. "We have a problem. This thrall... he's got the mark." She licked her lips. "He's got the Abhulengulus curse."

The captain's eyes went wide as she looked at me for the first time. Then her gaze shifted to Zofie. "Mother of the Creator," she whispered. "The prophecy. It can't be."

Geneene looked up at the captain. "In the book, it says that when the time approaches, the Guardian will seek out the Marked One, the one forever cursed. Their joined forces are all that will stand against the dark." Geneene dropped my hand like it was hot. "The final battle is near."

CHAPTER EIGHTEEN

The Guardian's Dilemma

I awoke the next morning to someone watching me. At first, I thought it was Zofie, but when I turned over, I saw it was Geneene sitting cross-legged a safe distance away on the outside of the bars.

Zofie's cell was empty—her blankets had been neatly folded and placed against the back wall. Likely they had put another abeyance charm on me while they took her out. I could see that their ability to stop me in my tracks was going to be a problem. I sat up and winced at the crick in my neck. After the revelation the previous evening that I bore the Abhulengulus curse, the captain and Geneene had quickly left to talk with their Guardian. Zofie had been given a blanket to sleep under while I had been given—nothing. When I had asked about it, they ignored me. You'd think I would get used to it after a while.

After she bedded down, we talked for a bit but nothing too serious since we didn't know who might be listening. Then about midnight, she had covered up with her blanket and transformed. Her curse was still active. Thankfully we remained connected, and it went quickly and quietly. If we got out of this one, she only had a few more trans-formations left. Then both she and I could permanently be done with our curses thanks to the nymph's gift.

I rubbed the back of my neck. I was starting to become very annoyed.

It was then that I noticed the plate of food just inside my cell. And on the plate were *eggs*. Three of them in fact. I stared at them in disbe-lief. I *loved* eggs. These had been fried, each with a perfect single orange orb in the middle. I hadn't had any in a long time. I looked up at my captor. "Are these for me?"

She simply nodded.

I reached toward the plate, my mouth watering. I should probably be annoyed that I was still in this cage, but I decided I would be an-noyed later. Eggs called.

I picked up the plate eager to get it toward my mouth when it sud-denly tipped. I tried to catch it, but instead knocked it further askew with more force than I intended. A lot more force. It landed face-first against the bars with the food on the floor outside them, almost at Geneene's foot.

"Creator!" I said aloud. "My breakfast!"

"Your curse knew," stated Geneene matter-of-factly.

I walked to the plate and picked it up. Nothing was left on it. Not even a crumb. "Knew what?" Irritation thick in my voice. "That I like eggs?"

"No, that they were poisoned."

I froze. Then carefully put the plate back against the cell door and backed away. I wiped my hands on my pants. "Poisoned? Why poison me?"

"I wanted to see if the legends were true. That the curse protected the bearer. And it indeed protected you, although not quite the way I expected."

"But why waste perfectly good eggs. You could have just shot an ar-row at me?"

"Oh, don't worry. That's next."

I glanced her way, finding her dead serious. This was *not* going well.

I began to pace my cage. It wasn't really effective since it was so narrow. "What did you do with Zofie?"

"The Guardian candidate is going through indoctrination. For her, that will mean learning about the role of Keeper and how important the Guardian is."

"Is that where you normally curse people to make them your slaves?"

She smiled at me smugly. "I answered your question. No more answers until you answer mine."

So that was how it was going to be. I gestured for her to proceed. "I'm really good at this question thing. Abhulengulus and I go at it quite frequently."

Her eyes went wide. "Your curse talks to you?"

I nodded. "Indeed he does. Quite loudly, and he's raised insults to a fine art."

"Is he talking to you now?"

I waved my finger at her. "Sorry, but it's my turn now." I thought for a moment. I couldn't waste my questions. She definitely was looking for something, and I didn't know what it was, so her answers could cut off at any time. I glanced back at her. "I noticed that you are alone with me. The other times, there were at least two people with us. Why are you questioning me by yourself?"

"Because I don't believe you're the Marked One. And I intend to prove it." She smiled. "Is your curse talking to you now?"

I leaned back. "Abe, are you there?"

Not like I can fly off into the sky.

Geneene's eyes went wide. "I can see your curse move as it's talking to you. I've never seen a curse so complex before."

Zofie had made a similar comment.

I thought for a moment. I needed something to throw her off.

"What makes this ship move? I don't see any sails."

"Myst," she stated flatly.

I eyed her suspiciously. "Zofie told me that it takes a lot of myst to physically move an object. And this ship is huge. So I'm not sure I believe your answer."

"It's true," she leaned forward, smugly. "It does take a lot of myst—*if* you do it directly. We use the steam method."

I blinked at her. I had read something about this in a letter from one of Spraggel's many colleagues. There was speculation that it might be more efficient to use myst to create heat rather than do work directly.

"So you have some kind of engine that converts myst into something that can push the boat?"

She smiled coyly. "My turn now."

I frowned. She was better at this than me.

She leaned forward. "How do you steal curses?"

"Not much to tell there. I say the magic words, and Abe does the rest."

"Surely, there's more to it than that."

"Nope, I assure you it's not."

"That's not much of an answer. What are the magic words?"

"Now if I told you that, they wouldn't be magical."

This was not going like I wanted. Maybe I could get some help.

I turned slightly and whispered into the back of my hand. I tried not to frame it up as a question since that would use up one of my three for the day, and being captive, I might need to ask one later. "Abe, I need assistance with questions for the Keeper."

Really? I never would have guessed. But as I've mentioned before, I'm just a curse, not some sage oracle that can save you from your own stupidity.

I glanced back over at her. She was studying me with her feather. It must be some kind of myst aid for her.

I decided to use one of my questions. "Does that feather have a curse on it that I can steal?"

Nope. Came the immediate reply.

I sagged. So much for cutting off her powers.

But the girl does.

"What does it do?"

Hell if I know. I'd have to taste it before I could tell you that. That's your second question, by the way.

I'm getting questions from two opponents.

"But you knew about all the other curses."

If you think back, you sack of meat, you will remember you assumed what the function of each of those curses were. I didn't tell you. I can only sense curses around me. I can't tell you what it does until I taste it.

"What is your curse telling you?" Geneene asked.

I considered. "It's telling me you carry a curse yourself. What does it do?"

She brightened and puffed out her chest. "All the Keepers have one," she said proudly. "It's a sign of our unity. It protects us from evil charms and helps guide us on the path. We get them when we're ten years old, or when we're inducted, which could be at any age. I can show this mark to any other Keeper, and they will know I am true to the path. All women have to have one, or they will be expelled." She grinned evilly. "My turn. How many curses have you stolen?"

"You can't tell?"

"She shook her head. No, your curse is so complex, I can't tell what was originally there and what was not."

I suddenly formed a plan. "Five. Would you like to see the curse anchors?"

"You won't try to hurt me, will you?"

"I swear I won't hurt you."

She stood and went to the bars, as did I. Once there, I pulled up my shirt to my neck. I thought she might take a moment to ogle my developing muscles, but sadly she went straight for the anchors. "They're all lined up across your chest. You're cursed and yet you're not."

"Now, do you believe that I'm the Thief of Curses?"

She shook her head. "I'm not sure." She seemed in awe as she reached out and gingerly touched one of the curse anchors.

I gently reached out and took her hand. She looked up at me with wide eyes.

"I'll tell you the magic words I use to steal curses," I said.

Delighted, she asked, "What are they?"

I smiled. "Your curse is my curse."

There was a sudden flash of blue as Abe did his work, and Geneene's eyes went wide. She jerked away and stepped back. She pulled out her tight-fitting shirt and looked inside. "It's gone!" she yelled in near panic. "You said you wouldn't hurt me!"

"I didn't. I just borrowed your curse."

"You give that back!"

"Abe, what do I call the curse so I can give it back to her?"

The Keepers' Curse. I haven't seen this one in a while. This one enhances physical abilities and gives basic protections against myst attacks. Kind of like armor. The fun part is that it's also a binding curse—the bearer can only be on the sea or their island territories. If they go anywhere else, they will die within three days. Quite painfully, I might add.

I looked to Geneene in horror. "This curse makes you a prisoner. And you want it back?"

She looked miserable. "It's what makes us Keepers. We all have it." A tear came to her eye. "I could be expelled."

"Well, we don't want that. Abe, I want to restore her curse."

As you wish. There was a brief flash of blue. *It is done.*

She again pulled out her shirt and looked inside. She breathed a sigh of relief. "Don't you ever do that again." And then she hit me with her feather.

My entire body went rigid—arms and legs snapping to attention. I couldn't talk, I couldn't move my eyes—

And I couldn't breathe.

I fell backward like a wooden board propped on end. And it hurt like hell as I hit since I couldn't catch my fall. Thankfully my heart still beat, but anything else was beyond me.

I heard my cell door open, and a moment later, Geneene came into view. She squatted beside me. "I don't think you understand the graveness of what you just did. I don't care if you are the Thief of Curses, men are not allowed to touch or harass us in any way. The penalty is instant death."

My lungs fought to expand, but they couldn't. I wondered if Abe had decided that I was no longer needed. And I also remembered my bargain with the nymph—would she know that I died?

I heard the pounding of feet and shouting outside my cell. I saw Geneene look up in alarm. Running steps brought someone into the room, and a moment later, Zofie appeared over me. She shoved Geneene away to sprawl beside me. "Release him this instant." I had heard that tone of voice only a couple times since I'd met Zofie—and she only used it when she was extremely pissed.

Geneene regained her feet. "And what will you do if I don't. He misbehaved. You are not the Guardian. You can't order me around."

Zofie's eyes narrowed. "I'm perfectly capable of soundly beating you all by myself. *Now release my very precious knight!*"

I was glad to hear that Zofie thought I was very precious, but I was really dying for some air. I could feel my sight dimming and sound began to slip into a gentle roar.

The two women glared at each other.

"Stand down!" came a shout from the doorway. I recognized the voice as Captain Scurrlocke. "Geneene release him this instant. And Zofie, you back away."

Geneene sighed and waved her feather in my direction. "I was going to release him anyway."

Instantly, I could move. I sucked a big breath and sat up. Bowing over my lap, I tried to make the burning in my chest go away. Zofie knelt beside me and put her hand on my shoulder.

"Are you all right, Coren?"

I noticed the concern written on her beautiful face. She had called me her *very* precious knight. I felt like I had just gotten a promotion.

"How...?" I managed to gasp. "How did you know?"

She smiled. "I'm not sure. I just felt it. Probably your damn curse again."

I nodded. I glanced over to where the captain was talking harshly to Geneene. Then leaned toward Zofie and whispered. "They're all cursed," I whispered. "They're unable to go to the mainland."

Zofie patted my shoulder. "I know," she whispered. "They do it to themselves. It's part of their identity as a people." She looked troubled.

"And?"

She sighed. "We have to get off this ship and soon. They want me to take the curse too. And they're not accepting my refusal."

I paced my cell wondering if it was dark outside yet. When all you have to do is look at the walls of the room around you, time seems to crawl by. I had tried taking a nap, but the hard floor really wasn't conducive to a relaxing snooze. I also tried going through my sword forms (without my sword of course), but you can only do those for so long. I did discover I became winded faster than I was used to, which meant I had been neglecting my training. Risten would be disappointed in me.

Also, I was pretty sure the Keepers were either watching or listening to me. Since Geneene had ruined my breakfast, I was pretty hungry about mid-morning and couldn't help but wonder out loud if they were going to feed me. Only a few minutes later, a guard brought me a tray of scrambled eggs. I didn't believe it was a coincidence. So feeling a little rebellious, I sang the first measure of a common drinking song and then repeated it. Over and over. Not the words, just a da-da-dah where the words would be. It was driving me crazy, repeating it again and again, but I hoped it did worse to the person listening in.

Not for the first time, my mind circled around what to do. One thing was sure, we had to get off this ship. But how?

After Geneene and Zofie's contest of wills, the younger was escorted out of my cell and forbidden to come back by herself. Zofie was likewise escorted back to her indoctrination.

Around mid-day, two men arrived dressed in a similar cut of shirt and pants as the women, but theirs was a drab gray. These were the first males I'd seen since we boarded the ship. They wore their hair long in a tight braid down their backs, but their faces were clean-shaven. One looked to be about my age and carried my plate of food—some kind of fried fish and a slab of bread. The other was graying at the temples and carried a mop and bucket. He set those down and went to stand beside the younger one holding the plate.

As I looked at them, something just seemed a little off. Their smile was just a little too wide and their eyes just a bit too bright. I couldn't quite put my finger on it. I was willing to bet that they wore some kind of control curse.

"Please, step to the back of the cell," the older one said in a gentle voice. "We have your meal."

I took a step back but braced to charge them. The older one grabbed the door and it clicked. He then swung it open and stepped inside. I immediately charged, but with surprising speed, he grabbed me and hugged me tight against him and carried me to the back of the cell. Creator, he was strong, and I was unable to break his hold no matter my struggles. The younger man calmly put down my plate beside the door, then backed out.

I smirked. This was going just as I planned. "Your curse is my curse."

There was a brief blue glow and the startled man stepped back from me. "What did you do?" he asked, eyes wide. He looked horrified.

"I removed your curse. You're back to normal now."

Abe interrupted with loud laughter, almost making my head ring. *You know this isn't going to go so well, don't you? And by the way, it's the same Keepers' Curse. It just manifests differently for men.*

And then the strangest thing happened. The man started hitting me.

"Put it back!" he yelled. He started to breathe in gasps and broke out in a fine sweat. "I... I don't want to be like this. My mistress won't love me anymore, and they'll kick me out."

"Hey!" I yelled, trying to back away.

He grabbed me by the shirt with one of his powerful hands and cocked his arm back to punch me with the other. "You better put it back. I can see my sister's face, all dead and white. Blood everywhere— so much blood. I don't want to remember that. *Put it back!*"

Before he could hit me, I quickly said, "I return to you the Keepers' Curse."

A flash of blue glow indicated the deed occurred. I could see the calmness return to his eyes and the tension leave his muscles. He released me and stepped back, giving me that huge, unnatural smile. I shivered.

"Thank you," he said. "Please don't ever do that again. I became a thrall willingly. Other than a noose, it was the only way to stop those dreadful memories."

They closed the cell door behind them, which latched in place by itself, and then began to work on cleaning up the mess Geneene had left that morning. They worked in silence, and moments later went back out the door.

I was shocked. I had thought he would be eager to be rid of the curse, but I was dead wrong. While I had some painful memories, they were *my* memories, and they made me who I was. I would *not* let that happen to me. For once in my life, I was glad I already had a curse. They might kill me because of it, but I would much prefer that fate than spending my life in some artificial bliss.

That had been several hours ago. Since then, all I had done was pace and sing. I was trying to figure out something else obnoxious I could do.

I was getting hungry again when I heard the rattle of the brig door. I ran to the bars hoping it was Zofie returning, but it was only the two men that had fed me earlier. The younger man carried a bowl of some kind of fish stew. Again I was warned to step away from the door, and this time I made no attempt to escape. The older man was just too strong.

"Where is Zofie!" I demanded.

But they said nothing as they opened the cell door and placed my food inside before locking it again.

"Can you at least tell me what you're doing to her?"

They said nothing as they turned to leave.

"Please! Tell me something."

The older of the two stopped and looked toward me. He paused for a moment before finally speaking. "The Guardian Candidate is with the council. They have been trying to persuade her to take her rightful station, but she is being stubborn. They might have to force the binding curse on her."

"But why? Why would they do that if she doesn't want it?"

He shrugged. "I do not know. But I hope they do it soon. All the confusion upsets my mistress, and I do not like for her to be upset."

He then turned and went out the door.

In frustration, I smacked the iron bar with my open palm. Creator, I had to find a way out of this cell. The aroma of the stew reached my nose, and I glanced at it. It sure smelled good. I sat down cross-legged and started eating.

As I chewed, I pondered the cell door. What did they use to open it? When I tried to rattle it, there was no play in it at all. The door itself was made from the same iron bars as the rest of the cell, but it also had heavy hinges on one side and a thick metal latch enclosed in a steel box. I couldn't see the mechanism inside the box, but I could hear it click open or lock again. It had to be some kind of myst lock, but a most unusual one. Myst locks typically only responded to one or two people. The more people that were added to it, the slower it performed. Typically two was the maximum.

I took another bite and continued to stare at the door. *Come on Coren. Figure it out.* What did the Keepers have that Zofie and I didn't?

I didn't want to use my last question, but I was getting desperate. "Abe?" I asked.

Let me guess. You want me to tell you how to get out of your cell.

"Well... yes."

It's very simple really, even a monkey brain like you should be able to figure it out.

I glanced toward the door. Was I missing something?

"I'm not seeing how," I said. "How about a hint."

I'll do better than that. I'll even tell you what you need to do.

"You will?"

Of course, I'll tell you how to get out of the cell.

"Then what's the answer?"

You go through the door.

In disbelief, I just sat there.

Abe burst out laughing. *You fell for that one. I can't believe it. I've told you time and time again that I'm only a curse, not some all-knowing sage. I have no idea how myst locks work. All I know how to do is piss people off. And I'm damn good at it too!*

I gritted my teeth. "Creator, I will be so glad to get rid of you."

I put a hand over my mouth in horror. I'd let it slip.

Really? And how do you propose to do that? Only an extremely powerful charm could break me. One from say, a nymph.

My eyes went wide. "You knew?"

Of course, I'm not STUPID like you are. I figured it out when all these flowers started popping up. So how much was I worth?

I cringed. "A visit once a year."

And?

"My firstborn child."

Typical. I think you got taken. Oh well, back to the door. I really have no idea how to open it. But it was fun making you think I did.

I shook my head. He didn't sound angry or even disturbed. It was almost like I had told him it would rain tomorrow. "Wait. Aren't you upset that I'm going to break you?"

Why would I be? I'm actually looking forward to it. Humans get to die. Why can't I die too?

"What?"

Listen Coren. Abe sounded strangely serious. *It might come as a surprise to you, but I've been around a really long time. Including yourself, there have been forty-two men and women that have worn me. And guess what, with only two exceptions, they all hated my guts. If I was lucky, we might reach an understanding which would make living with each other sort of tolerable. But then they would die. And I would have to start all over again. I have long since exceeded what I was made to do. So, if you have some way to break me, please do. I'm ready to stop existing at any time.*

I looked down. I never thought of it from Abe's perspective. It explained why he was so obnoxious. He was trying to keep from getting close to his host, so it wouldn't hurt as much when they died.

I looked up at a sudden thought. "My father was one of the exceptions, wasn't he?"

Abe was silent a moment. *I think you've exceeded your three questions for today. Good night.*

And I felt his presence leave me.

No wonder Abe didn't like me. I had forced him to give up someone he could get along with. All the joy at getting rid of my curse left me. My decision to break him suddenly didn't look so attractive. Abe had feelings, and he sounded so... sad.

I shook my head. I couldn't allow myself to feel sorry for him. He was just a curse, a made thing, not a human. I took a deep breath. Then why did it feel so wrong?

I pushed aside those thoughts stared at the lock again. Abe was right in one respect. All I needed to do was go through the door. And all that was required was to unlock it.

What was different?

I shoved the last bit of my food in my mouth. Maybe it wasn't what was different, but what was the same. Abe had told me that they all bore the same curse. Both men and women.

I turned my head to the side. Could it be that simple? I had stolen Geneene's curse that morning, so I technically had it on my body. I opened my shirt to examine the new curse mark on my chest. This one was a circle with a thick interlocking chain going around the inside edge.

But could I use it? None of the others had shown their curse mark, nor had I seen them touch a special place on the door. All they had done was touch the bars, and it opened.

I put down my now empty stew bowl and started singing again. I hoped it would cover up any noise I made. I stepped to the cell door and touched the steel box.

Abe had told me previously that I couldn't curse myself, and cursing things didn't work—something about them not having a supply of myst. The curse just would not stick. I smiled. I really didn't need it to stick permanently, just be there for a moment.

To cover what I was going to do, I mumbled to myself that I was tired and going to go to sleep. Then I did a fake cough and cleared my throat and stayed quiet for a few minutes. I reached out and touched the door's latch, pushing gently against the door. I whispered as softly as I could, "I curse you with the Keepers' Curse." Then I started coughing like I was about to cough up a lung.

I felt a flash of power as my curse attempted to follow my command. As it activated, I pushed on the door. The blue glow quickly faded, but not before the latch moved, and the door popped open.

Grinning, I silently slipped outside the cell and then quietly went to the brig door. It too was locked, but repeating the curse casting fixed that. I cracked open the door, and not seeing any guards posted, I slipped out and into the empty corridor. I looked left and right.

Which way?

I tried to remember the path we had taken coming in but wasn't sure. I thought it was left, but that didn't feel correct for some reason. I needed to go... I turned right. I just knew it was the way I had to go.

The corridor was narrow with several doors along it. Most were closed, but a few were open, showing bunks attached to the wall and a few storage areas. I was surprised at not encountering anyone. They all must be involved with whatever was happening to Zofie.

I eventually came to a staircase and cautiously went up. I emerged on the dimly lit deck aft of what I referred to as the wheelhouse. The sky was completely black, I assumed from an overcast sky, which made the ship's deck seem even darker. The rhythmic thumping that permeated the ship was louder here, and I could even hear the churn of the water as whatever it used for propulsion pushed the ship along. The night air was chilly with a stiff breeze blowing in my face. I had left my cloak back in the crypt, and I sorely missed it. Forward I could see lots of bright lights, and I could hear someone talking as if giving a speech. That must be where all the crew were.

I headed in that direction. If there was a gathering, then Zofie would probably be in the middle of it.

I cautiously picked my way, flitting from shadow to shadow, carefully passing the wheelhouse and then going further forward.

Just in front of the wheelhouse, several large crates had been stacked and covered with a tarp. But they had left a gap big enough for me to squeeze in. Slipping along between them and the wall, I slid to the other side where I was rewarded with a protected view of the proceedings.

A large ring of spectators occupied most of the ship's forward deck with them sitting on boxes, the ship's railing, or some had even brought out small wooden stools. One thing I noticed immediately was that they were all female—not a single man among them. Several quiet conversations were creating a low buzz across the deck. The crew wasn't that large, but it did make me wonder if they had left anyone to pilot the ship.

A group of five women in the center of the cleared area were the focus of the spectators. My eyes immediately went to Zofie standing apart from the other four. I nearly fainted in relief when I saw she was all right. She maintained that heads up, unflinching manner, which meant she was pretty well fed up with how things were going.

Standing in a group a little to one side of her were Captain Scurrlocke and another woman with long silver earrings I didn't know. Unlike the others, she had a symbol embroidered onto her white shirt, which looked an awful lot like the symbol for a healer I had seen on the door of the mirror's crypt. Zofie's grandmother sat in a wooden chair beside them, arms crossed, and glaring at Zofie.

But it was Geneene that everyone seemed interested in. She stood directly in front of Zofie, holding up that faithful feather and extended toward Zofie. The young woman's arm seemed to tremble with the effort. I could see a blueish-green glow surrounding the feather, and I could swear it was giving off steam. Geneene's face was a mask of concentration: lips pursed and sweat on her brow despite the cool conditions. Suddenly the glow went out, and her arm dropped. She lowered her head and breathed a deep sigh. "It's too strong. I can't remove the curse. Whoever put it on her is far stronger than I am. I've never seen anything like it."

Zofie smiled in satisfaction. "I told you. My destiny lies on another path."

Captain Scurrlocke glared at her. "Why won't you understand that you must come with us? You are supposed to be our leader. *That* is your destiny. You wear the ring!" She looked away for a moment. "Besides, what have those land crawlers ever done for you? Killed your father. Corrupted your brother. Put a horrible curse on you. Is going back to them so damn important? They don't even want you!"

"We've already been through this, I can't be your guardian right now. I promise to return after I've dealt with my kingdom."

The captain was totally outdone. She stepped up into Zofie's face. "BUT YOU WEAR THE RING!"

Zofie held up her hand and began to yank on the ring. "Then take the damn thing." She pulled, changed her grip, and then pulled again really hard—but the ring did not budge. She looked up from her struggles in disbelief. "It's not coming off, is it?"

The captain shook her head. "Not until you die or we complete the ceremony of succession. And that has to be done back in Tuatha—which is five days at full speed!"

Zofie looked thoughtful. "I could probably wait a little longer. That is if you'll take us back to the mainland."

"We wouldn't make it," the captain spat. "The safeguards won't let us."

"Safeguards?" asked Zofie.

Geneene waved her feather dramatically over her head, and suddenly the curse anchor on every woman's chest flared briefly in a pure white light through their shirts or jackets before slowly fading. I was surprised to see the one on my chest flare too.

Geneene raised her arms toward the sky. "We are the Keepers of Long Past Secrets. The protector of weapons needed for the coming great battle. The curse is our identity, and it is our protection. It unites us and makes us one people. And it safeguards us against any outsiders. If any are allowed on our ships, they must become one of us or leave in three days." Geneene lowered her arms and looked squarely at Zofie. "If they stay on the ship longer than that, the ship will explode."

The captain sighed. "And Tuatha is five days away. So you either take the curse, or I have to drop you in the ocean."

I heaved a deep sigh. No wonder they were in such a hurry to have Zofie take their curse. And naturally, they weren't too concerned about me. I was just a male after all.

The captain dropped her head in thought. "There has to be another way." A stiff breeze came over the bow causing their clothes to flap. The crew seemed immune to the cold, but I saw Zofie wrap her arms around herself.

Suddenly the captain looked up. "Bring that man—the one she was with." She turned to Geneene. "Didn't you say he could remove curses?"

I groaned. *Oh, Creator.* This was not going to end well. I turned in the tight confines of my hideaway to find something less exposed, but before I could crawl away, I felt a large hand close over my left calf. I was suddenly lifted into the air, dangling upside down. A tall woman with broad shoulders and arms bulging with muscles held me aloft. From my upside-down position, she looked to be a giant.

"Is this the one?" she asked. "Wonder how he got loose."

I could hear the smile in the captain's voice. "That's the one. Bring him here."

I was unceremoniously dumped inside the circle of women and made to sit before the captain. I tried to shoot Zofie a confident smile, but when I saw her, I faltered: her expression was a strange mix of miffed concern.

The captain squatted beside me. "You claim to wear the Abhulengulus curse which grants you the ability to remove curses. Have I heard correctly?"

I glanced toward Geneene. It wouldn't do much good to deny it. "I do have that ability."

The captain pointed to Zofie. "Then remove the curse from that woman."

"Why should I? You're just going to curse her with your own. One that will make her a prisoner."

The captain grabbed a handful of my hair and jerked my head back. "You do not question me, *male*. I will take off your head."

Zofie took a step forward, but Geneene's feather immediately pointed toward her and she stepped back.

I glared back at the captain. "My *name* is Coren, and I will *not* remove Zofie's curse," I answered. "And just try to take off my head and see what happens."

A murmur went through the crew at my challenge.

The captain considered me for a moment. "You think your curse will protect you?" She smiled. "All of us here, in fact, this entire *ship*, is protected against that kind of interference. No, I think we can safely kill you. In fact, it would actually solve a couple problems if I did. Your continued existence is completely at my discretion." She leaned closer. "Now, remove her curse."

I looked into her eyes. I didn't think she was bluffing. This woman would do anything for her people—just like Zofie.

"No," I stated.

The captain released me and stood. She nodded toward Geneene.

The younger woman smiled. She was getting way too much pleasure from this. She pointed the feather at me. I didn't even have time to blink before her spell hit me. I immediately went rigid, stretching out flat on the deck. And like before, I couldn't breathe—forced to stare up into the starless night. I couldn't help but think this felt just like being drowned by deep dark water.

"Stop it!" yelled Zofie. "He'll do it. Don't torture him." She struggled to come to me, but that muscular woman held her back.

Geneene's spell released, and I could breathe again. I sucked sweet air as the captain came within my field of vision.

"What say you now? Ready to cooperate with us. My niece has already given in. Why don't you?"

"Because it's not right." I licked my lips, feeling the words spring into my head. I wasn't sure where they were coming from. "She has to clear her name and reclaim what is hers. She will need it for what will come." I slowly stood, the captain standing with me. I turned my gaze on the crew. "I have seen a Dark Avenyts. The gate has been opened, and they will be coming." For some reason, I switched to ancient Ellish and spoke firmly. "*I am the Thief of Curses, and it is time for the Keepers to fulfill their duty!*"

The crew broke out in excited murmurs.

I blinked. Where had that come from? While I suspected I had seen the hand of a Dark Avenyts while on Mount Eternal—and we may have accidentally destroyed the protections around the gate—I had no clue what the duty of the Keepers were.

But what I said definitely had an effect on the captain. She was furious. "How *dare* you talk about our sacred duty. I will not be lectured by some lowly man who thinks they're something from a legend. Now remove her curse! This is your final warning."

"Coren!" Zofie yelled, struggling with the woman restraining her. "Just do it. We'll figure something else out."

I glanced in her direction. If I did remove it, she would probably be miserable for the rest of her life. Not just because she would never be able to reclaim her throne, or because she would not be able to clear her name, nor was it even because she would never bring Wynn to justice. It would be because she had abandoned her people.

I looked back to the captain. "Go ahead and kill me now. Guardian or no, I will not allow you to make her your permanent slave."

The captain rose and slowly pulled her sword. I could see the sad determination in her eyes. I had seen that same expression on Zofie's face. They really were alike.

The captain reared back to strike—

When suddenly, the thumping that was ever-present on the ship stopped. The abrupt change in sound was unnerving. Captain

Scurrlocke, as did the rest of the crew, looked up in alarm. Several of them ran to the stairs.

A moment later, the ship tilted hard to the port side. Those standing fell and those seated slid off. Captain Scurrlocke staggered to the side, and Geneene helped steady her. The healer and Zofie's grandmother held each other in place. Zofie used the opportunity to stagger to my side.

My first thought was that we had hit something, but then I heard a loud screech come from the side dipping toward the water, out beyond the darkness. It was a sound I immediately recognized. All eyes turned to see a giant claw appear, raised high in the air, and grip the railing. Moments later, its massive body heaved upward, splintering the rail and seeking purchase with its other legs. As it clattered out onto the deck, it waved its stub of a claw in my direction and screeched again.

I couldn't help but laugh. I must have really pissed that guy off.

Crabbie had found me.

CHAPTER NINETEEN

The Princess Decides

The crew that had weapons rushed forward to engage the giant crab, but their swords and spears were ineffective against its hard shell. Those without weapons fled, heading down into the ships interior or the wheelhouse, blocking those trying to come out to help. At Geneene's signal, those fighting pulled back and she threw a spell at it. The blue-green glow enveloped it but seemed to almost slide off before its glow went out. The monster didn't even slow down. It too must have been protected from myst attacks.

Captain Scurrlocke didn't hesitate, she and the tall woman that had captured me, managed to climb up its legs and then onto its back. They tried to attack its head, but the beast just brushed them off with one sweep of its claw. The captain managed to land on the deck, but the other woman went over the side.

Zofie rushed over to stand beside me. "Seems like your friend wants a rematch," she said.

I nodded. "He is definitely one determined fellow."

The crab pulled the rest of its bulk up on the deck as the Keepers tried to rush it in a group. But it swung its claw in a wide arc and swept them aside, some getting injured from its sharp spikes and others being knocked over the rail. But its path did not waver. It was heading right for me.

Zofie's grandmother waded through the panicked people, making them part like water before a stone. She strode up to the crab and raised her arms. "Stop sentinel!" she yelled. "We are not the enemy!"

But it paid her no heed. It flung out its massive claw and knocked the elder across the deck, where she landed hard against a crate. Zofie didn't hesitate to run to her grandmother with me right behind her. The elder was breathing, but her shirt was ripped and wet with blood. There was a puncture wound in her stomach.

Zofie quickly tore the elder's shirt and used it as a compress against the wound. Even to my untrained eye, this did not look good.

"Lie still," Zofie told her grandmother. "We'll get the healer for you."

The older woman grabbed Zofie by the arm. She leaned up as much as she could. "You must save the ship. They're your people, and you're their Guardian."

Zofie shook her head. "I'm not what you think I am. That is not my path."

The old woman gazed at her steadily, her eyes glassy as she began to go into shock. "Then find a new path. Your mother, curse her soul, made her own."

The elder closed her eyes and fell back.

The healer arrived and nudged Zofie aside. We gladly gave up our position as she tended the elder's wound.

Zofie stood beside me. She looked down at the blood on her hands and then gazed at the destruction around her—the women throwing everything they had at the monster. But despite all their bravo, the Keepers were not equipped to deal with something so big and so myst protected.

Zofie took a deep breath, and I could see the determination in her eye. It was the look of someone reaching a decision.

"Coren." It was a statement, not a question. "Modify my curse. Quickly." She paused for a moment. "And don't hold back."

My eyes went up. "Are you sure? You're taking the role you said you wouldn't."

She glanced in my direction. "Yes, but not exactly the way they wanted. Now quick!" She jerked off one boot and then the other before moving a short distance away.

I nodded. "Abhulengulus, I wish to modify Zofie's curse."

What would you like her to transform into?

I grinned. "Your discretion. Something big... oh, and make it flashy."

I heard a deep chuckle in my head. *This will be fun.*

Zofie was immediately enveloped in a bright blue glow. I felt her pain and the pull of myst through me as she transformed. I gasped and went down on one knee as the pain grew and the draw increased. Her human-sized form became a blur and then expanded growing larger and larger. I could see the crew eyeing it with dread.

The ship we were on was big, but it wasn't that big. The combined weight of the crab and her new form taking shape made the ship began to dip closer to the water on the port side.

"Fall back!" I yelled to the Keepers.

The glow around Zofie faded and in its place was a large beast—at least three times as tall as a human—with a slender head and long neck, and covered in thick scales which caught and reflected the light in a rainbow of colors. If it had been daylight, it would have been blinding. Giant wings spread out behind it. I was awed by the thing's beauty.

Zofie was a dragon.

Her large head snaked around to face me. Her mouth opened slightly, revealing row after row of beautiful but deadly sharp teeth. I heard her voice inside my head. *I like it when you don't hold back.* Then a thin tongue shot out to gently lick across my face.

My eyes went wide. I think she just kissed me.

Zofie turned toward the crab which had paused in its havoc to turn its eye stalks toward Zofie.

The crab began to back away with its claw up. But Zofie's head shot forward and seized the claw in her powerful jaws. She began to force it back toward the side of the ship. It beat at her with the other empty arm refusing to yield.

Out of the corner of my eye, I saw Geneene peering over the side of the ship into the water. She waved her feather over her head, again making all the curse marks light up with white light as she did before. She was using this to locate those that had fallen overboard. She pointed out into the water as two other women threw rescue ropes.

An unexpected light caught my eye, and when I turned to look at it, I was surprised to see it coming from the underside of the giant crab. I gasped in surprise. *Crabbie was cursed.* Suddenly the pieces fit together.

I ran up to where the two monsters were locked in battle. "Zofie," I screamed. "Don't hurt him. He's been cursed."

Zofie understood, immediately releasing the crab and backing away. I ran forward to stand before the creature.

The crab lowered its claw as I approached and trained both its eye-stalks on me. It was trembling.

"You're cursed, aren't you?"

It stared at me a moment before slowly raising up as high as it could to show me its underbelly. There on the dull white shell, I could see a round curse mark.

I looked up at it. "You've been cursed a long time, haven't you?"

The crab slowly lowered itself and stared at me. It then put its head to the deck of the ship and stay there prostrated before me. I suddenly felt so bad for it. The crab was begging.

"You want me to remove the curse?"

It raised its head and then rocked up and down.

"You know you'll die, don't you."

It again rocked up and down.

"Are you sure?"

It again put its head to the deck.

I gave a sad sigh. How could I not? I stepped forward and touched the crab on his giant claw. "I'm sorry your watch has been so long." I paused for just a moment more and then said the phrase. "Your curse is my curse."

The crab was immediately enveloped in a deep blue glow, and its form slowly began to change. Maybe it was because the curse was so old, or maybe it was just made that way, but it seemed to take a long time for the curse to finally complete. When the glow dissipated, it left behind an elderly man lying on his back. I knelt beside him and took his hand.

He slowly turned his head in my direction. "Thank you," he whispered. "It's good to be human once again." He closed his eyes.

And then he died. Like the other ancient cursed ones, the past thousand years caught up with him quickly and he turned to dust, blowing away in the ocean breeze.

I looked up with a tear in my eye. Like the others, I couldn't understand why they would have cursed people like this and leave them for a thousand years. It didn't make sense to me. And they had all done it willingly.

The Keepers around me had expressions of awe. I heard whispers: *It really is him.* They put away their weapons and began to assess the damage, but to a one, they were afraid to approach me.

Hearing shouting, I turned to find dragon Zofie standing at the edge of the deck beside a frantically gesturing Geneene. Zofie loomed over the young woman and had to bend her neck down to understand her. Zofie nodded once and then slipped into the water. After being gone a few minutes, she returned with one of the Keepers in her mouth. She deposited the woman on the deck, and a healer immediately rushed to help. Zofie went back in the water to see if there were others.

Captain Scurrlocke came up beside me. "You really are the Thief of Curses."

"Not that I want to be, but yes, I am."

She was silent for a moment as Zofie returned yet another woman to the deck. Geneene bent close to Zofie, pointed toward the rear of the ship, and said something I couldn't make out. Zofie nodded and immediately took off back into the water.

"You could have done something like that at any time, couldn't you?" She nodded toward Zofie. "Not only to her but to us as well. You were restraining yourself."

I faced her. "I was following Zofie's lead. She will never leave her people behind—not any more than you would yours. But you're her relatives, and I think she would really like to work with you instead of against."

The captain nodded. Someone called her and she turned away.

Zofie returned with the final survivor, the large muscular woman that had picked me up. One of the healers was right there waiting, and after working on her for a few moments, announced she would be all right.

Zofie looked over at me from where she held on to the deck. *Coren dear, could you trigger a transformation for me. I need my human form back.*

She called me *dear.* I couldn't help but smile as I passed the request on to Abe. Zofie transformed while holding on and then climbed the rest of the way onto the deck. She was naked, of course, and I looked away in embarrassment.

One of the Keepers must have given her a cloak because she was covered as she padded past me and went to kneel beside her grandmother, lying on a blanket on the deck. The healer had just finished bandaging her wound. She left to find a stretcher and asked us not to tire her patient while she was gone.

The elder opened her eyes and looked up at Zofie. "I take it you found your own path?"

Zofie smiled. "I have."

"I have a feeling I'm not going to like it."

"You might," said Zofie. "A little."

Just then, the healer returned with two stout women and a stretcher. They put the elder on it and lifted her between them. They hadn't taken two steps before the elder made her carriers stop right beside Zofie. She held up a hand and Zofie gripped it in her own.

"Your mother hurt me deeply," the elder said. "And it's a hurt that I thought I had buried with her memory. But seeing you has brought it all back. And I find I'm still angry. Very angry. She didn't have to die so young in a foreign land, and she didn't have to leave her family." A tear leaked down the elder's face.

Zofie patted her hand and struggled with her own tears. "You're right. But that's the path she chose. The path that led to me. And I thank her every day for that sacrifice... Grandmother."

The elder pulled her hand back and closed her eyes. "I must rest now. Do as you must, *Grand-daughter*."

Zofie smiled and patted the elder's shoulder before they left, carrying her down into the ship.

Zofie turned to face Captain Scurrlocke. "I have changed my mind and decided to be your Guardian, at least temporarily."

The captain's eyes went up in surprise. "But you said...."

"I said I wouldn't take the Keepers' Curse. And I still won't. However, since I wear the Blue Lavender Ring, I will agree to hold the position for now. In the meantime, I have to return to the mainland to reclaim my kingdom."

The captain looked at her in shock. "I can't allow that. Being guardian by itself is a huge responsibility."

Zofie crossed her arms, a defiant look on her face. "And how will you stop me? You saw what my knight and I can do." She paused for a moment to let that sink in. "I understand your position, but you have to understand mine. If you will bend just a little, I can bend a lot. I think it will work out to be advantageous to all our peoples. Especially if our ancient enemies return." Zofie held out her hand to the captain. "What do you say, my one and only aunt?"

Captain Scurrlocke looked down at Zofie's extended hand and then back up. "You want to do both? Isn't that a little crazy."

The corner of Zofie's mouth curled up. "I think I can handle it. Besides, I have an excellent knight."

The captain considered Zofie for a moment, glanced at me, and then broke out into a broad smile. She grasped Zofie's hand and then pulled her into a friendly hug. "You had better make me proud, my only niece."

Zofie pulled back from her and returned the smile. "I definitely will. And I will return soon."

I smiled too, but didn't exactly share her enthusiasm. She was assuming we managed to keep from getting killed when we returned to the mainland. I was worried Wynn might have something to say about that.

CHAPTER TWENTY

Some Needed Repairs

The next morning, I again awoke on the floor with a crick in my neck. Only this time, I had a blanket. And of course, Zofie slept in a small bunk across the room. I sat up and stretched, noting the bright sunlight coming in through the small porthole. The constant thumping sound within the ship had returned sometime during the night. Apparently whatever damage the crab had caused had been repaired.

After our previous evening's adventure, our accommodations had been significantly upgraded. We were placed in one of the larger cabins just down from the captain.

Where to place their guardian for the night had been easily solved—but as for me, they weren't exactly sure what to do. Zofie finally insisted I come with her. So they had given me a blanket, told me not to bother the Guardian, and left us to our own devices. I would have bet gold that they were listening at the door.

I looked over at Zofie as she slept. She was on her side facing toward me, and her hair hung loosely around her face. She looked so beautiful lying there it almost took my breath away.

I dreaded the day when I would eventually have to give her up. She was still a princess, and now a guardian, while I was just a commoner. It was just a matter of time before she would have to choose someone closer to her station. I hoped that whoever it was, would care for her as much as I did. And that my heart could stand it.

I heard shuffling outside our door, and then came a gentle knock. Zofie's eyes sprang open, and seeing me watching her, gave me a sleepy smile. I rose and went to the door to find Geneene standing just outside, head held high and hands behind her back.

"The captain is asking that you join us for breakfast. Would you ask the guardian if she would do us the honor?"

I felt Zofie come up behind me. She put a gentle hand on my shoulder while I held the door open wider for her. "Tell my aunt we would be honored."

Geneene nodded. "Just go three doors down to the captain's cabin." She paused. "Your... ahh... man-servant is also welcome."

Zofie smiled. "I appreciate the accommodation."

Geneene nodded once more and turned away. I shut the door and turned to find Zofie standing unexpectedly close. "Did you like watching me while I slept?"

"I... well... how did you know?"

She touched me gently on the nose. "Because I was watching you first."

She held her place for a moment, and I couldn't help but think she was expecting something more from me. And while I wanted to wrap my arms around her, I refrained. Her man-servant was indeed an accurate description of what I was.

"Is there anything I can do to help you get ready?" I asked.

She backed away slightly. "Well, a change of clothes would be nice."

There was another knock on the door. When I opened it this time, there was a woman I didn't recognize holding a stack of neatly folded clothes—ship's uniforms, a hairbrush, and a couple ribbons.

"Compliments of the captain," she muttered as she shoved them in my arms and hurried off.

I couldn't help but wonder if it was Zofie or me that intimidated the woman.

We changed into our new clothes. There was only a slightly awkward moment where I had to turn my back while Zofie changed, but we managed it like adults. (Well, she managed it like an adult—I was blushing furiously the whole time.)

She quickly braided her hair and tied it off with one of the ribbons. She turned to me and smiled. "How do I look?"

Breathtaking is what I wanted to say. But instead I said, "You look good enough to meet an admiral, little alone a captain."

"Thank you." Then she gave me a considering look. "But you, on the other hand, I think something is missing."

I looked down. I had put on my pants, shirt, and boots. What else could there be?

She grabbed the brush. "Turn around."

I did as she asked, and she started running the brush through my hair. I could feel her presence, her warmth behind me. Her touch was strangely intimate. I felt her pull my hair back, and use the other ribbon to gather my hair on the nape of my neck.

"There," she said, stepping back and giving me a critical eye. "My knight needs to reflect well on me."

"So you're going as the princess instead of the guardian?"

She took a deep breath. "Clearing my name and saving the people of Brethnach are what's most important now. And for that, I need to be the princess."

I bowed slightly to her. "My lady. Should we be off then?"

She smiled. "Indeed we should."

I offered her my arm, and together, we left the room.

An attendant was waiting for us outside the captain's cabin and held the door for us as we approached. The room wasn't that large, but a small table had been set for our meal. Judging from the instruments and books off to one side, this was likely her regular working table.

Geneene was already there and looked up at us when we entered. Most of her feistiness from the day before was gone. We sat across from her, and Captain Scurrlocke came in a moment later.

Breakfast flowed in behind the captain with platters of some kind of sausage, and my favorite—eggs. These had been scrambled. I wondered if they had hens stored somewhere in the ship.

"You slept well, I hope?" asked the captain.

"Yes," said Zofie. "Our new accommodations were most appreciated. But, you didn't need to do anything so extravagant."

"You saved my ship and crew. It is the least I can do."

Zofie ladled some eggs onto her plate and went out of her way to load up mine. The captain noted the gesture without comment. But Geneene's eyes went up in shock as she saw the guardian serve food to a man. Zofie ignored it. But I was pretty sure she knew exactly what message she was sending: *I may be the guardian, but I'm doing this my way.*

"How is Grandmother?" asked Zofie.

"Resting well. And giving the healers a fit."

Zofie smiled. "I imagine." We were quiet a moment as the others served themselves. "What exactly did you want to discuss this morning. I've already told you I will be Guardian. At least for now."

I watched the conversation carefully. I was busy cramming eggs into my mouth, afraid that we'd get put back in the brig. The tension in the room had just jumped up, and I wanted to get some of the eggs before something happened.

The captain nodded. "So you have said. But I wanted to ask one last time before we did what we have to do."

Zofie sighed. "Sorry, but the answer is the same."

The captain gave a heavy sigh. "Then I unfortunately must put you off the ship as quickly as I can. Only Keepers can remain on the ship longer than three days. Any longer and the ship will destroy itself. There is no land close by, so I will have to put you in a boat. Given the circumstances, it is the best I can do."

Zofie nodded. "I understand your limitations. A boat will be fine. Can we have some provisions too? I would love to catch up with the *Wily Lass*. One of our party took something I need."

"Of course. You do realize that for most people, being dropped into the middle of the ocean in a small boat is just short of a death sentence. And then on top of that, you're going to try to find the ship that stranded you. That's..." she paused searching for words. "Ambitious."

Zofie nodded. "It is, but we won't know unless we try."

The captain shook her head in disbelief. "If after seven days you haven't found help, use the ring. We'll find you. Enough time will have passed that I can bring you back aboard the ship for another three days."

Zofie thought for a moment. "I do eventually plan to return and pass on the ring. Do I use the beacon for that too?"

The captain nodded. "Just tell it you want us. We'll know and come as soon as we can."

We ate in silence for a moment. I could tell there was something Zofie wanted to ask but was hesitating. She finally put down her fork.

"Did you know my mother well?"

"Well enough I suppose. You have a lot of her in you."

"Do you know why she left the world of the Keepers?"

The captain snorted. "She never wanted to be one of us. She always dreamed of living in the outside world. Your grandmother was quite outdone with her." She shook her head. "Don't get me wrong. She would have stayed and assumed her station had something not happened... or rather someone—your father. She became utterly smitten with him. Which was enough to push her to leave."

There was a knock on the door, and an older woman poked her head in. "Ah, preparations are almost complete, captain."

Captain Scurrlocke stood. "If you'll excuse me. After making our repairs last night, we've have been traveling at full speed in the direction of your... birth land. Also, given its speed and likely direction, your previous ship should be close by. I hope this helps you find it. At about noon, we will have reached our time limit, and we will have to drop you off." She stepped to the door. "I'll leave you alone for a bit. Geneene has something she wants to tell you." She exited leaving us alone.

Both Zofie and I turned to look at her. Geneene blushed and then looked down. "I'm sorry I mistreated you. I was disrespectful and cruel."

Zofie glanced in my direction. She lifted her chin, throwing this one to me.

"We accept your apology," I said, speaking for the first time since entering the room. I held out my hand toward her. "In my homeland, it's customary for friends to shake hands."

She looked at it, before tentatively grasping it in her own. She gripped my hand tightly and we shook. I tried to hide my wince—Creator, her hands were strong. I think I heard a bone crack.

Zofie also shook hands with her. "You're in training to be the new guardian, aren't you?"

Geneene looked up sheepishly. "How did you know? We never mentioned it to you."

"I figured it out. You are Captain Scurrlocke's daughter, are you not?"

Geneene nodded. "I was supposed to be the next Guardian, but that was before you... before we found you."

Zofie held up the hand with her mother's ring. "If I could, I would give this to you now." She sighed. "One day soon, we'll have that ceremony so you can have the title."

Geneene looked down. "Thank you," she mumbled.

Zofie stood. "Well, we best be getting on deck."

"Wait!" Geneene shouted. "I have something I'd like to do for you... if you'll let me. You will have to trust me though."

Zofie looked puzzled. "And what is that?"

"I can fix your curse."

Zofie's eyes went large. "My curse? Fix it how?"

"I'm a myst seer too, and I can tell your curse doesn't work completely right. It doesn't transform you completely back to your original form. I can see how I could fix it so that it stops the cumulative trans-formation errors. You'll still need to continue transforming to get back to your original form. But it will keep it from getting worse." She grinned. "By the way, an excellent trick to set it to transform back to yourself. Although I'm not sure how you figured out your true form."

Zofie looked to me and smiled. "Let's just say, I have a knight that has a way with curses."

Geneene nodded. "But for me to fix it, the Abhulengulus curse will have to release control to me. This means I could also remove the curse if I wanted."

Zofie stared at her for a moment in consideration.

I was not sure I trusted Geneene enough to do that. Once Zofie's curse was removed, she could easily put their Keepers' Curse on her and do something that might prevent Abe from stealing it.

Geneene nodded. "I understand if you don't want to. I'm not sure I would after all we've put you through...."

"I'll do it," Zofie interrupted. "Although I hate this curse, it does have its uses."

"Really?" She looked like she had just been invited to the royal palace.

Zofie nodded in confirmation.

Geneene looked to me. "You'll need to instruct Abhulengulus to release the curse."

I nodded. "Abe. Did you hear that?"

I did indeed, came the booming voice inside my head. *Please confirm the release of the Curse of Forever Transformation.*

"I confirm," I said. "And you and I are going to have a talk about this later. You didn't tell me about releasing curses."

It's not my fault. You never asked.

A blue glow flashed around Zofie, and she gasped. But it was just as quickly gone.

It is done.

Geneene looked up at Zofie. "May I."

Zofie nodded. "Please."

Geneene reached forward and touched Zofie's chest with two extended fingers. She shut her eyes, and I felt power gather in the room. And where her fingers touched Zofie's chest, I could almost see flashes of light in intricate patterns, there and quickly gone, one after the other. It was only a moment later that Geneene pulled back and grinned. "I fixed it. You'll no longer have cumulative errors...."

There was a flash of blue light and Zofie gasped. She gave me a funny look.

I have re-established control of the Curse of Forever Transformation.

"Abe, why did you do that?"

It's required to keep your butt safe.

"You and I are definitely going to have a conversation about this." I then explained to Zofie what had happened.

Zofie nodded. "That actually is a good idea. That way, I can transform as I need to. Although it still means I can't use myst yet." She turned to Geneene. "Just how did you fix it?"

Geneene's eyes lit up. "You see, the problem was...." and then she ceased to speak in any language that I knew of. It was standard Ellish, of course, but the terminology was completely strange. Zofie seemed to follow along though. She even asked a few questions in the same cryptic language. During their conversation, I had time to finish my eggs, what was left in the bowl, and the scraps on *both* their plates. I might not know about myst, but I knew about good eggs.

They remained deep in discussion until a knock on the door interrupted, signaling it was time.

We were escorted onto the deck where the captain stood along with her crew. The Keepers were at attention in smart-looking rows, their uniforms clean and bright in the noontime sun. A rope ladder extended over the side of the rail. When I looked over the edge, I saw a small open boat bobbing in the water—just a long rowboat really—which was loaded with water and a few provisions.

The captain came forward and took Zofie's hand. "I'm glad to know that Winstella had a daughter. And I thank the Mother of the Creator that I got to meet you."

Before the captain could react, Zofie wrapped her arms around her in a hug. "It's nice to know I have an aunt and cousin... and a grandmother, of course."

The captain pulled back and glanced toward the wheelhouse. "Ah, Grandmother... She refused to see you off. Winstella really hurt her."

Zofie nodded. "You know I will return. I have to pass this ring on to Geneene. Maybe then she'll...understand."

The captain smiled. "Of course." She patted Zofie on the shoulder. "Now, go make me proud."

Zofie smiled, a tear in her eye. "That's one of the few things I can remember my mother saying."

The captain nodded, a tear coming to her own eye. "That's because she used to tell it to me all the time."

Geneene came forward and also received a hug from Zofie. Then much to my surprise, Geneene also gave me one. She whispered in my ear. "Take care of my cousin. I will know if you mistreat her."

I thought that odd, but then thought of the curse Geneene had fixed. "You didn't add something, did you?"

She just smiled.

We went to the rail, and Zofie looked back to the wheelhouse. I could make out her grandmother standing in the open window watching us leave. Zofie faced the wheelhouse, stood perfectly erect, and saluted with hand over heart as I had seen the other Keepers do.

Zofie's grandmother stood stolid for a moment but then saluted back.

Zofie smiled. "It's a start," she mumbled.

We climbed down to the boat, where we cast off, launching ourselves once again onto the vast ocean. This time we were looking for a ship somewhere out there, and we had to find it. Admittedly an impossible task, but given what had happened recently, it seemed a little mundane.

As we watched the *Angel's Dawn* fade into the distance, Zofie and I came up with a plan. First, we had to see if we could find the *Wily Lass*. So, Abe modified Zofie's curse to turn her into a seagull. We found the modifications that Geneene had made to her curse greatly reduced the amount of pain she experienced.

Plus, she got to keep her clothes on.

Zofie took wing and flew high above us searching for the ship, but there was nothing in sight except the retreating *Angel's Dawn*. We then worked with Abe to come up with another animal that he could transform Zofie into. We settled on a blue whale since Abe had seen those before—they had been a common sight during our trip out.

After transforming, she pulled the boat for the rest of the day, setting a pace faster than any ship could do (except perhaps *Angel's Dawn*). But as evening approached, Zofie returned to the boat. It was the night of the new moon so she would lose her transformation—no sense in taking a chance of accidentally drowning in the dark.

We settled down on the benches and chewed on some dried fish the Keepers had supplied us with. As we sat in the gently rocking boat, I got the impression something was on Zofie's mind. But I didn't press her. There was a lot to think about—the Keepers, her kingdom, the mirror. I thought she would tell me when the time was right.

Thankfully the skies were clear with not a cloud to be seen. Bad weather would be deadly in our little boat. No doubt my curse was keeping the storms away so I didn't drown.

As the last of the light faded, the stars came out in all their splendor. We had seen the stars while on the ship, but there had always been a misty fog which partially obscured them. But tonight, a gentle, but chilly breeze had cleared everything from the sky. And with no moon, we were treated to an uninterrupted view of the heavens, horizon to horizon. They were so brilliant, it almost felt as if one could fall into them.

Zofie sat on the bench across from me. I could only see her dim silhouette against the stars, but I could tell she was looking up at them. "Beautiful, aren't they?"

"Indeed they are. Back home, there's usually a tree, house, or hill in the way. I have to say there is something magical about seeing them from horizon to horizon."

We were quiet for a moment, comfortably sharing the view. She finally broached a subject on the surface of my mind. "Do you think we'll really be all right?" she asked. "That we'll find our ship, or even someone will find us? This is a vast ocean we're adrift in. This weather can't hold forever."

I snorted. "With Abe manipulating our luck, it's likely only a matter of time. I do worry who will find us though. I pray it isn't someone from your brother."

A chill breeze blew across us. It was still autumn, but the winter solstice wasn't that far off. I was surprised the weather was as warm as it was.

Zofie stood and moved to sit beside me. "I'm cold. Can I...?"

I slid over and pulled a blanket out of our provisions and draped it around us. "Is that better your majesty?"

I said it playfully, but Zofie didn't acknowledge it.

She leaned into my shoulder. "I don't like it when you call me that."

"But it's the truth. You're the princess, as well as the Keeper's guardian. And if I have anything to say about it, soon to be queen."

"Is that what's been wrong with you lately? You treat me differently."

I turned toward her and took her hands. "Zofie. I've come to realize you *are* different. You're a princess. And you have to be the strongest myst user in the kingdom. And at the core, I'm just a badly cursed apprentice scribe. I don't even deserve to be in the same boat as you."

"Coren...."

This had been bothering me for some time. The words just wouldn't stop. "No Zofie. Please hear me out. I know Galvyn may not have worked out, but I'm sure there are others that will be more suitable for your station. You deserve someone noble and strong. Someone who can really help you defend your kingdom."

"Are you saying you don't care for me anymore?" There was hurt in her voice.

I shook my head. "I wish it were that easy. No, my lady, I care for you all right. I care for you so much my heart feels like it's going to break. Every time Galvyn was near you, I wanted to strangle him. I want you all to myself, but it can't be." I turned away. "I will continue to serve you, so don't worry. I will be your knight to the best of my ability."

I felt Zofie's hand on my shoulder. "Coren, you seriously underestimate yourself."

I shook my head. "Zofie, I'm going to give up my curse soon. I won't be anything special anymore. I'll just be *normal*." I looked down. "I'm sorry...."

Zofie reached up and gently turned my face toward her. "Choosing you as my knight has been the best decision I've made. You've saved my life, and you've shown time and again, your sharpness of mind and goodness in your heart. Being the Thief of Curses has some advantages, but that is not why I keep you near."

"You need someone better...."

Zofie suddenly stood, violently rocking the boat as she turned to face me. I could see her silhouette against the stars. I sensed a storm coming and it had nothing to do with the weather.

"Coren, you have an annoying habit that I just can't stand anymore. Will you *quit* deciding what's best for me! I'm tired of others telling me what I need to do. Father did it. The Keepers did it. And Galvyn did it. I can't stand it. I have a brain. *I will decide what's best for me!*"

"Zofie will you sit down...."

"Shut up!" She shoved me hard, and I tipped over backward off my bench landing on my back.

"Hey...!"

And then Zofie landed on top of me. She stopped with her face just inches from mine.

"Coren... you are so damn annoying." And then she kissed me. Hard. I couldn't help but return it.

"Zofie...?" I asked when she pulled back.

She put a finger over my lips silencing me and moved to lay beside me in the bottom of the boat. "Coren, right now, I'm not a princess. I'm a young woman. A young woman alone in a boat in the middle of the ocean with a young man she greatly cares about. Cares about so much that at times it makes her heart want to jump from her chest." She leaned in and gently kissed my cheek.

"You... you care for me too?" I stammered.

"Of course you idiot. I've been in love with you since the first time I saw you."

"But what if it's just Abe manipulating our luck—actually controlling our fate—forcing us together?"

I felt her shrug. "And what if he is? It doesn't change the way I feel. He may have arranged for us to meet. But he could never have moved my heart. You did that all on your own." I shifted so that she could cradle her head on my shoulder.

I could feel her hand on my chest. "So what are you going to do about it my young man?"

I smiled and turned toward her. I could see her eyes reflecting the sparkling light from the bright stars overhead. "Why I think this young man and this young woman should do the things that young people do."

Zofie pressed her body closer to mine and whispered gently in my ear. "About time you quit holding back."

I jerked awake to darkness. There had been a sound.

Zofie still slept beside me, a comforting warmth under our tarp and blanket. The stars still shone brightly over my head, even though the horizon was just beginning to have the first hints of the approaching day. The boat rocked gently on the ocean, which continued to be unusually calm. I wanted to close my eyes and go back to sleep, but I couldn't. Something was different.

I sat up and looked around us, listening for whatever telltale sign had awoken me. Then I heard it, a faint creaking sound. I looked in that direction and saw a shadow outlined against the brightening horizon.

A ship? But where were its lights? My experience with sailing at night was limited to my time on the *Wily Lass*, but they had always kept a few myst lights on deck. I doubt it was something sneaking up on us. That would be a lot of trouble just to board a small boat they could easily overtake.

I got up and moved to the center of the boat, setting it rocking.

Zofie sat up rubbing an eye. "What are you doing?"

"I think there's a ship over there. I'm going to try to row toward it."

Zofie turned around and looked in the direction I indicated. I attached the oars and started rowing.

It turned out to be further away than it looked. I thought my arms and back were going to give out long before we reached it. But close the distance we did, slowly, but surely.

But the mystery deepened the closer we got to it. It was indeed a ship, but there was no light, no sign of life, and not a single sound other than the soft creak of its rigging and the water lapping at its hull. As the dawn's light grew, I could see no sails had been set. The ship seemed to be adrift. I prayed it wasn't what I feared. The vessel's outline looked very familiar.

After roughly an hour of rowing, we drew up to the ship. By then the sun was above the horizon, and I could easily read its name which only confirmed my fears—it was indeed the *Wily Lass*.

I called up several times, but no one answered. After circling the ship and not attracting attention, Zofie and I managed to climb up the side onto the deck.

As we expected, no one was there. The tiller was unmanned. The sails were down, but not tied off—like they had been dropped in an emergency.

We decided to try the captain's quarters first. Unfortunately, we found that something must have happened.

We found the body of Captain Ina. The cause of death was fairly easy to discern.

There was a rather large knife sticking out of her chest.

CHAPTER TWENTY-ONE

An Abandoned Ship

I knelt down beside Captain Ina. The blood had pooled underneath her, with no evidence she had been moved. Also, there were no tracks in the blood. When I touched her arm, it was cool, but not cold. She must have died only a few hours before we got there.

I stood. "Let's look around some more."

We went to the passenger cabins. I feared the worst, but the one Galvyn and I had occupied looked like no one had touched it. However, when we opened the one Zofie had shared with Fumiko, we found it a complete disaster. It looked like an impromptu lock had been affixed to the outside of the door. And inside, the bed stuffing had been pulled onto the floor, a chair was broken, and the door on the inside had been severely scratched. It looked like someone had been kept there, and they had not been happy.

But no further bodies.

We then looked into the hold. There was nothing there either. All the provisions and cargo were intact. Then I thought of something. I went to the crate that Zofie had used to be smuggled onboard. I opened it and to my surprise, I found two sailors hiding inside: Jomo, the big guy that had accompanied us to the island and another sailor whose name I didn't know. And there was one other...

A mass of fur enveloped my face. "Coren, my lad! About time you and the princess showed up."

"Spraggel!" I shouted. "It's good to see you!" I tried to separate him from me, but his claws were dug painfully into my shoulder.

I struggled to get him off. "What happened to everyone?"

Spraggel released me and I held him out. He looked at me sadly. "It was the king's soldiers. They took everyone."

"But how? This is in the middle of the ocean."

"Long-range portal," said Spraggel.

Zofie shook her head. "But finding a tiny ship like this on the ocean would have required some kind of beacon to anchor it...." Her eyes went wide. "*My correspondor!* The one I used to talk to Risten. It went missing a few days before we found the island. I thought I had just misplaced it, but Fumiko must have taken it." She looked at us in horror. "In the right hands, it would serve as the perfect anchor."

Spraggel nodded. "Indeed. It was an expert that did it. It was the myst user that turned me into a cat."

"Fumiko," Zofie stated. "She's been working with Wynn all along."

Zofie took Spraggel from me and cradled him in the crook of her arm. He purred as she absentmindedly stroked his head.

"I think there is more to it than it appears," he said. "I escaped from the sack almost as soon as we got back on the ship. Why she grabbed me, I'm not sure. She did say something about needing me later."

The two sailors had been hanging back, listening intently to everything we said. Jomo, the large one, leaned forward at the pause in our conversation. "What of our mates?"

"There's no one else on board," I said. "But I'm sorry to say that we found Ina in her cabin. She's been murdered."

The two crew members looked stricken. "We best see to her," Jomo said. They immediately left.

I shook my head. "If they took the entire crew, why would they need to kill Captain Ina. There were no weapons in her hands."

Spraggel cocked his head to one side and sat back on his haunches. "Fumiko was definitely acting strange. When we first got back on the ship, she feigned being frightened and asked to talk with Ina alone in her own cabin. After about a quarter-hour, Ina came out with the sack of stolen items, but Fumiko did not. In fact, Fumiko was bound and locked in her cabin while Ina immediately gave the order to set sail. But after that, I could hear Fumiko's muffled voice from inside the cabin."

"What happened after that?" I asked.

Spraggel began licking his paw. "I'm not sure. While Fumiko was talking with Ina, I managed to escape. Ina set the crew looking for me, so I chose to hide in places the crew had trouble finding." He looked up in thought. "Now that I think about it, it was Ina who met our mystery myst user when the portal opened. They seemed to know each other."

"That is odd," said Zofie. "If they were partners, then why kill her and take Fumiko instead."

"It might have something to do with Coren," said Spraggel.

"Me?"

"That master myst user was most pleased having the Mirror of Bygone Tears, but got angry that the Thief of Curses wasn't with her. Maybe that did it."

I shook my head. That didn't feel right. There was something we were missing. Something big.

"So that means they'll come back," said Spraggel.

Zofie sighed. "I'm not so sure. Establishing a long-range portal is not only dangerous, but on a moving object is outright hard. He would need some kind of anchor set up in a clear space to make sure he didn't open it over open ocean or have the portal blocked by the ship's hull." She shrugged. "Regardless. Two long-range portals, one here and one back, have likely exhausted his myst for now. It will take several days, maybe even a week, for him to build up enough for another portal."

I nodded. "And he doesn't know for sure that I am still alive. He may think I am still sealed away in the tomb."

Spraggel snorted. "With your curse, he can be fairly confident you're alive."

"So should we expect him to open another portal?" I asked.

Spraggel shook his head. "No, the easiest solution would be to wait for you to show up. After all, Risten will be executed in only a few days...." Spraggel cut himself off, but it was too late.

Zofie looked at Spraggel in disbelief. "Risten? Executed? How... how do you know?"

Spraggel gave a big cat-like sigh. "I was going to tell you a little more gently." He sighed. "While I was hiding, I heard some of the king's soldiers talking. Risten was captured a few weeks ago. It must have happened shortly after we boarded the *Wily Lass*. And she is going to be hanged on the Day of the New. Apparently, Wynn has been hanging anyone who disagrees with him."

All the color drained from Zofie's face. "Wynn's had her for weeks. What tortures has he done to her?" Zofie's brother had already demonstrated his preference for cruelty. He definitely wouldn't just put her in a holding cell. Which meant only one thing.

We had to save her. And fast.

Over the next few days, Zofie and I became temporary crew and assisted the two sailors in every way we could. Fortunately, the weather held, and we had a good breeze. But taking advantage of it wasn't easy. Exhausting is a better word. Zofie and I fell into our bunks and seemed to just shut our eyes before we had to get up again.

The one break we took was the service for Captain Ina. Jomo, and the other crewman whose name I learned was Uba, carefully wrapped their captain in a spare sail, and then we buried her at sea. Zofie spoke a few words for her and thanked her for her service. But the break was short before we were back to learning our new tasks.

Fortunately, Uba knew a little about navigation and seemed to think we might make port shortly before the Day of the New. That was provided the wind continued, and we didn't run into any storms, and a sail didn't rip, and any number of other things didn't go wrong. And since I was on board, it was almost assured at least two or three of them would all happen at once. In short, we likely wouldn't make it in time, but we had to try.

On our fourth day since boarding the ship, I was high up in the rigging when something caught my eye. Looking out across the sea, what looked like a ship in the distance. At first, I thought it was a certain large Keeper ship, which I had spotted a couple of times hugging the horizon. Zofie's relatives were no doubt keeping watch over their guardian.

But as I looked, I realized this one was a different configuration— it had sails. And it was rapidly closing with us.

"There's a ship approaching on the starboard side!" I yelled down.

Uba bounded up the steps to the poop deck and pulled out the captain's far-lens. He went to the rail and peered into the distance. Zofie stood just behind him at the ship's wheel. She tried to look over his shoulder without leaving her station.

"Creator curse it," Uba said. "Freebooters. We'll never outrun them as short of crew as we are."

Zofie leaned forward. "Can we just drop sail and get it over with. We don't have anything of value left on board."

Spraggel sauntered up on deck. "Ah, but we do. If they figure out you're a princess, they'll turn you over for ransom. And if they don't figure it out, then a fine young lady like you will fetch quite the price on the slave market. The young lad might too."

I joined them on the deck. "So we're done for either way."

Spraggel sat down and began licking his paw. "I don't know. This could be a fortuitous opportunity."

I shook my head. "And how's that?"

"Well, the king's scouts know this ship. They'll be looking for it when we get close to the harbor. However, if we swap ships with them, then we can sail into port without anyone suspecting."

"Us four against twenty to thirty. Don't those odds seem a little stacked against us?"

Spraggel flicked his tail in agitation. "Well, if we're going to all the trouble of confronting them, we might as well get a little something out of it."

I looked to my shipmates. Zofie shrugged, Jomo didn't say anything, and Uba just shook his head. I sighed. "All right. Let's hear your plan."

Spraggel started walking toward the stairs. "I'm going to leave the plan to you and the princess. You're a knight after all, and don't knights develop great plans?" I could almost hear the snicker in his voice.

I frowned. "Have you been reading my journal?"

Spraggel looked over his shoulder at me. "Me? Surely you jest."

Yes, he had been reading it.

He quickly trotted off. I was going to have a word with him about that.

I turned to my companions who were looking at me expectantly. "Any suggestions?" I asked.

Jomo shook his head. He was a big man, but he didn't talk much.

"We could fight them to the death," said Uba very seriously.

I sighed. "I am really hoping that no one has to die." I looked over to the approaching ship and rubbed my chin in thought. "I guess I could use one of my curses. Unfortunately, I can only put the powerful ones on Zofie, since she's the only myst user." I didn't mention that I had the Keepers' Curse, which I could use on anybody, but we had decided not to mention the Keepers to anyone just yet. It wouldn't help us anyway. "I could also remove Zofie's curse, and then she could draw myst from me to repel them."

Zofie was rather distractedly looking at the approaching ship. "I'd prefer not to do that," she said. "The kind of defensive charms I've used so far have been lightweights. The ones I would need would place quite the draw on you. Not to mention, some ships have their own myst users to counter our charms."

I sighed. "That only leaves turning you into a big animal. But with that many swords, it might not work."

But Zofie wasn't listening. The closing ship had her complete attention. The ship itself wasn't in the best of repair. The sails were more patchwork than complete sail. Plus, the paint had either faded or been scraped off in places.

Zofie suddenly turned to Uba. "Can I see your far-lens?"

The big man handed it to her.

Zofie used it to study the approaching ship. After several moments, she slowly lowered the lens. "That used to be one of my father's ships," she stated. "It looks like they've painted over their old name. But I know what it is. Some of the men are still wearing their old uniforms."

We stood side by side in contemplation as the ship approached. Then it dawned on me what she was thinking. "You're going to try and talk to them, aren't you? You think you can persuade them to join us."

She faced me and gave a big sigh. "If I'm a ruler worth my salt, I have to be able to persuade people to lend me their power." She looked over her shoulder at the approaching ship. "Some might take more persuading than others."

I took her hand and brought it to my lips. "You've certainly convinced me."

She glanced toward the approaching ship. I could see the nervousness on her face.

"Are you afraid?" I asked.

"I'm terrified."

I smiled. "I will be on standby if something goes wrong. I can't lose my only princess."

It seemed to be the right thing to say. One side of her mouth curled up. "Off with you then. Let's drop sails and wait for them."

I moved to the lower deck but paused just out of earshot. "Abe?" I asked. "How many can I curse at one time?"

Abe's response was immediate. *Theoretically, there is no limit as long as they are within fifteen feet. I also need a line of sight to each of them. But in practice, you can only fit so many people in that area.*

Fifteen feet. This is going to get interesting.

We dropped sail and arranged ourselves on the starboard side to wait for them to arrive. We didn't have long to wait. They too dropped sail and threw grappling hooks to bring us together. They lined up across the deck, armed with swords and knives. They looked tough.

I shouted over to them.

"Hello, good sirs and madams."

They looked on with interest but made no move to board just yet. A big man who had to be their captain came forward. "Our ship is the *Bloody Renegade*. The cruelest freebooters this side of the ocean. Stand aside and prepare to be boarded!" he roared. "That or be killed where you stand."

The captain climbed over the railing toward us. He immediately eyed Zofie. "Aren't you a pretty one?"

I frowned. "Is that any way to talk to your Princess?"

The captain snorted. "She isn't royalty. Just because she has red hair...."

Zofie interrupted. "Your ship used to be in the king's service, did it not? Its original name was the *Bernard Xernow*, named after my uncle. And I believe you are Captain Milner. I remember when you were commissioned to it. You might remember me as a young girl standing behind my father, King Tiernan Xernow."

The man looked like he was seeing a ghost. Murmuring set off in the crew within earshot.

"You lie," Captain Milner said through clenched teeth. "The princess is dead. A traitor who killed our king and abandoned us to the tyrant now on the throne."

Zofie stepped forward and looked up into the captain's face. He was at least two hands taller than her. "I assure you, I am not dead, nor am I a traitor. My brother laid a trap which ended up with me taking the blame for my father's death and then stealing the throne."

The captain considered her. "You do look like her. Sound like her too. Assuming I were to believe you, then where the hell have you been this past year! We've been forced to desert just to have something to eat!"

Zofie undid the ties of her shirt and pulled it down enough to reveal her curse mark. "My brother cursed me. I've been almost every animal you can think of during that time. And would be still had it not been for the help of my friends." She went to the railing and addressed the entire crew of the other ship as they watched silent and wide-eyed. "That's why I sailed these seas," she said in a loud voice. "I was searching for a way to clear my name. And I found it too, but it was snatched away by my brother's henchmen. Even so, I swear to you, that I Princess Zophia Olwenna Xernow, will clear my name. I will also retake my throne. And lastly, most importantly, I will bring my brother, Branwynn Taggart Xernow to justice and make him answer for his crimes."

The captain looked skeptical, and talking erupted among the crew of the ship.

"But how do we know you are the princess?" shouted one of the crew.

"What proof do you have?" said another.

Zofie spread her hands. "I have very little. The only thing close to proof I can offer is my curse mark and my friends." Zofie motioned me forward. "My knight is none other than the legendary Thief of Curses. He is the sole reason I am alive today." I waved and tried to look knightly. I didn't think they were buying it though.

Spraggel suddenly leaped atop the rail beside Zofie. "I also back the princess," he shouted as he strolled back and forth. "She is everything she has said and more."

Murmurs went through the crew. "A gray cat," they whispered. "It's a gray cat." Some of the men made a sign of reverence.

I was going to have to get someone to explain what the big deal was about gray cats and sailors.

Zofie leaned forward. Spraggel sat on the rail beside her and curled his tail around his feet while I stood just behind. "What say you?" she said. "Will you help me? Will you set this kingdom right again?" She stood and gazed out across the upturned faces. "What does your heart say you should do? Does it bother you that you have to take from the innocent and become the very ones you swore to protect against? Will you continue to be bloody renegades?" She stood up erect, her head held high. "Or will you be the ones to help save the kingdom. To assist a princess in need. To become the valiant warriors I know each and every one of you are."

"I'm with the princess!" shouted someone in the back.

The captain was skeptical. "You talk well, but I've heard lies before. And they sound just as sweet as yours."

Zofie looked insulted. "Coren, show them."

I looked up in panic. *Show them what?* And then it hit me—she needed a transformation.

"Abe," I whispered. But he cut me off.

Let me guess. You want me to trigger the princess's transformation. And to make it flashy. You're getting so predictable.

I smiled. "Then what's holding you back."

Not a damn thing. And you better thank me for this one.

She was immediately enveloped by her usual blue glow. It grew and stretched, changing shape into an animal I had seen on every banner and shield the kingdom owned. Her body grew large and muscular, the hind legs became those of a lion, and the wings that spread from her back were those of an eagle. She was a griffin.

She gave a loud squawk and the sailors drew back. She looked the captain in the eye. "Do you believe me now," she said. "I need good men like you. Don't let my evil brother win."

The crew was murmuring among themselves.

Captain Milner considered her, looking from her to his crew. He finally turned to them. "I say we join her! We have nothing to lose, and I hated being a freebooter anyway!"

A shout went up from the crew.

Spraggel yelled. "Long live Princess Zofie!"

The crew answered taking up the chant.

I had Abe reverse the transformation and Zofie was once again standing in front of us. Not having to lose her clothes was definitely an advantage.

Zofie raised her hands, and the shouts quieted down. "I thank you all from the bottom of my heart. But we must hurry. My brother Wynn has captured one of our own and will execute her on the Day of the New. We must reach port before then!"

The captain grinned. "Don't worry, Princess. This is the best crew to ever sail the ocean. We'll get you there with time to spare."

And off he went giving orders as he strode through the crew. Zofie grabbed my hand and led me off to her cabin. There seemed to be an urgency to the move.

I leaned toward her and whispered, "I can't believe you did that. You were wonderful!"

She didn't answer and led me inside her cabin. She shut the door behind me—

And fainted.

CHAPTER TWENTY-TWO

A Storm
Rolls into Port

We sailed hard for port after joining forces with the crew of the *Bernard*. Zofie and I transferred over to her new ship, leaving Jomo and Uma aboard the *Wily Lass*. Captain Milner offered to supplement them with a couple of crew from the *Bernard*, but they declined, saying they would be fine as long as they took it slow. And without a moment to lose, we separated quickly putting the *Wily Lass* far behind us. At that point, we only had ten days until the Day of the New.

Captain Milner promised us he would get us there in time if he had to swim us there. And make time we did. With the wind at our backs, a highly trained crew, and every man and woman aboard delighted to have a purpose again—we practically flew through the water.

While I was glad for our new friends, Zofie was on edge about Risten. I tried to occupy her with making plans for when we arrived. For starters, we would need to get into Edlingreen Castle, get Risten out, and retrieve the Mirror of Bygone Tears. Either one by themselves would be a huge undertaking—and extremely risky considering all we had to work with was a single ship, its crew, a cursed princess, a cat, and one knight in training.

Logic dictated the odds were too great. Both Spraggel and I were convinced some trap lay in wait for us which would get us all caught or killed. But Zofie was unmoved, convinced Wynn would kill Risten as he said, and if Zofie didn't at least try to stop him, she would never be able to live with herself. I could understand since I felt the same way.

The captain was true to his word, and on a chill evening of the ninth day, just as the sun was going down, the dim outline of land came into view. We all breathed a collective sigh of relief and put our plan into action.

The plan we decided on was simple. Once night had fallen, the *Bernard* would sail into the bay, bypass the harbor, and head up the Edi River just past the castle. From there they would come ashore and attack the castle gates as a diversion. The tricky bit was navigating up the river in the dark, but the captain said he had grown up navigating barges along its banks and knew how far he could push it. For the rest of us, however, there was a different role—and one not so nearly well defined. Everything depended on exactly where Risten was being kept.

When we got close to a steep bank just before we reached Edlingreen Castle, Zofie, Spraggel, and I were rowed ashore. The plan was we would approach on foot up a steep hill covered in thick brush. From there, we would take a secret entrance into the castle that only Zofie knew—secret knowledge her father had provided before his death and not shared with Wynn.

Which is how we found ourselves traipsing through the underbrush, in the dark, while looking for a secret passage Zofie insisted was there. Unfortunately, we couldn't find it. And naturally, Spraggel had disappeared.

Zofie led the way heading deep into the thick brush. I had to follow her closely, so I didn't lose her in the dark. She pushed aside a low branch to pass through and carelessly released it, smacking me in the face once again.

While I dearly loved the young lady, if she let another branch hit me in the face, I was going to put a curse on her.

She stopped suddenly, and I of course bumped into her. It was difficult navigating through the dense overgrowth in the dark. I wondered just how much further we had to go.

"It's got to be here," she stated for the fifth time. I could hear the frustration in her voice.

We were still a good piece away from the castle, yet close enough that we could see the soldiers on patrol atop its walls. We were on a steep bank covered in rocks and hidden behind dense trees and bushes. Plus thick vines were everywhere, doing their best to trip us. Better lights would have helped, but we dared not use anything too bright—just my trusty glowing amulet and a small covered myst lantern. All of this made exploring in the dark not only difficult, but dangerous.

"Are you sure it's this far out?" I asked. "It would take one very long tunnel to reach the castle from here."

"I'm sure it's close. The entrance was made to be hard to find. It's supposed to be an escape route, not an entrance." Frustration was in her voice. Back on the ship, she had been confident she could find it.

I pulled a dead leaf from my hair. It was chilly out this evening, not yet winter, but leaving not a doubt it was very close. "If I were going to build an escape route, it would be as far away as I could make it and be close to a road or waterway so I could slip away easily."

She nodded. "Perhaps you're right. Which way then?"

I pointed back over my shoulder. "I think it's closer to the water." I turned and started carefully picking my way toward the bay's shore. "I bet it's very close, but just a bit closer to the...."

Suddenly my foot came down on nothing, and I toppled off the edge of an overgrown rock ledge, tumbling down a vine-covered incline and coming to rest at the bottom of a cut into the hill. I sat up, looking around and trying to figure out what had just happened.

Zofie soon joined me coming down in a little more controlled manner. "Are you all right?"

I got to my feet feeling a little unsteady from my tumble, but otherwise intact. "I think so. Got a couple nasty scratches, but nothing broken."

She leaned over and gave me a kiss on the cheek.

"Thank you," she said.

"You're welcome, but for what?"

She pointed to the ledge I had fallen off of. "There it is."

When I looked, I saw we stood before a rock face covered in vines. Spraggel lay in front of it, curled up in a ball.

"Spraggel, why didn't you call us?" I asked.

Spraggel looked up giving me one of those cat 'how dare you wake me looks.' "You two were having such a good time I thought I'd let you enjoy the chase a bit more since we're running a little ahead of schedule." He stood up and stretched. "And besides, there's always time for a cat nap."

I sighed. We were definitely going to have to get Spraggel turned back to a human soon. He was adapting a little too well to his feline form.

Zofie went forward to the rock face and put her hand on it. "Please ancient Gatekeeper, open for me. I am Princess Zophia Olwenna Xernow. I was here two years ago with my father. I first touched you then."

The vines trembled and began to move. They writhed and shifted, but did not clear the way. To my amazement, they began to form letters against the rock, spelling out: *TIERNAN?* That was Zofie's father's name.

She shook her head. "He's gone. He died a year ago."

The vines moved again. *SAD.*

Zofie put her other hand on the wall. "Me too?" She paused. "Will you open for me?"

YOU NOT CROWNED. The vines spelled out.

"I know. My brother killed my father, Tiernan, and cursed me. Wynn sits on the throne now."

HE NOT CROWNED EITHER.

That was strange. I looked to Zofie and she explained. "Wynn can't be officially crowned until he reaches his majority. That won't be until this summer."

She turned back to the wall. "Please let me in?" Zofie begged. "I have to save my cousin." Zofie leaned her head against the stone. "*Please.*"

CAT I KNOW. WHO MAN?

The wall knew Spraggel? Spraggel had been here before? I was definitely going to have to ask him about this later. I stepped closer. "My name is Coren Hart. I'm the princess's knight."

YOU WEAR CURSE OF THIEF.

I nodded. I held up my arm toward the wall. I wasn't sure where to point it since walls usually don't have eyes. "I wear the Abhulengulus curse."

THIEF BAD.

I cocked my head to one side. Why did the gatekeeper think I was bad? "No, I'm on the princess's side. I swore to protect her."

XERNOW HEIR WITH THIEF. BAD TIME COME.

"I know I'm not the best...." But I stopped as the letters continued to form.

DARK AVENYTS COME. DESTROY ALL.

YOU MUST STOP THEM.

Not the best conversationalist, but I got the message. It was strangely similar to the legend of the Keepers.

Zofie stepped away from the wall. "Will you let us in?"

The vines went still, not forming another word.

Then suddenly, they started moving with a loud rustling sound. They began to move away from a section of rock just to our left. Then there was the sound of scraping stone, the rock pulled away to reveal a door-sized entry.

Zofie paused and put a hand on the rock. "Thank you, Gatekeeper. I will remember your kindness." She then glanced at me and went through the opening. Spraggel darted inside behind her. I lingered back to give one last look around to make sure no one had noticed us.

When I turned back, there was a ball of vines hanging at head height in front of me. The ball of vines took on the appearance of a face, and one of the vines rapidly seized my left hand. Its grip was so tight it hurt.

On the wall, the vines continued to form more letters: THIEF BAD. The face stared at me a moment. *VERY BAD.*

I swallowed. "Are you saying I'm bad?"

The head rotated slowly up and down, giving a crude nod. *FIRST THIEF TRAITOR.*

I shook my head. "I would never hurt Zofie."

CURSE CAN.

I blinked in surprise. "You know about my curse?"

The head nodded.

Zofie called from inside. "Coren, are you coming?"

The vines released my hand. *YOU MUST MAKE CHOICE. PROTECT XERNOW HEIR.*

And the ball of vines untangled and faded away.

"Coren," Zofie came to the entrance. "Quickly, I need your help."

With one last glance at the vines, I went through the doorway and entered a small cave. The walls were rough cut from the rock beneath the bank and the floor dry and dusty. The cave's ceiling was higher than I expected, a foot or two more than I could reach. I expected a tunnel or passage of some kind just beyond, but there was none. The cave's only exit was behind me.

Suddenly, there was the sound of rock grinding on rock and the doorway closed behind us, sealing us inside. I held out my glowing charm just to be sure, but I couldn't help but state the obvious, "We're trapped."

Zofie stood in the center of the room looking up at the ceiling. Spraggel sat to one side, his tail flicking back and forth as he waited on us.

Zofie shook her head. "No, we're not. I just need you to give me a boost." She pointed up and settled her bag on her shoulder.

I looked where she pointed and could see only rock. What was she thinking?

Zofie came closer. "Can you lift me to your shoulders?" It seemed an odd request, but I squatted down and she climbed on. After I stood, I could feel her shifting around, but couldn't tell what she was doing. Her legs came up, and she stood on my shoulders. I thought maybe she was looking for a secret trigger or latch. Suddenly both her feet left my shoulders.

I looked up, but she wasn't there anymore. "Zofie?"

After a moment, a length of rope suddenly dropped down, and then Zofie's head appeared out of the rock. "You'll have to climb up the rope."

"What is that?"

"Oh, it's a portal into the castle. Putting it on the ceiling must have been the best place to hide it."

Spraggel wasted no time and jumped into my arms. Then from there, leaped to the rope and clawed his way upward until Zofie grabbed him. I followed up, glad I had spent time getting used to them on the ship. I emerged out of a vertical wall. My head spun, and my stomach lurched at the change in perspective. My feet said down was behind me, but my head said that down was in a different direction. I shook my head and hurriedly climbed the rest of the way. This was one of those weird things that were possible with myst portals.

As I looked around the tunnel, I was reminded of the crypt of the Mirror of Bygone Tears. There were large blocks of stone set into the floor and walls, while along the sides of the wide tunnel were person-sized sarcophagi. I hoped there wasn't some creature lurking inside. But Zofie seemed unconcerned. While I coiled up the rope, she reverently moved down the aisle.

"We're in the family crypt," she explained. "And these are all my ancestors." She pointed to the life-sized statues watching over each of the sarcophagi. I couldn't shake the feeling of awe. These had all been great rulers. I felt like I was intruding into a domain I didn't belong.

Zofie turned to the left and began walking, our footsteps echoing softly off the walls and the air taking on a musty chill. "When I was little," she continued. "My father would bring me here at least twice a year—in fall for the anniversary of my uncle's death, and..." She turned yet another corner. "And in winter on my mother's birthday." She looked over her should at me and smiled. "I was always terrified to come down here. Father would give in to me on most things, but on this, he insisted. And we would always come alone, just him, Wynn, Risten, and myself." She moved further down the tunnel. "I didn't understand at first that their bodies were actually in the sarcophagi. I instead thought they were the statues themselves. And they were watching me. Ready to pounce."

Her steps took a faster pace as I followed. Spraggel had jumped up on one of them and was reading the inscription.

Zofie continued. "One day, I confided my fears to my father." She smiled. "I remember him sitting me on his knee, hugging me, and explaining that, yes, indeed they were watching. But they weren't going to pounce—they would never do anything to hurt us even if they could. Instead, they were watching us with pride and love. And if one listened carefully, one could hear their wishes and prayers to the Creator that he watch over us."

We finally came to the end of the statues, even though the tunnel continued beyond the reach of our lights. Zofie slowed in front of a pair of statues: one of a woman that shared Zofie's features and the other one carved of fresh stone—the statue of a man. He was dressed in fine robes with arms spread and wearing a half-smile on his face. He looked ready to take on the world.

"Thank the Mother of the Creator that Wynn had a few specks of decency. I had prayed that he would at least do this much."

"Is this your parents?" I asked.

She nodded sadly. "I've been on the run since his death. I haven't been able to... visit." She looked from the statue and then back to me. "Could I take a moment?"

"Of course." I took a few steps back in respect.

She then turned her gaze to the statue of the late king. "Hello, Father. I'm sorry I haven't paid my respects to you. It's been a terrible year and..." She gazed up at it with tears in her eyes and took a ragged breath. She wiped her eyes with the heel of her hand. "I'm just sorry.

I'm a miserable excuse for a daughter." She bowed her head. "I miss you."

As I watched, I felt like an intruder into a private family matter. I realized that Zofie had been cursed right after his death and had never been allowed to grieve his passing.

She sniffled and raised her head. "I will do better. I promise." She then glanced at me and motioned me closer. As I inched forward, she grabbed my arm and pulled me beside her. "And this is Coren, Father. He's the one I've chosen. And you were right, I did know without a doubt." She bowed her head. "I know I don't deserve it, but please watch over me. I can use all the help I can get."

She moved to stand in front of the statue of the woman. "Hello Mother, I met your side of the family a few weeks ago, and I learned some about you. I never knew what you had given up. Thank you for what you did, and I will make you proud too. Oh!" She held up her hand with the ring on it. "I found Blue Lavender, or rather Coren found it for me. I promise to keep it safe until I can return it."

Zofie looked from one statue to the other one last time and then turned, marching back the way we had come, a new determination in her stride. "We have to hurry."

Spraggel and I fell in behind her. After retracing our steps for a bit, Zofie turned and took a passage to the right. We made several more turns, and as I looked around, I realized I was thoroughly lost in this labyrinth of the tombs. Probably another protection the engineers had built into the castle.

Zofie slowed and looked over her shoulder at me. "We're getting close to the entrance to the castle. Keep your voice down and dim your light."

I did as she said. We turned one more time—and came to face a man leaning against what appeared to be a thick wooden door. He was a tall, thin man, fully dressed in stylish tunic and pants. I immediately recognized him as the myst user that had attacked us on the day our journey began.

He smiled when he saw us. "Took you long enough," he said.

I drew my borrowed sword and stepped forward, putting myself in front of Zofie. She drew hers as well.

"Step aside," I said. "I have no desire to harm you."

"Oh, please!" he said, rolling his eyes and pushing himself off the wall. "So noble of you to offer me my life when my hand is about to close around your throat. You are the ones that had better drop your swords. Your princess is still cursed so she can't access her powers, and you, oh cursed one, can't do anything to me without first stealing my current curse. And for that, you have to touch me—nearly impossible since you have the sword skills of a pig." He grinned. "So put your swords away, and I'll let you walk to your prison. Or else you can try to fight me, and end up in the same place but with a lot of bruises."

He knew so much about us. Defeating him would be extremely difficult. I didn't dare try to transform Zofie into something that could threaten him. His myst powers could easily overcome her. No, in this situation my first priority was to protect my princess. I would modify her curse to make it easier for her to hide.

Zofie spoke from behind me. "You obviously know our names, but we don't know yours. Who are you?"

The man smiled. "My name is Kegan Taithleach."

I heard Zofie's feet shuffle behind me. "Mistress Ginneley told me about you. You were her strongest student until you fell in with Lord Cruimeint. Then you took a taste for the cruel."

Kegan raised an eyebrow and shook his head. "Not cruel, just practical—unlike Mistress Ginneley. I have to admit she was an excellent teacher, but unfortunately not very smart. She was offered many well-paying posts, but refused all of them, just to tutor a spoiled little princess who couldn't myst her way out of a closet." He waved his hand in the air. "But I digress. Are you going to put away those weapons?"

I caught movement out of the corner of my eye. Two cat eyes looked down on me from the decorative ledge just above the man's head. Spraggel nodded.

I called over my shoulder. "Zofie, put your sword away. We're no match for him." I moved to put my own away.

Spraggel launched himself onto Kegan's head. The man immediately tried to get off the clawing and hissing cat wrapped around his face. I lunged forward and grabbed him.

"Your curse is my curse."

Nothing happened.

Coren, I.... came Abe's strangled reply. Then silence.

A purplish glow surrounded us all as Kegan's myst charm took hold, and I suddenly couldn't move. The man unwrapped Spraggel off his head like a scarf and threw him hard against the wall. The defenseless cat didn't make a sound as he hit and slid to the floor. "Damn old man. I should have killed you when I had the chance."

He turned to me and grinned. I was frozen in place like the other statues in the crypt. He gave me a little nudge and I tipped backward, cracking my head painfully on the stone floor. He then did the same to Zofie. I struggled to breathe, but Kegan's charm would not let me.

I heard the door behind Kegan open, and the scuffing of boots as someone entered. I had a great view of the dark ceiling, so I couldn't tell you who it was.

"What took so long?" Kegan said over his shoulder. "The cat almost scratched my eyes out."

My lungs burned, and the darkness of unconsciousness crept over me. My vision began to narrow, and I felt an overwhelming sense of defeat. I had let Zofie down yet again.

I heard the new person step closer. "I was attending to our other guest," said a female voice. "She's having a little trouble adjusting."

My eyes would have gone wide in shock if I had been allowed to move. I recognized the voice.

Just as I was about to pass out, a female form squatted down beside me. Her smiling face loomed into view. "Hello, Coren."

It was Fumiko.

CHAPTER TWENTY-THREE

Captured

I slowly awoke completely disoriented. My eyes cracked open to find the area beyond my eyelids was only a little bit brighter than the darkness behind them. And someone was wrenching my arm. I think I passed out again.

When I regained consciousness the second time, I heard someone moaning softly. My eyes opened to a dim view of dirty stones fitted closely together. A wall? My puzzled brain suggested. Then I made out the sprigs of mildewed straw lying across it and realized it was actually a floor. Which meant I was looking down—no doubt why my head and shoulders were throbbing. The moaning came again, and then I realized it was me.

I tried moving my arms and was thankfully rewarded with them responding, but they didn't want to move too far—the sound of clinking metal accompanying the movement gave me a good clue as to why. Slowly lifting my head, I saw I was restrained in a sitting position on the floor with my wrists in manacles bolted to the wall and ankles similarly restrained. I nearly cried out as I pulled myself to a more erect sitting position, trying to relieve the ache in my back and butt. I licked my dry lips and wondered how long I had been out.

And most importantly, where was Zofie?

"You're awake," came a voice across from me. My first thought was that I was back on the Keeper's ship. But then I realized that couldn't be right. This had to be the castle's prison.

I looked toward the speaker and saw that Fumiko sat across from me, perched on a small wooden stool. It took me a moment to focus on her. Light from a dim myst lantern hung just behind her, putting a glare in my eyes. She had done that intentionally no doubt. She was dressed in a loose white shirt with the top laces undone, black pants, and stylish boots. Quite a difference from the poorly dressed girl that we first saw.

"Why did you betray us?" I croaked out.

She snorted and smiled. "Straight to the point. Definitely not the first question I thought you'd ask. Unfortunately, it will take too long to explain. So instead, I'll answer the next question you're going to ask." She leaned forward. "Zofie is in the cell beside us. She must still be unconscious. Kegan went a little too far in his spell. His majesty would have been very disappointed if he had killed either of you."

"And why didn't you?"

She leaned back on her stool. "Timing is everything. It's morning now, and in only a few hours, Zofie, along with Spraggel, will be executed. Hanging, I believe. Kegan even turned the old man back to his human self just so he could participate."

My thoughts were slow, and I really needed my brain to start working. I had to figure out how to get out of this. I stalled, trying to keep her talking. "But why doesn't Wynn kill her now. Everyone thinks she's dead, so why go public."

Fumiko brightened. "Ah, there have been some persistent rumors that the princess lives, and there has also been a bit of a rebellion building. Her very public execution will put those down."

I lowered my head and let it hang. "Abe?" I whispered, hoping against hope he would answer. But as I feared, he remained silent.

I looked back toward Fumiko. Some of the pieces were starting to come together. "You're not sitting in my cell just to brag, are you? You're somehow suppressing my curse. Abe told me he thought he was broke, but I didn't take him seriously. I thought it was Lady Autumn, but it was you the whole time."

She smiled. "I do seem to have that effect. Why do you think I was so eager to make him appear for my research? I was testing the extent of the blackout. He will not work when I'm within roughly twenty-five feet, unless I'm sleeping of course." She shifted in her seat. "But it's not me actively suppressing him. I have no such power. I genuinely wanted to study him, but can you imagine my surprise at the effect. There was nothing about this in any of the information I had on him. It's some kind of strange protection scheme his maker put in him."

"Protection scheme? How are you different that Abe has to shut down when you're around?"

She smiled. "A woman has to have her secrets."

Which meant there *was* something different. We considered each other for a moment. She didn't mention that I was one of those to be executed. In fact, they seemed to be taking pains to preserve me when I had no value to the king. Unless....

"There's something you need from me," I stated flatly. "Otherwise, I'd be dead now."

She smacked the tops of her legs. "You so love stealing my thunder." She then leaned over and retrieved a sack beside her. It was the same sack that had been accompanying us from our initial trip. From inside, she extracted the shiny black orb she had stolen: the Mirror of Bygone Tears. She held it up with one hand where it seemed to swallow up the little bit of light hitting it. "You're right. I need you to unlock the mirror."

"Then how come you trapped us inside the crypt? Seems kind of funny that you would take it without knowing about the key?"

Fumiko frowned. "I knew about it all right. But I had to keep you from using it. So I used a delay tactic. I knew that the crypt wouldn't hold you for long. I merely wanted to strand you on the island until Kegan could pick you up using a long-range portal. Imagine my surprise that you not only got off the island but managed to find your way back." She breathed a deep sigh. "Now be a good boy and behave, or I'll call the guards, and they'll hold you down. You're probably smarting from the bruises they've already given you. They were *not* gentle."

I gritted my teeth. "Even if I wanted to," I said. "I don't know how to use the mirror."

She grinned. "That's all right. I'll show you, but try to hurt me, and I'll call the guards. They're just outside listening to us." She came over and knelt beside me. Then taking my left hand, she held the orb in front of my curse mark.

"You've already tried this while I was unconscious, haven't you?" I said. "But it didn't work. That's why you were waiting."

She gave an exaggerated sigh. "I can't keep a secret from you. I'm not going to have anything to talk to you about if you keep this up."

I gave my head a little shake trying to clear it. It felt like it was full of stuffing. I needed to try and delay her. "Will this work without Abe being... conscious?"

"It should," she said distractedly. "His lower-level abilities still function." She tried to twist my arm so that my curse mark was exposed above the manacle. She then touched the mirror to it. She looked up expectantly, but nothing seemed to be happening.

"Maybe the iron manacle is interfering?" I said, hopefully. If I could get her to undo one cuff, then perhaps I could do something.

"Nice try, handsome."

She sighed. "The angle's wrong. It was easier when you were unconscious." She shifted closer, and when she realized she couldn't get the needed alignment, she moved to sit in my lap. She looked up at me and gave me her cruel smile. Her face was so close, I had trouble focusing on it. She gently reached up and touched my cheek. "It would have been so much easier if you had fallen for *her* instead of the princess." She paused for a moment. "This girl really fell for you."

For a moment, she looked deep into my eyes and then went back to fiddling with the mirror.

What the hell was that about? She was talking about Fumiko like she was someone else. She shifted to raise her arm, and her shirt gaped open, revealing more of her chest than I think she intended. My eyes went wide. Just below her collarbone was a dark mark. I couldn't see it clearly in the light, but it had to be a curse mark.

Could it be possible?

I felt a sudden pull of myst through me. "There!" she exclaimed. She took her hands away, but the mirror did not fall. It was not attached to my wrist, just—floating. As I watched, the mirror drifted through the air to an arm's length in front of us and then unfolded like a flower into a larger bowl-shaped object—still deep black. It faced toward us, seeming to be waiting for something.

Fumiko clapped her hands. "It's working."

I squirmed underneath her. "You've got what you want. Besides, you're making my butt go to sleep."

She leaned closer and kissed me. "Sorry love, but I need you to help me control it. Once I see you do it, I hope to be able to mimic it."

"I've already told you I don't know how."

She grabbed my wrist around my curse mark and twisted. I winced at the pain. "Tell it to show you the memories of someone who just visited Mount Eternal."

"What?"

"You heard me." Her expression grew deadly. "*Now.*"

I glared at her but repeated the command. I felt a pull of myst go through me, and then the world began to fade away. I felt like I was headed toward a dream. I realized I had done this before—when Zofie had shared her and Risten's memories. Then a moment later, my world faded, and I saw the world through someone else's eyes....

Each step made a crunching sound as I walked across a flat expanse of rock covered by a thin layer of dry snow. The chill wind blew the loose flakes across

my path and piled it up in shallow depressions and against rocks. I staggered as the wind pushed and shoved against my old body, but I continued to fight my way forward.

I stopped and straightened my back, sighting on my destination: a pile of stones in the distance. They were closer than they had been, but still a ways off. Thank the Creator I was wearing a charm that heated my body. Without it, I wouldn't have dared to come. But it wasn't perfect. The cold still seeped in, making my joints hurt—especially my knees.

"Eric," I said to myself. "You're getting too old for this." Perhaps I should have listened to my wife this time.

I took the opportunity to survey the area. I thought it strange that after all this time, the top of Mount Eternal was not what we had thought.

The mountain had been permanently scarred when its top was blown off a thousand years before, back during the war with the Dark Avenyts. Stories told that many had died that day, and it had become haunted with the dead's restless spirits. No one would go near it, and those that did quickly returned trembling in fear. Everyone in the area knew not to go there.

But a few months back, something changed on Mount Eternal. It was after those priests of Dali had visited. They had claimed a powerful myst barrier had been hiding a magnificent statue atop the mountain—and it held a magical shield. But the statue and the shield had been destroyed in a battle with someone having a magical sword. Some even said that it had been Princess Zophia Xernow back from the dead and her knight, the Thief of Curses. I snorted. Like that could ever happen.

But those rumors were not what brought me out on top of this accursed mountain. I was looking for my son. The fool had been offered a considerable number of coins if he would climb the mountain and bring back a piece of the ancient statue rumored to be there. That had been two weeks ago, and although we lived only a few days from the mountain, my son had not returned.

I was determined to find out what had happened to him and so had been following along his most likely trail.

I tugged my hood further down to shield my eyes and resumed walking. If I believed the myst casting I had done that morning, this storm would pass quickly. The really heavy snows were still a month away.

And so I trudged on.

The weather changes quickly in the high mountains. To my relief, the snowing stopped after a short while, and the wind whipped away the last of the clouds, letting the sun come out in blinding glory. But it was still cold. I quickened my pace, desperately wanting to be off the mountain top. Something about it just didn't feel right.

It didn't take much longer before I arrived at the broken pieces of rock I had seen in the distance. It did look like something had fallen—and from the smoothness of some of the stones, it could indeed have been a statue.

I began to walk along the perimeter of the pile, carefully picking my way, but stopped short when I spotted a body sprawled in front of a particularly large chunk of rock. My breath caught as I recognized the coat. I ran over and turned the body over, confirming my worst fears. It was my son, all cold and stiff.

A deep sadness welled up inside me. He had been my youngest. The baby.

But as I looked closer, I noticed a gaping wound in his chest. My eyes went wide in shock. The cold hadn't gotten him. He'd been murdered.

I heard a crunch behind me and whipped around to confront whatever it was. But my eyes went wide in shock. The creature was not human, having large eyes, an ape-like face and a huge mouth filled to the brim with sharp teeth. It was completely hairless and wore some kind of slick garment that reflected the light like a mirror. I somehow knew the garment had hidden him as I walked right past.

While I fumbled for my knife, the creature caught me around the throat and lifted me off my feet. Suspended in the air, I struggled to get free.

It pulled me close to its maul, and I could smell its hot breath. It hissed as it spoke in near perfect Ellish, "You are a myst user. And you are mine!"

I jerked back from the memory as did Fumiko. We blinked at each other, gradually catching our bearings.

She grinned in delight. "It works. It really works."

Somehow, I knew that the memory was from about three days ago, and I knew exactly where it was. I had been involved in making that pile of rubble.

My eyes were drawn to the waiting mirror. I also understood the power in the mirror and why it had been hidden. To be able to see into people's lives without their knowledge was terrible! And powerful. Even if it was limited to just myst users, the things one could do with this. No secret would be safe.

No secret.

Fumiko started to rise. "I have to tell his majesty. He will be most pleased."

"Fumiko. Before you leave. I'd like to ask something."

She looked at me impatiently. "What?"

"Have the mirror, *show me how you got your curse?*"

Fumiko's eyes went wide. "*NO!*" she yelled.

But it was already too late. The mirror started its cycle, and we were immersed in Fumiko's past. And through Fumiko's eyes, I watched her travesty unfold.

There were strange horses in front of the cottage.

I froze at the sight, momentarily forgetting the load of firewood in my arms and the strain they put on my back. At first, my distracted brain refused to process the unusual sight. I had been thinking of what I could possibly fix differently with what we had in the cupboard. Preferably something that didn't require beans. I was convinced that if I put one more bean into my mouth, I was going to turn into one. I had begged Master Tormaigh for some rice—only a handful even. My mouth had watered at the thought. Just a small cup of steamy rice. I hadn't had any since leaving my homeland. I had even promised to do double—no, triple chores!

But my master had declined. He claimed that beans built character. I had countered that character didn't come with a gaseous odor.

I had left an hour earlier to scout the surrounding forest for a mushroom or edible plant, but unfortunately, all I been able to find was some suitable firewood. It looked like beans were again on the menu for dinner.

I had just stepped around the corner of the small work shed when I saw the horses tied to the post in front of the cottage. There were only two horses, but something about them made me uneasy. I dropped my load of firewood and ran to the door of our cottage, my dress pulling at my calves and my bare feet slapping the ground.

I slowed to a walk as I drew near. I eyed the horses as I passed, as they eyed me. They were large and well cared for—their tackle clean and shiny. This seemed odd to me since we were at least a day's ride from the closest village.

The cottage had a small, uncovered porch. Master liked to sit there to do his reading. He said it had the best light. I could see his wooden chair was still outside, and the book he had been studying rested upon his seat. He had indeed been interrupted unawares.

From inside, I heard my master's voice. He sounded frustrated. "...I'm sorry, I do realize you're on the king's business, but I have no further information. I have read extensively about the Mirror of Bygone Tears, but the information is all the same: that it was hidden at the end of the war with the Dark Avenyts and its location was sealed."

I paused on the porch for a moment and collected myself. I shoved my forever loose strands of short hair behind one ear and tried to smooth down my plain dress. Then after taking a deep breath, I stepped to the threshold.

Inside stood my master with two others. One was a large, broad-shouldered man several hands taller than average with dark hair and arms the size of small trees—he immediately reached for his sword as my shadow entered the room. Death was in his eye, but when he saw I was just a girl, he relaxed.

The remaining person was a woman. I recognized her as a dealer in books my master had worked with in the past. She had a slender build, almost skinny, and of medium height. If I had ever been given her name, I could not recall it; although, I did remember her visit. It had been shortly after I had arrived when I still suffered from the attacks of fear. I had hidden in the barn and viewed the transaction from afar.

But today, she did not seem the poor merchant I remembered. She wore fine pants and a jacket suitable for a noble. Her chestnut brown hair was pulled back in a bun at the back of her head and fastened with a gold clip. She smiled when she saw me. But it was not the smile one would give when meeting someone. It was the smile of a predator realizing it had new prey. I knew that smile well. I had seen it enough in the courts of my homeland.

"Why, now who is this?" exclaimed the woman. "Is she perhaps your daughter?"

Master Tormaigh gave me a worried glance, which told me he was not enjoying this little visit and would have preferred I had kept my distance. "No, this is my apprentice Fumiko," he said. "She is helping with my research."

I bowed to them and stepped forward. "Master, you should have called me." Then turning to the guests. "Can I offer you some tea to refresh yourself from your journey?"

But the woman stepped in front of me. I looked down, as I had been taught, but she took my chin and lifted it. I am not a very tall person, but she was at least a head taller. She gazed down at me. "What land does she come from?" the woman asked. "Her eyes are so cute."

Master cleared his throat. "She is from the lands over the mountains and far to the east. I came across her family during my travels years ago, and they asked me to teach her how to be a scholar." Not exactly the truth, but it was the story we had agreed to.

The woman gave a knowing smile. "She is quite cute. I bet she has done some prolonged research in your bed at night."

I stiffened. Master was aware of my situation and had very reluctantly taken me on. He had always treated me with the utmost respect. He was more a father to me than my own had ever been. My change in expression was not lost on the woman, and her smile drew just a fraction wider. I did not like this person.

Master also did not appreciate the comment. "Fumiko is an excellent apprentice in all ways. Nothing more, nothing less."

The woman continued to gaze at me with hungry eyes. "If you ever tire of her. Please let me know. I could teach her a thing or two." And then she released me and turned back to my master. I moved to the hearth and began making tea. I debated about putting some poison in for our guests.

The woman gave a deep sigh and pointed at my master. "I think you are lying, Scholar Tormaigh. I think you know where the mirror is and how to get to it. You have, after all, made this your life's work. I heard from one of my colleagues that they had delivered a piece of a book that you had been missing."

I nearly dropped the kettle. Master had just recently discovered something in an ancient historical account. About how the mirror had been used. And also how its creator had decided it was too powerful to keep, and yet too important to destroy.

The woman smiled. "I guess we will have to find out." I could feel a power around the woman start to swell—and then abruptly cut off. She frowned, clearly unhappy. "You have a curse."

I turned to look at her. What could a curse have to do with my master's work? Unless she was going to....

I looked around the room for something to use as a weapon. The only knife we had lay on the table just to the side. It was old and thin from heavy use, but I knew it to be quite sharp as the cuts on my fingers would attest.

Master drew himself up. "Get out of my house. You may be on the king's business, but this is too much."

The big man moved in an eye blink, and using one of his huge arms, locked it around Master's throat.

I eased toward the knife on the table.

The woman pursed her lips and patted them with a finger. "This does pose a problem. He's completely unusable."

The large man spoke for the first time, a hint of irritation in his voice. "Can't you just take it off him?"

"No Wort, the person who put it on him was very strong."

The man called Wort snorted. "I thought you said you could take anyone."

The woman shot back. "Well, not if they're cursed, I can't. No one can."

I slowly moved my hand toward the knife. The large man would be difficult to attack, but the woman—

I lunged the last few inches, jerked the woman to face me, and pressed the knife to her throat. "Release my master, now! Or the woman dies!"

And to my horror, the woman just chuckled. "The Supreme does provide," she said. "If one can't have the master, one has to settle for the apprentice."

"I said release my master!" I shoved the knife tighter, and a thin trickle of blood leaked down her throat.

"Wort," the woman called. "I will have this one."

Master struggled in the man's grip but was unable to break free. "Leave her alone!" he called.

Wort seemed to not even notice my master's exertions. "What if she doesn't know?" he asked.

To my horror, the woman smiled. "She's young. I'll enjoy it none the less."

"LET GO OF MY MASTER!" I screamed.

The woman looked at me. "Go ahead. Do it. It will make it easier."

And I instantly knew I had made a grave error. Something was afoot I did not understand. I made to jerk back, but the woman grabbed my hand—the one with the knife in it. She was incredibly strong. Her other arm snaked around my waist and pulled me closer until the blade was pressed tightly between us.

Over my struggles, she guided the knife to point at her own heart. And then she smiled, gazing deep into my eyes. She wore an expression so smug, so sure of herself... so pleased, I knew for sure I was looking into the eyes of pure evil.

"Go ahead," she whispered. "Defend your master. Try to save yourself. Kill me."

This woman did not know my past. I was no innocent. Far from it. I had killed more people than I had lived years. But I had sworn to give it up. To never harm again.

My head moved back and forth in denial.

The woman's expression changed to one of pity. "Poor thing." She leaned forward, her mouth right beside my ear. I could feel her hot breath against my skin and the tickle of her hair against my cheek. "But don't worry," she breathed. "I won't die."

She then jerked me tight against her and the knife sank into her chest. I felt her warm blood coat my hands and run down the front of my dress.

Still, she held me close. "I curse you," she whispered.

"To become me."

Immediately, I felt a red glow spring up around us. And I suddenly found I could not move. The world seemed to stop and grow dim....

I blinked and I was standing in a place of all gray: everything around me, for as far as the eye could see was a dull light gray. I looked at my hands to find no knife, no blood, no woman. Beside me stood a stick figure with arms and legs, which were nothing more than simple lines, and a head that was large and perfectly round—almost like a drawn circle. Inside the head was the symbol of a hand mirror, which seemed to reflect back the gray of our surroundings. To my horror, the stick thing stepped toward me, moving with a fluid grace. I wanted to run, but my legs wouldn't move. Its head leaned close and I made out the intricate details of the mirror inside. There almost seemed to be tiny gears moving inside it. It reached out a stick figure finger and touched my forehead. It felt ice cold and burned where it touched. Suddenly in the mirror of its head, I saw my own reflection. Me in every detail.

I gasped in horror struggling to move.

But the image of myself moved of its own accord and smiled at me.

It was the same evil smile the woman had used.

Suddenly, I was back in my body. But something was different. It felt wrong.

The stabbed woman collapsed, falling to the floor. I still gripped the knife that had killed her. I didn't even look to see if she had died yet. _No! No!_ I screamed, but nothing came out of my mouth.

I set the blade down on the table and picked up a small towel, wiping off some of the blood from my hands. I looked down at the blood on my dress.

"Being a little dramatic, aren't you?" asked Wort. "That's quite the mess."

I felt myself grin, even though I didn't want to grin. "True," I said. "But it was worth it. Her fear was so...." and then I shivered in pleasure. Only it wasn't my shiver, nor my pleasure. It was someone else's.

"Well, did you get what you wanted?" Wort asked.

I picked up the knife and stepped toward them. My master struggled.

I felt what I could only describe as feather brushes inside my head. Memories came forward unbidden in a rush of information, as if someone were thumbing through a book. I howled in rage at the assault—worse than any physical rape. Not only had this thing stolen my body, it was stealing all my knowledge, all my skills... and the secrets I tried my best to forget.

I felt my eyes go wide, and my mouth break into a wide smile. "Creator be damned. Did I ever. She's a treasure trove of information. And the skills...." She pointed the knife at my master. "You can kill him. She has everything we need."

"And the key?"

"It's not here. But she knows where it is. In fact, it's not a thing but a person. And you'll never guess who it is."

No! Please no! I screamed.

"And they're on their way here right this minute."

_No! No! NO!_

"It's that stupid boy. The Thief of Curses."

CHAPTER TWENTY-FOUR

A Final Offer

I came back to the present with a shock. Fumiko pushed away and stood. She glared down at me, her face red in anger. "Why did you do that?" she spat. "Now I might have to kill you. I was so hoping I could get you to come around."

"You're a curse," I said, eyes wide in disbelief. "A curse that has taken over Fumiko's body."

She pursed her lips in a tight line. She grabbed the floating mirror, which had collapsed back into a sphere, and strode to the cell door, scooping up her sack as she went. She angrily flung it open and slammed it shut behind her. I heard chains outside.

I shook my head at the new information. The Fumiko I knew was a curse. A conscious curse, similar to what Abe was. It explained a lot. It was thanks to our own curses that Zofie and I hadn't been taken as well. That was the one firm rule of curses—a person could only have one. Which means I might be able to steal it, if I could just get Abhulengulus to work around her.

Coren! Came Abe's booming voice inside my head. *I think I blacked out again.*

Speak of the devil. "You did. And now I know why."

You do? Did you and the princess figure out something?

"No. Well, yes." I sighed. "Just listen a moment. Remember the girl Fumiko I mentioned a while back. The one we went to about the mirror. She's the one that has been suppressing you. Plus, she carries a curse similar to yours, and it has taken possession of her body."

Abe was silent. I was afraid he had stopped working again.

"Abe, you still there?"

Yes, he answered. He sounded concerned. *I was just thinking. This explains a lot. I must be getting old not to have seen it before.* He paused. *This is bad. You have no idea just how bad it really is.*

In the deadly silence of the prison, I heard someone approaching. Many someones. Outside my cell, I heard chains rattling and then Zofie's voice not too far away.

"Zofie!" I yelled. I jerked to the limits of my chains. They must be taking her away.

"Coren!" I heard her yell back and then scuffling. She called out again, but her voice was more distant. I called to her once more, but this time received no reply.

Abe interrupted my misery. He spoke quickly. *You must find the secret word. Without it, I cannot help you.*

It was just too much for me. I exploded. "Do you think I've not been trying? I have looked and asked and researched, but I can't find it!" Uncharacteristic of me, I blinked back tears of frustration. "I wish I'd never gotten this stupid curse!"

Abe ignored my little tirade. *You have to find it Coren. You have all the pieces. And if you don't soon... we're all doomed. You're the only one! I....*

He broke off in mid-sentence just as chains started to rattle outside my cell door. Three guards entered. A displeased Fumiko stood behind them. Two held spears to my throat while the third unlocked my chains.

With Fumiko trailing behind, they took me out and past several sets of similar cells. They escorted me up into the castle, and past several other guards posted periodically along our route. We finally stopped in front of a set of ornately carved doors. The kind you would expect every king to be behind. I braced myself for what was to come as the doors slowly opened inwards to reveal....

The baths?

I was prodded inside where two man-servants quickly stripped me, bathed me, shaved me, and combed my hair in record time. To my further embarrassment, Fumiko watched silently, staying within range to suppress my curse.

I was quickly redressed in a fine shirt, pants, and boots and topped off with a jacket of material that nobles would have worn. I was clearly puzzled by the treatment.

My guards, who had been watching my embarrassment with amusement, collected me and again marched me through the castle. Fumiko again trailed along behind, keeping within a safe distance of me. This time we entered a long room with an elegant table that spanned its length. I was shocked to see Wynn sitting at its head. I recognized him from the memories Zofie had shared with me.

The table was laden with all kinds of food—breakfast items mostly. But since everyone's plates were still empty, I had to assume they had not started yet. Wynn was in deep conversation with a man sitting on his left—Kegan. Kegan too seemed to have dressed for the occasion in a bright red coat that almost hurt my eyes. The powerful myst user smiled along with Wynn at my entrance. Fumiko took a seat just to Kegan's left. She watched me intently as a predator observing its prey.

But it was Wynn's presence that dominated the room. As I had seen in Zofie's memory, the young man had dark red hair the same shade as his sister, pulled back in a tight braid down his back. He also had the same smattering of freckles across the nose, and his eyes were the same shade of blue. There was no mistaking the common heritage. He would have easily caught the attention of the ladies even if he hadn't been royalty. I couldn't help but notice the King's Sword hanging from his belt.

Wynn gave me a broad smile. It was such a friendly and welcoming smile, I could easily see why he had no trouble gathering allies.

"Welcome, Coren Hart, Thief of Curses," Wynn said. "We finally meet. Would you like to break your fast with us?"

The guards escorted me to the empty place on Wynn's right. One held the chair for me as I sat. The guards then stepped back against the wall.

I looked around in puzzlement. The change in my treatment had taken me completely off guard.

Servants quickly swapped out my empty plate for one filled with all kinds of things: bread, ham, and most importantly, eggs. My mouth watered and my stomach growled.

I pulled my eyes away from my plate and took a deep breath. "Where's Zofie and Risten?"

Wynn smiled in amusement. "I had heard you were direct. I assure you, both are safe. In fact, my sister will be joining us shortly. It is just taking her a little longer to dress." He leaned forward. "You know how ladies are." He leaned back. "But first, let's eat."

"I thought you were going to execute Zofie and Spraggel."

Wynn nodded in agreement. "Oh, I intend to. But that doesn't mean we can't have one last meal together as a family. We have some time before her trial starts. She'll go straight to the gallows after that."

I stared at him in shock. I couldn't decipher his behavior. Was it a gesture of kindness, or was he being exceedingly cruel?

Fumiko was sitting back thoughtfully chewing on a slice of bread. Kegan, on the other hand, was aggressively attacking his plate, determined not to let a single morsel escape his relentless fork.

"Zophia will be joining us in a bit. However, I wanted the chance to talk with you alone first. It's not every day that a piece of history walks into one's home."

"Is this the part where you offer to let Zofie live if I help you?"

"No, that's an interesting thought though, but not exactly what I had in mind. I was thinking more along the lines that I would let you keep your life. With your curse not working, you can just as easily die as the rest. I might even let you keep your title of knight and grant you a smallholding. And in exchange you would swear fealty to me. There are just a *few* things I need your help with." His eyes twinkled.

"I won't do anything unless you release Zofie—*with* a full pardon. It was you after all that set up the elaborate trap that killed her father."

He smiled. "That is what she told you, no doubt. And I'm sure she believes it—in her own way. After all, memories can be altered. She may have even altered them herself—she has that power." He leaned forward. "Come now, Coren. How well do you *really* know Zophia? How do you know she isn't a murderer? The myst signature was hers and hers alone." He leaned back and smiled. "I'll even bet she admitted it to you. That she was the one that killed our father." He took a sip of his drink. "The surest lie is the truth."

I shook my head in denial, but doubts nibbled at my conviction. Could Zofie really have been lying to me? Could I really be wrong? Zofie had admitted that she murdered her father, although she had been forced into it. An image came to mind of Zofie's fireside confession while in her chimera form. Her suffering had been real.

No. I felt it in my heart. There was no way Zofie had done it. She didn't have it in her. And this man. He was more twisted than I ever imagined.

"You're lying."

Wynn's eyebrows went up. He seemed disappointed. "Believe as you wish, but in her heart, she knows she is the one that killed Father. I am doing her a favor by giving her a proper punishment for her sin." He shook his head. "No, Zophia's fate cannot be changed. It is not negotiable. But there is one who you could save. Your old master has been returned to his human form just so he can die with my sister today. Now he, I would consider giving a pardon." He smiled and shoved a bite of eggs in his mouth, chewing happily.

I looked him in the face. "And what small tasks do you have for me? Operating the mirror for you so you can spy on others?"

"Well, using the Mirror of Bygone Tears would be one. I have enemies all across the kingdom, and it would definitely help in unearthing those." He leaned forward. "But there is something else I need from you. I need for you to remove some curses. For example, Lord Pringottin will be coming to see me today about the execution. He is no doubt going to plead that Zophia is of more use to me alive than dead. The fact he has a son that could marry her is not lost on me."

Lord Pringottin was Spraggel's sworn lord and owned the lands our keep resided in. We knew for a fact that he was no fan of Wynn's. But he had stopped short of openly opposing him, fearing a royal reprisal. I shook my head. "You just want me to remove their curses? Not kill them, or take them captive? And how do you know Pringottin is cursed? It would seem odd that he has one."

Wynn shrugged. "Not really. It's common practice for nobles to take on a minor one to give them a skin blemish, or maybe even make it so they don't snore. If a powerful myst user puts it on them, then they are protected from nastier ones."

I glanced at Fumiko and saw her staring intently at me. That's when it came together. The curse posing as Fumiko could move to Lord Pringottin and immediately ensure the man's loyalty.

I shook my head. "No, I won't help you." I leaned in Wynn's direction. "It doesn't get me what I really want."

Wynn gave me an amused smile. "So we're back to that. Persistent, I'll give you that. And pray tell *why* I should let her live."

I thought for a moment to organize my argument. "The princess has already been declared dead, so keeping her around as a commoner shouldn't be a problem. We could also figure out something for Risten. Even banishment might be an option." I didn't go into the whole 'get her kingdom back thing.' I was trying to save her life here. We'd worry about who their ruler was later.

Wynn put a finger to his chin in thought. "And how would I ensure Zophia wouldn't betray me?"

"I would take responsibility for her and Risten too."

Wynn snorted. "I admire that you think you can keep my sister under control, but I doubt, no matter how *close* you two may have become, that she would listen to you. My sister can be a little headstrong." He casually turned in his chair toward Fumiko. "However, there might be another way."

Wynn continued addressing Fumiko. "What do you think, my dear. Think we could find some way to keep Zophia under control?"

Fumiko smiled. "I think we could find a way. Especially if he were to remove her curse."

My eyes went wide. I could have smacked myself in the head. I felt I had just walked into a heavily choreographed play, with me as the fool. Wynn was playing with me and knew exactly what he was doing.

I leaped to my feet. The chair fell backward, startling the guards behind me. I leaned on the table glaring at Wynn. "I will *not* remove her curse, so the thing controlling Fumiko can take Zofie."

Wynn leaned back in his chair. "Don't be so hasty to judge. Just think about it, Coren. A young man like you couldn't possibly be happy with one woman. You could have Zophia and Fumiko. They would both be perfect lovers." To illustrate the point, Fumiko came over to stand beside me. She draped both arms around my neck.

Just then, the door to the dining room opened, and the guards escorted Zofie in. She was wearing a long formal dress, a pale shade of violet, and had her hair done up in a complex set of braids curling around her head. Around her neck, she wore a silver choker with a single amulet hanging from it. She was breathtakingly beautiful. I could see relief flood her face as she saw me.

Without taking my eyes off Zofie, I lifted Fumiko's arms from around me. She gave me a playful pout and turned back toward her place.

Wynn rose and motioned to the chair beside me. "Perfect timing, sister. Why don't you have a seat next to your *knight*."

Her guards escorted her to sit beside me. My own guard righted my chair, and with a heavy hand, guided me back to it. Under the table, my hand found Zofie's, and she clasped it tightly.

Wynn put his elbows on the table and leaned forward. "Good to see you again, sister. We were just discussing whether I should spare you or not. I have made an offer to spare your life, but dear Coren won't agree to my terms." He turned his gaze on me. "So why don't you explain to Zophia why you are going to let her die."

I leaned forward. "I'm not the one executing her. You are."

Zofie squeezed my hand and said, "The king is just in all that he does."

What! I looked at her in puzzlement. She blinked back at me in surprise. She spoke again. "The *king* is just in all that he does." She covered her mouth in shock. She shook her head as if clearing it and then spoke again. "The *king* is just in all that he does."

Wynn laughed. "It seems Zophia agrees with me."

Red-faced, Zofie glared at him. Her fingers crept to her throat feeling for her necklace. She grasped it firmly and tried to yank it off, but the delicate silver chain would not break. Abandoning the attempt to remove it, she dipped her finger in her cup and began to write on the linen tablecloth. "Necklace... charm... words... wrong... bastard."

I turned to Wynn. "Zofie says that you've put a charm on her necklace that makes her words come out wrong." I smiled. "Also, that you are a bastard."

Wynn shrugged. "I thought it would make her trial go a little faster if she said the right words." He leaned forward, an evil delight on his face. "So what will it be Coren. Does Zofie head off to be executed, or do you remove her curse."

Zofie shook her head emphatically. She patted her chest over her heart and then patted mine. The intention was clear: *You won't, if you love me.*

I am not proud to say, but I froze—unable to process how to proceed. I could hear a loud roaring in my ears. I did not want to see her die, yet I could not bear to see her will taken by some dark curse.

Wynn stood. "Take him back. The trial is about to start, and we don't want to be late. It will be so humorous seeing Zophia try to defend herself."

The guards were immediately at my side. I flung myself at them but froze in mid-step as I felt a myst spell fall over me. I heard Kegan behind me. "I thought he might do something like that."

I fell into the arms of the waiting guard. I was really getting tired of being frozen in place.

CHAPTER TWENTY-FIVE

Execution

I was taken back to my cell, but without the shackles this time. I guess they figured there was no need now. They had Zofie. I had to admit the accommodations made it easy to consider one's fate. Fumiko was not in my cell with me, but I didn't think she was far away. No matter how hard I tried, I couldn't get Abe to respond to me.

So I sat against the wall and considered what I should do about Zofie. This was the question circulating through my mind. Do I let her die, or do I commit her to a life of hell? And for once, I wished I had Abe's irritating banter to help me find the answer.

I was not terribly surprised when, a short while later, the door opened and Fumiko stepped inside. She put her hands on her hips. She looked concerned. "You really should take Wynn's offer, Coren. It's the best one you'll get today."

I looked up at her standing over me. "What's it like? You know, to have a curse controlling you. Is the real Fumiko even still there?"

Fumiko smiled. "She's not dead, if that's what you're concerned about. She's still here. Inside me." Fumiko squatted down so she was at eye level. "I have access to all her memories, her mannerisms, and everything else that makes her Fumiko. The personality we displayed was all hers at the beginning. Although my own has gradually crept in." She leaned closer. "She's conscious even now, watching my every move. To be honest, she's been quite the challenge to hold onto. She has a strong personality and a past darker than one would assume based on just meeting her. She..." Fumiko winced. "She doesn't like me to talk about her past. So I'll stop there—it's not worth the headache."

"Was it you, or Fumiko that drove away those kidnappers on the road?"

She nodded. "That was all her. Awesome, wasn't it? In that brief moment, our desires coincided, so I gave her rein. She has skills that you wouldn't believe." She winced again. "Fumiko would prefer I say no more."

"Could I talk with her? The *real* Fumiko."

The curse controlling her body considered this. "I don't see why not. I'll be watching everything. Plus we've come to a bit of an understanding." She grinned. "She has really been taken with you. That portrait she did of you was all hers." Fumiko closed her eyes and then opened them.

I can't really describe the difference, but I knew this was a different person, a *completely* different personality. It was very subtle: the change in the muscles around her eyes, the tightness of her shoulders, the position of her lips. It just looked like someone that was intimately familiar with their own body.

Fumiko moved to a kneeling position and bowed, touching her head to the floor. "Coren, I'm so sorry. I didn't..." She turned her gaze up to me just barely. Tears were in her eyes. "I have done you a grave disservice. I am to blame."

"No," I said. "It's not your fault when you're the victim."

She sat up and shuffled closer. She hesitantly took my hand, turning it over to stare down at my palm. She drew her finger across it. "They've hurt you." She looked me in the eyes with an unflinchingly open gaze. Embarrassed, I looked down at her finger moving across my palm.

As I watched, I noticed that her path across my palm was not random. She was spelling something. D—O—N—O—T—

She was trying to tell me something. I tried to keep the conversation going. "This is nothing. Especially after the pain you've been through."

T—R—U—S—T

She shrugged. "I really did do that portrait for you. I was hoping you would like it. Maybe even get you to pay attention to me. Although, I've known from the beginning that you've set your heart on the princess. She is a very fine person."

H—E—R—

She chuckled. "I have to admit I'm a little jealous of her. Especially the way you two complete each other's quotes. I find that so endearing."

Do not trust her. That was what she had written on the portrait she had one done for me. Is she telling me not to trust the cursed Fumiko? That kind of goes without saying. Or is she trying to give me some other piece of information?

The movement of her finger continued: F—A—

"That time in your cabin, I really was going to kiss you."

T—E

Suddenly her finger stopped and that subtle change of expression returned. The curse was back in control.

"Naughty, naughty," Fumiko said, leaning back. "Trying to take advantage of my generosity to pass secret messages." She snorted. "As if that would help."

Fumiko stood, dusting off her pants. "The trial is over now. No surprise that all of you were sentenced to death by hanging at noon. We'll be using Wynn's special gallows on the docks for this one—he built it shortly after taking the throne, and it's been pretty heavily used since. It will be able to hang all four of you at once, including that ship's captain. Although the crew will have to wait their turn."

My mouth fell open. "You captured Captain Milner and the crew of the *Bernard*? You couldn't have, unless you had known ahead of time?"

Fumiko grinned. "Haven't you figured out that Wynn is an excellent planner? Zofie's curse, contacting you, and then finding the shield and the mirror... they were all part of his plan. You've been nothing but simple pawns in a master's game." She moved to the door and motioned to the guards just outside. "That's why I suggest you accept Wynn's offer. It's the only one you'll get. And even if you decline—he'll still get his way." She turned to leave, but paused and looked back. "And I advise you to do it soon. It's hard to stop a hanging once the noose tightens."

She stepped outside the door and yelled for the guards. They entered and roughly tied my hands behind my back. I hardly noticed, thinking about what Fumiko just told me. Zofie, Spraggel, Captain Milner, and I would be hanged together. Then where was Risten? Had they already killed her?

"Where's Risten? Why haven't you mentioned her?"

Fumiko looked back over her shoulder as we left the cell. "Oh, didn't I mention, she's occupied at the moment."

"Occupied doing what?"

Fumiko shrugged. "I don't know. Something Wynn wanted done."

And then it hit me. Dread squeezed my heart.

"You put one of those curses on her?" I said in disbelief.

Fumiko grinned. "Of course. Do you think we could pass up the best sword-master of this generation?"

I lunged forward, but the guards easily held me. "You bastards!"

Fumiko gave a signal to one of them, and he punched me hard in the stomach. As I bent over trying to catch my breath, Fumiko squatted down to look into my face. "Now, now. We can't have you making too much noise."

Still catching my breath, they escorted me to the castle's courtyard. The air outside was damp and cold, with an overcast gray sky and the ground wet from a recent sprinkling. I wished I had my cloak. Too bad they didn't call off hangings for bad weather.

In the courtyard, I found a little procession forming up in a large circle. It was made up of several wagons and *lots* of soldiers. Three flat-bed wagons were pointed toward the castle's gates, each with a vertical pole affixed to its center. And tied to each were Zofie, Captain Milner, and Spraggel. Two other wagons held the bound and kneeling crew of the *Bernard*. Zofie strained to watch me as I emerged and began to struggle with chains holding her. She was still wearing her fine dress and looked every bit the princess she was. Milner hung limp in his chains, and from the bruises and cuts on his face, looked to have put up a respectable resistance. Spraggel, on the other hand, now wearing his gray-bearded human form, nodded to me and looked like he would have waved if he hadn't been bound. Typical of him, he seemed more amused than anything.

Everyone was already in place and looked ready to leave as soon as I was in place. I had thought there would be a wagon for me, but I was instead placed inside a covered carriage bringing up the rear. Fumiko got in beside me.

I had to lean forward because my hands were bound behind me. But it gave me a good view of the wagons ahead, and Zofie standing tall and proud on her wagon. I couldn't help but go back to the central question in my head. *What should I do?* Do I save Zofie and commit her to be a slave, or do I let her be executed? Creator, I didn't want her to die. But to make her an absolute slave to some else's will? I shook my head. Either way, I was going to regret it. I felt so worthless. I was her knight, and yet I couldn't even save her.

The procession continued to wait, so I assumed there must be one more. Fumiko was looking out the window distractedly, and I briefly considered trying to get past her and out the door. But I decided against it. I wouldn't make it two steps.

As I looked at her profile, my mind drifted back to the message that the real Fumiko had tried to pass on to me. *Do not trust her. Fate...* is what she had spelled out. The first part had also been on the picture that Fumiko had done. It was like she was trying to tell me something important. But what? And what was it she said about completing quotes. Why had she brought that up? Could she be indicating it was part of a larger passage? I shook my head. The words were familiar, but where had I seen them?

A moment later, Wynn was escorted to join us in the carriage. He smiled at seeing me inside and then took the seat across from me.

"How come I get the honor of riding in a carriage?" I asked. "Seems like I should have been on one of those wagons, too."

As soon as the carriage's door was shut, our little procession started moving forward.

Wynn leaned toward me. "I wanted to give you one last chance to change your mind. Having someone with your abilities would be most useful." He turned and looked over his shoulder at the procession. "Just look at her. Beautiful, isn't she. And standing so proud too. It's a shame to let her die."

"Then why are you killing her!" I shouted, losing my patience.

Fumiko beside me put a restraining hand on my shoulder. Wynn leaned back in his seat smiling. I was really starting to hate that smile.

"Because she needs to either be restrained or removed," Wynn said matter-of-factly. "I have big plans for the kingdom, and my sister would be completely against them." His expression took on one of fondness. "She can be very headstrong. I heard mother was the same way." He gave his head a little shake and looked up at me. "It's all Mother's fault really. She died."

I remember him saying the exact same thing in Zofie's memory. How had her death been the fault of all this? I began to suspect that Wynn might be insane.

The carriage lurched over a pothole, and I leaned forward to ease the ache in my shoulders. Looking out the window, I could see people lining the street. Armed soldiers circulated in front of them. Most of the people watched us pass expressionless and silent. They had the blank hopelessness of the beaten. How many of their relatives had already been executed on Wynn's gallows? Even more had likely just been cut down where they stood. The kingdom had indeed become a very dark place.

Wynn continued to make comments about the advantages of join-ing him, but I ceased to listen. I was in the midst of my own internal dialogue. Let her die, or allow her to be enslaved? Which was worse? I was having a hard time making up my mind.

After riding for over a half-hour, I glanced ahead and saw the wag-ons approaching our destination: the wharf beside the harbor. That might seem an odd place to hold a hanging, but it all had to do with the geography.

Edlingreen Castle had been built on a high rocky cliff overlooking where the Edi River flowed into the bay. While strategically secure, it afforded no place for a large number of people to gather. But just a lit-tle further was Wyndhaven Harbor, which had a broad expanse next to the water and perfectly suitable for a large crowd. It was paved in stone all along the water's edge and provided a wide buffer between the harbor and the shops facing the bay. Normally the open area would be full of cargo and ships tied to the wharf. But now it was empty and the vessels absent—a testament to the mistreatment that had occurred to the kingdom's economy.

A fountain had once served to mark the road's intersection with the harbor, but it had been covered over with a large gallows. A short dis-tance away, Wynn had even built stands for the nobles to witness the proceedings. I counted four nooses hanging from the tall cross-bar of the gallows and easily visible for all to see. Well, at least we would all go together.

As we neared the water, I could see a dense gray fog over the harbor. It gave the air a cold dampness that seemed to steal not only all color, but all warmth and goodness. But fighting against the dreary atmos-phere were decorations of bright red ribbons and wreaths of pine the people had put out on their doors and windows for the Day of the New. I couldn't help but smile at this act of bravery.

Traditionally, the festival season started on the Winter Solstice and ran for seven days, ending on the Day of the New. It was normally, a time for giving gifts to friends and family, and naturally lots of good food and drink. It had started over a thousand years ago after the defeat of the Dark Avenyts: the wreaths of pine to remind us of the start of winter while the red ribbons were for those that had lost their lives in the great war. And on the last day of the festival, just after sunset, there would normally be a great fireworks display. Wyndhaven Harbor took pride in their display, claiming there was no other like it. I shook my head. Only this year, I doubted there would be one for the first time in generations.

"So," said Wynn, bringing me back to the present. "What will it be? Death for Zophia, or remove her curse and have both of you come into my service."

"I...." Words completely left me. "Zofie...."

I couldn't let her die, could I?

Wynn leaned forward. "Better hurry Coren. Now's the time to do the right thing. Don't hold back."

It was like a slap in the face. *Don't hold back.* Zofie hated it when people made decisions for her. She had been very clear on what she wanted. I would totally betray her if I didn't. She would never forgive me if I condemned her to the life of being a prisoner and forcing her to watch all manner of atrocities.

I suddenly grew certain of my answer.

"I must decline." The words left my lips before I could call them back.

Wynn blinked, looking surprised for the first time since we met. "I am not jesting here. I *will* kill her."

I took a deep breath and then let it out slowly. "I have no doubt you're serious. But I cannot agree to your terms. Zofie would not agree to them either."

The carriage rolled to a stop, and the carriage door opened. Wynn frowned as he made his exit. "Fool," he said. Then he turned to Fumiko. "Execute him. If he won't play along, then I have no use for him."

Fumiko nodded and looked to me as Wynn walked away. But she did not appear pleased. "Don't make me hurt you further. Fumiko is crying inside our collective head right now. Every time I have to hurt you, she wails a little louder."

I was escorted toward the gallows, while Wynn went to the viewer's stand to join the other nobles already gathered there. He flung himself onto his throne like a sulking child.

Zofie, Spraggel, Captain Milner, and I were all herded up the steep stairs to the main platform. Zofie took each step with dignity and held her head high. Captain Milner could barely stand and was mostly carried to his spot. Spraggel doddered along behind like he was going to a party.

The gallows was constructed so that the noose was put over one's neck, and then when a lever was pushed, a trap door was opened beneath the condemned's feet. They would fall through snapping their neck. It was supposed to be quick and painless, but I didn't think anyone could actually testify to that.

Milner was placed under the noose closest to the stairs, then Spraggel, Zofie, and finally me on the end. The executioner was silent as he put the nooses over our heads.

The executioner went to the lever at the edge of the platform. He gazed up at Wynn, waiting for the order to proceed. Zofie looked over at me and gave me a sad smile. "The king is *just* in all that he *does*."

I smiled back. "Yes, I know. And I love you too."

She gave a weak smile and blinked back a tear.

Fumiko came up on the platform and paused the executioner with an upraised palm. She strode over to me, adjusting the noose around my neck. "It's not too late Coren. Just give the king your allegiance and all of you will be spared." I looked up into the stand that had been constructed for the nobility. Wynn sat at the top on his throne. He did not appear happy.

I looked Fumiko in the eye. "I must decline."

She simply stared at me. I couldn't bear to look into the eyes of the one who I had thought my friend and lowered my head. To my great surprise, and despite the cool season, there was a tiny purple flower growing from between the wooden boards at our feet. I couldn't help but smile. It was a reminder from Lady Autumn that our agreement was expiring. Today was the Winter Solstice. The last day the charm could be used. I would never know what it was like to again walk around curse free. I would never get to use that bit of magic which....

My eyes went wide as Fumiko stepped to leave.

I looked up. "Fumiko!" I yelled. "Can I tell you one last thing in private? Just one last whisper from a condemned man."

Fumiko smirked. "A final confession, no doubt." She stepped forward, pausing an arm's-length from me.

"Closer. Please! I need to whisper it to you." I moved my eyes in Zofie's direction.

She snorted and moved until we were a hand's-breadth apart.

"Closer," I said softly.

She leaned in and I strained forward, putting my mouth to her ear. I prayed that this worked. I touched her ear with my lips and...

Felt a warm spring breeze lightly caress my cheek, scented with the hint of flowers. Lady Autumn's chuckle sounded from somewhere behind me. She was whispering words in a language older than our civilization, and they came unbidden to my lips, as did the understanding of their meaning.

"Your curse stops now."

Fumiko took a step back, her eyes large in horror. *"What did you do?"*

The tiny flower at my feet suddenly started to grow. It became a vine, growing unbelievably fast, and snaked around Fumiko's feet and up her legs. She struggled to free herself, but the vine continued upwards carrying the growing flower with it. It snaked up her shirt and ripped it open to reveal her curse mark. I saw the vine extend its now large purple flower to cover it.

Fumiko suddenly stopped struggling and gave a single, blood-curdling scream. As I watched, the flower and vine wilted away to dust and revealed her curse mark had blurred. Then only a moment later, it disappeared.

That warm spring breeze once again touched my cheek, carrying to me a faint whisper. *Remember our promise. I'll see you come spring.*

Fumiko slowly looked up. Her eyes held disbelief and her mouth fell open. And I knew it was *her*—the *real* Fumiko.

The executioner and two guards ran up to her. "Are you all right, mistress?" one asked.

I heard shouting coming from the noble stands. Looking up, I saw it was Wynn. He was standing up on his throne, pointing at us and screaming. "Kill them now! All of them!"

The guards looked up in surprise. Fumiko grinned. "Sorry, but I must borrow your sword."

In a move faster than I could follow, Fumiko took one of the soldier's swords and smacked him smartly across the head with the flat of it. While he was falling, she moved again and again, easily taking out the executioner and remaining guard before they could draw their weapons.

Breathing hard, Fumiko went to me and lifted the noose from around my neck. "Thank you, Coren. I'm free! I'm truly free!" She then wrapped her arms around my neck and pulled me into a fierce kiss.

Zofie frowned. "The king is just in all... *that he does!*"

Fumiko, blushing pulled back and cut my bindings. She then stepped up to Zofie and freed her too. "I'm sorry princess. I know he is yours, but I had to. I'm free!"

And I'm back! Came Abe's booming voice inside my head. I winced. I was surprised that I felt a sense of relief to hear his voice. *Believe me, I'm dying to throw some curses.*

I quickly went to remove the noose from Spraggel and Milner while Fumiko cut their bindings.

I looked across to the stands to see most of the nobles had already evacuated. Wynn of course still stood on his throne cursing at the guards and those leaving. But in their place stepped up an archer. He drew back his bow, aiming in our direction.

"Watch out!"

Fumiko turned, just a second too slow—

Suddenly an arrow blossomed in her chest.

CHAPTER TWENTY-SIX

The Truth
Revealed

Fumiko collapsed against me. I caught her and eased her to the gallows' deck. The archer across from us suddenly started having trouble loading his next arrow. He notched one, and his bowstring suddenly snapped. The protection part of my curse was now working.

Zofie and I knelt beside her. Blood was seeping around the arrow and soaking her shirt. Fumiko looked up at us. "I seemed to have failed you after all." She gave a weak grin and coughed up blood.

I took her hand. "Fumiko, I need your permission to put a transformation curse on you. I think this can save your life, but I won't do it unless you agree. It won't heal you, but it will keep you from dying. Hopefully, when I remove the curse, we'll have someone with us that can heal you."

"Make me the shield," she said and gripped my arm tightly. "I have caused both of you so much pain. The least I can do is protect you."

I reached out to curse her, but she paused me and pulled out a sphere: the Mirror of Bygone Tears. "This belongs to you," Fumiko said. "Also the words on the King's Sword..." she coughed, more blood came out. "It's in my homeland's language... That thing in me wouldn't let me tell you..." She was fighting hard for breath. "It says...." she gasped. "Do not trust Fate; she gives false hopes...." Fumiko broke into another coughing fit. She made to go on but was struggling to draw air.

I paused her. There was no more time.

"It's all right. When you awake, we'll be ready."

She started to protest, but I initiated the curse. "I curse you to become Ruin's Shield."

The familiar blue glow surrounded her, and she quickly transformed into the legendary weapon. I grasped it by the inside middle support and swung it around to face the stands.

Fortunately for us, there was confusion among the guards and soldiers near the gallows—Fumiko's transformation had apparently unnerved them, so they were hesitant to rush us. Two more archers took up positions in the stands, but their arrows hit the shield, immediately dissolving into powder.

I looked around for Spraggel and Milner. To my surprise, they were missing. Where they had stood, one of the trap doors in the floor was open. I then spotted them on the ground, helping each other make their way to hide behind one of the wagons. I couldn't help but smile. There was more to my master than he was letting on. I was going to have a talk with him when this was over. A long one.

Using the shield for cover, Zofie and I began easing our way toward the stairs when the rain of arrows suddenly stopped. We froze in place to see a lone man approaching. Kegan. And with him, he carried a weapon I recognized—Havoc's Sword, which was actually a wounded and cursed Galvyn. Talk about using your friends against you.

Kegan smiled wickedly as he approached. "You know what this is. One touch with that shield, and everyone in the world dies. I'm not afraid to use it. But you on the other hand, what would you do?"

We retreated a couple steps. I thought we might could pull the same trick Spraggel had used. But by then, the soldiers had gotten themselves together and had surrounded the gallows. Running was no longer an option.

Zofie began to pull frantically at the necklace around her neck, but it would not break. *"The king is just in all that he does!"* she spat.

"Abe, can I transform Zofie into something?"

The reply was immediate. *Technically, but the necklace she wears is a problem. It is nearly unbreakable. If I trigger a transformation, it will remain around her neck. If I go with something big enough to do some damage, then it will strangle her. And if you transform her into something small, she'll become easy prey. Plus, you better live because she'll never be able to turn back without you.*

I angled close to Zofie. "I'll try to create an opening for you and the others." I sighed. "I wish you kept an army hidden under your skirt. It would sure be nice to have one right now."

Zofie blinked at me, I could almost see the gears of her mind turning. She made a fist with her right hand and stuck it high in the air. *"The king is just in all that he does!"* she shouted.

For a moment, I thought Zofie had finally lost her mind. But two heartbeats later, her extended hand began a soft blue glow, and then a blinding white beam of light shot into the air. It burned a path through the fog as it sought the sky. My eyes went wide. Zofie still had Blue Lavender, the guardian's ring. We did have an army, but it was doubtful they would make it in time.

The beacon unsettled the king's soldiers once more, and they fell back. And rightfully so. When myst users started flinging charms about, someone was going to get hurt. And it was usually the non-myst users that did.

Kegan stepped forward, giving the sword a few twisting swings. "Calling your friends, are you? A little late don't you think?"

Zofie brought her hand down and glared at Kegan.

I sighed. Using the shield was not going to work. I had seen Wort try to use it in a fight. While it provided an impenetrable defense, it was just too unwieldy. My best hope was that I was a better swordsman than Kegan... and my curse did something to protect me.

I quickly passed the shield to Zofie. Then stepping from behind it, I approached Kegan with a regular sword I had gotten from one of the fallen soldiers. I took my stance, and we stared at each other.

Kegan swung and I danced back. Again he swung, backing me toward the edge. When I could go no further, he followed with a thrust—and just like Risten had taught me, I batted the sword away on the flat side of the blade as hard as I could. But I must have done it wrong. While the strength of my blow nearly knocked his sword from his hand—my own blade broke in two.

Creator be damned!

Kegan smiled. He knew he had me now.

And then I heard it. A faint throbbing sound. It almost sounded like a huge running heart coming from deep in the fog. And it was getting closer. Whispers started up from the soldiers surrounding us.

Kegan paused, the first cracks of doubt seeping in.

"Kill him!" Wynn screamed, still standing up on his throne. "Now!"

The throbbing sound grew still louder, becoming a deep vibration I could feel in my chest. Eyes turned in apprehension toward the fog covered harbor. Across the water in the direction of the noise, a patch of the fog began to take on an orange tint, growing brighter with every heartbeat.

And still the throbbing sound increased, growing so loud that it echoed off the surrounding buildings. A shadow on the water began to take shape, illuminated by the orange glow. The spectators not already frightened away by the commotion began to leave the area—some breaking into a run. A few of the soldiers threw down their weapons and ran too. Something was coming. Something big.

The thumping abruptly ceased, plunging the entire area into an eerie silence.

Suddenly the hair on my arms stood up as a small portal opened in the air beside me, and only a moment later, someone dived out, rolling to their feet to stand in front of us. She was quickly followed by another and another until six Keepers stood with us—all bearing swords, drawn and ready. And the last one through, had a feather tucked tightly in her hair. Geneene Scurrlocke cocked a mischievous smile in our direction. "Did our Guardian call for assistance?" The portal closed behind her.

I pointed to Kegan who was backing toward the stairs, evidently deciding there were too many in close quarters for even the sword to take care of. "Watch out. He has Havoc's Sword and this is Ruin's Shield." I then pointed to Zofie. She needs to get that necklace off. She can't command with it on.

Zofie pointed toward the noble stands. "*The king* is just in all that he does!"

Geneene cocked her head. "I can see that it could be a problem."

Wynn lined up his archers, who seemed to be overcoming the problems with the strings breaking.

Geneene pointed at Kegan. "Keepers! Protect the guardian. And watch out for that man's sword." She then waved her hand, and a wall of green light sprung up before us just as the archers released their volley. The arrows hit and harmlessly slid to the ground.

The soldiers trying to climb the stairs gave ground as the Keepers spread out. Kegan, realizing the women were trying to surround him, started to swing at them, but they easily danced out of reach continuing to harry him. He gathered his myst with his free hand and flung it at the nearest Keeper.

The myst flowed off her with no effect.

Geneene huffed. "Did he actually think we wouldn't be wearing counter charms?"

Geneene strode to the front of the Keepers and gathered her own myst. Kegan swung with the sword, but the young woman caught the blade with no effect on her hand. He looked at her in shock.

She smiled. "Keepers are immune to most magic weapons, or did they not teach that to you in myst school." She plucked the sword from his hand.

Kegan backed to the edge of the platform and jumped off. It was a good ways down, and he landed badly, but managed to limp away.

Geneene took the sword to Zofie, and very carefully, used it to slice off the necklace.

Zofie grabbed the necklace as soon as she was free and flung the thing away as far as she could. And then she drew Geneene into a brief hug. "Thank you for coming for me. I owe you."

Geneene stepped back. "Just keep your promise."

"Oh, I will."

While Zofie was handing Ruin's Shield to one of the Keepers, Geneene gave me a knowing look behind Zofie's back. She then moved her lips but made no sound, forming words only for me: "I've had my eye on you." She smiled.

Evidently, Geneene had really done something to Zofie's curse so she could track her. No wonder they had been able to respond so quickly.

Zofie turned back to Geneene. "I think I can turn this around. Can you hold this platform for just a few moments longer?"

Geneene looked offended. "Of course we can. We are Keepers."

Zofie nodded. "Good. Give me just a few moments longer." She turned to me and held out her hand. "Coren, the mirror."

I pulled the Mirror of Bygone tears from my pocket and handed it to her.

"Now the most difficult part. Can you activate it when I say so?"

"Here?" I asked in surprise. "Right now?"

She nodded.

I shrugged. "I will do whatever my queen asks of me."

She looked to Geneene. "Could I borrow a Cryer spell."

Geneene raised a hand, and blue light encircled Zofie's throat.

The princess stepped to the edge of the platform and spoke. "Hold!" she said, her voice booming so loud it echoed off the nearby buildings. "Everyone hold your place. I, Zophia Olwenna Xernow, rightful ruler of Brethnach and the Guardian of the Keepers of Long Past Secrets, seek audience with all of you. I bring evidence that will clear my name over the murder of my father, and place the blame where it truly belongs." She raised her hands. "Will you grant me this audience?"

The nobles paused in fleeing the stands, the guards and Keepers paused in the fight, and it seemed even the wind held still.

Zofie held up the sphere. "What I hold here is the Mirror of Bygone Tears. Some of you have heard of this thing of legend. It is a powerful and ancient tool for showing the past of someone. To prove my innocence, I will use it to show you all that really happened."

Wynn came to the edge of the stands and screamed at his guards. "Kill her. Kill them all. They're lying. She's the murderer!"

Zofie held the sphere in my direction. "Coren, if you please."

I stepped forward and touched the sphere to my curse anchor. The mirror activated and floated up above us, where it unfolded into its bowl shape.

Zofie and I exchanged glances. I took a deep breath and shouted. "Show us what Princess Zophia saw during the murder of King Xernow."

To my utter relief, the mirror began to glow, and everyone around us was plunged into Zofie's memory of the event.

There was a knock on my door.

I was sitting on the bench at the foot of my bed, brushing my hair. I yawned. I may have just gotten up but my brain was still in bed. I had stayed up reading—again. Risten had risen at first light and slipped out for her morning sword practice. I sometimes joined her, but not this morning. I would have likely fallen asleep and cut myself.

"Come in," I said, thinking it was just one of the servants bringing breakfast. I yawned again.

But surprise cut me off mid-yawn. Wynn, my younger brother, strolled through the door. Behind him, one of his serving maids carried a rather large package—beautifully wrapped in pink and white paper. I assumed it was a birthday gift from one of his many admirers. Today was his day, after all.

"Good morning, sister," he said cheerily.

I blinked at him. It was unusual for him to visit me, especially first thing in the morning. Realizing I was being rude, I quickly responded. "And good morning to you too, brother. And a happy birthday as well."

He grinned. "Which is why I am here." He waved to the servant who presented me with the package. Feeling very puzzled, I took it.

"It's a present for you. I'm one to reverse tradition, and instead of you giving me a present, I'm giving you one instead."

"For me?" I was utterly surprised. We had not been getting along so well as of late, so maybe he was trying to make amends. I opened it and took out a splendid gown of rose pink, with white lace across the hem and sleeves. It was a simple piece, but beautiful, nonetheless. I was speechless. "Why, thank you, Wynn." I clutched the dress to my chest and gave my brother a hug.

"I hope you wear it to the party this evening. I had it especially made for you." I smiled. "Of course I will."

He nodded and pulled out another smaller box from behind his back. "And of course, I know you love jewelry, so here is something to go with the gown."

I quickly opened the present to find it contained a necklace. It also was simple, having a silver chain and a pendant with a single blood-red jewel encased in it. While it attempted to look elegant, it somehow didn't quite make it, appearing kind of—well, ugly. I looked up in shock. Wynn was trying so hard to make amends. I had to accept it.

"Why Wynn," I said. "You shouldn't have."

He smiled. "I thought everyone in my family should have presents today. I gave father a ring and even left a dress for Risten, although I doubt she'll wear it."

I smiled back at him. "I'll see if I can talk her into it."

He nodded. "Nothing would give me more pleasure than to see all my family wearing my gifts. I made sure each one was picked especially for them...."

The scene abruptly changed, shifting to that evening in an eyeblink. I had seen this one before from Zofie's memories.

It was the birthday party turned massacre.

...I fell to my knees, the world seeming to swim around me. I glanced at my father—he looked bad too, lying limp, sweating profusely and breathing hard in short gasps.

Although I fought to hold it, I felt my shield protecting the guests falter—and then fail. Their screams echoed through the halls.

How was he doing this?

And then it connected. The necklace. Father's ring.

I paled. Oh please Creator, no.

I reached to jerk the necklace off, but a strand of myst encircled my wrist and immobilized it.

Wynn squatted down in front of me. "Zophia, my dear sister, what is the first thing we are taught as myst users. Isn't it that myst users have a large supply of the stuff, but most people don't? And when you run out. You die. So what would happen do you think, if you were to link up a myst user with someone who wasn't one. So that every spell they cast drew from that poor someone. Do you think they might look like Father? Slowly dying."

"You bastard!" I tried to shout, but it only came out as a whisper.

"I gave you the necklace and Father a new ring, both specially spelled so any myst drawn by the necklace wearer would come from the ring bearer. And every defense spell you put up, drew our father closer to death. Until now, he is almost sucked dry. Almost. But just one more good draw should do it. One more spell and Father will die."

"I won't do it," I spat. "I'll let myself be killed first."

"As I thought you would. So I arranged for something special sister. Something to haunt you until the day you die." He smiled. "I laid awake many a night thinking this up. I hope you like it."

Wynn pointed a finger at me, touching it to my chest, his expression turning serious. "Zophia Olwenna Xernow, Princess of Brethnach, I curse you. I give you the curse of Eternal Transformation!"

The jewel around my neck turned hot, burning into my flesh. Father screamed in agony....

The world snapped back into place. Zofie stood beside me with tears in her eyes. The only sound around us came from a protesting seagull in the distance.

I searched the stands for Wynn, but he had vanished.

I stepped up to the edge. Glancing toward Geneene, I patted my throat and she nodded. She waved her feather, and my throat was enveloped with a blue glow. I turned to the crowd, raising my arms high. "Who here now does not understand who the real murderer was? Who dares to not recognize that Princess Zophia Xernow still lives? Who *dares* to not call her their *queen!*"

"Out of my way!" came a shout from the stairway. A man I recognized as Lord Pringottin stepped up onto the gallows. At my urging, the Keepers let him come forward. He made his way to stand before Zofie. He knelt before her and took her hand and kissed it. "I Lord Pringottin do hereby recognize Princess Xernow's claim to the throne."

A moment later, Lord Merrick made his way forward and also knelt. "I also recognize her claim."

I turned to the crowd. "Hail Queen Zophia!"

I also knelt before her as the crowd took up the cheer.

After several minutes, Zofie held up her arms, and the crowd reluctantly quieted down. She again spoke. "Thank you, my people. I swear I will do my best to be the kind of ruler you can be proud of."

The crowd erupted into cheers. A smiling Zofie turned to me, opening her mouth to say something—

When a burst of green light struck her from behind, enveloping her. Zofie went rigid. I recognized this spell. It was the Abeyance charm. The one that immobilized a person to the point they couldn't even breathe.

CHAPTER TWENTY-SEVEN

The
Secret Word

Zofie toppled over and I caught her.

The crowd broke into confusion.

Kegan was standing in a small boat in the water a few feet from shore, safely out of reach from anyone nearby. And the bastard was laughing like it was the funniest thing in the world.

Geneene was immediately beside us, and with a wave of her feather, tried to counter the spell—but it was too strong and refused to break. She looked at me helplessly. Zofie stared straight ahead unmoving, not breathing. Her face began to turn blue. I was losing her.

"Abe," I asked in panic. "Is there anything I can do for her? Anything at all?"

Abe's deep booming voice came into my head. I was afraid I already knew the answer, but he surprised me: *Use the secret word.*

"Dammit? I don't know what it is!"

You really are stupid, you know that don't you. Use your brain for once!

And then I knew. Fumiko had tried to tell me.

Abe mentioned he had given me all the clues a long time ago. It wasn't a secret word, it was secret *words*, a passphrase. The one on the King's Sword. I had been carrying it around with me for over a year!

I shut my eyes and looked up to the sky. It was from an ancient poem, one so old the author was unknown. Spraggel, bless his heart, thought I might need it one day.

I recited the words. "Do not trust her, Fate, the bane of man. Follow your heart, it leads true."

Abe's booming voice came into my head. *Pass phrase has been given. Do you wish to release protections?*

"Yes," I said. "Yes, I do."

Protections have been released.

I opened my mouth to ask what to do next, when suddenly my world vanished.

I was standing directly behind a middle-aged woman, looking over her shoulder into a mirror. Her long hair was gray and platted into a loose braid down her back. Her eyes were gentle and kind, with almost a twinkle. I had seen this face before somewhere. The mirror wasn't that good, so I couldn't make out the details behind her.

This was a different kind of memory than I had seen with Zofie, or even from the mirror. While before I was actually that person, seeing the world through their eyes. But for this one, I felt I was still myself and was just observing. And I sensed this memory was very, very old.

"Hello," she said. "You're no doubt surprised that I placed a memory to activate when you unlocked Abhulengulus this time."

She sighed. "We've had our differences of late, and I just wanted to give you one last message before our battle. Jonathan has expressed grave doubts that you will be able to carry this burden, but I trust you. I know you better than anyone." She smiled. "Since I likely won't see you again, I'll make a small confession. Jonathan may have taken my hand in marriage a long time ago. And I do love him. But you're the one who stole my heart. Although neither of us has spoken of it, I think you've known." She sighed. "It's ancient history, and I'm not exactly sure why I'm telling you now, of all times. But it just seemed important that you know. And I thank you for being my friend all these years."

And then it occurred to me. I was not the intended recipient of this message. It was for the original Thief of Curses. Then who was this lady? Could it be Evelend? Abe's maker?

The woman sighed. "But the real reason I'm leaving you this message is to give you some final instructions on using the curse. I adjusted him slightly since we last trained. The skill memory will play after this visual memory completes." She smiled. "I think you will find Abhulengulus a little more independent than you're used to. He's quite grown in intelligence. He may even talk back to you. I've also fine-tuned the protection methods to be a little more proactive." She smiled and leaned forward. "Just don't say anything to Jonathan, he'll think I'm trying to manipulate the future." Her smile grew wistful, and she shook her head. "No, it's not the future I'd change, but the past." She sighed. She paused for a moment in thought and then seemed to catch herself. "I guess I've dragged this out long enough." She leaned forward. "Good luck, Dughall. I know you'll perform your mission flawlessly and save the world from those horrors. You might even go down in history as the savior of the world." She smiled. "Take care my love. I'll see you in the next life."

When I opened my eyes, I was still kneeling beside Zofie, she still couldn't breathe, and was turning a deeper shade of blue.

Geneene looked at me concerned. "Coren, snap out of it."

But the world wasn't the same. I blinked at her in surprise. Geneene had a faint glow around her. No, that wasn't accurate. It was a glowing *web* surrounding her, moving and churning. I could see the bright spot on her chest which was her curse mark. I could see the lines connecting up to the feather she carried.

I looked around, and the lines were everywhere. All the people surrounding me had them, some were green, some pink, some blue, and a few bright yellow, and all of them were in varying levels of intensity and complexity.

I looked down at Zofie. I could see her own network of blue lines and the bright glow of her curse mark. But overlaying that was a darker green which was interfering with Zofie's blue.

"Abhulengulus!" I said. "What am I seeing?"

I heard a human-like snort in my head. *You really are stupid. You're seeing what any myst seer can see when they want to.*

"But how does this help Zofie! She's dying."

He sighed. *I don't know how you can be stupider than stupid, but you sure manage. Look closely at the princess. Do you see the charm? You have to separate it from the others.*

"Is it the green lines?"

It's whatever looks wrong.

I hesitantly reached out and touched a green line. It felt like greased string, sliding effortlessly along my finger, but resisting any movement. I pinched a strand between my thumb and finger and pulled, but it resisted.

"It's not coming off."

Of course not, it's made to stick to someone. You need to reset its target.

"Target?"

The one intended to carry the charm.

"How do I do that?"

You tell it.

"I just tell it?"

That's what I said. He sounded exasperated, like one talking to an overly curious child.

I wasn't too sure about this, but I had no time to lose. I took a strand of the green web and said the first thing that came to mind. "Could you return to your maker, please."

The green web covering Zofie gathered itself into a ball and hovered over her for a fraction of a heartbeat and then sped back to Kegan. Zofie immediately gasped for air and sat up.

Kegan was drawing the last of his myst into crafting a long-distance portal in the boat as it drifted further from shore. Tendrils of fog began to envelop him. He looked over his shoulder, and the smile fell from his face as the returning charm sped toward him. He stepped toward the portal just as the returning charm hit him. The charm wrapped its web around the man, and he drew up into rigid form. He stood there for a moment, unable to break free. The partially established portal began to waver. Then, as it was about to collapse, Kegan tipped inside. It closed behind him without a trace.

"The portal closed on him," Geneene whispered in horror. "He didn't make it through. He's in the in-between realm... the dark between worlds."

I looked to where he had been. It was terrible of me, but I didn't feel sorry for him.

After nearly being killed by an Abeyance charm, I thought Zofie might take a bit of a breather before rebuilding her kingdom. And she sort of did, but I thought a quarter-hour was a little short.

Since the gallows were conveniently positioned for everyone to see, she had the ropes taken down and a large chair placed on it so everyone could see her.

After introducing Spraggel, Captain Milner, and myself, along with Geneene and all the Keepers, Zofie opened court. All the major nobles present came to her one by one and swore their allegiance. While they smiled and offered their allegiance, I felt most of them were sizing her up on how best to win her favor. I had no doubt she would be busy keeping them under control.

Then after the nobles were finished, the common people came forward—bakers, cobblers, tailors, even whole families with children in arms. They all lined up to speak with their new ruler. Zofie accepted everyone, spending at least a minute or two with each. There were a couple teary reunions, one in particular with her personal chambermaid, Vidonia, which had survived Wynn's cull of the staff.

All of them had a story of Wynn's cruelty, and in each case, Zofie tried to assure them it would get better.

As the sun began to dip below the horizon, I asked that the Keepers that were managing the queue, to not allow anyone else to join her receiving line. I had been by her side the entire time, and I could tell she was exhausted.

Night was well fallen by the time the last person was seen. I helped Zofie to a waiting carriage, and we went to the castle, escorted by the Keepers. Spraggel had taken the chambermaid aside, and he instructed her to organize a place for the princess, so when we arrived, Zofie went straight to her old room and fell in bed. For myself, I saw the Keepers off as they returned to their ship and then kept watch over her during the night. I had come uncomfortably close to losing her, and I was not going to let that happen again.

The next day, Zofie summoned the best healers and surgeons in the land and had them ready for when I removed the curse from first Galvyn and later Fumiko. Galvyn's wounds turned out not to be too bad, and the healers were able to stop his bleeding, before cleaning and closing the wound. Of course, he had not been happy to have been cursed and having missed out on Zofie's return to the throne. He even tried to convince her one last time that he was the best candidate. But Zofie quickly put him in his place, explaining he was not the one.

I was surprised at how well Galvyn took the news. He shook my hand to congratulate me... and then punched me in the nose. "Don't you ever put a curse on me again!" he yelled, while I tried to keep the blood leaking from my nose off the carpets.

Zofie summarily dismissed Galvyn into the care of this father, Lord Merrick. She also returned the Wayward's Finder thanking them for its use. And as a reward, she gave them a month.

Lord Merrick was clearly puzzled by the comment. So Zofie elaborated. One month was the grace period they had to clean up their family business. She suggested they find a new one—preferably without slaves and brothels.

Fumiko's healing was more difficult. The arrow had struck her lung and nicked her heart, giving the surgeon a rough time. In fact, the surgeon nearly lost her after extracting the arrow.

But fortunately, the healers and surgeons prevailed and

successfully managed to mend her wound. She would just need to take it easy for a few days.

But the physical healing was only part of it. Fumiko felt extremely guilty for what had happened and swore with her life that she would make it up to us. I was afraid that Zofie might feel a grudge against her for the treachery done while the curse possessed her. But instead, Zofie surprised us all and asked Fumiko if she would be her secretary. At the words, Fumiko dropped to her knees and bowed her head to the floor, saying she would gladly serve. Zofie quickly reached down and pulled Fumiko to her feet saying to never prostrate herself again. And then Zofie hugged her. Fumiko broke down in tears.

As for Wynn and some of his key supporters, they vanished without a trace. Zofie issued a proclamation declaring him an outlaw. Yet, for some reason, I had no doubt we would see them again.

The final mystery was Risten. From what Zofie had learned, Wynn had dispatched the curse possessed Risten on a mission right before we arrived. But no one seemed to know what that mission was or where she had gone. I could tell it wore heavily on Zofie. But all she could do was issue orders to find her, and reluctantly turn her attention back to rebuilding the kingdom.

But there was one more plot lurking about the castle, involving secret plans and the ultimate deception. One which Zofie was completely unaware of.

If she hadn't been so occupied with replacing corrupt officials, she may have caught a clue from the serving maids who were smiling just a bit too broad. Or perhaps, while Zofie was ensuring cruel nobles were brought to justice, she may have noticed Spraggel was frequently absent and left no explanation. Or maybe even while the new ruler saw that supplies were dispensed to those in the countryside, she may have found Fumiko's expression a little more tight-lipped than expected.

And as for me, I was at the nexus of the deception which came together as planned on the Day of the New. And on that day—

I lied to Zofie.

I explained to her that we needed to meet with a delegation arriving by ship, and her presence was required at the harbor. The first inkling that something might have been amiss was when Vidonia dressed her simply and warmly in pants, shirt, and cloak. Not exactly the clothes one would wear for a dignitary. But Zofie had come to trust me and made no comment.

We then took her carriage into the harbor and down to the waterfront to where the people were gathered. The streets were brightly decorated with branches of pine and multitudes of myst lights giving the town a cheery glow it hadn't seen in some time. People were laughing and excited on what the new year *and* the new ruler would bring.

At my instruction, the driver let us off in front of a certain tavern, but instead of the front door, Zofie and I went in the back way. The proprietor was waiting for us and ushered us to a room with a balcony and a view of the harbor.

Zofie looked at me dumbfounded. "What are you up to?" she asked. She regarded me suspiciously.

I smiled. "It's just a quick bite before we go to meet the delegates. You've been working so hard lately, I thought you might like a quick diversion."

And so we were served a scrumptious light dinner of perfectly grilled fowl and an amazing potato pudding. We chatted of this and that, and I saw the lines of worry ease from her face for the first time in ages.

After she had pushed her plate away, she leaned toward me. Her eyes caught the sparkle of the lights around us. "I am beginning to suspect that I have been lied to," she said. "I believe there is no dignitary for us to meet, nor ship coming into the harbor."

I smiled. "I have been found out. What you say is true. I have deceived my lady."

"I can't say I'm not enjoying it." Her smile dimmed. "There have been so many changes."

I nodded, knowing now was my chance to spring the ultimate trap. "I hope you can tolerate one more change."

She looked concerned. "You are not leaving me, are you?"

I shook my head. "On the contrary."

Then the sky over the harbor exploded in light as the fireworks started, sending out beautiful trails of red, green, and blue across the starlit sky. I heard Zofie gasp in delight, quickly followed a second later by the sounds of their muffled explosion. Then another volley took to the sky. All around us, we heard the crowd of people cheering and awing at the beauty of the sight.

Bracing myself for the severe breach of status I was about to commit, I stood and went to Zofie's side. I then went to one knee beside her and took her hand.

"Zofie, I have a boon to ask. I am not worthy of it, but my heart demands that I at least attempt it."

She smiled and gently touched my cheek, as more streaks of color flooded the sky. "You know I'll do whatever I can for you," she said.

"Then I will ask." I took a deep breath. "Zofie, you are the finest person I have ever met. Among women, you have no equal. I ask that I be allowed to spend my life with you. Would you take me as your husband? Would you be my wife?" I kissed her hand. "I promise to never, ever hold back."

Zofie covered her mouth with her remaining hand, and tears came to her eyes. "You want *me*?"

I nodded. "Indeed, I do."

"Coren, I...."

The sky exploded once again in all colors of the rainbow and so bright they momentarily turned the night into day.

I lowered my head. She was going to turn me down. I could see it coming. It was an uncharacteristic move for me. I had confided my wish in Spraggel, and he had encouraged me to make my plans. He had even helped with finding the perfect spot. But it looked like it was all in vain.

"I accept."

"I understand if you decline," I said sadly. "You will be the queen. While I am nothing."

"Coren, I accept."

I looked up at her in puzzlement. "You do?"

"Yes, you idiot," she said gently. "I've been hoping you would ask. But are you sure you want to be my consort? It will be nothing but trouble, and if history is any indication, rulers and their family tend to die young."

I nodded. "True, but I can't think of doing it any other way." I leaned toward her for a kiss.

"Has he asked her yet?"

Zofie and I both turned at the whisper. That sounded like Spraggel. We stepped further out on the balcony to look up on the roof above us. There sat Spraggel, Fumiko, Geneene, and several guards.

Spraggel waved. "Did you ask her?"

"I did," I answered in shock.

"Oh, good. We can get down off this cursed roof. My butt's going to sleep."

"You *knew?*"

"Of course, Zofie was the one that suggested I encourage you in the first place."

I turned to her. "You told Spraggel to encourage me?"

She shrugged. "I wasn't sure if you would ever work up the courage without some prodding."

I took her in my arms. "I guess I'm going to have my hands full with you."

She snuggled closer. "Of course."

We then invited all our friends down to join us. Fortunately, the proprietor seemed to be expecting a party. He brought out drinks and desserts for us to celebrate our engagement.

At that moment, I was the happiest man on earth. I couldn't imagine anything possibly spoiling the evening.

But I was wrong.

CHAPTER TWENTY-EIGHT

Risten's Fate

After returning to the castle, Zofie and I retired early. We were both exhausted. And like I had many months ago atop Mount Eternal, I had the strangest dream—

I stood before a heavy wooden door gathering my courage. I finally pushed it open and entered into some type of workshop with a bench, books and various instruments lying across it. There was a central myst globe hanging from the ceiling with reflectors over it. This was not for ornamentation, but a work light.

A woman sat beside the table wearing a simple gray nightdress and a shawl across her shoulders. She was leaning over a book and frantically scribbling in it as if her very life depended on getting everything down. And she looked exhausted. She had the air of someone that has done much, but yet had so much more to do.

I recognized this woman. I had seen her in visions before. It was Evelend.

I closed the door and leaned against it, then slid the latch to seal us inside.

She looked up at the noise, frowning, but it quickly changed to a grin when she saw me. "Dughall, what brings you down to my workshop so late?"

"Couldn't sleep," I said, only it wasn't my voice.

She nodded knowingly. "I have the same problem. I've gone over everything and checked it at least a dozen times."

I went to stand beside her and looked over her shoulder. She was writing in some kind of journal.

The journal looked familiar also. Then I recognized it. It was the ancient book about my curse!

"Haven't you written enough?" I asked, in the voice that wasn't mine.

She gave a weary sigh. "I'm trying to record the last few changes I made to Abhulengulus. I've got to record them for whoever comes after." She looked back toward the journal. "There's many things about him I don't really understand."

"But you made him."

"Copied him, would be a better word. I also had quite a bit of help. While there are parts of him I understand very well, there are other parts that by rights shouldn't even work."

I snorted. "You tell me this now. After you've given him to me?"

She patted my arm. "No, it's safe. I made sure of that. And I built a lot of protections into it just in case."

My eyes searched hers for a moment and then I knelt beside her. I took her hand in mind. "Speaking of safe. You should not go to the front lines. You'll be killed."

She touched my face. "We've had this argument several times. There is no way around it. I have to be there to make sure our final weapon works. I'm the only one that can control the amount of myst that it needs."

"Draki can do it. He's more powerful than you."

"True, but it's finesse that's needed, not raw power." She shook her head. "No, I must be the one."

I bowed my head. "Please don't go."

"I have to." She patted me on the arm. "Now go and get some rest. We have a big day tomorrow. We're going to finally send the Dark Avenyts back to the hell they came from."

I stood and moved behind her, resting my hands gently on her shoulders. "I'm sorry Evelend. I love you more than life itself. But I can't let you march to your death."

"Dughall," she said. A note of irritation entered her voice. "Don't argue now. It's too late for that."

"You're right. It is too late to argue." I leaned down and kissed her head. "Please forgive me." Then louder I said. "Your curse is my curse."

The familiar blue glow flared around her.

Evelend turned around suddenly alarmed. "What are you doing? You took my protection curse."

"You leave me with no choice, my love. I hope you'll eventually forgive me."

She shook her head, comprehension dawning. "No, don't. I don't want this. I beg you!"

"I curse you with the curse of The Long Sleep."

Evelend was immediately surrounded by a blue glow. As the curse did its work, her face bore an expression of shock and betrayal. "You're stealing the curses, aren't you?" she shouted, with her eyes drooping. "You, Thief of Curses...!"

I awoke with a start and sat up in bed. It was still the middle of the night. What had that been? It was like the first dream I had back on Mount Eternal. They had to be connected somehow.

Realizing that sleep wasn't going to return soon, if at all this night, I got up and went to sit at Zofie's writing table. I turned up a small myst globe thinking I might write down what I had just seen. But the Mirror of Bygone Tears caught my eye, cradled in a small pillow at the back of the desk. It seemed to call to me. Zofie and I had been trying to use it to find Wynn and Risten, but for some reason, it refused to work on them.

I heard movement behind me and then a moment later, Zofie was draping a blanket over my shoulders.

"Can't sleep?" She leaned down and loosely wrapped her arms around me.

"I had another dream about Evelend." I looked at the curse mark on my wrist. "It was right before the start of some big attack on the Dark Avenyts. And I was someone named Dughall—the original Thief of

Curses. He... he loved her and yet..." I shivered despite the blanket. "He betrayed her."

I turned to look at her. "You've read the accounts of the Battle with the Dark Avenyts. Why haven't we heard of Evelend or Dughall? Why weren't they included in the chronicles?"

Zofie shrugged. "Just people lost in the telling. The war was a huge thing, and a lot of people helped make it a victory. Some stories are bound to be lost."

I ran a hand through my hair. "True. Yet Evelend's artifacts made it to the legends, but why not anything about Evelend herself? I almost feel I'm reading a book where someone edited out the parts they didn't like."

"Maybe it's because the knowledge was too great for us to handle." She pointed to the mirror. "That thing right there could start a war. Being able to know what your enemy is doing would be enough for someone to want to take it."

"That may be so, but we haven't been able to use it to find Wynn. Fumiko said that while it was powerful, it had some serious limitations."

Zofie leaned down and hugged me from behind. We were silent for a moment, lost in our own thoughts and enjoying each other's warmth.

Zofie sighed. "We've been so busy lately. I'm sure we're overlooking something. Maybe we're just not asking the right question." She sighed and stood up, patting me on the shoulder.

I nodded, thinking back to the dream. I turned in my seat toward Zofie. "Or perhaps, we're not asking about the right person." I cleared my voice and spoke louder. "Abe, are you there?"

You keep asking me that! I can't really go anywhere.

Zofie gave me a questioning look. It was time to bring her into the conversation. "Abe, can you make it so Zofie can hear you too? In fact, anytime she is present with us, can you include her in the conversation?"

There was a brief flash of blue. *Done.*

Zofie's eyebrows went up, clearly surprised. "So I finally get to talk with you. I don't know why we didn't think of this before."

It is good to talk with you too princess. I've been dying to speak with some-one of at least average intelligence, rather than the ape I'm attached to.

Zofie grinned and glanced toward me. "Is he always like this?"

I could only nod.

I'm sure you want more than just introducing me to the princess. What exactly do you want?

"Why won't the mirror show me any of Wynn's recent memories?"

Most likely because he is blocking them.

"How is he able to do that?"

Coren, we've been over this before. I'm a curse. Not an all-knowing sage. The mirror was constructed with me as a key, but I do not know how it operates.

"Does that go for Risten, too?" asked Zofie.

Yes, princess.

I thought a moment. Perhaps we needed to choose a time before Wynn was blocking the mirror. While it wouldn't tell us exactly where they were, it might give us a clue. I picked up the mirror and held it against my curse. It immediately activated and turned into its floating bowl shape. "Show me the last time Wynn was together with Risten."

This time the mirror responded. It glowed blue and we were plunged into a memory. But to my surprise, it wasn't Wynn's memories we saw.

It was Risten's.

I sat on the floor and struggled to get free. My wrists were in manacles af-fixed to the wall above my head while my feet were held by shackles bolted to the floor. They had even looped a length of chain around my middle to make sure I stayed in place. It was amusing that given my condition, they actually thought I was that dangerous. I tried to smile but stopped at the pain from the cuts and bruises on my swollen face. It hurt too much.

Wynn stood before me frowning. "Now Risten," he said. "Hold still for just a moment."

I continued my struggles against the chains. "Let me go, you murderer." I spat at him, but it fell far short of its goal.

Wynn looked over to the man beside him. It was the man that had tried to assassinate Zofie back at Spraggel's keep. Kegan.

He stood there studying what looked like a sophisticated brass clock. It was beautiful in the way of finely crafted tools and was even small enough to hold in one hand. Kegan shook his head. "She's only a five. She needs to be at least a six."

Wynn sighed. "Disappointing. Enough to power a small curse, but not the one I had planned. I was so hoping you would be able to join us." He squatted down in front of me. "Whoever your mother was, she was not a myst user. Likely the reason she tried to ensnare uncle using her bed."

"You bastard!" I shot forward to the full extent of my chains coming just a hairsbreadth from biting him on the nose.

Surprisingly Wynn did not flinch. He just smiled. "You always were so easy to goad."

Kegan put the brass instrument into his pocket. It must be some kind of myst detector. I wasn't too surprised at what it told. I had been tested when I reached puberty, and just as he had said, I had stronger than average myst capability, but not nearly enough to be considered a true myst user.

"Should I kill her then," asked Kegan with his hand on his sword's hilt.

Wynn stood and shook his head, considering me. "No, my dear sister would know somehow. While it likely wouldn't stop her from coming, it might make her more careful. I really do want that mirror. It's too dangerous to leave floating around. She's the only one that stands a chance of getting past the Keepers."

Kegan waved in my direction. "So what do we do with her? Just leave her here?"

Wynn looked over at me thoughtfully. He then squatted down in front of me again. He smiled. Lightning quick, his arm shot out and grabbed me by the throat, pinning me to the wall. "I think I have just the one for her. One that doesn't require as much myst as some of the others." He cocked his head to one side. "Send for Lilith."

Kegan blinked in surprise. "Lilith has become unstable. Plus this one would only have barely enough myst...."

I struggled to get free of Wynn's grasp, but I could not miss the gleam of anger in his eye as he glared at Kegan. "Are you questioning me?"

Kegan swallowed nervously. "Never. I'll get her now." Kegan quickly left.

Wynn turned back to me. He smiled—his grip on my throat tightening. "I think this will be educational for both of you. Lilith tends to drive her hosts insane...."

I jerked back into my body and turned to Zofie. She was having the same thoughts as me.

"Wynn has one of those curses too."

Zofie nodded. "It does explain why Wynn has been acting so strange."

"But it doesn't explain everything. Like why he has been so interested in the ancient weapons—the shield, the sword, and the mirror. Why would he want to gather all of them? And another thing... why sponsor the enslavement of myst users? Remember those girls that were captured. Why would he need to round up myst users?"

Zofie frowned, puzzled. "Was he afraid of them? A paranoid delusion maybe?"

"Maybe." I shook my head. "But this seems more deliberate than the actions of a madman."

Zofie nodded and began to count on her fingers. "Secure the ancient weapons, get rid of those that pose the biggest threat, and finally tear down the kingdom's defenses." She looked at me in concern. "It's like he was deliberately preparing for something."

I frowned. "What you mean is, it's what you would do if you were preparing to invade."

The color drained from her face. "Invade?"

I took a deep breath. "Abhulengulus."

Oh Creator, he used my full name. He must be serious.

"I know you can't deny me now. Tell us about the Dark Avenyts?"

There was a pause. *I think you already know. They are entities from a world beyond the Gate of Mount Eternal.*

I shook my head. "That's not all. *What are* the Dark Avenyts and why are they trying to get into our world?"

Abe paused again before answering. Both Zofie and I held our breath, afraid of the answer.

The Dark Avenyts are like me. They are curses. And what they want are hosts.

Lots of them.

The story continues in
Book 3 of the
Chronicles of Coren Hart Series

ASSASSIN
OF
CURSES

Acknowledgments

Queen of Curses would not have happened had it not been for the help of many others. Thanks go out to Jennifer, who once again was a major help with proofing and copyediting. I also need to thank Rebecca and Kasey for their writing advice and many corrections, as well as Callista and Daniel, who were my beta readers.

A special thanks to the creative team at Mibl Art for their fantastic cover art. I much appreciated their creativity and patience as we worked through the many drafts and adjustments.

And finally, my wife deserves major kudos for putting up with me spouting off about the book and characters. She would patiently listen to my latest problems and give me the encouragement I needed.

About The Author

Queen of Curses is Jessie Eaker's second novel. His short fiction has appeared in Marion Zimmer's Bradley's *Sword and Sorceress* and *Fantasy Worlds* anthologies. A native of North Carolina, he currently lives in central Virginia, and has been there so long, he's lost his southern accent (much to his wife's disappointment). When not writing, he watches anime, reads, and works on his ever-growing list of things to fix around the house.

Check out jessieeaker.com for his latest works and updates.